DELUGE

Also by Vincent Meis

Eddie's Desert Rose

Tio Jorge

Down in Cuba

DELUGE

Vincent Meis

FIRST EDITION
Fallen Bros. Publishing
29403 N. Enrose Ave.
Palos Verdes, CA 90275
ISBN: 978-0-9976728-0-0

*This is dedicated to the
one I love*

*Whom does Love concern beyond the
beloved and the lover?
Yet his impact deluges a hundred
shores.* –E. M. Forster

I. The Book of Byron

1 Plague of Insects

The first time Byron heard the call of the cicadas he was a boy of seven. On a hot, still Mississippi morning he ran out the back door and looked up at the sky. There was nothing to see, and yet he felt a presence, a vibrating blanket of sound gently ebbing and flowing through the tops of the live oaks. The sound then seemed to crescendo as if it were a wave gathering strength, about to descend from above and flood the land.

With his eyes still on the treetops, he ran to the front yard, tripped over a lawn sprinkler and fell to his knees. He got up quickly, brushed the grass from his arms and legs. The smell of grass tickled his nose. He went as far as the front gate and found the sound there, too. It seemed to be everywhere. Maybe the whole town could hear it. He spun around, scanning the upper branches of the trees, but still saw nothing.

If anyone could identify the sound, it was Sofia. She knew about all kinds of things—the plants in the garden, the weather, and what to do if you accidentally spilled salt. For every situation she had a saying like, "When the chairs squeak, it's of rain they speak." With his heart beating wildly, Byron crunched back up the gravel drive to the portico of the big house where he lived with his parents and Sofia. Through the sheer curtains he peeked in, hoping to spot her. At the same time, he wanted to avoid his mother who might drag him into the house to practice piano. He thought it best to return to the back of the house where he might catch Sofia at the kitchen window. But she was not at her station. Byron sat on a tree stump and kept an eye on the window.

With summer vacation came the excitement of having the whole day to wander, even slip into the woods behind the house where he wasn't supposed to go. By the third day, his legs were covered with chigger bites, and his mother made him stay in the house to practice his music. She even threatened to send him to music camp, and he felt his summer freedom sliding into the tedium of sitting on a piano bench, visiting relatives, and forced fishing trips with his father.

But surely this peculiar happening would change things, cause a break in the routine. How big a break he wasn't quite sure. What could the sound be? An invasion of some sort? Spaceships full of funny looking creatures? He really wished he could talk to Sofia about it.

From inside the house he heard his mother yelling and despite his reluctance to see her, he had to find out what was going on. His mother obviously knew something. He stole into the house and stood in the shadows of the doorway between the kitchen and the hall.

"Sofia!" his mother shouted. "I need you to help me pack some bags. And tell Junior to get the car ready. Where's Byron? Byron?"

He stepped into view. "Right here, Mother. Are we evacuating?"

Camille whirled around and saw her son in the doorway. "Evacuating? Why would...we're just going to Aunt Lidia's in New Orleans, sweetheart."

Under normal circumstances Byron loved to visit Lidia, who let him roam the Garden District unsupervised and talked about scandals and local corruption in front of him, which his mother thought was inappropriate. "Why do we have to go, Momma?" he whined.

"The cicadas are here!" she said, as if it explained everything.

"The what?"

"Horrible little creatures. They rise up every umpteen years. They'll be around for weeks and the incessant din gives me a headache. Sofia! Where is she?" Camille shook her head and passed by Byron in the doorway, patting him on the cheek. "Now, go get changed. Look at your shoes! You got mud on them. Can't go to the city looking like that!"

For the next hour Camille rushed around the house giving orders, and Sofia answered with, "Yes, ma'am. Yes, ma'am," a call and response chant, echoing through the house.

Byron sat on the edge of his bed and stared at the oxfords he had changed into. He scuffed them up by running the sole of one over the top of the other to diminish the shine. Sofia passed by and stuck her head in. "What is it, baby?"

"I hate these shoes."

She narrowed her eyes on his feet. "Chile, that don't mean you got to be scuffing 'em up. Ain't got time to clean 'em now. You got to go."

"I don't want to go. Something exciting is finally happening around here, and we're leaving. Why does Momma hate the cicadas so much?"

Sofia's eyes grew large. "They's people say them cicadas coming outta the ground is the souls of babies that never had the chance to cry. They singing the blues."

"Oh," said Byron, looking into her ancient eyes.

They heard Byron's mother calling from downstairs.

"We better go down," said Sofia.

In the back seat of the Lincoln Town Car, Camille breathed a sigh of relief and patted her forehead with a lace-trimmed handkerchief. "Junior, is that air conditioning all the way up?"

"Yessum."

Byron sat next to his mother in brown shorts and a starched white shirt the same wan color as his skin. With a devilish grin on his face, he reached over to the armrest and punched the button, lowering the window. The cool air of the car rippled with heat, and the eerie hum of the cicadas entered in waves.

His mother turned her head in horror. "Byron Purvis! What in heaven's name are you doing?" She leaned over the front seat. "Junior, please put that window up."

"Yessum." The window whirred and finished with a thunk, resealing the car.

"Didn't you just hear me verify that the air conditioning was all the way up? What were you thinking?"

"I wanted to hear it one last time," said Byron. "It'll probably be gone when we get back."

"I certainly hope so."

Byron was about to protest further until he caught the stunned expression on his mother's face. She gasped and grimaced, bent forward slightly, and put her gloved hand to her stomach.

"What is it, Mother?"

"Nothing, baby," she said through clenched teeth. "Please don't open the window again."

"I won't."

"Ma'am?" said Junior, squinting in the rearview mirror.

"Drive on," she said. "I'm all right."

Camille took a shaky breath. She patted her forehead again and turned to smile at her son. "You know, it's the males of the species that make all the noise. Some kind of mating call. Reminds me of the time, the one and only time, your father dragged me to an Ole Miss football game. My, what a clamor! The crowd was not still for a second. Why, you couldn't even carry on a conversation. You get a bunch of men together and they just want to make noise."

"I kind of like the cicada song," said Byron.

"Your father likes it, too. It's beyond my comprehension." She took a cardboard church fan out of the seat pocket and began fanning herself.

Byron moved his hand toward the armrest. "Can't I hear it one more time?"

"Don't be difficult, Byron. Mommy isn't feeling well."

"Are you sure it's just bugs making all that noise?"

"Yes, and if you ask me it's a harbinger of bad news. Puts my nerves on edge. Your daddy makes fun of me, but I *feel* like something bad's going to happen."

"Like an alien invasion!" He moved his cupped hands in the air as if they were spaceships descending to Earth.

Camille grimaced again and blanched slightly. Byron looked at his mother and shuddered. Perhaps opening the window had been a bad idea. What if his mother was wrong and it *was* some kind of invasion, alien insects that sent out eggs or spores or something on the air? His mother could have swallowed them. It could hurt the baby—the baby he wasn't supposed to know about, the little bundle of joy he had overheard his mother talking to Sofia about. Or worse, they could turn the baby into one of them.

Again Camille recovered. She took a deep breath and gazed at Byron with a far-off look. "Alien invasion! That's exactly what it sounds like, now that you mention it."

That night at Aunt Lidia's house a commotion downstairs woke Byron from his slumber. He got up and looked out the window. Down on Prytania Street flashing lights splattered the neighbors' houses, and paramedics eased his mother into the back of an ambulance. He ran out into the hall and down the stairs, but Lidia caught him before he could get out the door.

"Momma!" he screamed.

Lidia held him tight as he struggled to get by her. "It's okay, Byron."

"What happened? Is it the baby?"

His aunt stared into his eyes. "You know about that?"

"Yes," he said, stamping his foot. "Is she going to die?"

"No, sweetheart. They're just taking her to the hospital as a precaution."

"Can we go to the hospital?"

"Not now, dear. In the morning."

Byron knew it was serious when he and Lidia walked into his mother's room at Touro Infirmary the following morning, and his father, dressed in a polo shirt and cuffed linen pants like he'd just come from the golf course, stood beside his mother's bed, holding her hand.

"Hey, sport," Frank Purvis said to his son.

Byron stood at a distance, Lidia behind him with her hand on his shoulder. He looked around the room for some sign of a baby. "Hey, Dad," he mumbled.

Camille was propped up in bed, looking worn, but she had put on makeup and a brave smile. "Hi, sweetie. Come closer."

Lidia let go, and he took a couple of small steps toward the bed. "I'm sorry I opened the window, Momma."

"Oh, don't be silly, honey. It was nothing you did."

The look on her face when he had lowered the window was something he wouldn't soon forget, and he wondered if she was only defending him so his father wouldn't get mad. He was terrified of his father's temper, though his mother always told him not to worry. "You're father loves you and he would never hurt you. He got that temper from Grandpa Purvis and can't help it."

"Your momma tells me you took a shine to the cicadas," said his father.

"Yeah, I guess." He wasn't sure anymore. Something bad had happened. His parents couldn't hide it, and Lidia refused to talk about it on the way to the hospital.

After a couple of days Camille left the hospital, but they stayed in New Orleans. His father went back to Mississippi. There was no mention of a baby then or in the future. His much-anticipated sibling had just disappeared. Everyone pretended that his mother had had nothing more than a stomach flu. With gentle voices and exaggerated civility, the adults tried to set a tone of normalcy in the house. Byron couldn't help but notice the sadness behind their smiles.

2 The Splendor of Grass

What had been a distant hum was now a roar beneath Byron's window. He opened his eyes and looked at the clock. Thank God for summer! As a teenager home from military school, he could relish in the glory of sleeping late and would gladly have stayed in bed another couple of hours if it hadn't been for the grinding and sputtering of a motor outside. The night before he had stayed up late watching a Marilyn Monroe marathon: first *Gentlemen Prefer Blondes* that made him howl with laughter, and then *Niagara* that swept him up in its melodrama. He loved Marilyn, but for none of the reasons that might please his father.

The roar momentarily waned, and then a short time later reappeared right under his window. He threw off the sheet, went to the open window, and leaned on the sill. In the yard was a tall black youth pushing a mower back and forth across the side lawn in paths so straight it looked as if he had used a surveyor's level to mark the lines. The air was full of greenness, and bits of grass gathered on the youth's arms, settling like verdant rain in the tight curls of his hair.

The odor wafting up from below made Byron slightly

dizzy and excited him at the same time. His eyes lingered a moment on the sweat stains growing on the boy's shirt. With a fluttery flu-like sensation in his gut, Byron reached down to adjust the morning stiffness in his boxers.

But the more Byron watched the youth, the more anger rose up inside him. Leaning halfway out the window he shouted, "Could you cut that thing off?"

The young man didn't seem to hear him.

Byron then yelled as loud as he could and waved his arms. "Hey, you!"

The other glanced up at the window, and then back at the mower. He pushed harder and hit a small branch, sending out a crack that Byron felt up and down his spine. Of the many emotions tearing through him, Byron's annoyance at being ignored was the one he felt he could do something about. He made a slicing motion across his throat. The gardener turned off the motor.

"What are you doing? I'm trying to sleep," said Byron.

The youth looked up at the sky, calculating the position of the sun, a hazy glowing ball nearing the top of its arc. He shrugged and reached down to pull the cord to restart the mower. Byron thought he detected a wry smile on the gardener's lips.

"Who does he think he is?" Byron ran to the bedroom door, threw it open and shouted into the hall, "Sofia!"

In a tank top and his plaid boxers—the anger had quieted his erection—he stood in the doorway and yelled her name a couple more times. Sofia made her way down the hall, dust rag in hand and wearing an apron over a faded flowery dress. Byron's mother thought she was terribly liberal by not requiring a uniform like many of her friends did of their help.

"What is it, chile? What's all that racket?"

"That's what I'd like to know. The racket outside, I mean. Who is that idiot mowing the lawn at this hour of the morning?"

"Morning? Getting on close to noon, Mr. Byron. And that idiot, as you say, is my cousin, Thomas. He helping out his daddy with the yardwork."

Sofia normally called him "child" or "honey child" or "sugar" except when she was peeved at him, or when Byron's parents were around. When she called him Mr. Byron, he knew he was being an ass.

Byron groaned. "Sorry, Sofia."

"Somebody got up on the wrong side of the bed."

"I just don't like being woken up."

"Don't I know it?"

Byron looked back toward the window where the roar continued. "Your cousin, you say?"

"Uh-huh. He your age exactly. Play football over to the high school. They say he just like the Payton boy." People in town couldn't stop talking about Walter Payton, who a few years before had been a first draft NFL pick by the Chicago Bears and had already established himself as a stalwart on the team. His football career had started at Columbia High. Byron didn't understand why the town granted him such a favorite son status. It wasn't as if he was a famous writer or scientist. It was just football after all. He had suggested as much in a dinner conversation, and his father had lectured him for an hour on the importance of football in Mississippi.

"Well, good for him, but I still don't understand why he has to mow the lawn at such an ungodly hour," he said to Sofia.

"I'll go out and ask him to stop if you want."

"Already asked him. He just ignored me."

"Well, don't that beat all," Sofia said with a secret smile. "I tell him to behave hisself. Yes, siree, the Purvis family been good to us."

"It's not about that. It's just...I don't know. Can't they mow in the afternoon?"

"Maybe Joe got other yards in the afternoon. Come on, now, and have breakfast. Or would you be wanting lunch?"

She gave him the "Sofia smile".

Byron dressed quickly and went down to breakfast. In the background of his thoughts was the drone of the mower, moving farther away and then closer, back and forth. He couldn't get what he had seen from the upstairs window out of his head: the strong dark arms pushing the machine and the sweat seeping through Thomas' shirt. In the kitchen, where he ate when no one else was around, Sofia chattered away while she fixed his eggs and grits just the way he liked them, the eggs runny and the grits on the dry side.

She set the plate down in front of him, but he stared out the window, mesmerized by the sound of the mower.

Sofia stuck her face in front of his. "Byron, honey. You fixin' to wake up one of these days?"

He smiled. "Guess I need some more of that muddy stuff you like to call coffee."

"Humph. You free to make you own anytime you want." She shook her head. "You just like Thomas. Young'uns got no respect."

Byron laughed. He loved these breakfasts alone with Sofia and the banter they shared. As he mixed his eggs and grits and washed them down with chicory coffee, he half listened to her going on about how many people his mother had invited for the luncheon and how in the world she was ever going to get all the work done. Then the motor stopped.

Byron scooted his chair back and stood up. "I'm going out for a walk."

"But you haven't finished," said Sofia.

"Not that hungry. Thanks."

"That the first time I ever hear that!"

Byron went out the back door where the green odor of trauma from the cut grass hung on the sultry air, a smell that for years to come would send him into a state of excitement, a forever reminder of the day his sexuality came to life. The garage door was open. He saw Thomas bent over the mower, wiping it clean, his broad back stretching against the sweaty T-shirt. Byron stepped inside the garage where his nostrils were now assaulted by the smell of gasoline and oil. His sneeze sounded like a barn door slamming closed.

Thomas turned around quickly. "What the…?"

Byron sniffled. "Sorry. Did I scare you?"

"You got allergies or something?"

"Kinda." He stood like a statue staring at Thomas.

"What? You spectin' an apology?"

"Nope. Guess I should be the one apologizing. You were just doing your job."

Thomas turned back around and continued wiping down the mower with his rag. Byron was sure he was trying to stifle a smile.

"Sofia tells me you play football over at the high school."

"Yes, I do. Haven't seen you around there—or aren't you in high school yet?" he said with a smirk.

"Very funny. I said I was sorry."

Thomas, still on his haunches, folded the rag and turned to face Byron. "Don't take no offense. Momma always telling me I have a big mouth. Seriously, you about the same age as me."

"Going to a military school up in Jackson where my father went. I hate it. Thinking about transferring back to CHS."

"You wanna be a Wildcat, huh?" Thomas said with a big smile.

"A what?"

"You know, the Columbia Wildcats."

"Well, not much point in a military school when I have no intention of going into the military. Been going to private schools all my life. I just want to see what a regular school is like."

"Well, you ain't missing that much." He stood up, tall

and strong. "Guess I shoulda checked if anybody's sleeping, but I wanted to finish early. Pa told me I could go fishing after I'm done. You ever go?" He nodded toward the rods and fishing gear in the corner.

"That's my daddy's. He used to take me when I was little, but I hated it."

"Hmm. You don't like fishing. You don't like military school. And it seems you really don't like getting up in the morning. Tell me something you *do* like."

Byron took a step back and crossed his arms over his chest to confront the challenge. It took him a minute to think of something that didn't sound stupid like, Marilyn Monroe movies.

"I like to go out on the roof at night when no one is around and look at the stars," Byron said. As soon as it was out of his mouth, he realized it sounded only marginally better than saying he liked Marilyn Monroe. He fully expected to be mocked.

Thomas nodded his head and grinned as if pleased with Byron's answer. "You one of them romantic types, I guess."

Byron felt the color rising in his cheeks, still worried about how he might appear to Thomas. "I don't know about romantic, but as soon as I graduate from high school, I'm out of this town."

"I hear ya. I'm hoping for a scholarship to Jackson State or someplace."

"Like Walter Payton, right?"

Thomas smiled. "I suppose you don't like football either."

Byron shrugged and then let out a gigantic sneeze. Thomas jumped back as if from the force of the explosion. "Damn, that got to be the loudest sneeze I ever heard."

"Sorry," said Byron.

"Don't worry about it," said Thomas, folding the rag over and over in his hands.

"Well," they both said at the same time, and then

laughed.

"Guess you want to get going," said Byron.

"Still got a little cleaning up to do, but yeah."

"Hope you catch some fish," said Byron. With a buzz in his head he walked out of the garage on shaky legs. Then he sneezed three times in succession. "That damn grass does it every time," he mumbled.

3 His Hands Full of Sweet Innocence

Until the day Byron met Thomas the notion of transferring to Columbia High was a fantasy that had little chance of becoming realized considering his father's firm belief in the military academy's motto of "Give us a boy and get back a man." But looking out the bedroom window that morning, it was as if he had seen a whole new world. The five-minute conversation with Thomas in the garage—a casual conversation with a football player at the local high school—had awakened him from a deep sleep and given him the courage to confront his parents.

"I want a normal life," Byron told his parents in the summer between his sophomore and junior years.

"Have you been *bothered* at school?" asked his panicked mother, her implications obvious.

His father didn't let him answer, chiming in with, "Things get better in the last two years. That's when you get all the benefits," he said in an exasperated voice. "Give it one more year at least."

It took another year of sulky moods and carefully constructed arguments before his father gave in. His senior year he would spend at Columbia High.

It didn't take Byron long to realize that he didn't fit in any better at Columbia High than at the academy. While other students shuffled or bulldozed or paraded down the corridors in packs, he crept along like a shadow, avoiding stares and the occasional jostle.

Thomas was not in any of Byron's classes, but he knew that, at some point, he would he would run into him. Since that day in the garage, images of Thomas had frequently flashed in his head. To make matters worse, Byron fed his fascination by anticipating when the grass needed mowing and made sure he was home. He would look out his upstairs window (a couple of times Thomas had looked up and caught him staring), though he avoided talking to Thomas directly. He had no idea what to say, and he was absolutely sure Thomas didn't have the same curiosity about him.

One day Thomas came sauntering down the hall in all his football body splendor with a girl on each side. Since one of the girls had Thomas' attention, Byron thought he could get past the group unnoticed. Byron's eyes focused on the beige metal lockers to his right, as if they were of some anthropological interest, the scratchings in the paint like ancient hieroglyphics. He breathed a sigh of relief when they passed.

And then Thomas' joyful voice rang out, "Purvis, what are you doing here?" He had stopped and turned to Byron.

The two girls looked at Byron at first with surprise and then annoyance, as if he had barged onto the field during a cheerleader practice.

"You a student here now?" said Thomas in a voice loud enough to make Byron cringe.

"Uh, yeah. I transferred."

"Come on, Thomas," said one of the girls. "We're gonna be late."

Thomas ignored her. "That's cool," he said to Byron.

A group of boys known as Kelly's gang pushed past Byron. "You're blocking the hall, asshole," said Kelly.

"Sorry," said Byron, moving out of the way.

"Who the hell is that?" asked one of Kelly's friends.

"I don't know," said Kelly. "Some new faggot at the school." He guffawed and they went on. Byron wondered if Kelly really didn't remember him or was embarrassed to admit it. They had gone to the same grade school.

Thomas looked after them with narrowed eyes and a flared nose.

"I've got to go," said Byron.

"See you around," Thomas replied.

Byron stood plastered to the lockers, dumbfounded, watching Thomas catch up with the girls. Then Thomas looked back over his shoulder with a mysterious smile and what looked like a wink, though later Byron was sure he had imagined it. The fact that Thomas had acknowledged him at all made Byron's face hot and his stomach tighten.

It would take Byron a while to learn the dynamics of a public high school. Military school had been tough at times, but the rules of engagement were clear. Even harassment followed a certain protocol. Why would this black football player that he hardly knew be friendly while friends he used to play with as kids taunted him? Byron walked on, oblivious to the sophomoric antics spinning around him. He got lost in a daydream where Kelly and his friends were calling him names, trying to pick a fight. Thomas came up behind them and grabbed two of them, a neck in each hand, and smashed their heads into the lockers. It was sweet. It made him smile for a split second before the absurdity of his fantasy ripped the contentment from his face.

Byron came out of the cool basement office of the school newspaper into the airless drippy heat of late afternoon. The upside of being at Columbia High was spending time with his childhood friend, Julie. She had encouraged him to work on the school paper with her, and it made him feel, in a small way, like he belonged.

He crossed the nearly empty parking lot toward his red Mustang. The car was a gift from his father who, relegated to the somber automobiles of his grown-up life, had taken upon himself to buy Byron a muscle car, fulfilling his own teenage fantasies. At first Byron was embarrassed by the gift, though he wasn't immune to the way other students admired it, or to the rush he got from the roar of the engine when he stepped on the gas. He sometimes wondered what Thomas would think of it, if he would want to ride in it.

From a distance he saw Thomas come out of the gym after football practice and start walking up Bryan Avenue toward Church Street. The smile earlier that day sparked a recklessness in him. Byron jumped in his car and pulled up alongside Thomas who walked with his head down, deep in thought, the sweat rolling down his cheeks.

"You need a ride?" Byron yelled out the window, his voice slightly cracking.

Thomas bent down and looked in the car. "It's outta your way I'm sure."

"I don't mind."

Thomas opened the door and paused a moment to take in the expanse of the car, whistling his appreciation. "Guess it's better than walking. You ever been to my part of town?"

"I don't know. Where is it?"

"Out Owens Street. You know, that *rough* area," he said with a grin.

They rode in silence, Thomas hugging the backpack in his lap.

"You could put that in the back. Be more comfortable."

Thomas turned to throw his backpack in the back seat, and Byron glanced at the taut muscles of his arm and the smooth hardness of his bicep. He forced his eyes to return to the road, just in time to see a stop sign right in front of them. Byron slammed on the brakes and they both lurched forward. Thomas put his hand on the dash.

"Damn! Who taught you to drive? Maybe I should get out and walk from here."

"Sorry." Byron's jaw fell like he'd been punched in the stomach.

"I's just kiddin'. No biggie."

In a neighborhood of modest homes with laundry flapping in the wind and black children playing in the yards, Thomas directed Byron to pull over in front of a white house with a porch swing. Unlike many other houses on the street, the yard was clear of rusted debris, but the grass needed mowing.

"I appreciate the lift," said Thomas, staring out the front windshield.

Byron breathed the odor of his own sweat and caught a whiff of Thomas' as well. While his heart beat an off-rhythm, Byron became aware of Thomas' hand in front of him, waiting to be shaken. Byron took it and felt the calluses of an athlete and worker. And then he sensed the tingling of embarrassment that his own hands were so smooth. He imagined the intermingled palms of their contrasting colors, but didn't dare look down. He had the urge to lift the giant paw to his lips and kiss it. Thomas started to withdraw his hand, but Byron, trembling with his own recklessness, entranced in a lazy afternoon cloud where his hand acted on its own, wouldn't let go. Thomas extricated his hand with a forceful jerk. "What are you doing?" Thomas said with more astonishment than anger.

Byron quickly put his hand in his lap. "Huh? Sorry."

"Sorry? You been sorry all day." His voice sounded more disgusted with Byron's sorryness than the prolonged handshake.

"Sorry. I mean, cancel that. It's just that no one has been very nice to me at school." As soon as he said it, he regretted it. It sounded whiny. But what most amazed Byron was that Thomas was still in the car. He hadn't fled in revulsion, or at least confusion, as any other teenage boy might have done.

Thomas opened the door, cutting into the moment and bringing them back to where they were. Byron felt panicked to come up with a clever line, or perhaps an invitation for something they might do together.

Before his thoughts could transform into words, Thomas blurted out, "Thanks again, Purvis."

"Uh…Byron. I don't like Purvis much."

Thomas was out of the car. He closed the door and shook his head. "It's your name."

"I know."

As Byron drove away, revulsion rose up in him. Kelly had been right. He was an asshole. He knew he wasn't supposed to have these feelings. Two blocks up the street, he saw in the rearview mirror two small boys standing in the road staring after him. In the same moment, he saw Thomas' backpack in the back seat. "Oh, Christ," he said. He turned around, parked in front of the house, went up on the porch, and knocked. Thomas' father, Joe, came to the door.

"I gave Thomas a ride home and he left his pack in my car," Byron said quickly. "Here." Joe opened the screen and took it.

"Hey. You's the Purvis boy, ain't ya?" Joe had taken over the yardwork after Byron went away to military school. During the summers, Byron had seen him a few times, but they had never spoken.

"Yes, sir."

Joe chuckled at being called sir. "Tell you daddy I'll be over on Saturday for the yard."

Thomas came up behind his father. "Oh, thanks." He took the bag. "Pa asked me to help out on Saturday, so might see ya."

The punches to Byron's heart kept coming. "Oh, sure. Maybe. I mean if I'm around and all."

Byron backed away and trotted down the steps.

On Friday afternoon Byron forcefully removed the chain from the sprocket of his bicycle. On Saturday, he stayed around the house until Thomas had finished mowing. Like the afternoon a couple years before, Byron went in the garage while Thomas was bent over, cleaning the mower.

"Pretty hot out there, isn't it?" said Byron.

"Uh-huh," Thomas said without turning around, his back showing no signs of being startled or surprised at Byron's sudden appearance. "I didn't start mowing too early. Then I saw you's out on the porch reading, so I guessed it was okay."

"I was a jerk that time. Sorr...I mean..."

Thomas swung around and laughed. He shook his head in a slow, downward side-to-side motion that Byron had seen several times and had begun to associate with his character. Byron stood in that catatonic state of not having the slightest idea what to say. "So?" said Thomas.

"Oh, my bike." Byron pointed to his olive green Raleigh sitting in the corner. "I was going to ride downtown, but the chain's off. Was wondering if you could help me fix it? Should only take a minute. I don't want to delay you if you're going fishing or something."

"Let's take a look."

They turned the bike upside down and hunched down on either side of it.

"I don't know. It looks pretty complicated." Thomas screwed up his mouth as if he knew it was a ruse, but didn't seem to care much. He began to thread the chain back onto the sprocket and Byron watched the grease make its way to Thomas' fingers. Byron hated getting his fingers greasy and felt bad he was making Thomas do it.

Through the spokes Byron stared at Thomas, his image cut into a kaleidoscope of pieces, parts of a puzzle that changed with a slight movement of his head. Who was this boy, Byron's opposite, possessed of a gentle and playful spirit, strong and self-assured? Byron stared at the spinning wheel as if it were a wheel of fortune that might stop on a prize, or land on "Bankcrupcy" where he would lose everything. He stood up, took a couple of steps back, pulled out a handkerchief, and wiped his forehead. "Man, it's hot."

"Uh-huh," Thomas mumbled. "Okay, looks like we got it."

"Thanks. You want a Coke?"

"That'd be nice for sure. Got me a thirst."

Byron ran into the house for the Cokes. When he came back, Thomas was spinning the wheels of the bike to make sure they were working. "If you ever get over your fear of fishing, we might try it sometime."

"It's not a fear, Christ. I just didn't like it. 'Course that doesn't mean I wouldn't try it again."

"Is that a yes?"

"Well, when are you coming over next? Bring your fishing stuff and maybe we could go after."

"Me and Mr. Purvis going fishing. Ain't that something?" He let out one of those chuckles like a brook dancing over smooth rocks.

"Mr. Purvis is my father. Byron, please."

"Like the poet."

Byron tilted his head and was on the verge of saying, "How do you know about Lord Byron?" but figured it sounded patronizing. "Yep. It was my mother's idea. Guess she really liked some of his poems she read in college." Byron had done his own reading of the poems as well as a biography. "At her college, I doubt they delved much into his personal life."

"Like what?"

"Man, the stuff he did reads like a scandal sheet. He did it all."

Thomas laughed. "You still young. Maybe you can, too."

Byron felt a shot of electricity pulse through his nerves.

He was on the verge of telling Thomas what he had read about Lord Byron having male lovers as well as female, but he held back. He forced a laugh and said, "We'll see about that."

"Hmm." Thomas pursed his lips and looked away. It was the first time Byron had seen him turn pensive.

4 Make Thee a Fiery Serpent

On a muggy afternoon when the fish had stopped biting, the Pearl River, with its long, crooked finger, beckoned Byron and Thomas to cool their bodies in its flow. They stripped down to their shorts and felt the bottom sludge ooze through their toes as they stepped into the water.

They were the only two people in the area, and yet they maintained a distance as if strangers who had happened on the same spot by chance—Byron floating on his back and Thomas showing off by swimming laps across the river as fast as he could.

Since the day Kelly had seen Byron give Thomas a ride, Byron thought it better to avoid Thomas at school and not offer him any more rides. Kelly and his gang had stepped up their campaign of hallway torments, added "nigger lover" to their repertoire of taunts, saving for it a hostility that far surpassed the regular insults of "queer" and "faggot." But Byron still looked forward to the Saturdays when Thomas would come to cut the grass. Later they would decide on a place to meet, and then discreetly head into the woods to go fishing.

As Byron continued to lie on his back treading water, he listened to Thomas' hands slapping the surface as he swam back and forth. With his head in the sky, Byron thought back to an incident that happened about a month after the new insults started, a confrontation which gave Byron his knight-in-shining-armor fantasy, though it wasn't as delightful as he had imagined. On a day that Byron had a particularly large load of books and papers in his hands, Kelly slammed Byron into a locker, causing his books and papers to spread across the floor. Byron recovered, but when he bent over to pick up the mess, a couple of Kelly's friends knocked him to his knees.

Kelly cocked his leg back, poised to soccer kick Byron's French book down the hall when Thomas appeared out of nowhere and stuck out his leg to block Kelly. It threw Kelly off balance, and he fell against the wall.

"Stop messing with him," Thomas growled in low voice.

Kelly's friends immediately surrounded Thomas, saying "Yeah? What are you going to do about it?"

One by one Thomas looked each bully in the eye. "I don't want no trouble. Let me pass."

All action in the hallway stopped and a hundred eyes looked on. Just then the history teacher, who also happened to be the football coach stuck his head out of a nearby classroom. "What's going on, Davis?"

"Nothing."

"Get moving, everybody," the teacher roared.

Thomas pushed through the gang, picked up the French book, and handed it to Byron.

"Thanks," said Byron, not looking at him.

Thomas leaned forward and spoke in voice low enough that no one would hear. "See you Saturday."

On Thomas' fourth or fifth crossing of the river, Byron heard the sound of Thomas' strokes stop.

"Shit," said Thomas. "Look!"

Annoyed at being disturbed, Byron let out a lazy "What?"

Thomas swam to Byron and yanked his arm. "Over there."

They gaped at a snake plodding through the murky water, its head bobbing on the surface. It seemed headed straight for them.

"Is that a cottonmouth?" said a horrified Byron.

"Go," yelled Thomas, and he pushed Byron toward the shore.

They swam as if in an Olympic race, Thomas arriving first, grabbing Byron's arm and pulling him onto the patch of beach. Full of the remnants of fear and the exhilaration of escape, hearts pumping at a new rhythm, they stomped along the sandy shore, and then stopped to gaze with relief at the snake drifting down river.

"Damn! Damn! Damn!" said Thomas, his excited toes kicking up sand. "That close to meetin' our maker." He laughed hysterically, and Byron joined in.

Byron watched Thomas continue to pace up and down the water's edge like a Great Dane, his powerful body twisting and glistening with river water, his jaw hanging open to take in every part of the moment. And then he made a sudden turn, ran toward Byron, his arms outstretched. Byron stood wide-eyed, imagining that Thomas was about to tackle him. He turned at the last minute in an attempt to run away, but Thomas managed to grab Byron around the waist and bring him to the ground.

Their laughter had faded, replaced by panting. Byron felt Thomas' breath on the back of his neck. He tried to push Thomas away and squirm out from under him.

"Oh, you want to wrestle, huh?" said Thomas.

"No," Byron answered flatly. "Get off me."

They were on an embankment, and Byron thought that if he pushed Thomas' weight with all his might toward the river he might escape. They rolled and grappled, arms flailing, but Thomas held tight in a contest absurd in its inequality. Thomas soon had Byron pinned to the sand, sitting astraddle him and holding his arms above his head.

The breathing of exertion pumped Byron's chest, and under the weight of Thomas, he became painfully aware that he wasn't just pinned under someone much bigger and stronger, he was at the mercy of a man with black skin. Distrust ripped through him, dredged up from his whiteness, his privilege. But why this distrust? In the time they had spent together the most threatening thing Thomas had done was to tease him, play on his insecurities as boys will with each other. Thomas could be quiet at times, obsessively serious in his training, but seemingly a soul who wished no harm on anyone. He was, as Byron had dubbed him in the school newspaper, Sweetness Two. And yet the thread of terror still ran through him as he felt the power of Thomas' limbs, limbs that perhaps didn't know their own strength or what resentment might lurk in a dark memory, limbs that could crush him like a gnat. He also had an inkling of why Thomas liked playing linebacker: the tackle, its permissible nature of hunting someone down and bringing him to the ground, the sheer domination of it.

Byron continued struggling to get free and with it came a dreadful stirring inside him, a frightening expectation that Thomas' domination might take a different form, that something he hadn't yet dared put into words might happen.

But the torment Thomas had in mind was something Byron couldn't have imagined. Thomas worked his jaws and produced a gob of saliva, which he let dangle from his lips just above Byron face. Then, like a frog recoiling his tongue, he slurped it back up.

"That's disgusting," said Byron, and bucked in another futile attempt to get free. "Get off me. I mean it."

Thomas started working his jaws again. "Don't move or it will fall," he said, his eyes sparkling. Several dark shades of delight were painted on his face. He produced another stream of saliva and let it hang inches above Byron's mouth. It appeared a practiced gesture, a prank he had done a hundred times while straddling boys in the neighborhood, maybe his brothers and sisters.

Byron no longer saw the dangling spit above him, but stared instead at the lips from whence it came. He had never kissed anyone before and found himself wondering what it would be like to touch those lips to his. The delinquent thought paradoxically calmed him as though he were abandoning himself to death because in the mere ability to formulate that thought, a part of him was dying. His body went still.

"Do it," Byron whispered.

There was a moment of frightening silence, where the only sounds were the rush of the river and the breeze rattling the trees. They looked into each other's eyes and in a moment were brought back to who they were: boys from two families that lived less than a mile from each other, and yet they might as well have been from different planets.

Any vestiges of merriment came to a complete halt. Thomas sucked the saliva back into his mouth and wiped his face. He blinked and looked away. His face now had lines as if he had aged twenty years in a few seconds. He let go of Byron's hands and jumped up. "We should go."

"I was just kidding."

As Thomas moved away from him, Byron was overcome with a sense of ugliness, that Thomas couldn't in any way find him desirable with his hairless concave chest and thin arms, the pallor of his skin. And yet the ugliest thing of all was the monstrous desire churning inside him. Thomas must have sensed it and been disgusted. But in the moment before Thomas turned his back, Byron's astonished eyes landed on the bulge in Thomas' shorts. Thomas quickly ran to the river and dove in, seemingly oblivious to the snake they had seen earlier.

Byron got to his feet and ran into the woods, at first with the impulse to jump in his car and leave Thomas stranded. He trembled with what he thought was anger, and horrible thoughts about Thomas came into his head, racist ideas that he would have sworn were not part of him. For a moment he hated Thomas, the broad nose, his brutish body with its need to dominate, the charcoal patches on his elbows, the springy little wires of hair on his head. He hoped the snake got him and he would never have to see him again. In his blind rage he stumbled on a tree root and fell, skinning his knee and feeling a sharp pain in the hand that he had thrown out to catch himself. Tears formed in his eyes. Sprawled on the ground he stared at a trail of ants happily marching toward some unforeseeable goal.

"Are you okay?"

Byron sat up, but couldn't look at Thomas. He stared instead at his bleeding knee and listened to the water dripping from Thomas' shorts onto the leaves as he stood above him.

Thomas crouched down and touched Byron's leg below the knee. He took the T-shirt from the elastic of his shorts and brushed some dirt off the wound. Byron tried to move his leg, but Thomas held it steady.

"You don't have to do that," said Byron.

"I saw the snake again. But it wasn't close." They spoke without looking at each other's eyes.

"I worried about that."

"Yeah, so much that you ran off and left me."

"Sorry."

"You are the sorriest person I know." And then he did something that left Byron dumbfounded. He bent down and kissed his wounded knee. Then he raised his head and found Byron's eyes. "Momma says it makes it better," he said in a man-child voice.

Ah, Thomas distant, Thomas playful, Thomas rough, Thomas sweet. All the facets connected. Byron offered his hand. "I hurt my hand, too." Thomas took it and began to massage it, bringing out sensations of pain and pleasure. Byron was lost. He closed his eyes.

With Byron's hand tucked in his, Thomas stood up, pulling Byron with him. They were two streams merging into a river, and the river rushing toward an endless sea. With his other hand, Thomas pulled the drawstring on Byron shorts and pushed them down. Byron let his head fall into the crook of Thomas' neck. He smelled the river mixed with Thomas' essence, a pungent blend of earth and sweat. He smelled different from anyone he had ever been near, a wonderful difference that made Byron's blood roar.

"Turn around," Thomas whispered in his ear.

Byron didn't move. He wanted to hear that whisper again and again, feel the hot breath fill his head and drown out the negative voices forever.

Thomas gently twisted Byron's torso as though it were a lump of clay that he was about to mold into something new. He wrapped his arm around Byron's chest and pulled Byron back against him, this time with force. He lowered his own shorts and with his head resting on Byron's upper back he forced him to bend forward.

It was, like stray dogs, over in less than five minutes. Byron had cried out in pain at first and then could feel Thomas slow down though he seemed unable to stop. When it was over, Byron fell to his knees. Snot ran from his nose and tears down his cheeks. Thomas pulled up his shorts and knelt beside him, resting a hand on Byron's back. "I'm sorry."

"Now you're the sorry one," Byron said in a voice rattled with mucus.

"Yeah," Thomas said, suppressing a chuckle. "But I

mean it. I couldn't—"

Byron exploded in a sneeze that seemed to shake the trees. "Oh, God!" he said, with huge sigh of relief. They both began to laugh. Thomas put his hand behind Byron's neck and pulled their faces together. Their foreheads touched. Thomas kissed him and their spit, and tears and snot all mixed together, and there was something in that elixir that enchanted them, made them happy and sad at the same time, and very, very far from home.

5 Giveth and Taketh Away

Thomas was in a mood. He walked back to the car with his head down, stabbing the air with his fishing pole. All afternoon they had only caught two scrawny carp. Thomas threw them back. Might have been the cicadas causing the fish not to bite. Byron remembered how enthralled he had been when the cicadas had emerged thirteen years earlier, his boyish fascination with their song. Now he leaned toward his mother's irrational fear of the creatures, the hum from the trees taking over his body, making his head light and his senses distorted. Colors took on a heightened intensity. Smells seemed outside of their normal limits. He pictured the nymphs tunneling up from the ground in the millions, shedding their skins, and emerging as winged adults. A part of him wanted to flee, get in the car with Thomas, and go far away. At the same time he remembered his mother telling him about the song being a mating call. His body made the connection as his mind tried to pull him away.

He and Thomas were home for the weekend—Byron from Tulane in New Orleans and Thomas from Jackson State—the meeting arranged through discreet hallway phone calls from their dorms. The fact that they hadn't done it yet had been in Byron's mind all afternoon; the urgency was more than the rampant hormones of youth. As much as he tried, he couldn't trust what he and Thomas had. They had been having sex for a couple of years now and after each time, Byron got the tumbling feeling it was the last, that Thomas' desire would wane, that the forces against them—the external pressures to conform to the wishes of family and society, and the internal fears that following their sexual inclinations was wrong—would make it impossible for them to go on. And Thomas, with his enigmatic manner, was no help. Outside of the facial contortions and moans of pleasure during throes of passion, Thomas acted like they were nothing more than fishing buddies.

"Do you even like me?" Byron said one day, though immediately regretted it.

"Stupid question." Thomas looked toward the ground and shook his head. "What? You want me to hold your hand walking down Broad Street?"

"No, of course not."

"Don't upset the apple cart. We got a good thing." That was about as expressive as Thomas would get: They had a good thing. "You *know* we can't make it more than it is," said Thomas with a tilted head and a negotiator's smile. Byron didn't know that, but he had to accept it.

Thomas was under enormous pressure to follow in the footsteps of Walter Payton, though he hadn't come close to the records Payton set at Columbia High and it was unlikely he would at Jackson State. Still, it seemed he had a shot at playing professional. Thomas was a fanatic about his training, sometimes dropping his fishing pole and sprinting up and down the sandbanks and steep levees alongside the river during the heat of the day. Other times, when they walked through the woods, he would drop down and do fifty pushups.

Byron and Thomas emerged from the trees to the dirt road where the car was parked. "Hey, By. What's going on with you? You been awful quiet."

"Nothing. Just thinking."

They put the fishing gear in the trunk and Thomas started to get in the front seat.

"Wait," said Byron.

Thomas gave him a look like he knew what was coming. "What?"

"Come on," said Byron with his hand still on the trunk. He tilted his head back toward the woods and arched his golden eyebrows. He was tired of Thomas always being the one who decided when they would have sex. And he was damned if he was going to drive back to New Orleans the following afternoon full to his throat in pent-up desire.

Thomas stood by the passenger door, dropped his head, and let out a puff of air.

"Forget it—if it's that much of an imposition," said Byron. He started for the driver's side.

A gust of wind moved through the trees, and a hickory nut plunked onto the roof of the car, startling them both. They gazed up and saw a squirrel prance toward the end of a high branch.

Thomas smiled at Byron, enjoying Byron's pout. "You're right. No reason the afternoon should be a total loss." He stood up straight and shook out his shoulders.

Byron flipped open the trunk and pulled out the blanket. They went to a spot under an old magnolia tree replete with white blossoms beginning to turn brown. They were on Byron's daddy's land, twenty acres along the Pearl River near Morgantown just south of Red Bluff, a canyon on the bank of the Pearl showing a colorful palette of reddish hues. People liked to call it Mississippi's Little Grand Canyon. The area was wild and densely forested, but they still had to be careful. There were no fences and people sometimes strayed onto their land, hunters mostly or visitors searching for a short cut to Red Bluff.

Against the din of the cicadas, they heard a mockingbird in a seemingly endless repertoire—from staccato chirps to a two-note rising and falling tweet to a high-pitched honk that sounded more like an alarm. They liked to think it was always the same one—their bird, their tree. Not far away were the ever-present crows, cawing like angry crones. Byron kept waiting for the day when the mockingbird, with its gift for mimicry, would produce the sounds he and Thomas made under the tree: his own short gasps going up the scale and Thomas' guttural mumblings that sounded as if he were unconsciously speaking in a forgotten African language.

They hadn't bothered to undress completely. Shorts around the ankles. T-shirts pulled up. Sneakers still on. They had been in a hurry to get at it, and they could dress quickly if they heard people coming their way. Byron lay face down, his head over the edge of the blanket, inhaling the crisp nutty smell of leaves and the astringent bite of the grass. Thomas settled himself on top, nuzzling the back of Byron's neck. All around them were the sounds of insect and animal life echoing their own stirrings, the fulfillment of desires, while the sun peeked through the leaves and landed in patterns on their backs. The forest was their temple, their sanctuary from the ignorant world around them.

Thomas stopped.

"What is it?" Byron gasped.

"I don't know. Our friend." They looked up. The mockingbird had gone into alarm mode, twisting its head around, opening its beak and screeching like a rusty door. The crows had gone completely silent.

"Probably nothing," said Byron. He was anxious to continue, get to that edge and fall into the selfish place where a man cares only about his own fulfillment.

The bird amped up her alarm. Then there was a loud

crack. They often heard the pop of a hunter's rifle in the distance and Thomas would play like he was hit, grab his chest and fall to the ground. Now Thomas' body jerked. He let out a short, violent groan and slumped on top of Byron.

"Stop it," Byron mumbled, assuming that Thomas was playing.

Then he felt a hot liquid spreading over his back. "What the...? Thomas, did you...?"

In a voice thick with bewilderment, Thomas said, "I think I been shot."

Thomas' full weight was on him now, flattening him to the ground. Byron reached back and touched the wetness running down his sides. He brought the red-stained fingertips in front of his eyes. A gust of panic rattled him from head to toe. Byron heard voices—shouting, arguing, coming closer.

"Fuck, they're coming," said Byron. "We've got to get out of here. Let me up."

Byron thought of the silly war games they used to play at military school, exercises he never thought he'd have to use in real life. He now pictured them doing the low crawl over to a fallen log surrounded by brush about twenty yards away.

"Over there," said Byron, motioning with his head toward the log. "We crawl. Can you do it?"

Thomas was on his side now, his hand on the wound. Blood flowed through his fingers. The grass was wet with it. Byron's stomach pitched as if he were going to vomit, but he didn't. He turned away and started to inch over the ground. "Come on, Thomas."

Thomas moved about a foot, and then slumped flat to the ground, his face turned to the side. Byron looked back and saw it was worse than he thought. He went back and grabbed Thomas' arm, tugging and pulling, but couldn't move him.

"I can't," said Thomas. "You go. Get out of here." His

voice now sounded like a small stream gurgling over rocks.

Byron kept trying to pull on Thomas' arm. "I can't leave you. Please, come on. Try."

"No, Byron. Just save yourself."

"I'm not leaving you." Tears of frustration choked Byron. "Please try," he gurgled.

"Don't," said Thomas. "I'm telling ya. Run. Go!"

Byron shook his head. He pulled his T-shirt over his head and covered, Thomas' wound. He had no idea what to do, but instinct told him he had to stop the bleeding.

The voices edged closer. "Whadja do, you dumbass? I told you we were just gonna have a little fun."

"Did I hit him? Hell, I was just aiming. Didn't mean to pull the trigger."

"Probably the first time in your life you ever hit something you was aiming at. Christ!"

"You done good," said a third voice. "You nailed a nigger raping a white girl."

"You guys are idiots," said the first voice. "That ain't no white *girl*. Now what do we do?"

Byron felt the pulse of blood under his hands. He looked at the three hunters staggering through the pines toward them, the pines that had always hid them, but today had failed. The woods were never so silent. Even the cicada song seemed to have stopped. The sun hid its face in a cloud.

And then a glimmer of hope. Byron knew them. Kelly and his two minions, Jasper and Preston, the same people who had made his life miserable in high school. But they were the devil he knew, especially Kelly, who had been a schoolmate since childhood. They were bullies, but Byron never thought of them as murderers.

"Somebody get help!" Byron screamed.

"Well, lookie here. This chick's got a dick," said Jasper.

Byron ran his hand through his shoulder-length hair and tucked it behind his ear. "Don't just stand there. Get help!"

"Don't fight with 'em, By." Thomas' voice was barely a whisper.

Byron looked down into Thomas' black eyes, watched the life fading. "Hold on. I'm going to get help." He took Thomas' hands and placed them on the wound. He stood up and pulled up his pants, giving Kelly a hard stare. "You gonna shoot me, too, go ahead."

"Stop squawking," said Kelly. "We ain't gonna shoot ya."

"We ain't?" said Preston.

Byron started in the direction of the car.

"Where you going?" said Kelly.

"Get help."

Jasper lifted his gun and pointed it at Byron's back.

"Put your fuckin' gun down, you bozo," said Kelly. He knocked the barrel to the ground. "One could be an accident. The faggot is Judge Purvis' son. They'll come after you."

"I'd be doing the world a favor," said Jasper.

"Just shut up," said Kelly.

Byron began to run. The adrenaline surged, and imagining the gun pointed at him, he became a deer, bounding from side to side, jumping over fallen logs. But he didn't get far before Kelly tackled him to the ground with a heavy thud. Kelly had thirty pounds on him, and as hard as Byron struggled, he couldn't get up.

Kelly's labored breathing smelled of tobacco and whiskey. "That what they teach you in college?" He hissed in Byron's ear. "Take it up the ass from a nigger?" He made a single hard thrust with his crotch into Byron's backside.

"Fuck you," said Byron. "If he dies, you're going down for murder."

"Not me. I saved your life. Now I'm gonna let you up. Don't try to run again or we *will* shoot you."

Kelly held Byron by the arm and dragged him back to

where Jasper and Preston were standing under the magnolia, smoking cigarettes. They kept glancing over at Thomas with his pants still down around his ankles.

"That's sick. How could you be all up on that?" said Jasper.

Preston looked at Byron. "Yeah. Cover that up, would ya? Gettin' sick a lookin' at it."

"Take a good look," said Byron. "You've just shot the next Walter Payton. The town's going to put you away for this."

"What? The town ain't gonna do shit!" said Jasper. His eyes were bloodshot and his speech slurred. He still hadn't registered who Thomas was.

Kelly moved closer and studied the man on the ground. "Shit, Jasper. You messed up. That's Davis, football Davis."

"All look the same to me."

Byron felt a hatred so profound he wanted to grab Jasper by the throat. Squeeze the life out of him. Why couldn't he act, ride on the wave of rage the way other people did?

Kelly stepped in between Byron and Jasper. He took a rope out of his backpack and threw it to Preston. "Take this and tie Purvis' hands and feet," he said. "Then we're going over yonder and have a powwow about what to do."

"Tie him your damn self," said Preston. "I don't wanna touch him. Seems you got no problem with that though."

"Fuck you." Kelly grabbed the rope. "You turds go on over there. I'll be over in a minute."

Byron felt time goose-stepping toward disaster. He glanced at Thomas' blood soaking through the shirt. Byron's body trembled.

"Hold still, damn it!" said Kelly, wrapping the rope around Byron's wrists.

Byron stared at the tobacco stains on Kelly's fingers. For all Kelly's bullheadedness and posturing, Byron knew he was someone who could be reasoned with, someone who could see the consequence of his actions. "K…Kelly, you can't let him die." Byron took a couple gulps of air, tried to slow the thumping in his chest. "You could be a hero, saving Columbia High's old football star. You could say it was just an accident. You aren't like those guys."

Byron saw a spark in Kelly's eyes as if he wanted to do the right thing. But Kelly seemed torn; he probably didn't want to seem weak in front of his buddies. Over the years Byron had watched Kelly establish himself as the alpha male in his little band of rednecks. It would be hard for him to put that position in jeopardy.

"Just shut up. The last thing I need is you telling me what to do." Kelly looked away a minute, stared at his friends under the tree. When he looked back at Byron, his momentary softening had vanished. "We was just gonna scare you. Have a little fun. But you had to be doing the nasty and got my friends all upset. If anyone's to blame, it's you, Purvis."

Byron opened his mouth to present his defense, but no words came. Kelly was already standing up, walking away. What could he say to soften Kelly's accusation, words that crushed him under their weight of their possible truth?

Kelly, Jasper, and Preston sat on their haunches under a tree about twenty yards away, cradling their rifles, spitting, and occasionally glaring at Byron. Kelly did most of the talking, Preston and Jasper most of the spitting. Jasper pulled a flat bottle out his back pocket and they passed it around.

Byron scooted closer to his friend. "Thomas," he whispered. "Try and keep the pressure on. Don't give up." Tears welled in his eyes. He felt something that had to be love. Never before with Thomas had he allowed his heart go to that place he knew so little about. They stared into each other's eyes. Thomas' eyelids fluttered. With one hand he reached over and touched Byron's shoe. This is what they had. A touch on the shoe. A look. The slightest hint that

Thomas might have loved him back.

The three returned and stood over him. The afternoon sun was in Byron's eyes, so he couldn't see their faces. But he had a feeling that the decision wasn't good.

"Get up," said Kelly. "We're going."

Byron rose to his feet and Kelly untied his ankles. "I don't think we should move Thomas. It might—"

"Not him," said Kelly.

"But we're going to get help, right?"

"Come on."

"No!" Byron screamed. "You can't do that!"

"We can and we are," said Kelly with a sneer.

Byron was horrified by the notion that they were leaving Thomas to die. But his only option was to go with the gang and get away as soon as he could to get help for Thomas. "Give me a minute," he said to Kelly.

"Jeez," said Kelly. "You got thirty seconds." He started walking and the others followed.

Byron laid his hands on Thomas' arm. "I'm coming back no matter what. I promise. They'll have to kill me to stop me."

"Take the medal, okay?" Thomas nodded toward his chest. His voice was shaky with fear. "You need it. Please. Take it."

With his hands still tied in front of him, Byron managed to grab the St. Christopher medal he had given Thomas, pull it over his head, and drop it in his pocket. He gave a pat to the coarse hair he loved to run his hands over. He thought of the time Thomas had teased him. "You don't never touch a black man's hair," he had said like he was angry. "You muss it up." And then he had laughed like a crazy man when he saw Byron's startled expression.

"Hold on," said Byron. "I'll be back."

Thomas just blinked his eyes. Byron jumped up and ran after the others. The sooner they left, the quicker he could come back. In his mind he was sure that it couldn't be the end.

Kelly stroked his chin and turned around, addressing Byron. "The idea I got is how 'bout we tell your daddy what we discovered in the woods, huh?" He laughed harshly, pulling on the week's growth of his beard.

"Why are you doing this?" Byron looked back at Thomas, his body fading into the green and browns of the forest as if it had already taken him.

"Listen up. This is what's gonna happen."

"Please, Kelly, I'm begging you."

"Shut up. I'm doing the talking. Here's the story. It weren't one of us. We just came upon this guy bleeding in the woods. Musta been another hunter shot him. Tragic accident. You weren't here. You seen nothing. Heard nothing. Next you git in your car and we follow you to your house. I suppose you're just home for this little ron-day-voo. You gonna pack up your stuff and go on back to that faggot college in New Orleans. If anybody's home, you make up an excuse why you gotta go back right away. Then you git outta town and don't come back. You breathe a word of this to a single soul, you will be a dead man. Maybe we tell your daddy what we saw first, and then shoot you."

Byron hung his head. There had to be an escape. He would pretend to be on his way, and then double back as soon as he could.

Kelly untied his hands. "You're driving and I'll be right next to you, watching every move." He threw his keys to Preston. "You guys follow in Blue and don't fucking wreck it."

Into the orange light of the setting sun angling through the thick trees, Byron drove his Mustang. It seemed wrong that it was such a beautiful late spring day, the light bathing everything in richness, the breeze warm and not yet heavy with the dampness of summer. They had the top down and his face felt tight with dried tears. He contemplated gunning the motor and running the car into a tree, and kept looking in the rearview mirror as Kelly's truck rattled with every bump behind them. Kelly must have sensed his thoughts and said with an unlit cigarette stuck to his bottom lip, "Don't be getting no crazy ideas."

They pulled up outside the gate to the Purvis mansion, an old Greek revival home with a guardian of four columns across the front.

"We'll wait here for ya," said Kelly. "Don't dilly dally." He looked at Byron's bare chest. "Wait a sec. You can't go in the house like that." He pulled his T-shirt over his head and threw it at Byron. "Put this on."

"I can't wear your stinking shirt."

Kelly gave him a hard stare. "You ain't calling the shots. Ain't you figured that out yet?"

Byron wondered why Kelly had adopted the redneck speech of his buddies. He wasn't one of them. His family was what his mother called nouveau riche, educated, his father a banker. They had gone to the academy together for grade school, and Byron remembered him getting pretty good grades. He had been to Kelly's house for a birthday party once. Then something happened in high school. He had dumbed down and started hanging out with the likes of Jasper and Preston. As a freshman he had gone to dances with a girl who would later become the homecoming queen. By senior year he was dating a tough girl with a mullet haircut, a troublemaker who was always getting into fights with black girls.

Kelly's shirt was too big and smelled of stale beer and tobacco. He felt sick as he pulled it over his head.

"Remember, we're waiting out here, so no funny business. No phone calls. Then we're escorting you outta town."

Nobody was home except Sofia. He tried to get up the stairs, but she intercepted him. Nothing got by her.

"Byron, sugar, your momma left a message..." She stopped mid-sentence and stared bug-eyed at his T-shirt.

"That is one nasty looking shirt. Don't look like none of yours."

"What did she say?"

"She spectin' you for supper."

The story of what happened was about to tumble out of his mouth, but he didn't want to involve Sofia. He no longer knew what Kelly and his friends were capable of. He could be putting Sofia in danger. "I can't. Something's come up. There's an emergency in New Orleans. Gotta go back right away."

She raised one eyebrow that was split in two by a scar. "And how you know that? Ain't nobody called here."

"I called my roommate from Josh's. I promised I'd check in with him. Seems somebody broke into our dorm room." He was amazed at his own ability to perform. He took a breath and forced a smile. "Don't you worry about it," he said with a wink. He had a way of charming her. Always did. "Just tell momma I'll call when I get back to New Orleans." As he edged toward the stairs, she moved closer and looked him in the eye.

"You don't look so good. Let me git you something to eat."

Sofia knew him about as well as anyone. If he'd looked in her eyes a moment longer, he would have burst into tears. Byron turned and started up the stairs.

"Don't have time."

"At least change that shirt."

"I will."

Byron stood in the center of his bedroom; the door closed. He was divided in two. In half of his brain, images of bloodstained leaves, trampled grass, long shadows of trees, and grotesque faces raced by. In the other half, he wanted only to escape. He stared at the bed. Suddenly, all he could think of was being awakened by the lawn mower, and leaning his head out the window to see Thomas for the first time. He wanted nothing more than to collapse, be lulled into a dream that would roll back time, wake up as he had that morning, excited and joyful that he and Thomas were going fishing. Their woods, their tree awaited them.

He put his hand in his pocket and felt a chain. He pulled it out. Thomas' medal. There were flecks of blood on it. It felt cold in his hand, so cold that it burned. *Do something. Move.*

The clock on the wall ticked. *Time. Blood flow. Life.*

The plan. Yes, the plan. Follow their orders. Get away from them. Get back to Thomas. He ran into the bathroom and caught his reflection in the mirror. Time drifted again. What an odd T-shirt! He peeled it off and threw it in the trash. Now he saw dark stains on the side of his torso. His first thought was dirt from the filthy shirt. *Wash it off. No. Wait. Blood. Thomas' blood. Wear it. Something of him. Thomas is bleeding. Needs help.*

His head spun, thoughts galloped, and then backed up onto themselves. From behind the door he took a faded Pink Floyd T-shirt and pulled it over his head, stabbed his arms through. In his bedroom he grabbed his bag from the floor. From the bottom of his closet he dug for the coffee can with money in it. He took it all.

Make a 911 call. They won't know. But Sofia was all eyes and ears. He didn't want her to hear. She would panic. It would delay him. She would know everything. Then everyone would know everything. He would be the one no one could look in the eye on the street. *That doesn't matter. Thomas' life matters.*

What's that sound? Vacuuming. Sofia was vacuuming his parents' bedroom. There was a phone at the bottom of the stairs. He ran down to it, lifted the receiver. Before he could dial, he heard banging on the door. He turned and saw Kelly with his face smashed against the glass of the front door. And then Kelly was inside the house, creeping across the foyer, looking up toward the sound of the vacuum cleaner. He grabbed the receiver and slammed it down. "I told you no calls," he said in a harsh whisper. "Let's go. Now!"

Outside the front door Byron said, "Kelly, please. I beg you. Let me call somebody."

"Too late."

Byron hurried in front of Kelly, walking backwards, trying to get Kelly to look at him. "Don't say that. We can save him. We'll make up a story. I'll give you money. Whatever you want." Half of his brain listened to the pleading, the whimpering, and it sickened him. The other half heard the wall clock still ticking in his head.

Kelly kept his head down and continued walking.

They got to the car and Byron threw his bag in the back. Kelly got in the passenger seat.

"What are you doing?" Byron screeched. "I think I know the way to New Orleans."

"Ha ha. You thought we was just gonna let you go? I'll ride with you."

"I promise I won't tell anybody you guys were there. Please let me go."

"Just drive and shut up."

They headed out Highway 98 with Jasper and Preston following in the truck. When they reached the interstate outside Hattiesburg, Kelly told him to pull over and he jumped out. "Now git and I ain't kidding. Don't even think of going to the police. Remember what I said." Kelly walked back to his truck and slid into the driver's seat.

In his rearview mirror Byron saw the three men sitting stone-faced in the cab, waiting for him to leave. Byron stepped on the gas and merged onto the freeway. Looking once more in his rearview mirror, his heart leapt for joy that he was free. He pulled off at the first exit and found a phone booth at a Texaco station. He dialed 911 and told the operator that a man had been shot and exactly where to find him. The woman kept asking his name and location.

"It doesn't matter who or where *I* am. You've got to get

somebody there. He's shot and dying."

"But, sir, I need—"

She was interrupted by a loud pop and shattering glass.

"Fuck!" said Byron. He crouched down to the floor of the booth. The receiver dangled above him with the woman's tiny voice coming out of it. "What was that?" she said. Byron felt a sting in his cheek and then touched the blood. He thought he might have been grazed by the bullet, but realized it was just a cut from flying glass.

"Sir, I need to know what's going on."

He rose up enough to talk into the receiver. "It was nothing, a car backfiring. Please go to the location I told you. It's a matter of life and death." And then he crawled out of the booth and sat on the ground against the car, a barrier between him and where the shot had come from. He expected them to pull into the gas station any minute.

But they didn't. He waited, staring at the dangling receiver and the shards of glass on the ground. He could still hear the woman's voice, and he thought he should get back on the line and tell her to call the police, have them come to the gas station. But it seemed that was happening already. A man over by the pumps was shouting for someone to call the cops. Byron stayed on the ground, shivering and praying that the operator would send someone to get Thomas.

Byron had to leave now. If the police arrived he'd be delayed again. He had an 8-cylinder Mustang and Kelly had a beat-up old truck. He opened the door, crawled in the front seat and started the car, keeping his head down, all the while expecting another shot to ring out. He gunned the motor and it roared. He peeled out of the station and got back on the freeway. As soon as he was on the open road, he stepped full on the gas. Surely they would head back to Columbia now, thinking they had put enough fear in him, that he wouldn't dare go back to town.

Byron flew past the exit for the town of Purvis, named

after one of his ancestors, and turned off on Highway 13 to get to Columbia the back way. He drove the narrow, winding highway at eighty to ninety miles per hour, passing the few cars with little room to spare. Now he was focused, the car an extension of his sole purpose in that moment: getting back to Thomas.

On Old Morgantown Road, an ambulance pulled out of the turnoff to his daddy's land. It raced past him with its lights spinning and the siren on. Byron's hopes surged and he made a quick U-turn, following the ambulance to the hospital.

Inside the emergency room he headed for the double doors, but a nurse stopped him.

"You can't go in there."

"I'm looking for Thomas Davis, the boy they just brought in."

"Only family," said the nurse. "You can wait over there."

"But I...I've got to see him." He started for the doors again.

"Don't be making me call security." She pointed to the waiting area. "Sit. I'll keep you informed."

He fell into a hard plastic chair and stared dumbfounded at the TV. *As the World Turns* was on. The nurse, back at her station, picked up the phone and looked over the top of the counter at Byron as she talked.

Byron's mind was back in racing mode. The nurse had probably called the police, and they would arrive soon. They would want to talk to him. Thomas' father could arrive any minute. Kelly and the boys would be back in town and hear of Thomas being taken to the hospital, would snoop around to find out what happened. He started to shake so bad— he must have looked like a windup toy to the nurse. He asked for the bathroom and staggered down the hall, wanting to be hidden, and yet near Thomas. He ducked into the bathroom and locked the door. The glossy tiled walls closed in on him and the stale urine-tainted air made the room even smaller as he sat on the floor, feeling his life spiraling down into the floor drain. The world had become a sinister place. This was more than just a fear of being taunted or beat up for what people suspected. Now he had real enemies, enemies that had threatened to kill him. And yet what terrorized him most was the power Kelly and his friends held. They could destroy not only Byron but his family, Thomas' family, and any chance of Thomas having a career as a football player—if he lived.

He found an exit and walked around to the main lobby. The receptionist directed him to a phone and he called emergency.

When he asked about the condition of Thomas Davis, the nurse said, "You the boy that was in here before? Where you at?"

"Please tell me. I've got to know how he's doing."

"Who are you?"

"I'm...I"m his friend."

There was a long pause. "I'm sorry. He didn't make it."

Byron dropped the phone and slid to the floor. His chest heaved and he thought his head would explode. Everybody in the lobby turned to look at him. Several rushed over to help.

"Get a nurse," someone yelled.

The concerned faces hovering over him only increased the desperation of the moment. Rejecting their assistance, Byron pulled himself up and walked outside. As the door slid closed behind him, it seemed that his old world stayed on the other side. He saw his past fading into the background as the urge to flee rose up like an animal inside him. Running away seemed his only option. Cut the strings—the expectations of his parents, the hapless cruelty of Columbia, even the Pearl River Valley with its periodic plague of cicadas—everything that had controlled his every move since he was born. And then, from a dark hole in a corner of his mind, an unexpected notion emerged. Byron was free of Thomas as well, cut loose from the incomprehensible hold that Thomas had over him.

His stomach began to churn ferociously and he leaned over to vomit on some newly planted marigolds. He stared at the bits of the sandwich he and Thomas had shared earlier in the day, and hoped that acidic thought had been purged forever. Free? Just the opposite. If there was one thing that shined through his darkness, it was his love for Thomas. He desperately needed to be chained to that love, to something, as his old life receded like a riptide, making its last attempt to pull him under.

In the car, he let go. Tears flowed down his cheeks. He took out the medal again and brought it to his lips. He had never felt so alone and an uncontrollable sobbing overtook him.

Through his tears Byron gazed out the windshield at the purple light announcing the finish of the day. Earlier, he had wished they'd shot him, too. Now he knew he had to stay alive. Staying alive would be a sort of revenge for the moment. Any other action would have to wait.

6 Exodus

Byron's desk was gouged and inked with the crude etchings and graffiti from the endless stream of bored students. Skulls, hearts, geometric shapes, and what appeared to be an ancient script rose off the weathered surface and danced in front of Byron like holograms. He was tempted to stick his fingers into the eye sockets of the skull, touch the dripping blood of the heart, and rearrange the three-dimensional letters and symbols into a new language. With his lack of sleep, and all the drugs and alcohol floating around in his system, Byron was only vaguely aware of the lazy vowels and diphthongs flowing from the lecturer in the front of the hall. He couldn't focus on the words, but he *had* noted that the professor's smooth drawl ran antithetical to the violent subject matter of the day's lesson, the lesson that, of course, he had neglected to read.

"The Mayans, like the Aztecs and Incas—in fact most pre-Colombian cultures—engaged in human sacrifice to appease the gods," the professor said as if he were reading a nature poem. He held up a picture of a ninth-century vase. "As you can see, a Mayan in full-feathered regalia is standing over the victim draped over a large stone. The priest is holding the still-beating heart in one hand and a ceremonial dagger in the other."

The heart from the desk and the one in the photograph merged in the air halfway between Byron's desk and the lectern. It looked so real that he tried to reach out and grab it. The professor noticed the gesture and stopped. He stared at Byron over his half-frame glasses, causing Byron to drop his hand and lower his eyes. In the lingering silence, he could hear the syncopated tapping of rain on the elephant ferns outside the window, sounding like a primeval drum.

The dampness and heat of late spring had turned the hall into a sauna. The lecturer mopped his brow, took a wheezy breath, and started anew. "The Spanish clergy were horrified by these practices, yet much of what we know about this barbarism comes from the writings of Diego de Landa, the Franciscan charged with bringing Catholicism to the Yucatan."

In the front row, a student's hand shot up so fast he might have been a shill.

The professor glanced up from his notes. "Yes, Mr. Wentworth?"

"But didn't de Landa unleash an inquisition of cruelty and torture against the Maya? Seems a bit hypocritical to me."

"Excellent point, Mr. Wentworth. I see *someone* has read the material."

The girl sitting next to Byron turned to him and rolled her eyes. He had seen her hastily applying her makeup just before class, and now he noticed an errant swath of eyeliner pointing toward her ear. Her gaze was both comical and terrifying. He faced front and shook his head in an attempt to clear his hallucinations. But in a short time his chin fell to his chest. Minutes later, the dreaded nightmare began. The angry trees rattled their branches, the hum of the cicadas dominated the air. Menacing faces, their features a strange combination of Mayan and backcountry inbreds, looked down on him. There was a loud crack and he felt a hot stickiness on his back.

"Mr. Purvis. Excuse me if I'm disturbing your sleep," said the professor in a notch above his lecture voice.

Byron's head jerked up, and several of the students chuckled. "Sorry," he mumbled.

It had been three days since his heart was wrenched from his chest, exposing a love that was offered one moment, and in the next, destroyed. In a vicious cycle he plied himself with downers and whiskey to kill the pain, and then diet pills given to him by a girl in his Art History class to keep him awake, so he wouldn't fall into the cicada nightmare.

He made one last attempt to shake the visions, but it was no use. And then, as if suddenly finding the formula to extricate himself from the prison-desk, he jumped to his feet, gathered his books and left the room.

"Mr. Purvis?" the professor called after him. "Mr. Purvis!"

Byron staggered down the hall and out the door. In the pouring rain, he walked across the quadrangle. Halfway to the dorm, he realized he was done with school. Better to drop out than fail. But what would he do? He couldn't go back to Mississippi where he feared for his life.

As he pushed open the door to his room, Byron was hit by the sour smells of dirty socks and his roommate's overflowing ashtray. The windows were closed tight against the rain. He stripped off his wet clothes and put on gym shorts and a tank top. On his desk was a message that his parents had called again. He sat down and ran his fingers over the letters of his roommate's childlike scrawl. ASAP was written extra large. With his arms he swept his desktop clean of books and papers, half of them tumbling on his unmade bed and the rest on the floor. He opened a drawer and took out a bottle of Jack Daniels and a Quaalude from his stash. He downed the pill with a swig of whiskey.

In the pile of books on the floor he caught sight of *The Columbian-Progress*. His mother had the newspaper sent to him through the mail, though most of the time it went straight into the trash. Not this week. It was folded open to the article, "Football Star Loses Life in Hunting Accident." He had read it three or four times, and each time a tsunami rage overwhelmed him. He took another swig of whiskey and considered downing a second Quaalude.

Columbia, Mississippi—On Saturday afternoon, local hunters Kelly Price, Jasper Downs, and Preston James, all recent graduates of Columbia High, came upon a severely wounded Thomas Davis in the woods near Red Bluff. Davis, who achieved great success on the gridiron at Columbia High, was home for a visit from Jackson State where he was in his freshman year on a full sports scholarship. The police believe that Davis was accidentally shot by an unknown hunter who panicked and fled the scene.

"We recognized him right away," said Price, obviously still shaken by the incident. "We tried to stop the bleeding, but it was clear he needed an ambulance. So we jumped in the truck to find the nearest payphone. We were afraid to move him."

Paramedics reported that Davis had lost a significant amount of blood. He was pronounced dead at Marion General Hospital at 5:36 p.m. on Saturday.

Marion County Judge Frank Purvis, owner of the land where the wounded youth was found, said he had no idea why Davis was on his property. He also stated that hunters frequently strayed onto the land from the nearby hunting reserve. Police are asking the public to provide any information, which might shed light on this tragic accident.

Byron dropped the paper and looked out the window,

watching the rivulets of rain slide down the glass. He realized that he was the only thing that stood in the way of Kelly's gang getting away with it. Threat or no threat, he needed to tell somebody. A door slammed down the hall and nearly made him jump out of his seat. Someone was playing "Another Brick in the Wall" by Pink Floyd at full volume. He began to feel the sweet tingle of the drug, had the urge to slide down onto the cool linoleum of the floor, curl up in a ball. He put the bottle to his lips and felt the burn of it going down.

He rose to his feet, staggered to the phone, and dialed home. With his back to the wood paneling he slid down to a sitting position. The ringing sounded a million miles away. Bryon studied his bare feet, thinking how nicely formed they were. He plucked at the golden hair on his legs and then ran his hand very slowly from his knee to his ankle, delighting in the sensations of the drug. After countless rings—in his distorted sense of time it might have been hours—his father answered.

"Hey, Daddy."

"Byron. Glad you called. You okay?"

"Yeah, well, you know…"

"No, I don't know. Your mother's near hysterical what with you taking off and not saying goodbye, not returning our calls. And of course those damn cicadas." His father must have been on the extension in the breezeway because he could hear the hum in the background. The sound made him shudder. "What's going on?" his father said on the upbeat. Byron always recognized when his father was trying to sound chipper to cover up that he was really pissed off.

"I want to talk to you about something."

"You having problems at school? Sofia said something about—"

"No. It's not that."

"You sound funny."

"Just listen, would you?" Byron shouted. His tone of voice was laced with the false courage of alcohol and drugs.

"I'm listening."

"You know that boy that was shot?"

"That was a crying shame. Felt bad for Joe, the guy that takes care of the yard. It was his son."

"I know, Dad."

"Your mother and I sent flowers. You read about it in the papers, did you?"

"That article was a big pile of horseshit!" His voice was shaky and full of phlegm.

"Have you been drinking or taking dope or whatever you kids do these days? I'm not paying for you to piss away your education."

"I was there. I saw it. It wasn't an accident," said Byron, making an effort to annunciate each word, as he knew he was beginning to slur.

His father went silent for a moment. Byron could hear his breathing. "You know what, son? You need to go sleep it off. You're not making any sense. We can talk when you're sober. I'll tell your mother you're all right."

"Wait! You don't want to hear what I've got to say?"

His father huffed. "Go on." Byron pictured him examining his fingernails for a hangnail to bite off, a gin and tonic at his side.

"Did the police think to check the rifles of those guys that found him?"

"How do I know, Byron? Are you saying you think they were involved?"

"I *know* they were involved."

"How's that?"

"I was there."

"What the hell were you doing there?"

"Thomas and I were fishing."

"Fishing?" his father screamed. "You hate fishing!"

"I hated fishing with you."

"Jesus Christ! I can't believe we're having this conversation. Let me get this straight. You and the boy that mows the lawn were fishing, and the Price kid and his buddies came up and shot him just like that?"

"More or less."

"More or less won't stand up in a court of law." Frank Purvis had been a criminal attorney before he became a judge.

"You don't believe me?"

"I'm trying, Byron. I'm trying. So what did you do?"

"I tried to get away and find help. They threatened to kill me." His speech became more garbled with each word. Emotion played havoc with the timber of his voice.

"So you ran back to school and didn't say a word for three days!"

"Are you listening? They were going to kill me."

"I thought the Price boy was a friend of yours."

"He was never a friend. He's an idiot. All I'm asking is that you go to the DA and tell him I'm willing to make a statement."

"I will do no such thing. They would ask you all kinds of questions, starting with why you ran away and what you were doing there in the first place. Who knows what kind of bullshit would come up?"

"Want me to tell you what kind of bullshit?" Byron's tongue was loose and ready to fly.

"Now, son, let's slow down and think of things rationally." The tension in his father's voice belied his counsel to be rational. "We've got ourselves a situation where we have to weigh things. There's a good possibility those boys would never see the inside of a jail, and then what have you accomplished? Any evidence there might have been is gone for sure. It would be their word against yours. If that isn't enough, Bob Price plays golf with the Chief of Police. The whole thing could turn into a big scandal. It would kill your mother."

"You mean it would kill your chances in the next election."

"Byron, Byron, Byron. You don't know the law like I do and you don't know this town like I do. You've been sheltered. Always told your mother it wasn't the right way to go. I want you to think long and hard about this. Maybe it's best you not come home for a while, until this all blows over and you've calmed down."

"Blows over? Are you serious? It was murder!"

"Byron, please. Just think a minute—not just what it would do to your family but Joe's as well. The defense would drag that boy's name through the mud until he would look like the aggressor. Use your brain. You know how things are here."

Byron didn't know if he had gone crazy or the world had. "This is NOT the end of this!" He slammed down the phone.

Byron stayed on the floor and thought again about the newspaper article. Kelly playing Nurse Nancy, trying to stop the bleeding. That disgusting fabrication alone made Kelly deserve a prolonged and arduous torture. Byron imagined needles through his eyeballs. But he knew that one thing his daddy said was right. The good ol' boys had a way of protecting their own. With the courage and blunt logic of his inebriated state, he said out loud, "There is more than one avenue to justice." He wasn't sure what his words meant yet.

He got up, went back to his desk, and took another gulp of Jack. On his bed he saw that his anthropology text had fallen open to a picture of Tulum. He picked it up and with bleary eyes started to read the lesson he was supposed to have read for that day's class. Along with the reading were pictures of other sites in the Yucatan, Coba and Chichen Itza, surrounded by dark jungle. Mexico looked like a country where someone could disappear. A person who disappeared could become a ghost, an avenging angel that could strike when it was least expected. It flashed like clear white light in his head.

The next morning the flash was gone, replaced by a million dead brain cells cluttering the attic of his mind. He remembered little of the night before, but one image had survived the mass destruction of cells: the avenging angel, all burnished sword, suit of armor, and a wingspan that didn't quit. In the light of day, he scoffed at the idea the angel could ever be him. Everything in his life had prepared him to be a southern gentleman—take on a cushy white-collar job, nurse a couple of cocktails every evening sitting on the veranda. That is, until the day he met Thomas, and his life took a major detour.

On his desk he found a scrap of paper where he had jotted down a reservation from New Orleans to Cancun scheduled for late that afternoon. He had made the reservation the night before; in a stupor of drugs and alcohol it had seemed like a brilliant idea. He had been staring at the anthropological map of the Yucatan Peninsula in his textbook for what seemed like hours, the deep green of the land undulating and the blue sea rippling. Consulting an atlas he found that Cancun was the closest airport.

In his mind, his future had narrowed to a jagged path illuminated by a golden light in a faraway place where he could vanish and be reborn. Staying on the Tulane campus, surrounded by the rites of spring, flowering shrubs, couples holding hands with budding love in full bloom, only made the pain of losing Thomas more unbearable. In the jungles of Mexico he could fake a kidnapping, or even a suicide. He would learn to be strong, though he didn't yet know how, rid himself of the sensitive boy that fell into tears at the slightest provocation, and return a man ready to find justice. As he told his father, this was not the end.

Peter—the roommate of the childish script—edged into the room as if he were entering the space of a psychopathic cellmate. Byron looked up from packing his bag.

"Are you going somewhere?" asked Peter.

"I need to go away for a while."

"You in some kind of trouble?"

"Why do you say that?"

"You've been weird the last few days, especially the stuff you were saying last night."

"I was a little high."

"A little? Do you even remember campus security bringing you back to the room? You were out in the middle of the quadrangle in the pouring rain, shouting and running around in your boxers."

Byron turned to Peter with a baffled look on his face. "Really? What was I saying?"

"I guess you were pretty upset with your father. And then a lot of crazy things about cicadas taking over the Earth, and bloody hands not getting away with it."

Byron looked at the empty Jack Daniels bottle on his desk next to the books that had been restacked. "Sorry. I know I've been a little crazy lately. That's why I have to get out of here. If anybody asks, tell them I went to Mexico."

"You mean like the police or something?"

"Just forget everything I said last night. It was the alcohol and…other stuff talking."

7 Land of Milk and Honey

Cancun was abuzz with jackhammers, pounding steel, and swinging cranes. From his taxi window Byron saw the skeletons of new hotels emerging from the white sand next to calm azure waters, wide boulevards of bleached concrete ending at the edge of the jungle, and young Mayans in drab, ill-fitting uniforms walking to work along the road. It was "the Mexican miracle of 1980" someone had told him on the plane.

At the Hotel Playa Blanca he went straight to the pool bar where he drank margaritas, occasionally sticking his finger in the drink to feel the pleasure of cold. The air around him was like hot paste on his skin, and the inside of his brain was on low boil with images of Thomas' face in pain repeatedly rising to the surface. Not the distance nor drugs nor alcohol had managed to quell the guilt that he hadn't been able to save Thomas. Nothing diminished the rippling sense of loss, the expanding emptiness he felt inside.

Byron leaned his head down and hovered over the drink, letting the coolness rise to his face. Nearby, a parrot in a cage squawked, as if it, too, was irritated and forlorn.

He felt so very far from home—aimless, drifting. And yet, in the back of his mind there was a plan, a purpose to his venture that he must attend to. But not now.

A loud voice, sounding as if it had descended from the heavens said, "You part of the boom?"

The only other patron was a man with longish hair and a beard, sitting a few stools down. He might have been Jesus Christ drinking a Tecate. Coming out of his stupor, Byron's first thought was that it was a very odd way to begin a conversation, and whatever did he mean? It must have been Byron's khaki chinos and blue Oxford cloth long-sleeved shirt that made the man take him for a businessman. His mother was a firm believer in looking one's best for travel. Some things just stuck.

Byron turned his heavy eyelids toward the man. "No, sir."

The man chuckled. "So what *are* you here for?"

Byron was struck by the intrusiveness of the man's question. Had to be a Yankee, probably big city, but Byron's upbringing made it impossible to be rude and not respond. "To escape, I guess."

The man looked Byron up and down. "Can't imagine what you would have to escape from. You get in some trouble at school?"

Byron hesitated a moment and then answered with a snort. "Oh, yeah, failing grades at college. Not to mention I was witness to my black friend being shot down in front of me. A bunch of rednecks with rifles threatening to kill me if I came back to town, one of whom was a childhood friend. And my daddy telling me to stay away to avoid a scandal."

The man's brow wrinkled, his eyes narrowed, and finally a smile spread across his face. "Good one," the man said with a laugh. "You must be a Southern writer." He moved closer and extended his hand. "My name's Terry. Hope I'm not intruding. Been in town a couple days and all anybody talks about is the miracle of Cancun."

"Got the same from a guy on the plane."

"Hotels and fast food joints as far as the eye can see," said Terry. "Gonna be worse than Miami Beach."

Byron took the man's hand. "I'm Byron Boudreaux." He felt a chill up his spine. It was the first time he had used his mother's maiden name. If he were going to disappear, a name change would be necessary. Years ago Lidia had suggested that a slight adjustment in his name could make a world of difference. "How on God's green Earth could she have married someone with the name Purvis?" said Lidia in the midst of a tirade against his father. "Wouldn't Byron Boudreaux be a wonderful name for a writer or an artist?" She had always tried to encourage Byron along those lines, taking him to cultural events whenever he came to visit, introducing him to a colorful array of New Orleans characters that his father would not have approved of.

"I once met a Boudreaux from Louisiana," said Terry. "That where you're from?"

"Mississippi, actually. My mother's from New Orleans though."

"Now that's a great town. Corrupt to its very soul, but at least it's got a soul. This place is a Disneyland."

"If you dislike it so much..." His voice trailed off, not wanting to be further dragged into a personal conversation.

Terry narrowed his pale blues. "You're not CIA, are ya?" He laughed again, a guffaw that set Byron's nerves on edge. "You ever hear of the Venceremos Brigade?"

"Spanish, right? The *venceremos* part."

"It means 'we will win' or 'we shall overcome,' like in the Civil Rights song. In a couple days I'm meeting a group of *brigadistas* from the West coast and we'll sail over to Cuba to do a little work in support of the revolution. I brought my boat down here from Tampa."

Terry continued to stare at him, his face not two feet away. This guy was a bore, thought Byron. Why wouldn't he just let him get drunk in peace? He wanted nothing more than to get up and walk away, but his upbringing again demanded decorum. Byron sighed. "I thought Cuba was off limits. It's communist, right?"

"Don't make communism sound so much like a disease." Terry reached for his bag and took out a book. It read *Venceremos Brigade: Young Americans Sharing the Life and Work of Revolutionary Cuba*.

"When people ask me that question," Terry continued, "I love to quote this little poem." He opened the book and read. "'Communism is not a religion. I neither believe or disbelieve, nor have I tasted pure water, but I am often thirsty and drink, fight for the springs of the earth'."

The words meant nothing to Byron. "I'm not political myself. One politician in the family is enough. My daddy's running for office."

"Oh, hell, man. Everything is political. Every little decision we make every day is political. Politics is about power, who's got it and who doesn't. If I decide to be a vegetarian, I might say it's because I don't believe in cruelty to animals. But ultimately it's political, a slap in the face of the almighty meat industry. If I decide to shop at a small store instead of a big supermarket, I'm supporting small business rather than corporate America contributing to political candidates who will support their point of view."

"But you could go crazy," said Byron, "worrying if everything you say or do is politically correct, down to the last minute detail."

"It's a goal, of course. We're only human. But we've gotta try. And that's what they're doing in Cuba. Don't take my word for it. Take this book back to your room and read what these people have to say. They were on the first brigades ten years ago. It's not all rosy, but it's honest. Come back and tell me what you think. Maybe you'll want to join us. If you want to escape, escape into something that has meaning." Terry stood up, downed the last of his beer, and squeezed Byron's shoulder on the way out of the bar. This was absurd. He would never read it. It was only his complacency that kept him from running after the man and returning the book.

Byron took a sip of his drink and looked down at the cover. The photo showed a group of men and women of mixed races in a cane field. Byron's eyes fell on the black men in the picture with their shirts off, and his stomach took a turn. He opened the book and looked for more pictures.

Byron stood in line at the Cancun bus station ticket window, staring at the board of possible destinations: Chetumal, Mahahual, Tulum, and the impossible-to-pronounce Xcalak. The names jumped in and out of focus. That morning he had awakened to a hammering sound of construction, reminding him that he was in a far-off corner of Mexico. But why? Oh yes, to disappear. Little by little the rocky and jagged path stretched out before him, but he hadn't been sober long enough to formulate a reasonable plan.

At the window, the Spanish words to buy a ticket tumbled out of Byron's mouth, handing the agent a puzzle of morphemes he was obliged to piece together. The older man looked down in embarrassment as if he were the one at fault. Byron simplified matters by reducing his request to one word, "Tulum," and the agent nodded. From the photos in his anthropology textbook he seemed to remember that Tulum was surrounded by jungle. Could it be the scene of his disappearance?

He took his seat on the first-class bus and let his head fall against the curtained window. On the open road the bus dipped and swayed on the uneven surface, causing his head to bounce against the glass, and the breakfast buffet items to play leapfrog in his stomach. From the banging in his head down to his cramped feet, his body was one long highway of pain—each muscle, joint, and nerve screaming for relief.

Just outside the window the scenery baked and the

road buckled, but inside the air conditioning system achieved arctic conditions far beyond the manufacturer's wildest dreams. Byron was forced to wrap his beach towel around his shoulders, as he hadn't thought to bring a jacket. Could he possibly be more at odds with his surroundings? And yet, the rapidly arranged flight from New Orleans, the excessive consumption of alcohol and drugs, and now the freezing bus into the wild were a necessary—though perhaps illogical—remedy to stop the squabbling voices in his head and give his heart a nudge to keep going.

The tiniest hope appeared on the horizon. The extra-strength headache medicine had, in the last few minutes, begun to kick in like an unfathomably slow morphine drip. It didn't so much ease the pain as blanket it with a thick cloud.

Byron pulled the book Terry had given him out of his bag. The night before he had been too drunk to do anything more than look at the pictures. Even now he doubted his brain had the wherewithal to concentrate, but he was pleased to see that the entries were short: poems, excerpts from diaries and letters, taped interviews—a compilation of emotions and dreams from the first *brigadistas* of 1969-1970. Most of the writers were from various movements on the left—the SDS, the Black Panthers, young socialists—but there were a number of entries from middle-class kids that hadn't yet formed their political ideas. Some of them seemed like him.

When he tired of reading, he again focused on the pictures: a group of exhausted workers in a cane field with machetes dangling at their sides, high-spirited faces on a crowded bus, a meeting around crude tables in a thatch-roofed pavilion. In one photo, two men, one brown and one black, stared at the camera in defiance, cigarettes hanging from their lips. But their arms were draped over each other's shoulders, and bare torsos leaned together in the kind of intimacy men allow themselves in hard work, sports, and war. Byron was plucked from his suffering, and allowed to float for a mere second on the edge of excitement. In the next moment, the feeling had traveled down to his lower belly and emerged as a twitch of desire. He quickly turned the page.

Byron stepped off the bus at the intersection of Highway 307 and the road to the Tulum ruins. He was hit by a wall of heat under vast blue skies only broken by a sun that glowed like the point of white-hot poker. In the mile walk to the site, his body thawed and his spirits were uplifted by a sense of adventure in a part of the world completely foreign to him, by new sights and smells, the peculiar way the dense air settled on his skin. Each step on the road took him further away from small world he had known—the Louisiana-Mississippi delta and several capitals of Europe on a high school graduation tour—and with few tourists at that early hour he could imagine himself one of the first Spanish explorers entering a new world.

The road to the ruins was lined with rustic stalls selling trinkets, food, and drinks. Men in straw hats and baggy, drawstring pants conversed in a Mayan dialect. As Byron passed by, they quickly switched to a mix of English and Spanish, attempting to sell him "authentic" figures dug up from the ruins or to offer guide services. Byron ignored them and continued until he reached a clearing where he heard the shrill notes of a small flute. From a ninety-foot wooden pole four men in white embroidered shirts and red pants hung from ropes tied around their ankles and wrapped around the pole. They flew like exotic birds; their arms were outstretched and colorful ribbons streamed from their hats. As the ropes unraveled from around the pole, the men gradually lowered themselves toward the ground. A fifth man remained on top of the pole, dancing and playing a flute and a tiny drum. The ritual caused his mind to wander, imagining the road leading to the gates of the city as it had been in ancient times with vendors and performers.

He could smell the sea and see the dark gray tops of the temples in the distance.

A group of small brown children surrounded him, chattering and giggling as they touched his skin and pointed at his golden hair. One of them took his hand, pulling him toward the ancient city. Were they idolizing him or leading him to be sacrificed, a particularly novel offering for the gods? The children were held back at the entrance, and he passed through the narrow arched gate. From what he had seen so far, the area appeared too busy to fit into his plan. He needed a more remote location.

Directly in front of him, Byron saw the building that dominated the complex, el Castillo. He trudged up the steep steps to the top of the temple-fortress, positioned on the edge of limestone cliffs that tumbled down to a pale-sand beach licked by the turquoise waters of the Caribbean. From the top he took in a commanding view of crumbling empire and tropical vegetation. Mayan priests had stood on that very spot, presiding over an assembly of commoners in the plaza below, anxious to witness a sacrifice.

Over a large square stone in front of two thick columns, Byron draped his body as he had seen in his anthropology book. He was the sacrificial victim, his heart ripped out, his body in agony, but still able to think and feel.

"Are you all right?" a voice said.

He opened his eyes and saw a tall, thin woman leaning over him, wearing fossil-colored travel clothing. Her sunglasses were down on her nose and she had lifted the brim of her floppy hat to get a better view. Her accent was American. Not from the South.

"I'm fine. Just trying to imagine what it would be like to have your heart carved out of your chest."

"They actually cut in about here." She drew an imaginary line above Byron's stomach. "Then the priest would reach in under the diaphragm, detect the heart by its pulsing, grab it, and wrench it from the body." Just above

Byron's chest she did the motions of grabbing and pulling. "Sorry," she said, and dropped her hands. "I get a little carried away." She looked to be in her late twenties and was attractive in a tomboyish way, with pale blue eyes, a thin nose, and no makeup.

Byron sat up. "That sounds so much better than cracking the rib cage."

"The victim would be conscious throughout the process until, of course, the blood flow to the brain stopped, and he would pass out. Then they would chop off his head and burn his heart."

"Oh." Byron felt like he was going to faint. He ran his hands over his face.

"Are you sure you're okay?"

"I think I sat up too quickly." He took a bottle of water from his pack and poured some over his head. "You seem to know a lot about this."

"I should. My field is Mayan culture. I'm doing research on human sacrifice. If you're interested, I could explain a few things to you. Have you seen the Temple of Frescoes? It's not to be missed."

"Are you a guide?"

"No," she laughed. "I just like sharing things that I find fascinating." She looked away as if embarrassed by her forwardness.

"Sure," said Byron. "Why not?"

Samantha showed Byron the remains of the red frescoes on the outside of the Temple. They visited palaces, watchtowers, and the House of the Cenote. She pointed out how often both the diving god figure and the serpent motif appeared throughout the site. She went deep into the significance of human sacrifice and other rituals, though most of what she said couldn't be absorbed by Byron's still-mushy brain. He found her pleasant enough, and the distraction made him forget himself for a moment. After an hour, during which they had covered most of the site, she asked him if he'd like to have a beer. The offer took him by surprise, and he had the awkward feeling that she might be coming on to him. He had also promised himself, after his three breakfast mimosas, that he would try to face the rest of the day sober.

"Come on," she said. "You look like you could use a drink. Hair of the dog?"

"Is it that obvious?"

Just outside the gate they sat on low stools at a long weather-beaten table and sipped their cold Negra Modelos. The wide-eyed barefoot children were back, and now they had two people to stare at and try to touch. Samantha spoke a few words to one of the little girls who giggled and ran away.

"You speak Mayan?"

"A little. Enough, I guess, to scare people away."

Byron asked about other sites nearby. He was especially interested in Cobá for its remoteness. She told him that it was a large site in the middle of the jungle and most of it was unexcavated. "If you go there, be careful. It's a little wild." Byron took note.

After their beers, Byron said he was headed to the beach.

"At this time of day? How brave you are! I'm a SPF50 person myself. Don't go near the beach until sunset."

"I'll try and find some shade."

"Here you can even burn in the shade."

She gave him the name of her hotel and told him to stop by for another beer if he came to Playa del Carmen.

Byron headed down the long wooden stairway leading from the precipice of the ruins to the beach. A couple of times he stopped to watch the iguanas skittering among the rocks of the cliff face, and looked back up at the temples from different angles. On the beach he stripped down to his board shorts and dove into the warm water. When he came up to the surface, Byron imagined Thomas treading water next to him, smiling, and then dunking him. He wiped the saltwater from his eyes and saw the sun slicing through the temple on the cliff. Mississippi was far away and Thomas was still dead.

He left the water and found a triangle of shade up against the cliff where he could read more of Terry's book. Several times during the tour of the ruins, bits of the book worked their way into his thoughts, and he was anxious to get back to it. When Samantha talked about the ceremonial knives used in sacrifice, he saw the machetes dangling from the arms of the people in the pictures. When she talked about the harvest and the commoners who worked the land outside the city walls, he saw the workers in the fields of sugarcane.

Byron opened the book to the pages about the work in the fields. The writers described it as grueling, but most of them expressed joy at pushing through to the other side of their pain. Still, Byron found it absurd that Terry had suggested he try this kind of manual labor. The Cuban revolution had nothing to do with him. What could he solve by doing volunteer work on a backwater island whose leader shouted epithets at his native land?

Nevertheless, there were, in addition to the photos, parts of the book that interested him—discussions of Cuba's attempt to build a non-racial society. Though a good part of the population was of mixed race, prejudice had been widespread before the Revolution. It was an issue the revolutionaries addressed, and laws had been passed to create a more equal society. It made him think about the mistrust between blacks and whites back in Mississippi. Could Thomas' murder have happened in Cuba? Everything he read, every picture he saw related in some way to Thomas, and each time his heart was stabbed again, the pain bringing tears to his eyes. Was it really racism that had killed Thomas? Were things better in Cuba? He wavered between thinking the idea of going to Cuba was absurd, and curiosity about a place so unlike home.

In the hotel lobby Byron ran into Terry. "Byron, my man. Did you get a chance to look at the book?"

"I did. A bit."

"Are you ready to join us?"

"I haven't really done much in the way of manual labor. I probably couldn't hold up."

"Don't let the book scare you. They worked the first *brigadistas* pretty hard. These days it's more about solidarity. We do a couple weeks of cane cutting, and then break up into various groups to do everything from picking fruit to construction. Of course it isn't going to right what's going wrong with you. But there's nothing like hard work to take your mind off problems."

Byron hesitated a moment, distracted by a curly strand of gray that had escaped from Terry's pulled back hair. "You're sailing your boat over? You can do that?"

"Yep." He glided his calloused hand over the air as if it were a boat crossing the sea.

"Do the Cubans share information about comings and goings with U.S. officials?"

"There are no formal relations and the Cubans don't even stamp your passport, just give you a tourist card. Come on. I want you meet someone. He's Cuban-American, but he doesn't buy into the whole anti-Castro crap."

He led Byron over to an armchair where a handsome dark-skinned man sat reading, one long, hairy leg draped over the armrest.

"Rafael," said Terry. "This is Byron. He might be joining us."

Rafael's eyes peered over the top of the book as if he were annoyed at being interrupted, but his full lips quickly rose up into a smile. "Oh, we are including movie stars in our groups now?"

Terry laughed, but Byron turned red and felt the urge to slip away. He wasn't accustomed to compliments from men, especially from a man that at first sight confused him. Rafael was a black man with a foreign accent and an easy style of interaction. He continued to stare unabashedly at Byron, acting as if neither his skin color nor anything about Byron would inhibit him from doing what he wanted.

Terry cleared his throat. "Rafael, give the kid a break."

"Where you from?" asked Rafael.

"New Orleans, well, Mississippi originally."

"*Por dios*, a real live, how you say, cracker man?"

Terry gave Rafael a warning look. "Don't mind him. He had some rather unpleasant experiences traveling through the South."

"Sorry," said Rafael. "I have problem to say everything what come to my head. When we come over in the seventies, my parents they take me to live with an uncle in Miami. Those Miami Cubans are crazy. I had to get out of there. I hitchhiked to San Francisco. Thank God, I find San Francisco. Took me two weeks cause nobody want to pick me up. Can you imagine the people not wanting to give a lift to a handsome devil like me?" His eyes bore into Byron again, making Byron feel like tiny creatures were crawling on his skin.

"You know we're not all racists," Byron said. He wanted to announce to the whole lobby where his hands and lips had been, that he knew how black skin felt and tasted. That proved he wasn't racist, didn't it? Instead he lowered his eyes. "But I know what you mean." In thinking about Thomas, his blue eyes glistened and his jaw quivered slightly.

"Seems like I make you sad," said Rafael. "Sorry."

"I guess nobody likes to be stereotyped."

"You're absolutely right. Anyway, sit down. Talk with me."

"I'll leave you in Rafael's care," Terry said to Byron.

"I've got stuff to do." And to Rafael, "Be nice."

Rafael explained why he had joined the brigade and what it meant to do something for his homeland rather than scream and moan like many of his fellow Cuban-Americans did.

"I love my country. I only come here because my parents bring me. I think there is much good with Revolution."

Byron was mesmerized by Rafael's voice, the extraordinary accent, his penetrating eyes that shined when he told Byron how the brigade worked hard, but played hard, too. And Rafael claimed to know all the places where they could have fun. Several times he touched Byron's arm while he was talking, and a couple of times broke into a laughter that made heads turn in the lobby. Rafael wasn't like anyone he knew back in Mississippi, or even New Orleans.

Byron stayed awake most of the night contemplating his plan to disappear. He got up early, and bought a backpack and some new clothes. He left about half of his belongings in his old bag in the room, making sure to take his passport and traveler's checks. At the front desk he asked about visiting the Cobá ruins. If anyone inquired later, the hotel could say he had gone to visit some remote jungle sites.

Off the trail outside the Cobá ruins, Byron heard the cawing of birds and what sounded like monkeys chattering, adding a haunting soundtrack to what he was about to do. Next to a large *ceiba* tree entwined with ancient stonework, he changed clothes, hid his hair under a beanie and put on aviator shades. He scratched himself on the thorns of the trunk and wiped off the blood with his shirt, which he dropped along the trail. He took off his watch, stomped on it, and left it in the woods. His plan was to not go back to his hotel near the beach, but rent a small room in town. Once authorities had discovered his disappearance, they might conclude, with the signs of foul play, that he was lost and injured in the jungle, or even kidnapped.

When he got back to Cancun late in the evening, he called Terry and said he would meet him at the marina in the morning.

"Been worried about you," said Terry. "Called your hotel several times. Really glad you're all right and going with us."

"I just have one request. Can it not be officially listed that I'm making this trip?"

"Well, as far as the States goes, they don't have to know anything. But Cuba has to know your stats. It won't be a problem, like I said before." Cuba suddenly made sense to Byron; there, he couldn't be tracked down. His name wouldn't appear on flight manifests going out of the country.

"See you in the morning," said Byron.

"Five a.m. sharp."

8 Parting of the Waters

In the dark they clambered onto Terry's thirty-five-foot Pearson yawl. By the time they were out of the bay, calm waters reflected a rosy dawn. Terry was at the wheel, and his crew, Maggie and Jason, were perched on either side of the cabin. Byron leaned over the stern railing and lost himself in the gentle wake, thin white trails gradually dissipating. He felt a sense of peace, almost letting go of the events that had battered him in the past week.

Byron declined the Dramamine. He had never had a hint of seasickness, though he forgot to take into account that his experience on boats had been limited to calm waters—his father's fishing boat and canoes on the river. Two hours after leaving shore, he was stretched out on the deck bench, his pounding head resting on Rafael's thigh while saltwater sprayed over the side and the mainsail popped and fluttered. He had spent the second hour vomiting until there was nothing left. Rafael mopped the sweat from his brow with a damp washcloth; the intimacy felt at once awkward, soothing, and exciting. Already he felt a strange ease with Rafael that he had never felt with Thomas.

Until Rafael had come along, no one had comforted him. He hadn't been able to talk to anybody about his agony—not his Aunt Lidia nor Sofia nor even his mother. Rafael's kindness and simple flirtations didn't lead him out of his hell, but made it slightly more tolerable.

In the afternoon, Byron's stomach had settled enough that he could keep a Dramamine down, and he crawled into a berth to sleep. Sometime in the night Rafael slipped into the bed they had to share. He gave Byron a brotherly kiss on the back of his head and threw a protective arm over his back. In the morning he felt better until they told him it would be at least another twenty-four hours before they arrived in Havana.

The following day around noon they docked in Marina Hemingway near Havana. Byron tested his wobbly legs on the dock, looking around at the marina full of boats sporting an assortment of flags, including American, Canadian, Mexican, Spanish, and Venezuelan. The five of them hired a taxi, a 1952 Chevy, to take them into the center of Havana where they would spend one night before the bus took them to their work camp early the next morning.

The car bumped and rattled along Avenida Quinta toward Havana, and the poor suspension along with the tired seat springs caused them to bounce up and down as they gazed out the windows. Byron and Rafael were pressed together in the back seat—they had taken on a sixth passenger soon after getting on the highway—and their legs rubbed together, causing sweat to run from their knees down to their ankles.

"How do you hold these old things together? I mean parts are hard to get, right?" Terry asked the driver, a short wiry man of mixed race.

"With rubber bands and paper clips," the man replied in heavily accented English, and then laughed as if he had given the answer a thousand times. "No, my friend, we take parts from the dead cars, you know, like the cannibals. This got a motor from an old Russian truck. We got to rebuild everything."

They saw many other American cars from the fifties—nothing after 1959, the year the revolutionaries took control of the government—alongside later model cars manufactured in the Soviet Union and Eastern Europe. While Terry and the others marveled at the cars, Byron focused on the people. Cubans of every skin color—from black African to pale European and everything in between—walked along the road and sometimes stuck out their hands, wiggling them to solicit rides. Others rode bicycles, often with two or three people on a single bike. At bus stops, men, women, and children waited with expressions and postures of resignation as if it could be a long time before the bus showed up. Poverty was evident in the number of simple structures needing repairs or a coat of paint. And yet, the people didn't look unhappy. Women swayed their hips, men strutted, and children laughed.

Terry had a reservation at the Habana Libre, the pre-revolution Habana Hilton, located just off La Rampa in Vedado. Byron offered to pay for a room in the same hotel if Rafael wanted to join him. "A room with two beds," Byron added.

Rafael grinned. "As you like, *señor*. I only agree because I know you need help in this new city—the new places, the new food, everything. Don't worry. You can count on me."

"Soak up the luxury, boys, before we descend into Hades." Terry laughed with his belly and slapped Byron on the back. Byron wrinkled his forehead and squinted in a stunned look that people closest to him frequently teased him about.

The next morning a group of about a hundred *brigadistas*, plus a large number of Cubans who would be joining them at the work camps, assembled at the Plaza de la Revolution alongside a string of old buses, many of them donated by Canada, Venezuela, and Mexico. They were flanked by the giant statue of Martí on one side of the Plaza, and the steel silhouette of the iconic Che portrait attached high up on the Ministry of the Interior.

"Do you not feel the eyes of these two great revolutionary figures smiling down on us?" said Rafael.

Byron nodded, the stunned look still on his face. What the hell was he doing? It was bad enough that he was breaking U.S. laws by being in Cuba, but associating with revolutionaries? His original idea of disappearing had morphed into something bigger, more otherworldly, and questionably the decision of a sane mind. But he had to admit that no one would search for him here. It had been forty-eight hours since he left the signs of his disappearance. He wondered if anyone had started looking for him yet.

Rafael leaned close to Byron and whispered that the two men in berets standing next to him were Black Panthers. On seeing Byron's expression, he squeezed his shoulder and laughingly said, "Don't worry. I protect you."

Of the hundreds of people milling about the plaza, there were men already in work clothes and others looking like they were about to spend a day at the beach: white girls wearing straw hats and overalls, black girls wearing bandanas and tight shorts, men and women of every skin color, most of them smiling in awe. A rumor weaved through the crowd that Fidel might stop by to see them off. Though Byron pretended that none of it mattered to him, he was genuinely disappointed that the Man didn't make an appearance.

When Byron had looked out the scratched windows of the bus the previous afternoon, he had found the cane fields of Matanzas Province beautiful, a sea of brilliant green, the stalks upright with lazy tops swaying in the wind. Now he stood in the middle of those fields between the thick, tight clumps, each one growing from a mound of soil. Up close its jointed stalks reminded him of bamboo; in addition to the green, parts of the plant were yellow and red in a way that showed nature's bounty.

Rafael stood over Byron and instructed him how to cut the cane. "Take machete firmly in hand, better not to use gloves. Well, okay, maybe use gloves. Put the leg opposite the machete, hand well forward. Step up and whack the stalk like you mean it. Maybe you want to imagine it is that devil of your dreams."

"What do you know about my dreams?"

"I heard you the other night in the hotel. Was tempted to go comfort you, but you were so sure about the two bed thing."

Byron looked around to see if anybody was listening.

"You can talk to me, you know," Rafael continued. "You don't have to keep it inside." He leaned over Byron, slid his arm along Byron's, and grabbed his wrist. "Now with a quick, down motion, strike the stalk at ground level, cutting it from its Mama Earth. If you leave stumps, it maybe makes the rot and grow back wrong. Yank the stalk up, cut it into lengths of about four or five feet, and cut off the leafy top. Throw the stalks behind you and someone will pile them. Keep moving. Try to keep even with your partners in the next row. That's all there is to it. Now you try it."

Byron aimed the blade and slammed it into a thick clump of stalks. The machete stuck in a stalk and his hand came away empty. Rafael chuckled and shook his head.

"Shut up," said Byron. He grabbed the machete, pulled it out, and swung heavily into the clump.

"Watch your leg!" screamed Rafael.

The cane toppled over, but Byron came within an inch of lopping off his left kneecap in the follow-through.

"*Por Diós*, By! Be careful!" Byron shuddered at being called By. The only other person who had done that was Thomas.

It took Byron most of the morning to be able to make a clean cut. Sweat dripped down in his eyes and his hands were numb. The muscles of his back felt like burning ropes. The physical exertion was beyond anything he had ever experienced, and he also had to deal with the added pressure that Malik, one of the Black Panthers they had seen earlier, was his crew boss. As Byron began to fall behind in his row, Malik walked over and gave him an intimidating stare. At first Byron cringed and forced himself to work harder. But then he stopped and let out a little snigger. The irony of the scene hit hard: He the blond Southern aristocrat doing slave work while a black man watched over him.

"What's so funny, Boudreaux?"

Byron was shocked that Malik knew his name. "Nothing," said Byron, and he slammed the machete as hard as he could into a thick stalk. It toppled over.

By the time they broke for the long lunch and siesta to avoid the hottest part of the day, Byron was so drained he skipped the dining hall, went to the barracks, and flopped on his lower bunk. Later Rafael came in with a plate of food. "You gotta eat. You need strength for the afternoon."

"What afternoon? I'm done." He rolled over and faced the wall.

Rafael took him by the shoulder and gently shook him. "Come on. You'll get it. Each day gets better, and then we are finish before you know it."

Byron shook off his hand. "I really don't need you to take care of me. This was a mistake. I don't know what I'm doing here." His voice cracked from exhaustion and pent-up emotion. He bit his lip to stop the flow of tears.

"Is okay, buddy. Just eat something."

"I'm serious. Can you just leave me alone?"

Rafael returned his hand to Byron's back and rubbed it. "I'm only trying to help. Talk to me."

"Stop it! Shit! What if somebody comes in?" His sharp words belied the deep appreciation he felt at Rafael's compassion. Someone cared about him. His body began to shake.

"Hey, come on. Don't do that." Rafael now had his hand on Byron head, smoothing Byron's hair like Sofia used to do when he was a little boy with a cowlick.

The screen door slammed shut and Malik came in, trudged past them, staring hard at Rafael.

"What are you looking at?" said Rafael.

"That shit got no place here."

"And just what shit you talking about? Comforting a compañero who's down? No human kindness in your kinda revolution?"

"You know what I talking about. The Cuban Revolution put people like you in camps for a little reeducation."

"You don't know the history. The Cuban government, including Fidel, recognized that the UMAP camps were wrong and they are closed a long time ago."

"If you ask me, they oughta bring 'em back, them camps, teach people how to act proper."

"Well, nobody ask you." Rafael wasn't a big man, about five-nine, a hundred and sixty pounds. But he didn't back down. The Panther, who had several inches and about forty pounds on Rafael, walked toward his bunk, looking over his shoulder a couple of times with a sneer. Malik got his clipboard and walked out.

Rafael hanging tough with a Panther impressed Byron, made him sit up and wipe his eyes. "You really don't care what people think, do you?" said Byron.

"I care about what people I care about think."

Byron produced a half-smile. "Not sure you'd care about me if you knew what I'm thinking about."

"Try me."

"Revenge." The word, elongated and frightening, rose up from deep in his gut. It was the first time he had uttered the word out loud.

"Don't worry about that guy. He just have to maintain

an image."

"Not him. Something much bigger."

Since that day in the woods, vengeance had consumed Byron, a slow burn like pages of a book going from yellow to red, curling up into a delicate black ash. But the pages kept rising. For each level of hurt that drifted upward there was one beneath to replace it. He had the guilt of a survivor and the righteous anger of the wronged. But he knew he was weak, had never even been in a fight, at least nothing more than a childish shoving match. Why couldn't he learn to be a warrior like Rafael? It wasn't impossible. His training could start with the challenge of cane cutting. Two weeks of it wouldn't make him a warrior, but it could be a start. He saw it now. He would get stronger day by day. He would not cry again. Nothing in his short indulgent life had prepared him for this, but people could change, couldn't they?

With this realization he went back out in the fields that afternoon and every day after, even when he was filthy, sweaty, sick, exhausted, lower back screaming, and whole parts of his body numb. He learned to work through the pain because now he had a goal: to lose the genteel person he was raised to be, and become a person who fought for what he wanted. At times he looked up to see Rafael in the next row, staring at him with a look of consternation on his face, witness to a metamorphosis.

In the evenings, the workers had meetings where they talked about the day's problems, listened to a report on the yield, and discussed politics. In the years since the first brigade made a significant contribution to the 1970 *zafra*, or harvest, in its goal to reach ten million tons, the focus of cutting cane had shifted to a more psychological and social contribution than an economic one. The meetings were part of educating the workers so that they would go back to their respective countries and inform people about what was happening in Cuba.

Near the end of the first week, after an exhausting day of cutting, the best in terms of yield, the sunburned workers trudged into the meeting room. Some of them had bandaged hands and others limped, but on many faces was the satisfaction of making a contribution to something they believed in. The meeting moved to the open discussion portion. Rafael indicated he had something to say and stood up. Byron, sitting next to him, cringed; he had a premonition of the topic Rafael was going to bring up. Since the day Malik had implied they belonged in a reeducation camp, Rafael had broached the topic many times. "Who does he think he is?" Rafael would say to Byron. "They want revolution, but they want it their way, their terms."

"*Compañeros,*" Rafael began, "I would like to know why some people believe that the gay people cannot be revolutionaries. Is not a revolution about changing the old order and eliminating discrimination in all forms? This new socialist man that everybody talks about seems to have new ideas about everything except gay people."

Silence fell on the room like a dark cloud with a storm tucked inside it. Malik swung around in an exaggerated motion and glared at Rafael. "What? You really want to talk about this shit?"

"Language, Malik," said the moderator, a tall sandy-haired woman who was the camp doctor.

"Yeah, all right," said Malik. "But really, comparing what the black man has had to endure to the plight of the homosexual. Man, it's not even in the same ballpark."

The air in the room crackled with murmurs. Byron felt his face go hot, and now Malik's tough stare seemed to be on him rather than Rafael. Byron gripped his seat and his anxious heart thumped. He had never heard the word "homosexual" uttered in a public forum. Even the private talks he had had with Rafael left him distraught. Rafael kept telling Byron he shouldn't let his emotions stew in his gut or they would boil over. With Thomas they had never talked about their feelings. It had been a ride down a river of white rapids, an emotional run that quickly reached beyond what his brain could put into words. Rafael's openness posed new complexities: the anxiety of facing who he was mixed with the guilt that he was on the edge of being untrue to Thomas. Any attempt Byron made to understand his feelings always arrived at the simple equation: Following your heart equaled death.

And yet he admired Rafael's courage, asserting his right to be who he was in the face of people like Malik. Rafael stood strong, and the moderator asked for silence. Rafael continued, looking straight at Malik. "You know the Nazis kill not only millions of Jews, but also hundreds of thousands of homosexuals."

A young Cuban man, a representative of *Juventud Rebelde*, rose to speak. "Of course is wrong the killing of homosexuals, but we in Cuba see that the homosexual is concerned only with himself and his desires. This way he can't be a revolutionary. We do not hate him and we invite him to be with us in the Revolution, but he wants only his own world and not be part of good for everybody." Several people nodded and mouthed their approval.

The next to speak was a woman whose nasal vowels pegged her as a New Yorker. "I would like to make two points, if I might. First, why is the topic of homosexuality always dominated by the discussion of gay *men*, always using the pronouns 'he' and 'him'? And while we're at it, isn't it time we start talking about the 'new person' rather than the 'new man'? I have been in the revolution movement since the late sixties and have been involved in every group you can name. Believe me, lesbians have played a huge role in every organization I know." She turned to look directly at Malik. "And I have known more than a few gay sisters in the Panthers, including a prominent figure whose name I won't mention. But again, nobody wants to talk about lesbians or even the closeted gay men who pass for straight. Men are obsessed with the out and sometimes effeminate man."

"Right on, *compañera!*" said a petite black woman who Byron had observed whacking cane stalks with the force of someone twice her size. "Once I heard brother Huey Newton talk about the urge of a man to hit the homosexual in the mouth and the tendency to make women shut up in the same breath. He said it stemmed from a man's insecurities, fear that he might be a homosexual himself, and in the case of women, that he felt castrated. Newton advocated for both women and homosexuals being considered oppressed groups, and that the women's rights and gay rights movements must be part of the black man's fight for freedom from oppression. I remember him distinctly saying that not only could a homosexual be a revolutionary, but the most revolutionary."

A wave of surprise serpentined through the room and arguments rose up among the various groups. Some of them had probably known Huey from his years in Cuba, where he had fled prosecution for a murder.

All eyes turned to the front of the room when the camp doctor rose up to speak. "This does not surprise me at all, the words of *compañero* Huey. When I am not a camp doctor, I teach at the University of Havana Medical School. These negative attitudes toward homosexuals I see all the time among my students. I remind them they will be doctors and are sworn to help people. Prejudice against homosexuals, like treating women as inferiors, is machismo, pure and simple, and it has no place in a socialist society. I do feel that in this country, we are on the verge of changing our outdated opinions, but machismo dies hard."

Malik had turned back toward the front, his arms crossed over his chest, head down. He seemed to be listening intently, but with his shoulders slightly arched. Rafael had told Byron that Malik was one of the Panthers who got into trouble with the police back home and fled to Cuba like Huey Newton. Now he worked as an organizer of foreign groups. Malik swore he would never go home and stand trial the way Huey had. Seeing him now, defeated, in a place he maybe didn't want to be, made Byron feel a surprising pang of sympathy.

9 No Rest for the Weary

Byron walked in the comedor and saw Malik sitting alone.

"Okay if I sit down?" said Byron.

Malik dropped his fork, leaving the last few bites on his plate. He looked around the almost-empty room. "Suit yourself. I'm leaving anyway."

Byron put his tray down across from Malik, and at the same moment the scraping of Malik's chair on the floor echoed through the room as he stood up. "Wait. I want to talk to you," said Byron. "Nothing to do with the discussion last night. I need your help."

"My help? Really? Look, what you do with your life is your business. I won't mess with you. But I ain't gonna be your friend, neither." He picked up his tray and started to walk away.

"Some white boys gunned down my friend," Byron said a little louder than he had intended. "Right in front of me. He was black."

Malik stopped, his body leaning toward the door, but his feet wouldn't move. He set his tray on the far end of the long table and turned around. "So you had a black friend.

That supposed to make me like you?"

"I'm not asking you to like me. Just need some advice."

Malik pulled out the chair, put his foot up on it, and rested his arm on his leg, giving Byron the full force of his stare. "And you think I'm the one to give it to you? Because I'm a Panther?" To Byron, a Black Panther was someone hard, someone who didn't put up with shit, someone who could kill, if it came to that.

"I need someone who knows how to take care of things," Byron said. "Maybe you're not that person."

Malik turned the chair around and straddled it, keeping the back as a barrier between him and Byron. "Let me guess, those white boys didn't go to jail."

"Weren't even arrested."

"And you did nothing?"

"They threatened to kill me if I said anything. What would you do?"

"I don't know, man. Buy a gun. Waste the muthafuckers. Why you bothering me with this?" Malik stood up and looked around the room as if afraid someone would see them talking. When he came back to Byron, he had a hard time looking him in the eye. "Damn! I can't get mixed up in your shit." He picked up his tray and walked toward the counter.

The door banged. Rafael walked in and came over to Byron. "Was he bothering you?" said Rafael.

Byron dug his fork into the plate of *congri*, rice and beans mixed together. "No. I just asked him a question."

While Byron concentrated on his food, Rafael sat across the table and tried to make eye contact. "Sometimes I don't get you."

"Don't worry about it."

The following Saturday was only a half day of work and they had Sunday off. By one o'clock Byron and Rafael were on a local bus that took them into Cárdenas, a town of low buildings, bicycles, and horse-drawn carriages nestled on the Cárdenas Bay, which in turn was protected by a finger of land that jutted out into the Caribbean. That lean peninsula, Varadero, was their destination. They changed buses at the terminal and headed out the Via Blanca highway, arriving at the white sand beaches and aquamarine sea of what had been a playground for the rich in the fifties.

A taxi took them to the Kawana hotel—not the finest in the area, but a decadent luxury after the conditions at the camp. How would they ever be able to go back? At the front desk, two women sat behind the counter. They glanced up at the boys, and then went back to their conversation, which had the ease of gossip rather than work.

Rafael drummed his fingers on the counter and said, "*Hola?*"

"*Un momento, por favor, señores.*"

The women continued to ignore them, speaking in low voices, peppering their conversation with expressions of surprise: *No me digas!* and *No puede ser!* Rafael and Byron turned their attention to a blond, shirtless young man, burnt to an inch of his life, flip-flopping through the lobby. Rafael arched his eyebrows at Byron, who immediately turned to look back at the women behind the counter. The women still conversed in a languorous world where the ceiling fans seemed to rotate at the speed of a merry-go-round that a parent had tired of pushing.

A few more moments passed before one of the women rose to her feet with some effort and sauntered over to them, looking first at Rafael, then Byron. Her face transitioned from carefree to the steely gaze of a party member. At home she was probably in the local Committee for the Defense of the Revolution, volunteers who made sure all the neighbors were adhering to the principles of the revolution.

"*Sí?*" She drew out the word as if it were several syllables instead of one.

"We'd like a room," Rafael said in forceful Spanish.

The woman looked over at her co-worker, and then back at them. "Together?"

"Of course," said Rafael.

"You're Cuban, right?" Cubans always recognized other Cubans. The accent was a giveaway.

"Yes."

"Well, then you should know that's not possible."

Rafael stared her down, not in a nasty way, but rather in amusement. In the short time Byron had known him, he recognized when Rafael was having fun with people, keeping them guessing. At times he enthusiastically supported the Revolution, the parts he agreed with, but laughed about the parts that didn't make sense.

The co-worker got up and stood next to her friend. Her uniform blouse was a size too small and you could see her bra in the gap between buttons.

"There's a hotel down the road for Cubans. Your friend can stay here," said the other woman.

"What's going on?" Byron's Spanish was still too weak to follow the conversation.

"She wants to separate us. What do you think of that?"

"Let's go," said Byron.

To the women Rafael said, "See, you've upset my friend, a fine tourist from *el yuma*." Cubans often referred to the United States as *el yuma*, though Byron hadn't been able to find someone who could explain why. "But I think we can resolve this." He reached in the pocket of his backpack, pulled out his passport, and slammed it on the counter, making the women start.

"Soy Cubano con pasaporte Americano!"

They stared down at the passport like he had just produced a letter personally signed by Fidel Castro. Even the staunchest revolutionaries had a touch of *envidia* when they saw a passport that could open thousands of doors for them. But they quickly recovered and forced a smile. "Why didn't you say so?" one of them said in good English.

"With a sea view, please, upper floor," said Rafael.

Rafael jangled the key in his hand and draped his arm over Byron's shoulders as they walked to their room. As soon as they had unlocked the door, Rafael looked at the two double beds that had been pushed together and said, "I like it." Byron felt a dead weight in his stomach and moved quickly toward the arched door that led out to the balcony.

"Look at this," he said, throwing the door open and stepping out on the tiled area with a table and two rattan chairs. They had a view of the giant swimming pool and, beyond that, the tranquil deep blue of the sea, edged in a beach so white it looked like snow.

Later at the beach they kicked up sugary sand and dove into warm water that Rafael described as the color of Byron's eyes. They lay side by side, nearly touching, and no one seemed to mind. On the way back to the hotel, they came upon an impromptu street party. It happened anyplace there was a boombox playing salsa, a bottle of rum, and hips that longed to move, which was most everywhere in Cuba. Byron watched a little girl, perhaps five years old, moving her body to the music of Cuba's perennial pop group, Los Van Van. She wore a skimpy halter-top, shiny red nylon shorts, and sandals with big plastic sunflowers on the toes. She danced as if she were born to do it, her body attached by invisible strings to the music. The girl's parents stood by smiling as she swayed and gyrated and spun, out-dancing the teenagers and adults around her. At such a tender age she knew how to move her body in the world, and felt not the slightest hesitancy to do so. She was remarkable for her age, but all the Cubans who danced around the crackly speakers cranked up to maximum volume—svelte and squat, old and young, wearing clothes tattered or new from Miami—had the same sensuality, owning his or her little square of broken concrete, saying, *I'm here, look at me.*

This same sense of self and lack of shame Rafael brought back to the room as heat lightning streaked the late-afternoon sky. Byron stood at the window, his back to the room and its possibilities, and focused on a place far out at sea. Rafael came up behind Byron, wrapped his arms around him, and wedged his nose behind Byron's ear. He inhaled deeply. "This is the spot. It is beautiful, this sweet smell of Byron."

Byron tensed. "I really don't think..."

"Shhh," Rafael breathed into his ear, sending a cascade of pure oxygen down Byron's spine.

"I can't."

"Yes, you can and you want."

Byron's half-hearted resistance was no match for Rafael's charm, the beers they had been drinking all afternoon, and the sultry air of Cuba that infuses everything with sensuality.

Later, when they collapsed in a tangle of sweaty limbs, Byron felt as if he had just had sex for the first time, sex in its three stages: teasing foreplay, a desperate, animalistic fucking, and then a gentle rocking embrace.

There was something perfect about the way Rafael cradled him while a salty ocean breeze made the sheer curtain dance in the copper light of sunset. Rafael sighed contentedly in his ear, one arm over his chest and a leg on top of Byron's, creating maximum skin-on-skin contact. He played with the few hairs on Byron's chest until he fell into the heavy breathing of sleep. And yet, it was not perfect. Shame latched onto Byron like a leech, sucking out all the joy. That was nothing new. But now it was combined with the notion that pleasure was not due him as long as Thomas' ghost roamed the Earth looking for justice.

Further clouding his mind, the inevitable comparisons between Rafael and Thomas cropped up. Though Thomas abandoned himself to the second stage of sex, he got quickly bored with foreplay and wasn't keen on being touched afterward. Once Thomas had come to New Orleans for a weekend and they got a room in a French Quarter hotel, where no one cared what they did in any shape, form, or fashion. Previous to that, they had always had sex outdoors under the trees, smelling the grass, listening to birds and insects.

It had been late on a Friday night when they got to their room in the French Quarter. Thomas immediately went into the bathroom to take a shower. Byron took his turn, but when he came out, the light was off and Thomas was in bed. Byron dropped his towel on the floor and quickly got under the sheet.

"Ain't this fancy?" Thomas mumbled with no thrill in his voice.

Byron's hand slid over to find Thomas had his underwear on. He pinched the material and said, "What's with the boxers?"

"I don't know about this."

"This meaning what? The hotel? The bed? Us?"

Thomas had never been shy before, not when he was out amongst the trees, the sights and smells of nature acting like an aphrodisiac on him.

"It's just so different."

"Oh, shut up," said Byron and stuck his hand in Thomas' shorts. A minute later they were grunting like a pair of wild boars they had come upon one time in the woods over by the John Ford pioneer house. When it was over, Byron had fantasized they would sleep entwined. But Thomas would have none of it. He rolled over and hugged his side of the bed.

Now that Byron had his fantasy embrace in the Kawana Hotel, with salsa music in the distance and playful shouts of children from the pool below, he felt trapped. He tried to move, but even from the depths of sleep Rafael held him tight. Byron watched the sun descend below the horizon and his thoughts drifted to his recent conversations with

Malik.

In the downtime between the end of the workday and dinner, most of the workers went to their quarters and crashed on their bunks. Others anointed their cuts and scratches with antibacterial creams, conversing in low, weary voices. They started calling it the Tiger Balm Hour because the smell of the ointment—camphor and menthol—often hung in the air as they passed around the small jars of the Chinese balm and massaged it into aching muscles.

Malik came into the bunkhouse with a clipboard. As a group leader he was supposed to meet with everyone on his team and write up a weekly report. Byron noted that Malik had gotten around to everybody except him and wondered if he was going to skip him altogether. Since their previous conversation they hadn't shared so much as a nod.

"Boudreaux, you're up," said Malik.

Rafael leaned over the edge of the upper bunk and looked at the surprise on Byron's face. He also seemed to have noticed that Malik was avoiding Byron. "It's no big deal," said Rafael. "Just a few questions."

Byron and Malik went outside and sat on a crude bench in the shade of a giant Ceiba tree. Malik wore sunglasses and a beret tilted to one side atop his limited afro. Rafael had told Byron that the Panthers in Cuba were trying to keep up appearances with their signature look, but back in the States membership had dwindled to a few dozen.

In a flat voice Malik read the questions off his clipboard and jotted down Byron's answers. He asked about Byron's experience, any injuries he had had, and what he would prefer as his next work assignment after they finished the cane cutting. In the quiet between questions, Byron heard the angry scratching of pen on paper.

After a few minutes, Malik retracted his ballpoint and said, "We're done."

Byron stayed seated with his hands folded in his lap. "I was hoping we could talk a little more."

"We've done all the talking we need to do. I've got to write up this report."

Byron took a deep breath. "Correct me if I'm wrong, but as a member of the Black Panther Party, I assume you believe in justice for victims of racism."

"So now you telling me what I believe? You're really pushing it, man."

"Look, I've got to do something. I want to do something."

"And you think you're ready?"

"I'm ready."

"Saying ain't being."

"You have your doubts because of me being…because of the way I am?"

"See, you can't even say it."

"I'm not like Rafael. I wish I was. He's fearless."

"Rafael is Cuban. One thing I learned here is that Cubans are born fearless. A little bit crazy, too. He wasn't raised in a Mississippi plantation family that probably had slaves up to the very last minute and then servants who were just a step above slavery. Y'all got soft having other people do the work."

"I never said my family had slaves."

"You denying it?"

His father had always been vague about family history. "It wasn't something we talked about."

Malik shook his head and blew out some air. "I have no idea what you want from me. I don't even know what we're talking about here. Your friend got killed by some white trash and you got it up your head you gonna get revenge. Is that it?"

Malik moved to the edge of his seat as if about to stand

up and go. Byron started talking and wouldn't, couldn't stop. He told a redacted account of what happened to Thomas, leaving out some of the details that might disturb Malik's sensibilities. His voice cracked a couple times in the telling. As he talked, Byron noticed tiny changes in Malik's demeanor—he leaned slightly forward instead of back and he took off his sunglasses with the excuse that he needed to clean them. He hadn't run away this time.

When Byron's story came to an end, Malik stood up and shook out his legs. His face went through the contortions of someone trying to understand. Malik stared up at the sky and pulled on his right earlobe. "He meant that much to you?"

"Yes. He did."

A couple days later they spoke while on an afternoon break. Instead of going over to where he usually sat with Rafael, Byron collapsed on the ground near Malik, rubbing his sore legs. He took off his bandana and rung it out, forming a puddle in the dirt.

"You were cutting really hard today," said Malik. "You trying to prove something?"

"Nah," said Byron.

"Maybe you're trying to impress your friend who, by the way, keeps looking over at us. I think he's jealous."

Byron laughed, but he was baffled. In a few short days, Malik had gone from hateful stares to teasing comments. It was partly the camaraderie of the Brigade that demanded it—they were all in the work together. And since that meeting where Rafael had broached the subject of gay revolutionaries, the majority had agreed that they had to respect each other, no matter their differences. At the same time Byron wondered if Malik was really as down on homosexuals as he professed. Sometimes out in the fields or across the meeting room, Byron would feel eyes on him and look up to see Malik staring—not hateful staring, but curious. Their eyes would meet for a second, and then Malik would turn his head.

"You ever kill anybody?" Byron asked.

Malik twisted his lips to one side and looked up at the murky sky. "Don't rightly know. I was in a shootout once. I had a gun in my hand and fired it. There were bullets flying ever which way. We escaped. The next day we read in the newspaper that one of the cops took a slug and died at the hospital. That's when I knew I had to leave. I came here."

"But if you knew it was you that killed him, how would you feel?"

"They were shooting to kill. Plenty brothers have lost their lives at the hands of the pigs. So what? If you worried your revenge is going to run up against your moral fiber, you better forget it right now. We didn't ask for that fight. They brung it to us. And you didn't ask for your fight." Malik paused and used his hand to wipe the sweat from his face. "Ya know, there's something about that incident you're not telling."

"What do you mean?"

"What were you and that brother doing out there in the woods? I mean, there are plenty of crazy-ass honkies that'll blow a nigger away for no good reason, but you said y'all were just fishing. Really?"

Byron had spared him the sexual details both because he didn't think Malik could handle it and he didn't want to say it out loud. Now Malik was practically begging for it. His eyes dropped to the ground and he spoke in a quiet voice. "I had let my hair grow long. From a distance, they thought I was a girl."

"What? Shit! There ain't nothing they hate more than a nigger messing with their white women. I guess second would probably be queers. In this case they sorta killed two birds with one stone. Of course, you're still alive 'cause you're white."

"There was a moment I wished they'd shot me, too."

Malik twisted his lips. "But they didn't. That's the point. Shit."

10 Displaced

Descending from the treetops, the call of the cicadas circled him in a tightening grip. And then, just as the cacophony was about to squeeze the life from him, the sound elongated, changing from a deafening hum to a chorus of celestial voices, an ethereal repetition of a two-note melody. Pressed to the ground, he felt the bitter green of the grass smart his eyes, the scent of earth, its decay and rebirth shooting up his nostrils and exploding in his brain. The magnolia tree above him was filled with the winged red-eyed males, shaking their tymbals like there was no tomorrow. With a gust of wind came a sudden crack, a thick branch snapping of its own weight began its descent with great speed toward him. He needed to move, but the incubus pressed down on him, sending him into a panic of labored breathing and voiceless shouts. But instead of crashing down on him, the branch was stopped by something or someone.

His mother's face danced in front of him—the way she looked that day in the Town Car so many years before, her chestnut-colored eyes full of fear and her lips warning of the curse of the cicadas. He felt the weight still on top of him, felt the hot viscous liquid dripping down his sides. With a trembling gloved hand his mother brushed his side and put her fingers in front of his face. The kidskin gloves were smeared with blood. "See?" she said.

"Help me, Momma," he whimpered.

His eyes opened to the sound of his own weeping and he clambered to consciousness. He touched the stickiness on his chest. It wasn't scarlet like in his dream, but rather sweat pooling in every crevice of his torso.

The terrifying dream, his "cicadamare," had haunted him since the day Thomas was killed. Each time he awoke his first thought was of what had been taken from him: the days when love was sweet and birds sang and the sun fell through the leaves in dappled patterns on their backs. That thought was immediately followed by another: his inability to get justice for Thomas.

Over the last few weeks Byron had awakened from the dream in so many different places that it took time each morning to orient himself. He sat upright and surveyed his surroundings. Ah, a studio apartment in Barcelona. He had gone from New Orleans to Mexico to Cuba, and now Spain. His meandering at times seemed without purpose, though there was, in fact, a certain logic to each move, if not a carefully designed plan.

When the *brigadistas* had returned to Havana before their next work assignments, Byron stole away on a night flight to Barcelona, the city he had most enjoyed on his brief senior-year trip through Europe. There was no message left behind, no parting kiss, no promises to keep in touch. He felt the wretch for abandoning Rafael, who had been so good to him, supportive without question, and loved him without expecting love in return. After a time Rafael's admirable qualities, which once had bolstered Byron, over time threatened to drown him. Byron had his moments of loneliness and panic, moments when he regretted his decision, but it couldn't be undone.

Soon after arriving in Barcelona he rented a *sobreatico* atop a fifth-floor walk-up with a terrace three times the size of the interior. It was in Barceloneta, a triangular spit of land facing the sea. From the narrow streets below he heard people speaking in a language he didn't understand, the voices as loud as if they were next door. He felt the buzz of a sleepless metropolis, an ancient city perched on the sea. If he listened carefully, he could hear the water sloshing onto the beach.

It was a dazzling city, and yet he had already grown tired of wandering the crowded streets, sitting in cafes blank-faced while people in fashionable clothes swirled by, everyone going somewhere. He hated their relevancy, their smug European sense of belonging. At night he would sit in bars, whiskey in hand while bleary images danced in front of him, smiling people trying to talk to him—men, women, some he wasn't quite sure of. And then in the darkest hours before dawn he would fall into bed almost forgetting his past until nightmares would rattle his memory, bring back the horrible image of the light fading from Thomas' eyes. He kept going back to Samantha's description of the sacrificial victim's heart being wrenched from his body, and feeling that same pain, that emptiness.

At the sink in his closet-sized bathroom, he ran water over his hands still raw from the labor he had done in Cuba. For a brief moment he had felt alive, on a path to becoming the man he wanted to be, a man who could cut sugarcane until his hands bled. As he whacked the sugarcane stalks he also had the illusion he was a man who could take matters into his own hands. The sudden flight to Barcelona had shaken his resolve, and doubt again reigned.

In the shower Byron turned on the cold water to wash away the remnants of his nightmare. With each shivering breath, he had a feeling that today could be a kind of beginning. He had an appointment at a modeling agency with a woman who had nearly accosted him at the Café de

L' Opera on the Ramblas. It wasn't clear—like most of the things that happened to him since he left the States—how a modeling job would fit into the overall plan; but it was something to keep him busy.

The woman had told Byron he needn't look so glum, pointing out that he had his youth and his looks. He wasn't immune to kind words, and he smiled, noting that she had once been beautiful. Now the afternoon light fell on her lifeless, repeatedly dyed hair, and her skin stretched tautly over her face, giving her a slightly traumatized look.

At first she had addressed him in French.

"Sorry, I don't speak Catalan," he answered automatically.

She giggled, and then realized he wasn't kidding. "Catalan? I was speaking French. No matter. So you're English then?"

"American."

"Heavens. I never would have guessed it." She commented on his thick blond hair, his brooding lips, his doubting eyes. It was just the kind of face they were looking for, one that expressed youth with a lingering sadness just under the skin, like Barcelona itself. It was 1980. Barcelona was emerging from the dark days of Franco, she explained, poised to become a great European city again. Designers and architects and ad companies were working tirelessly to put a new face on the renaissance of Catalan culture.

"I'm Byron Boudreaux," he told her. Again it felt good to use his mother's maiden name.

Her eyes lit up. "See, a French name. I wasn't that far off." She stuck out her hand. "Montse Ferrat. A pleasure. The truth is I've worked with French models and I'm a bit tired of them looking down their aquiline noses with the belief that Africa begins at the Pyrenees. It might be a pleasant change to work with an American such as yourself." She smiled and batted her eyelashes in a mildly flirtatious way.

"But I don't speak Catalan and very little Spanish," said Byron.

"My dear, it's the face. You won't have any speaking parts," she said with a wink. "I think we'll do quite well together."

Byron had arrived in Barcelona with two things in his favor: his looks and an income, one thanks to the dumb luck of genetics, and the other thanks to Manny, his Aunt Lidia's dear friend and investment broker extraordinaire. Manny was a drag queen at the French Quarter clubs by night and an Armani-suited businessman by day.

In the summer before he started at Tulane, Byron sat on the sofa at Lidia's house and felt the intensity of Manny's eyes upon him. "Gold!" Manny said, and let out a high-pitched laugh. "Like your hair." And to Lidia he said, "My dear, where in the world have you been hiding this lovely gift to humanity?"

Blood rushed to Byron's cheeks. No man back in Mississippi had so unabashedly flirted with him. It was a sort of awakening for him, the first time Byron became acutely aware that he had a gift he didn't quite ask for and wasn't sure how to handle. Thomas had been more than happy to engage in physical pleasure with him, but he never gave Byron any indication that he found him attractive.

With Lidia's assurance that Manny was a wizard, Byron had taken his savings and a good part of his college trust fund to buy gold at close to $275 an ounce. Gold went up and up and up. In mid-January of 1980, Manny said it was time to sell. Others said no. It could hit $1000 or higher. Manny was insistent. Byron followed his advice, which turned out to be right. By the latter part of January the price was falling, but Byron had come close to tripling his money. Manny continued to invest Byron's money, helping him to amass what felt like a small fortune. But a few months later Byron would have gladly given the eighty thousand dollars he had in the bank to bring back Thomas alive and well.

Now Manny, who sent Byron regular checks, was the only person from home who knew of his whereabouts. Byron had sworn him to secrecy, and because of Manny's great fondness for Lidia, Byron knew it must have been a gargantuan task for him not to reveal what he knew about her lost and possibly dead nephew.

So Montse's proposal held little financial interest for Byron, but he knew that something had to change in his life. He couldn't forever wander the streets all day and drink all night

In Montse's office he had a formal interview and a photo shoot with a photographer in the same building. Montse was so sure about Byron that she offered him a contract before even seeing the photos. He walked out of her office into the heat of a late summer day, feeling the best he had in weeks. To be admired for his looks was still somewhat disconcerting, but the fact that he would be paid for doing nothing more than standing in locations while he was photographed changed his usual shuffle to a walk with a slight bounce. A few paces down the sidewalk, he encountered a disheveled beggar with all hope erased from his eyes. Byron dropped a rather large peseta note in the hat beside the poor man.

11 From the Rib of Adam

From a café window up the street, Byron watched a young woman smoking a cigarette as she leaned against the wall under the marquee of the Cine Verdi. She wore a black vinyl trench coat over a flower-print mini dress and red boots. People glanced at her as they walked by, raised their eyebrows, and turned to their companions to make comments. But even more than her distinctive sense of attire, the woman stood out because she was alone—Spaniards had a tendency to rove in packs. The only other loner in front of the theater, a young man with wild hair and hunched shoulders, inched closer to her, pulled out a pack of Ducados, and asked her for a light. A twinge of concern brought Byron to his feet, but he stayed inside the café.

The woman took a lighter from her coat pocket and held it at arm's length. When he returned it, she took a step back. He lingered, puffing nervously, seemingly trying to think of something to say. She glanced at her watch again, and then up and down the street.

Byron settled back on the stool and twiddled a coffee spoon in his hand. He bounced his knee to the pop song blaring from a speaker just above his head. He thought up different excuses for how he might get out of this date, imagining how they would play out. With others he had begged off by claiming a photo shoot had run over. But he was reluctant to lie to someone who had already become dear to him.

Byron and Georgette had met at a club in the Barrio Chino, a dank and crowded neighborhood known for prostitution and crime near the port. Byron had spent the evening drinking at a sidewalk café on the Ramblas with a couple of female models from France and a male photographer from Kentucky. Someone suggested they go to La Concha, a bar frequented by drag queens and dedicated to the Spanish diva Sara Montiel. Byron had tried, unsuccessfully, to escape.

In the cramped bar Byron's friends marveled at the dozens of movie posters and portraits of Montiel lining the walls, while he surreptitiously watched Georgette, much as he was now doing from his perch by the window on Verdi Street. She was petite with a head of tight black curls and milky skin that looked as if it had never seen the light of day. She obviously wasn't a drag queen, though Byron had been fooled before. That night at the bar she sat alone, nursing a fruity cocktail. After another bourbon he got up the courage to approach her and try out his fledgling Spanish.

"Darling," she answered in English. "Let me see. You're definitely American, and most likely from the South! Would you mind too much if we spoke English?" She flashed her coal black eyes that seemed like patches of night sky dotted with tiny stars.

His jaw fell as if he were mortally wounded. "How embarrassing! You got all that from 'Buenas noches. Como estas?'" he said in a drawl.

"Oh, don't worry. We all go through the ungodly accent thing our first few months here."

"I've been here over a year."

"Oh…" She put her hand to her mouth and giggled. Her movement was slightly awkward, and she had to catch herself from falling off the stool. "I'm Georgette." She stuck out her hand. "From New Orleans. Born, raised, and forever corrupted by it."

He took her hand and held on. "You look like a Georgette. All perky and French." He continued to stare at her, the small hand tucked in his. She wore a slinky black dress with little trees of white coral printed all over it. It was low cut. A single strand of pearls cascaded down toward her cleavage.

"I guess if I had to say where I come from, I'd say New Orleans as well. But I was born and raised in Mississippi, and certainly far more corrupted by that. All hail Mississippi, last in everything with the exception of corruption and religion, where it's number one."

"Now that we've verified our credentials of degeneracy, let's have another drink." She turned to the bartender. "Javi, another one of these bombs and whatever he's having," she said in flowing Spanish. Inside his chest, Byron experienced a sudden quaver, something he had never felt with a woman: the urge to scoop her up and run away with her to a deserted island.

Byron watched as Georgette lit another cigarette and paced under the movie marquee. The wild-haired man had disappeared. Downing the last of his coffee, he stepped out of the café. The sparkling sensation he had felt the night at La Concha confused him, but it had been verified the couple of times they had gotten together since then. Last Sunday they had spent the afternoon in Parque Guell where they made a date to see Almodóvar's new film *Laberinto de Pasiones.*

She was by far the most delightful person he had met in Barcelona. And the fact that she was from the same part of the world was comforting—comforting and frightening.

When she would sit across from him, her eyes seemed to pierce the membrane of his cerebrum. He wondered how much Georgette could really see with those penetrating eyes.

Byron hurried toward her, and she discarded her cigarette, and with it her annoyance that he was late. As she watched people turn to take a second look at him, Georgette was reminded why he worked as a model. But something other than Byron's youthful good looks caught her attention. The charming innocence and the careful walk reminded her of someone. And then it struck her; it was that embarrassing fantasy from her youth, Tab Hunter. She recalled the pubescent thrill of watching reruns of *Operation Bikini* and *Ride the Wild Surf* on late night TV with her friends at pajama parties, squealing with delight and declaring their love for the blond heartthrob. In her rebellious later teens, when she saw the world as a much more volatile place, she berated herself for those earlier whims of innocence. But recently she had seen an older Tab Hunter in John Water's *Polyester* and felt somewhat vindicated for her early crush. Neither she nor Hunter had turned out as expected though his transition was the more striking. She had failed as a debutante, but Hunter had gone from teen idol to the smarmy, corvette-driving Todd Tomorrow who proposes to the overweight housewife Francine Fishpaw played by "Drag Queen of the Century" Divine. Throughout the movie Georgette had sat giggling with her hand over her mouth.

"Really sorry," said Byron, out of breath. "The time got away from me." They kissed and Georgette smelled Armani. His haircut was recent, and it looked like they had taken thinning shears to his golden waves.

"Why are you looking at me like that?" asked Byron.

She touched a finger to the center of his chest. "Tab Hunter."

He rolled his head back and laughed.

"You've heard it before," she said, letting the corners of her mouth droop.

"Not for a while," he said. "I do hope you mean the young Tab Hunter."

Georgette pinched his arm. "Don't do that again. I thought you weren't going to show."

"Why Miss Lacroix, how did you ever get it in your head that I might pass up an opportunity to be in your presence?"

She took his arm and they headed to the ticket window.

A couple of hours later they exited the theater, feeling like they had just returned from the bizarre planet of Almodóvar's mind. "I need a drink," said Georgette. "I've got a bottle of Rioja at home and I live just a couple blocks up the street."

"Fabulous idea," said Byron.

"Thank God I don't have any early classes tomorrow," said Georgette. She had gotten an ideal job that paid her well and left her with a lot of free time: tutoring several of the Spanish Federation tennis players who were based in Barcelona. "In the afternoon I have the Sanchez family— Emilio, Javier and their little sister Arantxa. They're like this tennis dynasty fixing to take over the tennis world. Can't have them flubbing up their English in interviews."

"You never told me how you got that job."

"I was an English major in college—not that it really prepared me for this kind of teaching. When I was at the University of Barcelona for junior year abroad, there was another American student, this Mexican-American guy from Dallas. He was obsessed with Sara Montiel, and she became his favorite drag persona. He dropped out of college and stayed here. Can you imagine a Mexican-American drag queen not chomping at the bit to get back to Dallas?" she said in her thickest Southern drawl. "When I moved back to Barcelona, we reconnected. Now he's my roommate,

Frankie. He had a two-bedroom in Gracia, so I moved in."

"And I bet he was the one who turned you on to La Concha?"

"Oh, honey. Big time. Turned out he was tutoring tennis players. Mild-mannered teacher by day, outrageous drag queen by night. He said they were looking for another teacher and I got the job."

They hurried up the stairs in Georgette's third-floor walk-up on Verdi Street to beat the timed hall lights. Just as they reached her landing the lights clicked off, leaving them in total darkness. Her hand fumbled along the wall and found the switch to give them another ninety seconds of light. Georgette pushed open the heavy wooden door, and then eased it closed, in case Frankie was asleep. She turned on a small table lamp with a beaded shade that cast the hall in a gentle light.

"The tile!" Byron gasped. He sank to his knees to examine the floor more closely.

Georgette put her finger to her lips. "Isn't it amazing?" She whispered.

It was a dizzying array of pyramids topped by circles in repeated combinations of Kelly green, pale blue, wheat yellow, and rust red. The pattern was reminiscent of the Freemason Eye of Providence on the back of a one-dollar bill. But even more amazing to Byron was that he had seen this tile before. His last night in Havana, in his gutless escape, he had gone to a small hotel in Vedado. The exact same vertiginous pattern and colors were on the floor of his room and he had spent a considerable amount of time staring at them, wondering if he were doing the right thing, leaving Cuba, leaving Rafael. He thought of Rafael's face and how it must have looked when he had discovered that Byron had skipped town.

She sat in a chair by the door and took off her boots. "Tile is great in the summer," she continued in a low voice, "but in winter your feet practically stick to them like a tongue to an ice cube." She noticed the distant look on his face. "Byron?"

"Oh, yes. Tiles *can* be very cold," he said.

"Shhh," she said again.

She led him down the hall to the living room in the back. "Sorry, don't have much furniture. But I do have wine glasses. Priorities, you know." The living room had a rattan loveseat, a coffee table that looked like a reject from the street, a tree lamp in the corner draped with a pink scarf, and a stereo on the floor. She went to the kitchen to get the wine.

On her way back into the living room she put on a Ana Belén cassette and opened the shutters to the balcony, letting in a jumble of sounds from the surrounding buildings: clipped dialogue from late-night movies, the clang of washing dishes, and a whine that could have been the mewl of a cat or a child. Georgette stood a moment, watching a neighbor cradle a phone between her ear and shoulder while scrubbing a pot. Then she joined Byron on the dingy flower-print cushions of the loveseat.

"What did you think of the movie? Were you able to follow it?" Georgette asked.

"My comprehension is getting better all the time, but I have to admit I missed about half the dialogue. Thank God for the overacting and the exaggerated facial twists."

"Did you get the part about Sexilia wanting a different kind of relationship with Riza?"

Byron looked at her, not sure what she was trying to say. "Uh, yeah. Seems like he was the only man she didn't jump into bed with."

She ran her hand through her black curls, fluffing them up. "Sometimes I feel my life is an Almodóvar film."

"Are you identifying with Sexilia?"

"Oh, God, no. I'm about the farthest thing from a nymphomaniac right now. I've sworn off sex." She looked over and surveyed his face. "Don't look so relieved," she said with a wry smile.

"I find you very attractive," he said. His boyish looks and the tremor in his voice gave the impression of an awkward sixteen-year-old on a first date.

"Why thank you, Mr. Boudreaux!" She cranked up her Southern accent and batted her eyes.

"Don't make fun of me."

"You're right. That was unkind. Maybe I just don't know how to accept a compliment anymore. One's personal history does have a way of polluting things. Damaged goods, you know. And I've got this funny little feeling that you might be, too."

"Are we still talking about our pernicious Southern upbringings?"

"That you learn to cope with. Other things hit you all at once and the wound is deep, hard to heal." Georgette finished her glass of wine and contemplated the dark remnants at the bottom.

Byron saw a story brewing behind her onyx eyes and he wasn't sure he wanted to hear it. He refilled their glasses. "Let's toast to the South and may it *not* rise again."

Georgette half-heartedly clinked his glass. "What I said before was a little odd. I feel like it warrants an explanation," she said.

"You don't have to." The mood had changed and Byron didn't like it. He just wanted to get drunk on the wine and enjoy Georgette's company.

"The reason I'm here in Barcelona. I haven't told anyone, not even Frankie."

"Really, Georgette. Maybe right now isn't…"

Her voice began to shake. "Please bear with me. I don't know. I have to tell someone. If I don't, I'll go crazy. You're so sweet I feel that I can trust you."

The words came out slowly as if they had been trapped inside her, waiting to be freed. "The summer after I graduated from Loyola back in New Orleans I got involved with a sweet guy, a hippie type with long hair and a beard. He sold cocaine and we lived in a basement apartment near Tulane where a lot of his customers were. The guys upstairs were students and sold pot. One night the police busted the whole house. Luckily, that night I had gone over to visit Sybil, a friend who was distraught over a breakup with her boyfriend. I didn't want to go, but she was in tears on the phone. On my way home, I saw the flashing lights from a block away and knew what it was. What I had feared for a long time had come to pass. I went back to Sybil's and spent the night. Early the next morning Johnny called from jail and said I should get out of town. He thought the police might be looking for me.

"I had no idea where to go and felt guilty about abandoning Johnny, but he had been insistent. He suggested I leave the country and mentioned Barcelona, the place where I had spent my junior year abroad. I needed to get some of my things, so one night I went back to our apartment. Johnny was *not* making a fortune, so the apartment was hardly the Ritz. He kept saying he was saving to move us to a better place. I unlocked the door and stepped into the dark low-ceilinged living room. I thought it was strange there was light spilling into the hall from the bedroom in back, but I imagined the police had left the light on. For some silly reason I was worried about the electricity bill.

"I heard what sounded like a creaking drawer and then a low voice. I knew I had to get out of the house immediately and ran back to the front door. But two men rushed down the hall and grabbed me before I could get it open. I tried to scream, but one of them put a hand over my mouth. I remember how strange it was that this calloused hand smelled of the lilac sachet from my underwear drawer. They had been going through my things. 'Where's the stuff?' one of them said. Then he let go of me. 'You scream again you're in big trouble.' 'What stuff?' I said. 'Are you cops?' The guy looked at me like I was crazy. 'Cops? That's funny. Just give us the coke and we'll leave.'

"Johnny had told me the police had found it all, but I was afraid to say that for fear they would get angry. 'It's my boyfriend's. I don't know where he keeps it.'

"One of them looked like Fats Domino and had an idiotic smile. The other had long wavy hair and a scar that went from the corner of his mouth to his ear. For years I saw it in my dreams. They carried me into the bedroom and threw me on the bed. They told me to stay there and shut up. They continued to ransack the apartment, but came up with nothing. 'Now what we goin' do?' said the fat one. 'Go get that duct tape I seen in the kitchen,' said the other.

"I was scared, but there was a part of me that still believed I would get through it unharmed. I should have fought. Screamed at the top of my lungs. The neighbors might have heard. They might have gotten scared and left. But it was too late. Still I tried to reason. 'I'll give you all the money I have.'

"The fat one started tearing off pieces of duct tape. That ripping sound still makes me want to jump out of my skin. They taped my mouth and hands, and then fell on me like animals, taking turns. The smell of their bodies was horrible. It lasted no more than half an hour, but it seemed like an eternity. I wanted to die. And yet they had let me live.

"When I opened my eyes it was quiet." Georgette didn't look at Byron. "It seemed that they had left. My body felt like it had been trampled in a stampede, but I managed to wiggle to the edge of the bed and stand up. In the kitchen I held a knife between my knees and cut the tape from my hands. I was so anxious to remove the tape from my mouth, I yanked out hunks of my hair with it. I hobbled to the neighbors' house, and they called Sybil who came and took me to a clinic. They did all the tests."

"How did those guys know your address or that you had drugs?" asked Byron.

"That's what I said to Sybil. Johnny was very careful who he sold to, students mostly. She told me about a section in the paper where they list all arrests, what they were for, and if you can believe this, the address of the person. She said I ought to go to the police, and if they couldn't find the guys, which was likely, I should at least file a civil suit against the newspaper, the police, or somebody.

"But I wanted nothing to do with the police, facing rapists in court, or seeing my name in the newspaper again. Instead, I cleared out my bank account and got on a flight to Barcelona, the last place I remembered being truly happy."

Byron was shaking inside from her story. It sickened him, but he wanted to pretend they could still have a normal conversation, that what she had told him was just one of the nasty incidents in life that everybody had to deal with. And then one had to get up, brush oneself off, and go on. "I don't know what—"

"You don't have to say anything," she said quickly.

Georgette fell silent; the story hung like a bad painting looking over their shoulders. Byron again grasped for a word, a phrase, something that might sound more or less normal. He took a last gulp of wine.

Georgette stood up and hurried from the room, calling out, "I've got another bottle."

"I'm so sorry," he said when she returned to the sofa. He reached for her hand, which twitched at first like a sparrow unaccustomed to being confined, and then settled into his. She let her head fall on his shoulder. "What about you? Do you have some equally enchanting story to tell me?"

What did she mean? Was there something that made her suspect he had a tragic story as well? Or was this the time he was supposed to confess that he'd never had sex with a woman? He had tried, gone to his high school prom with a girl he quite liked. After the dance they went to a friend's house whose parents were out of town. They got drunk on cheap champagne. Instead of losing his virginity, he lost everything he had eaten for the previous few days. The poor girl spent the night mopping his brow with a wet washcloth and cleaning up the bathroom floor. He often wondered if there was something portentous about that night.

Despite the breeze coming in the open balcony door, sweat seeped onto his forehead. "I have a story, and I *will* tell you, but it's no big deal. Nothing like yours. I should probably go."

Georgette squeezed his hand. "You don't have to. It's late. I don't want to be alone." She felt his body tense. "As a friend, I mean. Sometimes when I'm scared, I go and crawl in bed with Frankie, just to feel close to someone."

"I'm *not* Frankie," he said with a bite to his voice. "I might want to kiss you."

"Oh! Really?"

"I told you I found you attractive."

"I just want to sleep and have someone there. Am I being selfish?"

"A little maybe. But I must admit I'm not anxious to slog home at this hour."

Georgette wore an extra-large T-shirt. He wore his boxers and a tank top. They lay in bed in silence, their hands touching. After a time, she turned away from him and fell asleep.

Byron stared at the shadows on the ceiling and listened to the angry bark of a dog echoing off the walls in the courtyard. He couldn't banish the image from his head of the two men violating Georgette. It felt like someone was twisting his intestines into a knot. And then he thought of the violence perpetrated against Thomas and him. He was glad to be away from the racial tension of Mississippi. A history of racial violence ran through his state like a tapeworm, eating its fill. He pondered, as he had a thousand times, all the scenarios of what would happen if he went back to his town. None of them included forgiveness.

He had started taking martial arts classes to increase his confidence and ability to defend himself. He read murder mysteries, looking for information about ways to kill that left no trace, imagined enacting them on Kelly and his friends. Georgette's body jerked, and she let out a whimper, reminding him that he was not alone. She looked so vulnerable, her small bones twisted into a self-embrace. He had to stop himself from throwing his arms around her in an effort to keep her safe. How easy it would be to seal off the dark tunnels to his past and start anew, create a life with Georgette in this awakening city, immerse himself in the streams flowing toward a modern Spain.

But the ghost of Thomas was not through with him, his dying eyes appearing at the most inopportune moments, breaking down the walls Byron tried to build against the past. He could not, he decided, even think of pursuing anything with Georgette until he dealt with the men who had caused Thomas' death. Even if he failed, Byron could at least be comforted by the fact that he had tried.

12 An Eye for an Eye

Byron and Georgette were squeezed into a corner in the overcrowded 4 Gats restaurant, pleased that they had snagged a window seat until they saw the people outside staring longingly at their table.

"What a marvelous thing to do with spinach!" Georgette said of the Espinacas a la Catalana. The nearly black spinach leaves had been sautéed with raisins, pine nuts, and garlic.

It was her third attempt at getting Byron to speak since they had sat down. Silence from him was not unusual, but she was having a particularly hard time this evening.

Then he opened his mouth and the words dashed out. "I have to go away for a while. I'm leaving day after tomorrow. Don't know when I'll be back." He picked a raisin out of the spinach with his fork and moved it to the side of his plate.

"Oh, and you waited until now to tell me?" said Georgette, trying to tamp down the shock, though the feeling of falling off a ten-story building is hard to hide. Their progress toward closeness had been "as slow as the Second Coming," as her grandma used to say with a wink, but he was the first man she had been able to trust in years. It had been a couple of months since their first venture into sex. After a night of drinking, they went to Byron's apartment. She could tell he wanted to please her. And she wanted to please him. When you love someone, that's what you do, right? Sex hadn't brought them much closer, but it hadn't been a disaster that drove them apart. They were two broken and discarded toys that had found each other in the corner of a dark closet. Being physically close to someone, particularly being held, brought Georgette closer to healing, and she was determined to help Byron get there, too.

"I'm glad I didn't have to come by one day and find out from a neighbor that you'd flown the coop," she said.

"I'm coming back," he said with the conviction of an itinerate preacher.

She realized she had been holding her fork suspended in the air, draped with weeping spinach, and quickly put it down. "I've heard that before."

"No, really. I'm keeping my apartment and leaving most of my things here. I'll give you a key. Perhaps you'd be kind enough to check on things and make an attempt at reviving the plants you're always reminding me about. You're good with them."

"Better, it seems, than with people."

"Please try to understand. I've got to take care of some business. Could take a couple months."

"Understand what?" Her voice rising. "You tell me nothing. I pour out my heart to you and get little in return."

Byron had broken the promise he made the night Georgette told the story of her rape. He avoided talking about Thomas, only mentioning that, once, a friend back in Mississippi had died. No details. How could he tell the person he was desperately hoping to love that his heart had been destroyed?

"The less you know the better," he said.

"What? Mission Impossible? If you tell me, you'll have

to kill me?"

He responded with a laugh gutted of any humor. "Georgette, you are very important to me. But we can't move forward until I take care of this. I'll be in touch. I promise. I have to do this. I've been planning it since I came to Barcelona."

The truth was that he had no plan, or rather, that he had so many plans they seemed like none. The weight of time had become unbearable; if he didn't do something now, he never would. Malik had sent him the name of a guy in Atlanta, someone who had experience in arranging things. He and Malik had kept in touch since Cuba, writing letters where Byron expressed his frustration with himself for not doing anything, and Malik expressed his frustration with being a foreigner in a closed society, wanting to go home, even if going home meant returning to the belly of the beast. The only thing that kept him going, Malik said, was his association with the Brigades—despite having to deal with a few perverts like Byron, which he followed with a quick "just kidding." Since Byron had cut short his Cuban adventure, he hadn't had a chance to convince Malik of his sincerity to seek justice. But in letters it seemed that Malik had been won over, and he had agreed to help.

In Madrid Byron picked up a false passport. It had taken weeks of going through channels, but the original connection was again from Malik. Though stuck on a Caribbean island, Malik had associations all over the world. The passport looked good. They used the name Brian Wilson. "Oh, God," thought Byron. "Now, I'm a Beach Boy."

He got on a nonstop flight to Atlanta and from the airport went to a downtown hotel. Later, out on the street, he used a payphone to call the number Malik had given him. His hands shook as put the coins in the slot. "Your cousin Paul sends greetings from Nantucket," said Byron.

"And how's Aunt Beatriz?" answered a tired voice. It sounded unbelievably corny, but it was the response he was supposed to get.

The man told him a time and location to meet, a Burger King not far from his hotel. He took a taxi, ordered a Whopper meal, and sat under the milky glare of fluorescence that seemed so foreign after his time in Barcelona. In the corner, a young couple sat, feeding each other French fries. The only other customer was a workman in overalls with paint-splattered hands holding his hamburger as if somebody might take it away from him. Byron didn't have to wait long before a heavyset balding white man in his fifties approached him. He was on the verge of getting up and running. He glanced out the window, expecting the screeching tires of unmarked cars and flashing lights.

The man stuck out his hand. "I'm Randall. You look surprised."

"I guess I expected, well, my associate is a Panther," he whispered, "so I just assumed—"

"That I'd be black?"

"Yeah."

Randall sat down. "Don't worry. I'm the one you want. We can talk here. What kind of person are you looking to hire?"

Byron hesitated and rubbed his damp palms on his jeans. "Hire?" And then he remembered that hire was code for "eliminate." "Actually there are three."

Randall knocked his head back. "Are you shitting me?"

"They were all involved. Only one shot—"

Randall held up his hand.

In a lower voice Byron continued, "But the three of them, you know…they could have saved him."

"All right. Just tell me a little about them. Don't mention any names or anything personal. What are their habits, hobbies? You know these guys, right? I think that's the story I got."

"We weren't exactly in the same circles, but yeah, I knew them." Thinking about them made his voice begin to shake. "They fucking blew him away. And they won't be punished. They'll just go on hurting people, maybe—"

Randall shook his head and put his meaty hands on the table. "Okay. Calm down. I don't need to know any of the shit, the why or wherefore. If our mutual friend says you're a stand-up guy and you've got a legitimate beef, that's good enough. If you wanna make a confession, there's a church down the street," he said wryly. "I need to know their habits, what they do together. My guess is you don't want to hire 'em one by one."

"Hunting and drinking mostly."

"That's good. Very good. But we need patterns, habits. Here's what you're gonna do. Follow them. Keep track of their schedules. Find out where and when they go hunting. If we're lucky, they spend the night away on those trips, somewhere remote. Come back to me with the info and we make a plan. I don't participate. I advise. Each situation is different."

"Why are you doing this?" Byron asked.

"We don't sweat the why or wherefore, remember? Oh, and create a disguise. Grow a beard if you can. Get a good wig to cover those golden locks. You know, hats, sunglasses and stuff."

"I'm already officially disappeared. A lot of people probably think I'm dead."

"And above all, don't be tempted to contact family or friends. Stay away from people who might know you." Randall held up his hands. "Now, last thing. What *don't* you see on my hands?"

"What?"

"Gloves. Always wear gloves!"

Randall stood up, ran his hand through the few thin hairs on his head, and then stared out the large windows at the vacant parking lot. "I'm doing it because of my wife. She wouldn't approve, of course. No way, no how. If you're really interested, look up the *Montgomery Advertiser*, March 3, 1962. Front-page story. She was a good woman. The best."

Byron rented a car to drive from Atlanta to Mississippi. Since he had to cross Alabama, he decided to take I-85 and make a little stop in Montgomery. He went to the public library, and on microfiche found the story that Randall had referred to: "Men Acquitted in Freedom Rider Nurse's Death." The article gave the basic facts: Two men accused of manslaughter in the death of Betty Sedgewick had been found innocent. Betty (whom Byron had to assume was Randall's wife) was a nurse at the St. Jude's Hospital, where the Freedom Riders had been taken after they were attacked by an angry mob at the Montgomery bus station in 1961. He read several more articles including a firsthand account of the Montgomery beatings in a journal called New South. He not only was able to piece together Betty's story, but learn about a part of history he knew almost nothing about.

The Freedom Riders had been protesting the South's segregated buses, waiting rooms and restaurants, and for their efforts were beaten with baseball bats, bottles, and pipes in Montgomery and in other cities along the protest route. Betty heard about the trouble at the Montgomery bus station, and even though it was her night off, volunteered to work. When the white mob tried to come in the ER to continue beating the Riders waiting for treatment, she stood in their way while a colleague quickly gathered the victims into a room and locked the door. For that action she was branded "the Freedom Rider nurse." When she left the hospital that night, some of the men waited for her. A witness said they saw several men get in a car and follow her. Another witness looked out her window and saw a car tailgating a vehicle that matched the description of Betty's Chevrolet. A few minutes after leaving the hospital, her car was smashed against a tree, her lifeless body slumped over the steering wheel. When the prosecution noted that the police hadn't bothered to look at flecks of paint from her badly damaged bumper, the defense lawyer brought up the bad driving record of female drivers, as well as a fender-bender Betty had been involved in some five years before. It was not surprising that a conviction had not been reached in the impossibly charged atmosphere of those days in the South. Before the trial, the woman who had seen Betty's car being tailgated by a black sedan, recanted her statement and refused to testify.

One of the articles included a photo of a man who looked like a much younger Randall, except his name wasn't Randall in the caption. Identified as "a local inventor," the man was quoted as saying the trial was a travesty, and they would continue to seek justice.

Byron went to the microfiche index and looked up the names of the two men who had been acquitted. About six months after the acquittal, there was an article about one of them being killed in an accident on a mountain road up in Talladega County. He drove for a company that delivered auto parts all over the state. The other man's car had been found a month later by Lake Martin. His body washed up on shore a few days later. Seems he had drowned. The authorities hinted at the possibility of foul play, but had no proof.

The stories made Byron shudder. At the same time, the notion that justice had been served somewhat cleared the murky pool of his conscience. He became stronger in his resolve. When the courts failed, people had the right to take action. When a woman like Betty was killed simply for protecting victims of racial violence, and Thomas' life was taken away for sport, something had to be done. It wasn't revenge. It was justice. In the couple hours he spent in the library, he read about countless examples of racially motivated violence, including a lynching that had taken place in Alabama just the year before. A lynching in 1981? It seemed impossible.

Byron arrived in Mississippi and took a motel room in Hattiesburg rather than Columbia. It was only a half-hour drive to his hometown, and he wanted to avoid running into someone he knew, possibly one of his high school classmates who might have aspired to a job as a desk clerk in a local motel. If someone recognized him, he might as well jump on a plane back to Barcelona and leave his plans behind. In a small town, gossip flies like squawking crows flitting from power line to power line.

In a room smelling of stale tobacco, he looked at himself in the mirror—new white linen suit, light-brown oxfords, a Panama hat, and a briefcase in hand. He looked like a traveling bible salesman. He also had dyed his hair dark brown and filled in a new mustache with the same hair dye. He donned a pair of sunglasses and barely recognized himself.

Columbia only had one bar, a run-down saloon out North Main just beyond the city limits. Byron pulled into the parking lot and immediately spotted Kelly's truck, bringing back memories of seeing it in the rearview mirror and his own eyes blinking back tears while every fiber of his body was wracked with pain. He parked in a dark corner of the lot, far from the lone streetlight near the road. The blinking neon Ruby's sign bathed the potholed terrain in red light, making it look like the surface of Mars. He fell into a trance, watching the sign flash on and off, vaguely noting the comings and goings of the customers. He imagined the inside as a place where the crowd was as miserable and undone as the country music they listened to, where slack-faced women were subjected to a constant string of crude propositions, and whiskey flowed until it killed the pain or knocked the wounded to the floor.

At around one in the morning, Kelly, Preston and

Jackson exited the bar and staggered to Kelly's truck. They seemed as inseparable as ever, and Byron wondered if Thomas' murder brought them even closer. They were bound tight like criminals or gang members or rogue policemen, knowing that if one fell, he would take the others with him.

Preston danced around, squirming and howling, and then headed straight towards Byron's car on the edge of the lot. Byron quickly put his window up and locked the door. He scrunched down and lay his head back as if he were sleeping. Right in front of his bumper, Preston stopped and squinted through the windshield. Byron's heart was thumping, his eyes barely open. He picked up the imaginary gun off the seat and emptied it into the man's face. Preston teetered, cocked his head, and moved his face closer to the windshield, not realizing he'd just been eliminated, feeling no pain, seeing no blood.

Preston tipped his cowboy hat, grabbed his crotch, and sprinted to the edge of the parking lot. There he stood swaying and peeing for what seemed like an inordinate amount of time, and then walked back to join his friends. Preston hopped in the truck, and Kelly backed up and took off like a racehorse kicking up gravel.

At a safe distance Byron followed them through town, out 98. And then they made a surprising turn onto 587, as if they were going back to the scene of the crime. Had Preston somehow recognized him? Were they playing with his head? But soon after getting on 587, they turned onto a gravel road that weaved through a cluster of mobile homes. Kelly parked and the three of them entered a small, ramshackle trailer on the edge of the park. Byron went past them, pulled onto a side road, and cut the lights.

Kelly stayed about an hour, and then got back on the road. Byron followed him to his parents' home on the east side of town, pulling over a few houses down. He watched Kelly climb the outside steps to a room above the garage.

Feeling certain that Kelly was in for the night, he drove back to the trailer, turned off his lights, and eased the car into the parking lot of Beulah's Grocery and Grill across the street from the trailer park. There was a "Closed" sign on the door. Beulah's was known for its barbecued pork sandwiches, and a number of times he and his father had stopped there for lunch. In later years he went there with Thomas. Thomas would sit in the car while Byron went in. They would take the sandwiches and eat them sitting under a tree or by the river, smacking lips and licking the sauce off their fingers. In the short time he had been back in Columbia he had already been bombarded by a hundred memories of Thomas that rattled his spine and made his blood run cold.

He sat watching the trailer and made mental notes. Lights went out about three. Little traffic on the road. No life from the other trailers or neighboring houses. He heard crickets and frogs. He calculated the distance to the trailer doors, one on the side facing him, and the other on the back facing the woods. A car parked by the back door wouldn't be seen from the road.

Byron was yanked out of a dream by a knock on the window. He sat up and gazed at a man with a gaunt face and stringy hair, his back bent awkwardly, staring at him with cloudy eyes. In the hazy dawn of coming awake, he thought it was Jasper or Preston. His hand reached in a panic for the keys to start the car. The man continued to stare without saying anything, and Byron recognized him, an older man he had seen a number of times over the years emerge from the back of Beulah's, perform a task, and then return to the shadows without a word.

"What you doing?" said the man. "This is private property."

Byron rolled the window halfway down. "Uh...you got any of those pork sandwiches made?"

"Are you shitting me? You sitting out here all night

waiting for a pork sandwich?"

"I was just passing through," said Byron, searching for the words of his story. "I've stopped here over the years. Traveling salesman. Got to be in Hattiesburg this morning, but last night I was so bushed I couldn't drive another minute. Just pulled over to catch forty winks."

It was getting light, and out of the corner of his eye Byron saw activity around the trailer. A county truck pulled up with gardening equipment in the bed. Jasper and Preston stumbled out and got in the truck belonging to the crew that cut weeds along the highway.

"Looks like you got a far sight more than forty winks." The man's voice was surprisingly high and uncalibrated. "I come to open the store. Don't get much call for sandwiches at this hour. But if you ain't in a hurry, we can rustle one up."

There was something about the way the man tilted his head and widened his eyes, as if to let in more light, that made Byron feel the man was testing him, that he didn't really believe his story. "How about some coffee?" said Byron. "I think I can wait on the sandwich until the next time I pass through."

"Uh-huh. I see. Let me go check on the coffee."

This was the first person he had encountered since being back in Columbia, someone who might later report him as suspicious. It was a stupid mistake, but with the old man's compromised vision, any description he made would be unreliable. Byron resolved to be more careful. He started the car and got back on the road.

Later that day he found a side road where he parked the car, walked into the woods, and observed the trailer through the trees. The home was in poor shape, with two broken windows covered with plastic and duct tape. At one end was a pile of tires next to a few rusty rims. He didn't see anyone go in or out, so it appeared that Preston and Jackson were the only ones living there. There was no activity in the closest trailer about fifty feet away, but seeing a baby stroller next to the door disturbed him.

In the heat of the day when few people were out, he emerged from the woods and crossed the tracks. He got close to the stroller and saw that it was broken and unusable, likely abandoned a long time ago.

Since most people in town didn't lock their doors, he wasn't surprised that the back door of the trailer was open. Inside he was walloped by the smell of dirty clothes, cigarette smoke, and stale beer. It was pretty much as he had imagined: shabby furniture and clothes strewn throughout the rooms. He stood in the middle of the kitchen bathed in a pale green light coming through the faded curtains. Without knowing why, he went to the refrigerator and opened it. It contained a few condiments, a six-pack of Schlitz malt liquor, and a Pizza Hut box with a couple of petrified slices in it. Almost humorously he thought about poison. A nice dose of arsenic. No, too messy and discoverable. And too Agatha Christie.

While closing the fridge, Byron's eyes fell on his hands. No gloves. Randall's parting words already forgotten. He grabbed a crusty towel and vigorously rubbed the handle, and then spun around, looking for anything else he might have touched. From the pocket of his trousers he pulled out a pair of thin black leather gloves and put them on.

The heat in the trailer was oppressive, bringing to life a mélange of volatile odors, but he didn't plan to stay long, only long enough to make note of the things Randall had suggested: air conditioner, gas stove, air ducts. Earlier that day he had checked the hours of county road crew workers and figured he had time to spare—but why push it? Sickened by the rancid smells and the eeriness of being in the devils' den, he headed for the door. Then a sudden urge to pee stopped him. He could wait until he got to the woods, but he stood frozen, gazing down the narrow dark hall that led to the bedrooms and bathroom, fighting the urge to see more.

The sparse bathroom had a couple of mildewy towels on racks, a can of Gillette shaving cream on one side of the filthy sink, and an uncapped, mangled tube of toothpaste on the other. He relieved himself and stared out a small, partially open window. Just as he was about to flush, he heard the popping of a car rolling over gravel. *No, it can't be. Delay equals disaster. Think.* He ran into the living room and parted the blinds to look out the window. There were two doors, one on each side. If he saw them going in the direction of one, he could go out the other.

An Oldsmobile Cutlass came into view and pulled up next to the neighbor's home. An elderly man got out, and as he walked around the front of the car, he stopped and bent down to examine the bumper. "What's that?" he screamed. A woman huddled in the car and shook her head. "Get out and look at this," he yelled. "When did this happen?" Then with great difficulty she extricated herself from the car and waddled up the steps of the trailer without looking at him or answering his question. The man continued to yell in her direction and after looking back twice at the bumper, he stomped up the steps, opened the trailer door, and slammed it behind him.

Byron went back and flushed the toilet. He knew he had to leave, though the urge to stay kept tugging at him, a compulsion like that of a hot prowl burglar who is more interested in violating the privacy of the occupants than stealing. If he hadn't already peed he might have urinated on the floor or he spit in the water glass by the sink, some primal token that he had been in their territory.

Unable to stop himself, his feet moved along the rough brown carpet, and he found himself in one of the bedrooms. It must have been Preston's because the cowboy hat hanging on a hook looked like the one he had worn the previous night. There was a Confederate flag above the bed and a Lynyrd Skynyrd poster on the opposite wall. Sitting on a bedside table was a teddy bear with a sign around its neck that read, "I love you." In a second Byron's resolve turned to dust. *What are you doing? They are people just like you. They have people who love them. They like to drink and have sex, leave the cap off the toothpaste, discard their clothes wherever they take them off. You're done here!* He took the first steps that would be his trajectory back to Barcelona—leave the trailer, get in his car, go to the airport, and fly away.

On the way out of the room, he spied a cartoon taped to the fake wood paneling, next to the light switch where it could be seen often. It looked cut out of a magazine, yellowed, the edges curling. He leaned in to get a better look. His spine turned to ice. In the cartoon two hooded Klansmen sat on a stump, drinking beer. In the background, three black men hung by their necks from a tree branch. The caption read, "This has always been my favorite hangout."

All his disgust and anger and pure revulsion came rushing back. He felt drunk with it as he staggered to the door and left the stifling trailer.

Byron sat in his car, suffocating in emotional turmoil. Sweat dripped down his face. He lowered the windows, letting in the sounds of crickets and katydids clicking and buzzing, insects that needed the heat to warm up their instruments for their songs. Nature, in its waves of unpredictability, echoed the turbulence that always seemed to surround him. He was nothing if not a product of this town, most of his life spent under its relentless sun that melted his spirit one minute and, in the next, restored it under the shade of its big-leafed trees. In summer, lakes and ponds turned to bathwater, and in winter, the garden was painted with a delicate coat of frost. Mornings he woke up with hope and evenings went to bed with doubt. Even the layout of his town had its dichotomies, segregated neighborhoods and opportunities doled out according to race. As a child he didn't understand the dynamics of the world, but he knew there was something unfair about it. He remembered, as a small boy, asking Sofia one day why her skin was so unlike his and why she always wore the same clothes while his mother had a new outfit every day.

And then Byron From The Hill met Thomas From The Other Side Of Owens Street. He began to believe there could be a bridge between the two sides of town. With Thomas, his life changed in ways subtle and great. For the first time Byron took an interest in football, went to games and cheered Thomas, felt proud that they were friends. He started writing sports articles for the school newspaper, often spending hours in the library learning the fine points of the game. And yet there was an instinct—also echoed in Thomas' eyes—that made him only discreetly acknowledge Thomas at school. When they went fishing he would tell no one, and sneak the poles and tackle in and out of the garage.

The only person he talked to about his new friendship was his best friend from childhood, Julie. One day, as they worked on the school newspaper together, he announced as casually as he could, "I went fishing with Thomas Davis last weekend."

"Fishing? I thought you hated fishing." As children he used to complain to her how much he dreaded going fishing with his father.

"It was fun. We had a good time. Don't tell my parents, okay?"

"I think blacks and whites should be friends," she said in a cautious voice, and he was tempted to ask her how many black friends she had. But he knew the answer.

Sometimes he would give her a ride home from school, working Thomas into the conversation. "We caught four catfish last weekend," Byron said. She must have detected the unmeasured enthusiasm in his voice when he talked about Thomas. Her eyes widened with the tiniest strains of fear that she might be losing her friend, if not her future husband. When they were growing up, everyone teased them about one day getting married.

"How thrilling. Did you finish that article about the drama club?"

"I will. You know, I was thinking about writing some of the sports stuff, like about the football team."

Later Julie would look over his football articles, telling him they were much too wordy, and that she didn't want to waste so much space on a game she thought barbaric. They argued about it, and their friendship suffered.

But when Byron and Thomas tumbled into intimacy, Byron stopped talking to her about Thomas altogether. She would occasionally ask him, "You caught any catfish lately?" and follow with a snigger. He would lean down closer to the copy he was working on and ignore her, thoughts of Thomas' skin shivering through him like a gust of wind. He wished he had never told her about the fishing trips; her inquiries threatened the wall he had built between what happened in the woods and the rest of his life.

Before going back to Hattiesburg, Byron felt a desire to drive by Thomas' old house. He had no news of the family and wondered if he might see signs that they were okay. While traversing the streets he had known all his life, his mind slipped into a daydream where he knocked on the Davis' front door and Thomas' mother answered. He would introduce himself, and they would fall into each other's arms sobbing.

A blaring horn brought him out of his reverie, and he slammed on the brakes. He had gone through a stop sign, nearly hitting a car crossing the intersection. With the screech of his tires and the shouting of the driver, several people on the street stopped and looked at his car. He was on Main Street, right in the middle of town, an area he should have avoided. His father's office was right across the street. And then, in what also felt like a dream but was real, his father appeared, hurrying toward a shiny maroon Cadillac, a new purchase, Byron noted. Byron began to shake and angled into a parking space. In his side view mirror he watched his father as if he were a stranger. He thought of their last conversation and regretted the way it ended. Maybe if he had tried harder to convince his father that he needed to go to the police, they might have turned those boys in, gotten justice for Thomas. Instead he had run away and faked his disappearance with signs of foul play, in part to punish his parents. The guilt of making his parents suffer these past couple of years weighed on him.

Before his father had a chance to get in his car, Kelly's father walked out of the hardware store and shouted a greeting. "Hey, Frank!" His voice filled the street. The two men shook hands, perhaps shared a joke as both their heads tilted back in laughter. It had happened again. Just when his anger had softened, when a glimmer of hope made him regret certain actions or thoughts from his past, fate came along and shook a finger in his face. It was as if the Almighty reached down and moved a piece on the chessboard just to see what would happen. Though his time in Europe had made him momentarily forget how things worked in this town, that simple handshake reminded him that the old guard had to stick together in changing times.

Byron started his car and headed out Main Street. He slipped into the part of town where no one knew him, the streets he had only entered the few times he had dropped Thomas off. Though he had never been invited inside the house—Thomas hadn't been comfortable with the rides—he found the small, wood-frame house, recognizable by the large cactus hugging a fire hydrant in the corner of the lot and the huge long-leaf pine fanning out behind it. There were three little boys playing marbles in a patch of dusty ground on the side of the porch. He knew that Thomas had a younger sister, but he couldn't imagine who the boys were. A neighbor got out of her car and took a bag of groceries out of the back seat. Byron pulled up alongside her.

"Need some help with that, ma'am?"

The woman looked startled. "Uh, no thanks. I got it."

Byron smiled. "Sorry to trouble you, but is that still the Davis house?"

"The who?"

"Davis. Joe Davis."

"You a reporter?"

"No, ma'am. Friend of the family."

She slowed her pace and took the bag in both arms in front of her. "Shame what happened to their boy."

Byron felt a stab in his chest, but tried not to show his emotions. "I know. Do they still live there?"

"No, honey. They moved on. New Orleans, I believe. Hattie, she took it real hard, but I shouldn't be telling you that."

"Sorry to hear it. You wouldn't have an address, would you?"

"No, I don't. It all happened kinda fast. A big truck come by one day and they's gone the next."

"Well, nothing important. Might try to look them up in New Orleans."

"That where you're from?"

Again he thought how these small encounters might come back to haunt him: people remembering a stranger, acting odd and asking questions. "Yes, it is. Well, I'd better let you go so you can get those groceries out of the sun. Take care now."

"You, too."

13 Day of Reckoning

After a long drive back to Atlanta, Byron and Randall sat in the ghastly fluorescent light of a donut shop. Byron told him about the previous two weeks tailing Kelly, Preston and Jasper. They had a booth near the large windows and no one sat nearby, but still they spoke in low voices. Randall took interest in the trailer where Preston and Jasper lived, and the fact that Kelly often accompanied them there after a night of drinking at Ruby's. The girls they sometimes took to the trailer were a problem; Randall wanted to know if they stayed the night. Byron reported that, on the two weekends he had sat in the woods with a view of their home, the girls had left between four and five in the morning.

"Obviously, you don't want the girls in the mix. You've got to wait for a night when the three of them are there, hopefully very drunk, and no one else."

Randall asked a lot of questions about the location of the trailer, distance to other homes, if it was old or new, if there was air conditioning. He told Byron he had to reach the ventilation system and explained how to find the main duct. It meant removing a section of the skirt around the lower part of the home and crawling under the trailer.

Byron listened, but his mind was elsewhere. Randall instructed him how to introduce the Penthrane gas into the trailer ventilation system, reminding Byron that it would only anesthetize them, not kill them. When they were clearly out, Byron would have to put on a gas mask and enter the trailer, turn off the air conditioning, and close all windows tightly before turning on the gas stove, making sure the pilot lights were not functioning. Randall pulled a small device out of his pocket. "This little baby was invented by a buddy of mine. It's a carbon monoxide monitor. Here's the catch. When it reaches a level way beyond what would kill an adult heavyset male, instead of sounding an alarm it activates this Bic lighter attached to it. Bang. If the Carbon Monoxide poisoning doesn't complete the job, the explosion will. And if by some miracle they survive the gas, there's no way they could survive the noxious smoke of a trailer fire. It also destroys any evidence, though there shouldn't be any." Randall sat back, crossed his arms, and looked satisfied.

"And like I said before, gloves, gloves, gloves," Randall continued. "A small flashlight. Duct tape. Knife. Little things can be the difference between life and death, being caught and not. Park your car at a distance, but not too far so you can't get away quickly. You should already be in your car by the time of the explosion. Then get as far away from there as you can, preferably out of the country. I don't want to know where."

Byron felt sick to his stomach. During the drive from Mississippi back to Atlanta, he had gone over his revenge plot a thousand times. By some psychological mechanism, on the eve of carrying out the plan at last, his hatred for these men began to waiver. They were a product of their environment. It wasn't their fault. His thoughts even slithered into territory that what he and Thomas had been doing was reprehensible and they deserved to be punished.

The reality of committing a triple murder began to sink in. Who did he think he was? God? He felt more like the Devil. He wanted to take the bag with the gas canister and the igniting device and throw it in Randall's face. Denounce him to the police.

Byron stared at the swirling patterns of the Formica tabletop. He turned his hands palms up and examined them as if checking for dirt. "I can't do it."

Randall took a deep breath. And then another. "To have cold feet is human. To have doubt is human. Every thought you've got in your mind right now needs to be purged. This is not revenge. It's justice. You've known what you wanted the moment that bullet cut down your friend, and you have been preparing for it. A warrior who doesn't feel fear before a battle is an idiot. You can do this, and I admire you for it."

"I can't kill anybody," Byron said more forcefully. "I don't have the guts that you did."

"You read about it?"

Byron nodded.

Randall didn't look pleased, but he also seemed to accept the conviction in Byron's voice. "So?"

"Don't worry. I'll pay you for your time."

"I'm not worried about that. What I'm worried about is that people who commit acts of violence and get away with it almost always do it again."

"I'm not completely letting them off the hook. I have an idea, and I might be able to use the gas and stuff."

"I'm listening."

"I still want to get them together in the trailer. I want to scare the shit out of them. I want a confession. On tape. I want them to feel, if only for a moment, that there's a price to pay for what they did."

"The police won't do anything with it. What has it been? A year and a half? And in that town?"

"I just want it. Later I'll decide what to do with it. Maybe nothing. And I need help. An associate. Preferably a large African-American man. Do you know anybody?"

Randall lowered his eyes and started to shake his head. Byron had the feeling he would soon be dismissed, that he had been a disappointment to Randall. And then there was a sudden change in the lines of Randall's forehead, as if something had occurred to him. "I know some people in Hattiesburg. We might be able to find someone."

"We? Are you an organization? I always wondered about that."

Randall shook his head. "No questions. Call me in two days. It won't be cheap."

"Money is no concern. The man must understand there will be no violence. Kelly and the boys need to be subdued and then persuaded to confess with minimal force. I'm thinking that with a menacing-looking man standing over their shoulders and an unloaded gun pointed at their heads, it might work."

The last thing Randall gave him was the unregistered handgun he had requested, a SIG Sauer. "You know how to use it, right?"

"Been going to a firing range for the last year. I'm a pretty good shot. But I don't want live bullets."

Randall narrowed his eyes and shook his head.

"I've also been going to Karate classes."

"Ah, the way of the hand and foot! Good. It doesn't hurt to be prepared."

Byron dropped him off in downtown Atlanta. They didn't shake hands or really say goodbye.

It was around midnight when Byron walked into Ruby's, bathed, he sensed, in a spotlight of not-belonging. He was repulsed by the sour smell of cigarettes and stale beer, the country music, and the ramped-up voices of people on their fourth or fifth drink. Right away he spotted the boys in the corner: Preston with a skinny dark-haired girl on his lap, Jasper with his thick paw on a bleached blonde's shoulder, and Kelly dominating the conversation while ignoring the overweight but pretty brunette at his side.

Byron had bought a pair of Levis and a light-blue western shirt with pearl buttons at a secondhand store in Hattiesburg. He wore a John Deere cap, Clark Kent glasses and work boots. From his stool at the bar he ordered a Pabst Blue Ribbon and stared at his reflection in the behind-the-bar mirror, wondering who he was. Beyond the unfamiliar face, bruised by blues and reds of neon, he could see the boys in the corner. The jukebox, trimmed in electric purple, produced the opening chords of Hank Williams' "Dixie on My Mind." Hoops and hollers ricocheted around the room like stray bullets. A woman with blonde hair the texture of cotton candy and a little too much green eyeshadow tried to catch his eye from the other end of the bar. He ordered another beer. She edged off her stool, making her way toward him, looking vaguely familiar. In a state of panic he jumped up, but she was a fast mover.

"Hi, how ya doin'?"

Byron spoke in his best "New Awlins" accent. "Doing quite well, thank you. How you doin'?"

"I knew it," she giggled. "You're from the city. I said to myself, 'He's not from around here.'"

"Is that a problem?" Byron held his beer bottle tight and took a swig.

"Are you kidding? It's a relief to meet someone not from here. You see, I got goals. I'm taking classes over to the junior college. I dropped out of school a while back and now I'm trying to finish my education."

"That's good."

"I was in New Orleans once. Went there with my....a friend of mine. The Quarter is something else."

"Sure is." He took a sip of beer and wiped his mouth.

"My name's Lucinda by the way."

Her name set off a flash in his head. He was talking to

Julie's sister, older by at least ten years. Byron had only seen her a few times when he was a boy. He and Julie must have been around ten when Lucinda became a pariah in her family and Julie stopped talking about her. But Columbia was a small town, and rumor had it that she dropped out of college and ran off to Atlanta with a black man. She and Julie had always been opposites, Julie being studious and quietly ambitious. Julie admired Eudora Welty and went to the University of Iowa for the writing program. Lucinda was known for running with the wrong crowd.

"Nice to meet you," Byron said in a faraway voice.

She tilted her head with a questioning look. "Uh, and your name?"

"Oh," he said with a chuckle. "I'm William."

"I love that name! It is such a pleasure to meet you. Don't get many like you in here."

She was a nice girl, soft-spoken with eyes that were curious about the world but would never understand it. It must have been hard for her having a sister who was far more intelligent, and no doubt she wasn't allowed to forget it. He felt sorry for her and would have continued the conversation, but he didn't want to get distracted. In the mirror he observed the boys again.

"You sure do get lost in your thoughts, don't you?" said Lucinda.

"Sorry. Are you going to be here a little while? I've got to run to the men's room."

"Sure enough. I'll watch your beer."

At the urinal he wondered if there was any chance she might recognize him. He would have loved to ask her about Julie. He had lost touch since she went away to college. Just as he was finishing, he heard the door open. He shook off and turned around almost face to face with Kelly. Byron bowed his head and hurried past him.

As he came around the corner back into the bar—every minute louder and more crowded—he saw movement in the corner. Preston and Jasper, and their two honeys, got up to leave. Kelly still hadn't come out of the men's room. Byron hurried out of the bar and saw Preston and Jasper get into a car, driven by one of the women. They were leaving Kelly? He needed the three of them together.

Earlier that day he had set up everything with Samuel, Randall's connection. Samuel avoided small talk. Every time Byron switched topics from the actual plan to the rationale for his actions, Samuel would draw him back. "Just tell me what you want me to do. If our friend gave you my number, everything's cool."

"Do you know Malik?"

Samuel didn't answer, but didn't seem surprised by the question. "The plan?"

Byron described the trailer park and a small side road where Samuel could wait. If everything was a go, Byron would flash his lights four times, two times if he needed to talk.

Byron had spent the day preparing, pumping himself up in the motel room with some Karate exercises. He was ready. But if he couldn't get the three of them together, the plan was off. Byron followed the car to the trailer. Preston and Jasper got out, and the girls drove off. Perfect. He flashed his lights twice and pulled alongside Samuel's car. "One of them has disappeared," said Byron. "I'm going to see if I can find him."

"And if you find him?"

"I don't know yet."

"What do you want me to do?"

"Wait here."

Kelly's truck was in the driveway of his parents' house, but his apartment was dark. Not even the blue light of Kelly's TV was on, a light Byron had grown accustomed to seeing during his late-night stakeouts. Why had Kelly gone home so early? The fact that the TV wasn't on bothered him. He always left the TV on.

Byron sat in the car with the window slightly open. It was extremely quiet, not even the sound of buzzing insects. He stared at the Spanish moss dripping from the oak trees on the side of the road. Suddenly the car bounced like someone had stepped on the bumper. Byron's spine stiffened, and he turned around. But the sound of heavy feet was already on the roof, the thud and pop of metal depressing and then retaking its shape. A second later there was a crashing thump on the hood, and a large man stood in front of him. He crouched down and gazed at Byron through the windshield, his hunting rifle cradled between his knees. It was Kelly. He shook his head and laughed. "Stupid fuck," he said. "Get out."

Fight or flight? Byron figured he could start the car quickly and peel out before Kelly got off a shot, probably throw him off the hood. Then what? He'd been spotted. He might not have another chance. His heart raced. Would the Karate training of the last year and a half mean anything? Would he lose his nerve? He threw the door open and the interior light not only flooded the car, but seemed to light up the trees for miles around. Kelly jumped off the hood.

"I told you not to come back. You think I wouldn't recognize you sitting in the bar and then in the john with your pussy mustache and Lady Clairol hair? Guess I have to take you over to the boys, so we can figure out what to do with you. We shoulda taken care of you way back when."

Fear coursed through Byron's body, but in his head he heard the voice of his Karate teacher. *When someone has a weapon and you don't, your tendency is to move back. But you need to move in as close as you can. Hold their eyes. An assailant needs space to use a weapon, especially a rifle.* In a second, Byron had leaned forward, and using a distracting gesture with one hand, cupped his hand under the rifle butt and flipped it up in the air. It landed with a clank and slid across the pavement. Kelly started after it, but Byron tripped him, and in another second had Kelly on his stomach with a knee in his back. He pulled the handcuffs from his pocket and clamped them on Kelly's wrists. He grabbed the pistol tucked in the back of his belt and held it at Kelly's head.

"What the fuck? You are so dead," said Kelly.

"Oh really? I've never felt so alive. This wasn't exactly my plan, but sure is nice we're going to have a little one on one." Byron was high on his own actions. He never believed he could do something like this. His mind was racing, but clear. There was no turning back. "You're right, though. We need to go discuss with the boys what we should do."

"You'll never get away with this," Kelly growled. Still sitting on his back, Byron took a handkerchief out of his pocket and tied it over his mouth. Kelly continued to rant in muffled phrases like "fucking faggot" and "all for a damn nigger."

"Shut up," said Byron. He yanked Kelly to his feet by the cuffs, keeping the gun to his head and pushed him toward the car. He put him in the back seat and locked the doors. Then he collected Kelly's rifle and opened up the trunk. As part of his kit, Randall had also given him injectable diazepam at a dosage that would sedate. He filled the syringe, and with the gun in one hand and the needle in the other, opened the back door. With his foot he pushed Kelly face down on the seat. He set the gun on the roof of the car and pulled Kelly's jeans down to expose his ass.

"You motherfucker, don't even think about it..." said Kelly.

Byron jammed the needle in. Kelly struggled, but quickly lost his fight.

"Don't worry. I wouldn't waste my time with your sorry ass. Can't have you thrashing around in the back seat though." He hardly recognized his own voice, saying things in both content and manner that he had only fantasized about.

Byron got in the front seat and sat a minute. He imagined a scene where he had the three of them lined up, wetting themselves with fear, and reminding them why he was doing it, giving a speech about the promising life they had snuffed. But Kelly had already made him detour from his plan, and with each new variant, something could go wrong. He glanced at the back seat. Kelly moved less and less, his muffled epithets now slurred. Byron checked the cuffs one more time. He grabbed the light blanket he had taken from the motel and draped it over Kelly.

By the time he reached the trailer, Kelly was out cold. He cut the lights and turned onto the side road where Samuel was parked. He flashed his lights four times, jumped out of the car, and ran over to Samuel's open window. "I've got the third one in the back, cuffed and sedated."

Samuel shook his head and smiled. "Damn. Not bad for a college boy. What now?"

"I'm going to look in the windows. Wait here."

Byron saw Jasper and Preston passed out on the couch in front of the TV. He checked the door to make sure it was unlocked, and then returned to Samuel.

"Okay," said Byron. "We pull around to the back door in my car. We get Kelly inside. I'll have a gun to his head in case the other two wake up and want to make trouble. You'll have your gun drawn as well. Unloaded."

"Unloaded? No way, man."

"That's what we agreed on."

"We agreed on no unnecessary violence. I never agreed to walk into a trailer full of crazy rednecks with no bullets."

"All right. Just keep it cool."

"Don't worry about me. But if they pull any shit, I'm goin' defend myself."

Byron pulled his car around the back with the pop and grind of the gravel sounding like explosions that might wake the whole neighborhood.

Samuel helped Byron get Kelly out of the back seat and to the door. "How much of that shit did you give him?" he whispered.

"Enough, I guess."

Byron held on to Kelly and waited for Samuel to get in position at the other door. It was all Byron could do to keep him upright while he opened the screen door. Out of the corner of his eye, he saw that the old couple's trailer was dark and the air conditioner groaned, reducing the chance they'd hear any noise.

Swinging the door open cautiously, Byron maneuvered Kelly into the trailer. Preston and Jasper were asleep in front of the late-night movie *Alien*, the TV's greenish light coating the room and the haunting, heart-pounding music echoing from wall to wall. Kelly stumbled and fell to his knees with a thud that made the whole trailer shake. Jasper's eyes popped open. Slowly he came out of his stupor and struggled to his feet. "What the—?"

"Sit down!" shouted Byron.

With the shout, Preston woke up and tried to stand up, but fell back. They looked at each other, and Jasper nodded toward the other door.

Byron stuck his gun against Kelly's head. "I said sit down! You try to leave and your buddy's done for."

"What? You gonna shoot all three of us?"

Everyone froze. Kelly began to mumble something through the handkerchief. *Where was Samuel, dammit? What if he split?* Preston and Jasper made a move toward the door, and at that moment Samuel burst in, gun drawn. "Going somewhere? You heard the man. Sit down and put your hands on your head."

They ignored him. Samuel moved in front of Jasper and with a simple punch to the chest, Jasper collapsed on the sofa with a grunt. Preston dropped down next to him of his own accord.

"Hands on your heads," Samuel said again. One by one he cuffed them. And then he helped Byron get Kelly to the couch. Byron removed the handkerchief from Kelly's mouth and pushed him back. His head rolled like a bowling ball and ended up on Preston's shoulder. Preston leaned hard against Kelly's head and forced it to tilt in the other direction. Within a second, his head rolled back onto Preston's shoulder. "What the hell's the matter with him?" said Preston.

"You chose the wrong damn trailer," said Jasper. "We got nothing."

"As a matter of fact, you do have something I want," said Byron.

Samuel pulled a kitchen chair close and trained his gun on the men. The room filled with angry breathing and mean looks. Byron went outside and came back with a handheld cassette recorder and a roll of duct tape. He tossed the tape to Samuel who bound their ankles.

Byron flicked off the TV, bringing quiet to the room now dimly lit by a tree lamp in the corner with only one low-watt bulb. Byron smiled. "You don't remember me, do you?"

"Not a clue," smirked Jasper.

"Last time we met, I had a lot less clothes on."

"Oh, shit," said Preston. "Is this about that ni…" He looked over at Samuel. "…that negro?"

Samuel's face was expressionless. He adjusted his dark glasses and picked a piece of lint off the lapel of his sharkskin jacket.

Preston shifted ever so slightly away from Jasper. Worry crept into his voice. "It wasn't me. I had nothing to do with that."

"Shut up, Preston," Jasper said.

Byron looked at Samuel. "Isn't it great how quickly the rats turn on each other? I think it's time we wake up Kelly so he can participate." Byron went to the sink and filled a glass with water. He threw it in Kelly's face, to little effect. Kelly mumbled, opened his eyes briefly, and then his head fell forward.

"Slap him," said Samuel. "It'll feel good."

Byron hesitated. Disarming someone and throwing them to the ground was one thing; hitting them in the face quite another.

"Go on," said Samuel.

"Yeah, be a man," taunted Jasper. "Like that's possible."

Byron backhanded Kelly across the face, harder than he had intended. Kelly's eyes sprang open with shock and anger. Byron's hand hurt, but he wanted to keep going. He slapped Kelly a couple more times.

"Woo hoo," said Jasper, but Preston remained quiet, his dark eyes widening.

Kelly looked around the room as if he had awakened into a world where everything was turned upside down. Water dripped down his chin. His nose was bleeding and his cheeks were red. In a raspy voice he said, "Water." Byron refilled the glass and poured some in his mouth. It was going down too fast and Kelly spit the last of it back at Byron. Kelly stared at Byron with intense hatred, as if being trapped and then slapped by a queer was the lowest thing that could befall a man.

As Byron stared down at Kelly, a memory from childhood rushed into his head. He and Kelly were playing toy soldiers in Kelly's room. They must have been about eight years old. Kelly's father opened the door and stumbled into the room with a scowl on his face and reddened eyes.

"What are you doing in here with the door closed?"

"Nothing," said Kelly.

Mr. Price looked at Byron as if he were a source of loathing. "Get out," he said.

"He didn't do nothing," said Kelly.

Mr. Price leaned down and walloped Kelly across the face. "Don't talk back to me, you little shit." Then he walked out of the room.

Byron was stunned. "Are you okay?"

"Don't worry about it. You'd better go."

"Does he do that a lot?"

"Just go, okay?"

From that day on Kelly ignored him at school.

Byron blinked, bringing the adult Kelly back in focus. "What happened to you?" said Byron. "You're not like them. You chose to degrade yourself."

"And you chose to be a fuckin' faggot. So what?" Kelly mumbled.

Samuel shifted in his seat and the wood of the chair creaked.

"Just do what you're going to do and get it over with," said Kelly, his voice still sounding as if pushed through a rusty pipe.

"It was Kelly told us to leave him," Preston blurted out. Both Jasper and Kelly turned toward Preston with looks so fierce he shrank like an admonished dog.

"You're jumping ahead, Preston," said Byron. "But that's exactly where we're going. Y'all get to tell your stories. Get it off your chests." He picked up the tape recorder. "And I'm going to make sure that it's saved for posterity."

Kelly was awake now, though his breathing was short and labored. Drool hung from his chin. "What if we don't cooperate?"

"We can do it the easy way..." he nodded toward Samuel, "... or the hard way."

Samuel stood up and took off his jacket, folded it carefully, and put it over the back of the chair. His shiny mauve T-shirt accentuated his broad chest and huge biceps.

"Just do what they say," said Kelly to the others. "It don't mean nothing."

Jasper looked at Samuel. "You know what your friend here was doing with one of your people in the woods that day?"

Samuel ignored him.

"What? He your bitch, too?"

Samuel stood up again, towered over the couch, and stuck his gun under Jasper's chin. "One more word out of you, and you and me's going for a little walk in the woods." Jasper's eyes widened, but the snarl never left his face. Preston looked like he wanted to curl his body into a ball.

"Jasper, for once in your life keep your mouth shut," said Kelly. He still spoke as the leader, but his rueful smile showed fine cracks of worry. It was the same expression Byron had seen on Kelly's face that day in the woods: on the edge of losing control but masked with the calculated bravado of a leader. Underneath it all was fear. Even as a child Kelly had always tried to get the other kids to do what he wanted. When anyone resisted, he belittled them in whatever way he could. His way of getting at Byron was to call him "chicken." Now it was with great satisfaction that Byron looked at Kelly, bound and helpless. Let him suffer a while. Byron no longer wanted his life. Just that he suffer.

Samuel applied a little more pressure, sending the barrel higher into the soft flesh under Jasper's jaw.

"I'm ready to start," said Byron to Samuel who backed away, wiping off the barrel of his gun as if it had been sullied.

Byron pushed the record button on the cassette player and announced the day, date and location. "Start with your full name, age, and where you're from. Then you'll tell in your own words where you were and what happened on Saturday afternoon, April 19, 1980." Byron stopped the tape. "Tell the truth and you walk out of here unharmed. Kelly, we'll begin with you."

It sickened Byron to relive that day, and if he had hoped for any sign of remorse, he didn't get it. In Kelly's version, the shooting was an accident, pure and simple. It had nothing to do with what they had witnessed, though it was pretty disgusting. They were drunk. When Byron pressed him, Kelly admitted that they might have been able to save Thomas, but that was not the choice they made. He also admitted threatening Byron if he told anyone. Jasper owned up to pulling the trigger and had no regret. In his opinion neither Byron nor Thomas deserved to live. Preston claimed he tried to talk the other two into getting help, but he was outvoted.

While the boys bumbled through their stories, Byron kept glancing at Samuel, though he could read nothing in Samuel's stone face, his eyes hidden behind sunglasses. If it hadn't been obvious before, the slurs that tumbled from their mouths made it clear that the nature of Byron's relationship with the slain boy was homosexual, and Byron couldn't imagine that Samuel was totally comfortable with that. If Samuel got up and walked out, Byron would lose the threat edge, and the boys might refuse to talk further. There was also the fear that Samuel might find his behavior so repugnant he would turn on him. But Samuel remained impassive.

At a certain point Byron became disgusted listening to their half-truths and excuses. He wondered why he had come all this way. In the middle of a Jasper rant, he clicked off the recorder. With gloved hands they replaced the handcuffs with duct tape. They gagged them and turned the TV back on, upping the volume. Byron grabbed the tape recorder, and in the darkest part of night when even the trees across the way were obscured, Samuel and Byron stepped out the back door of the trailer. The fresh air felt good. Byron gave Samuel an envelope and said goodbye.

Samuel walked toward his car on the side road about fifty yards away, and Byron got in his. With no lights on Byron eased over the popping gravel of the driveway. Almost to the road, he saw in the rearview mirror a shadow move across the park in the direction of the trailer. He put his foot on the brake and caught sight of the brake lights reflected in Samuel's glasses as he turned toward him. Had Samuel forgotten something inside the trailer? A minute later there were three flashes of light against the dimly lit windows and reports of gunfire, spaced a few seconds apart. Byron felt as if each bullet had ripped through his own body. "No!" he screamed. He didn't want more death. In the throes of his original anger and hurt, it had been what he wanted, but reason had taken him down a different path. He had prided himself on his new plan to elicit confessions even though it would mean little to anybody except him. Now his gut convulsed with the fire of betrayal. Though Randall and Samuel had acted as if they were indulging his whim, it seemed they had an agenda of their own.

And then Byron's revulsion quickly turned to thoughts of self-preservation. He was a witness. The snake he had unleashed might circle around and turn its poison on him. Byron stepped on the gas and got on the road. With nothing but escape on his mind, he drove with the same frantic energy he had the day he tried to get back to the dying Thomas. But this time he was in a rented Honda, not his Mustang.

To his advantage, he knew the back roads and took several turns within the first mile. Keeping a sharp eye on the mirror to see if he was being followed, he circled around and went south on Highway 35, the back way to New Orleans. As the road behind him remained dark, the reality of what had happened began to settle in. Again he pulled onto a side road that led down to the Pearl River. He exited the car and vomited on its banks. It was mostly dry heaves as he hadn't eaten anything since lunch the day before. Bent over, his hands on his knees, he looked out at the mist hugging the opposite shore of the river. He thought he saw something, shadows moving through the trees, rifles pointed at him, but it was just his mind playing tricks. When the retching stopped, he opened his trunk and took out Kelly's rifle. He threw it as far as he could into the middle of the river. Then he removed the tape from the machine and threw it, along with everything Randall had given him, into the water.

By the time Byron crossed the bridge over the eastern end of Lake Pontchartrain, with New Orleans rising out of the swamp in front of him, the sun pointed its early rays into the driver-side window. The Avis office at the New Orleans airport was just opening when he arrived. He turned in his car. Then he got in a cab and told the driver to let him out a couple of blocks from Lidia's house.

14 Prodigal Son

It was unlikely that anyone was pursuing Byron or knew of his presence in New Orleans, but still he scurried liked the city's giant cockroaches from shadow to shadow. Making his way down Prytania Street, he felt bathed in dampness, a wetness that never leaves you in a city below sea level. The early morning light barely filtered through the canopy of oppressive trees in the Garden District while jasmine over-perfumed the air, and the morning call of birds rang shrill.

Aunt Lidia's old Double-Gallery mansion loomed over a small front yard, and he swung open the creaky gate with trepidation. For the second time in two years he escaped to New Orleans after a horrific event in his hometown, but this time he sought his dear aunt who might offer solace.

He rang the bell and the sound seemed to reverberate through the whole neighborhood. After a few minutes, a light flipped on, and through the cut glass doors he saw her refracted shape come down the stairs and glide across the wood floors. He wondered why she didn't let the maid answer it, though she wasn't the type to leave everything to servants. She had abandoned a lot of the conventions his mother still clung to.

"Who is it?"

"It's me, Tata," said Byron.

The locked clicked and she threw the door open with a force. Then she stepped back with fire in her eyes. "Boy, you'd better be a ghost 'cause if you're not I'm going to make you one. What the Devil?"

Byron had always admired his aunt's ability to go from a genteel lady to a streetwise gal in the blink of an eye. "I need help," he said humbly.

"Most dead people do. Get in here and close the door. My God, your hair!"

"I can explain."

"There isn't enough explaining in the world to make up for the pain you caused your family. I'm of a mind to turn you over my knee right now. What? You faked it?"

"I had to."

Anger wrinkled her well-moisturized skin. "Damn you," she said. But her eyes were pools reflecting the special connection they'd always shared. In her face he saw a weariness that hadn't been there a year and a half ago, and he knew he was the cause. He reached to embrace her. "Forgive me."

"Not on your life." She put up her hands to push him back, but he was a lot bigger and stronger than she was. He enveloped her and held her tight. "You're the only one I can trust."

She softened in his embrace. "You look like hell warmed over. What in the world is going on?" she said in a voice on the verge of tears.

Byron didn't answer, but holding onto Lidia made his body unwind a fraction.

She led him into the library and they sat on a sofa.

"It's done," he said in a distant, strained voice as if he were a medium channeling a spirit. "They're all dead from that day except me. What's done can't be undone and I am doomed." Byron thought he had long ago abandoned the Catholic Church and its guilt he had been born into, but moments of crisis brought it all rushing back. Imminent punishment ran like a searing message through his veins.

Lidia felt a chill and pulled her blue satin robe around her. "Byron honey, I need a little more to go on if I'm going to help you."

"I'm so tired," he said. He curled up like a child and laid his head in Lidia's lap. Surrounding them, as thick as the motes in the air, was the history of his mother's family, the elegant curvature of the furniture, the musty intelligence of books, and the worn, lived-in quality of the décor. In was in this room Byron sensed most strongly the Boudreaux name, a name as old as New Orleans itself, a name that held a vitality that straddled both the economic and racial gap. Lidia used to love saying in his father's presence that it was highly likely there was a touch of color in the family.

Byron had always felt more comfortable in this house than his father's back in Mississippi. The furnishings and drapes of the Purvis house felt oppressively heavy and full of woe while the similar fixtures in the Boudreaux house seemed elegant and infused with culture. But the greatest appeal of the New Orleans house was the joie de vivre that surrounded Lidia. She had never married, and since her parent's tragic death, had turned the family home into a gathering place for people in the arts. She often had soirees to promote an artist or writer she had befriended. Byron's mother had chosen such a different path. Camille craved security and had left New Orleans for the backwater town in Mississippi to marry Byron's father. Against his father's better judgment, Camille often sent Byron to the city for a visit and a little sophistication where Lidia would dote on him and take him to movies, ballets, concerts, and lunch in the French Quarter. Once, when Byron was ten, he and Lidia stayed up late watching *Auntie Mame* on TV. Byron turned to her and said, "That's you, Tata."

Lidia smiled. "I'm hardly Rosalind Russell and you, my dear, are not an orphan."

"Sometimes I wish I was," said Byron.

"Don't say that, honey. Your parents love you, and I'll always be here for you no matter what."

With Byron's head still in her lap, Lidia played with his once golden locks, now dyed a hideous brown. Byron went in and out of consciousness. He hadn't slept well for days, but the shattering turn of events in Columbia kept him from drifting off.

Lidia began in a low, soft voice. "Despite the bad news from Mexico—I don't know why people always imagine the worst of Mexico—I maintained hope that you were all right. People talked of kidnapping or worse, but I didn't feel you were gone. I just kept on praying that you would come back to us."

"I'm sorry," mumbled Byron.

"I'm not forgiving you, but I know it must have been something terrible to send you away and stay away. I pleaded with your mother to tell me what she knew about that last day at home, but she kept saying it was a mystery to her. I knew she knew something and I wouldn't give up pressuring her. She finally let it be known that several days later there had been a very disturbing phone conversation with your father."

Byron groaned and readjusted his head.

"Your mother was torn up inside, but you know how good she is at putting up a façade. She said you were just being temperamental and would show up any day. You know, your father sent a private investigator down there, though he came back with nothing but a few clues that led nowhere. Your mother had the gall to imply that your disappearance was a deception I was party to."

They heard someone come in the front door, and a moment later Angela walked into the library. "Oh, señora!"

she said.

Angela wasn't Lidia's maid so much as her project. A couple of years before, Lidia had found her sitting on a stoop down the street, head in hands. She wore a long skirt and a colorful blouse typical of Guatemala. Her long black hair was braided and arranged in an elaborate nest on her head. Lidia asked her what was wrong, but she didn't speak a word of English. She held a crumpled paper in her hand. It had the name of her father on it, and an address on Prytania Street. When they couldn't find her father, she came home with Lidia and never left.

"Angela, you remember my nephew, Byron, don't you?"

"Yes. I remember, but I thought he—"

"He's just been overseas and he's here for a little visit."

"Okay. I go make coffee."

"Wonderful idea."

Byron rose into a sitting position. "Tata, no one can know that I'm here. And I have to leave this afternoon."

"Oh, heavens, Byron. You just got here."

"Something terrible happened in Columbia a year and a half ago, the last time I was there. Of course mother didn't want to talk about it 'cause she couldn't accept that it had any relation with me."

"Truth is," said Lidia, "when I couldn't get anything out of her, I had to work on Sofia. It wasn't easy, but I got her to tell me about the death of her cousin. Said he was a classmate of yours. The authorities had determined it was an accident when three local boys said they had come across the body. She also admitted that you had come home mighty upset that day."

Byron's eyes sharpened on Lidia's face. "Those boys were the murderers. Sofia's cousin, Thomas, wasn't just a classmate. He was my friend and he was shot down in front of my eyes."

Angela entered the room with a tray of coffee, and set it

down. The air was heavy with secrecy. "You want I make breakfast?"

"Not now, Angela." Lidia's whole body was a series of taut ropes. "I'll let you know later."

"Byron, honey, I can't imagine how horrible that must have been."

"He wasn't just my friend. He was…" Byron choked on his words. Thomas was still so strongly in his heart and everything had gone terribly wrong.

"It's okay. I've known for a long time, I mean, not about Thomas, but…" Her hands tightly gripped the neck of her robe. "And you know I love you and support you in all your endeavors and choices."

Byron let out a gnarly laugh that made Lidia shiver. "In all my endeavors? Tata, you don't know what I'm capable of."

Lidia leaned over and poured two cups of coffee. She handed one to Byron and tried to look in his eyes, but he only stared into the cup. "What did you mean earlier when you said you were the only one alive from that day?"

"They said they would kill me if I ever went back. They threatened to tell my father what they saw. I should have gone right to the police, but I didn't. After a few days I couldn't stand it anymore. I called Dad and said I wanted to tell my story to the police. He said no, that it was a bad idea, that my running away looked suspicious, that they probably wouldn't be charged. It's hard to believe in this day and age justice is so hard to find for the killing of a black man."

Lidia put a hand to her mouth. "Byron, what have you done?"

"Yes, I wanted revenge. It was all I could think about for months. But as I got closer to the reality of taking three lives, I couldn't do it." Byron went on to tell her about meeting Randall and bringing in Samuel. And then the twist that had not only left him haunted, but made him an accomplice.

He took a sip of coffee. One minute the previous day's events didn't seem real to him, as if it were a movie he had watched, and in the next his whole body shook like a man dying of a fever. "Are you horrified?"

Lidia's hand shook and the china cup rattled. She set it down. "Yes, I guess I am. And no. I can't judge you. I wasn't there and don't have the capacity to know how the horror of a friend's senseless killing can change a person. My only concern is you. Are they after you? Did anybody see you?"

"I was meticulous. The only people who knew I was in Columbia are now dead. I'm traveling on a false passport. I've been living in Spain for the last year and a half. The only person who knows that is Manny."

She let out a sigh. "I knew he was holding back something. He kept giving me some song and dance about your assets being frozen until...anyway, that's not important now. What are you going to do?"

"Live with it. Go back to Barcelona. I have a semblance of a life there. Manny has done well by me. I have money."

"I wish you had come to me before."

"So you could have talked me out of it?"

"What you have done frightens me to the very depths of my soul. I would have done anything to talk you out of it. I'm not concerned about the ethics. I'm concerned about the danger this puts you in, the physical danger of you being caught, and also the psychological danger. You are a civilized, intelligent, kind, loving person. Nothing in your upbringing has prepared you to weather the mental storm that I already see you going through. Do you have someone in Barcelona, someone you can talk to?"

"Georgette. We've become quite good friends, but I don't want her to know."

"Can you trust her?"

Byron laughed. "Of course. She's from New Orleans."

"Go to her. Every day. I don't care what kind of relationship you have with her or what you tell her, but you have to talk. You're going to give me a number and I will call you to check in. You better answer your phone. And another thing—I have to tell your mother you are alive."

"Please don't tell her I was here in the States. She will hear the news about the shootings. I don't want her to make any connections with me. A sharp detective—if any exist in Columbia—could still put two and two together. A neighbor might have seen something. They could question her, and you know Mother, never good under pressure. She can't know where I am just yet. Tell her I'm living in Europe and that I'm fine. I will contact her when things have died down."

In the next couple of hours, Byron gave Lidia a detailed account of his flight to Mexico, how he made it look like a disappearance, his trip to Cuba, and eventually ending up in Barcelona. He talked about the people he had met, the Black Panthers who had fled to Cuba to avoid spending the rest of their lives in prison whether they were guilty or not. He talked about Randall's wife who had been killed simply because she was trying to protect the lives of Freedom Riders, and how the perpetrators had never been brought to justice, at least in the courts. He realized, as he told his story— focusing on certain events, leaving out others—that he was, in a way, trying to justify his actions.

"We must get you out of the country as soon as possible," said Lidia. "You know you always have a home here if you should want to come back some day." Her eyes filled with tears. "Will I ever see you again?"

"Oh, Tata. Of course you will. You would love Barcelona. Come and visit."

15 Sodom and Gomorrah

The first thing Georgette noticed when she opened the door to Byron's apartment was that the shades were closed. She always left them open for the plants she had come over to water. With her hand frozen to the door handle, she started to back out of the apartment. She was furious at him for not contacting her in the last month and didn't want to face him.

"Georgette?" Byron's voice came from the other room.

"Oh, you're back." She entered and closed the door behind her.

Backlit by slivers of brightness coming through the shades, he appeared from around the corner. She could only make out his silhouette; he looked ten pounds thinner. As he came closer she made a little gasp as if she were encountering a stranger. The hair. The mustache. And then closer still, the eyes gave everything away. In them she saw a frantic need for comfort that he dare not ask for. Her anger began to fade. She knew he must have gone through something terrible.

With her mouth agape, she continued to stand near the door in a no-man's-land between actually entering his ambivalent realm and retreating back into the not-knowing on the other side of the threshold.

"Do I look that bad?"

"I'm not sure bad is the word. Changed. I hesitate to ask, but I can't not ask. What happened?"

"I wish to God I could tell you."

Her profound exhale was somewhere between a sigh and a moan. "Oh, Byron of the eternal secrets! Are you ever going to trust me? How are we supposed to have a relationship in this fog?"

"A relationship? Is that what we have?" Her face started in fuck-you mode and ended in complete devastation. "I'm sorry," said Byron. "That was cruel."

"I didn't necessarily mean relationship relationship."

"Yes, you did." They stared at each other for a moment, strangers in a bar car on a train hurtling through a tunnel. "Georgette, if I thought I was deserving, I would jump in with both feet." On the flight back he had thought a lot about Georgette, and how his relationship with men had brought him only pain and confusion. He felt peaceful with her. And the stories he had heard about this new "gay cancer" frightened him down to his toes.

"You know deserving has nothing to do with it," she said. "And I'm not sure humility becomes you, my dear. But if you just can't do it, I understand."

Byron wasn't exactly sure if she did understand how much he wanted it emotionally, and how much of a stretch it was to go from the black muscular male body that he had eroticized in Thomas to the petite white softness of Georgette. At the same time, he knew that putting it in those terms made it all about sex, as if it were only the galloping soldier between his legs that led the charge to find a mate. There was sex and there was love. And as the months passed, the intensity of sex with Thomas faded in his memory along with the possibility that there had been love in those black eyes. On the other hand, his need for the comfort he found in Georgette had flourished. The war he had been through the last couple of years had blinded him to the wider spectrum of choices, he told himself, and if the final battle in Columbia had not brought him satisfaction, it had brought some kind of closure. He was ready to end that chapter of his life; the person that had gone fishing with Thomas that summer day bore little resemblance to the one he caught in the mirror over Georgette's shoulder.

"I honestly don't know," said Byron, placing one hand on Georgette's shoulder and, with the other, taking a strand of curls that had fallen into her eye and returning it to the nest on top of her head. "I want to try. I just don't know what it would look like. We are brought up to think in terms of picket fences and little Georgettes and Byrons running around. That seems so foreign to me right now."

"That's not what I want either. Believe me, I never imagined I could feel something for another man after, you know, what happened. I missed you terribly while you were gone." And then there was a shift in her eyes. Her Southern accent went from parlor room to down by the river. "Shit! I can't believe I said that. That's a sure way to make you hightail it."

He pulled her into his arms and cradled her head against his chest. She was adorable at such moments, trying so hard not to be soft. "I have to tell you something," he said. "If I don't tell you now, I'll keep putting it off."

"I think I know," she said delicately. "Shall we sit down?" Their embrace now felt awkward. Byron's legs were at the point of buckling. They edged toward the sofa as if their ankles were shackled.

Byron collapsed onto the sofa and grabbed a cushion, holding it to his chest. "It is way, way more complicated than anything you could imagine. If you can stand the sight of me after I tell you…I thought a lot about it on the flight back. I want you in my life. But you have to know who I am, what I'm capable of."

"The first thing I wanted to do when I met you was unburden myself of the secrets. You kept yours locked inside. I can't imagine that anything you'd tell me would make me turn my back on you."

"I'm not a good person. I've done terrible things." He hugged the cushion tighter. A jackhammer started up on the street below and echoed through his jet-lagged brain. His palms were sweaty.

"Good God, Byron! Just tell me."

"Remember the nightmare I had the second night we spent together? I told you that it was about the cicadas, that as a child they scared me. That's not exactly true. At first I thought they were wonderful. I wasn't particularly happy as a child, and I thought the cicadas ushered in something new, a change. In fact it was just the opposite. Every time they emerged something bad happened. In high school I had a friend. He was black and on the football team, if you can imagine that. We used to go fishing together." Byron paused. He picked up the glass of whiskey he poured earlier and took a drink. He lit a cigarette. "Would you like a drink?"

"At this hour?"

Byron chuckled. "I'm a few hours ahead." Rays of light sliced through the cloud of smoke. Construction noise wafted up from below.

"So this friend?"

"Thomas. I liked him a lot. He was everything I wasn't: athletic, popular, easy-going. And someone that my parents wouldn't want me hanging out with. That in itself gave me no end of pleasure."

"Did you love him?" Georgette liked to go straight to the heart of the matter.

"At that age, you know, the hormones. Emotions get mixed up with sex."

"You had sex!" Georgette blurted out. "Sorry. I didn't mean it to come out like that. You were in Mississippi, darling. I have a feeling where this is going."

"I don't think you do. If we had just gotten caught, it would have been a scandal. There would have been hell to pay, but I would have survived it. I had one foot out of that town already, anxious to go to college. And Thomas...it might have ruined his football career, but he would still be alive."

Georgette gasped. "Alive?"

"He was shot down in front of me by three guys I knew. I already hated that town, the church-going hypocrites, the racists, well, you know the South. I went a little crazy. At first I was afraid to go to the police, and then when I thought I had to, my father wouldn't support me. All I could think about was revenge. I wanted to wipe those three killers off the face of the earth. I fled to Mexico, then to Cuba, ended up here. I met people who let me believe it would be justice, not revenge. That's why I went back. Everything was set up. But I chickened out at the last minute. Just wanted to teach them a lesson. I learned, however, that when you open a door to hell, it's mighty hard to close. The man I hired to help me 'teach them a lesson' took matters into his own hands. Four people are dead because of me! How does one keep living?"

Georgette nodded her head slowly and took a deep breath. "You think I didn't want revenge on those bastards that raped me? If I'd had a gun in my hand, I don't know what I would have done. Of course, that would have screwed up my life even more. But you don't think about that at the time."

"The thing is, I had concluded that it was wrong to take their lives. I was walking away, literally. And then I heard three shots."

"You were at the scene? My God, are they after you?"

"I flew there on a false passport. I didn't contact my family and didn't see anyone who would recognize me. When I first fled to Mexico, I officially disappeared. That's part of why I ended up in Cuba. And then from Cuba to here. No one knows where I am except my Aunt Lidia."

"I think I do need a drink."

Byron got up to get the bottle and another glass. Horns honked their frustration at the backup caused by the construction down in the street. The smell of battered concrete drifted up. Byron stood at the window a moment, and then closed it.

How often he thought back to that day of his return from his disastrous mission. How naïve they both had been. Love was not the problem. He truly loved Georgette and knew he would, in some way or other, love her for the rest of his life. She stuck by him those first weeks when he teetered on the edge, filled with ample remorse and scant satisfaction about what he had done. When he drove home from Mataró drunk one night, he went off the seacoast road, totaling his car but not seriously injuring himself. Georgette came and got him. She never asked where he had been. Another time when she stayed over at his place, someone pounded on the door in the middle of the night. Byron got up and told her to stay in bed. He closed the bedroom door behind him. Georgette could hear Byron arguing with a man, who spoke heavily accented English. She opened the door a crack and saw him give a Middle Eastern-looking man money from his wallet.

He didn't come back to bed. She went to the living room and found him staring out the window at the night sky, a tumbler of scotch in his hand.

"I'm sorry," he said.

"Be careful," was her response, and she went back to bed.

Byron was in his twenties, with a sexual appetite the size of the Mediterranean, and he would not be satisfied until he had feasted on all her shores: the passionate gypsies from Andalucía, the chiseled-faced Italians, the mysterious

North Africans, and unfathomable Greeks. And yet, he had come to enjoy warm sex with Georgette. It was like sitting by the fire on a cold day, or taking a bath after his Karate exercises. Soothing, but not completely satisfying. At times he hated himself for his meanderings though he didn't know how to stop.

A few months after his return from the States, they moved in together and lived a life between veils and curtains in a chamfered corner apartment in the Eixample district of Barcelona. They married a year later, a civil ceremony attended only by their closest friends. Byron had desperately wanted a family member to witness his marriage, as if he were proving something. He called Lidia to invite her, but she was committed to several functions and couldn't make the trip.

When Byron and Georgette went out together—and that was often—he was the devoted husband. They were a striking couple that turned heads. His eyes did not stray. But there were afternoons at the saunas, and an occasional solo trip to Morocco. She knew. Of course she knew. It was a time of sexual freedom and no one was supposed to care, certainly not their group of offbeat friends—models, artists, musicians, minor drug dealers, and major fuckups— products of the post-Franco years. They all seemed to look up to Byron and Georgette in unspoken admiration: an ideal couple, a couple dancing on the grave of traditional marriage.

On weekends the gang would often pile into Byron's Peugeot and speed down the coast to Sitges where partying had reached a level comparable to *la movida* in Madrid. Georgette's old roommate, Frankie, had a new boyfriend, Lluc, whose family owned a beach chalet on Passeig Marítim where they all crashed. They would party all night at L'Atlantida disco, famous for its foam parties where revelers frolicked in mountains of suds on the dance floor. The foam would climb to waist-high and Byron would jump into the fray. Hands groped below the waist, unseen under clouds of bubbles reflecting the tinted rainbow colors of the disco lights.

Other nights, Frankie and Lluc, would convince them to go to Trailer, in the gay heart of Sitges, a stark, high-energy disco where gay men were predominant. Byron would casually try to discourage gay disco ventures, but if he protested too much, it would look like he couldn't handle the temptation. Georgette often turned a watchful eye toward him when the suggestion was made. It was almost as if she liked to see him squirm a bit.

On one particularly drugged-out night, Byron found himself at four in the morning in Trailer's sparsely lit men's bathroom, making out with a caramel-skinned British tourist of West Indian descent. In a Quaalude and alcohol blur, the man's velvety skin and lips awakened the beast he tried to tame, the unrelenting addictive surge that had brought both rapture and agony to his life. He was speeding through a wormhole to a dimension where Byron Boudreaux Purvis didn't exist. He was a mass of vibrating cells hurdling toward an orgasmic explosion.

The Brit unlocked his lips and sought Byron's ear. In a breathy whisper he said, "Let's go to my hotel. I'm at the Calipolis."

Byron opened his eyes and looked at the walls of the DayGlo-graffitied stall. Something inside him screeched and ran dry like a rusty faucet being turned off. He released the grip on the man's arms he had been holding against the wall over their heads. He took a step back and the man's black eyes danced in confusion in front of him. "I can't," Byron mumbled. "I'm here with my wife."

"For bloody real?"

"For real."

"Tomorrow maybe? Room 417. Jefferson Marlowe."

The invitation had killed the mood, but having a name attached to the person in question put it in the ground. In

Byron's world of slippery mores, a prearranged date was taboo.

Byron opened the stall door and exited the restroom. He stopped at the bar to order a whiskey before rejoining his friends. Georgette had her back to him as he approached the group. Everyone watched with raised eyebrows as he threw his arms around her and snuggled his nose in her hair.

He felt her tenseness, exacerbated by the cocaine she had done earlier. He massaged her shoulders. When they partied, their drug preferences always sent them in opposite directions. She became aloof, not wanting to be touched. He became a puppy, wanting to paw and lick everybody in sight.

"Are you wearing cologne?" she said.

"Oh, well, they have these dispensers in the bathroom. I thought I was smelling a little funky." Perhaps the wrong choice of words, he realized. "I've got that nasty caffeine sweat from all the coffee we drank earlier."

"Oh."

"Let's go dance," said Byron.

Georgette was not a big dancer. To beg off she said she was tired, which played right into Byron's real desire: To leave as soon as possible. He suggested they take a walk on the beach. The last thing he wanted was to run into the Brit again.

They told the others they were leaving and walked down the streets barely wide enough for a small car toward the sound of waves lapping at the shore. It was a muggy night, and they strolled in silence past hulks of stacked-up beach chairs and stepped around couples entwined and giggling on the sand. They arrived at the chalet just as the sky turned a lighter shade of gray. "How about we go to Cadaqués next weekend?" said Byron. "Have a quiet weekend just the two of us."

Georgette plopped down on the porch swing. "Sure,"

she said, gazing toward the sea.

Byron sat down next to her. "What is it, darling?"

"Nothing. Just tired." But the way she chewed her lip and kicked her feet belied her claim. Byron, still under the effects of the Quaaludes and whiskey, only wanted everything to be all right. He was a boy who needed comfort. Moving closer, he tried to embrace her. "Byron, please. I'm hot and sticky. And I hate that cheap cologne!" She got up and leaned on the porch railing.

"We need to stop taking opposite drugs," offered Byron.

"Oh. Is that what we need to stop doing? Don't you worry sometimes about what we have become?"

"Don't, Georgette. I can't have one of your mind-fuck conversations right now. Why can't you just live? I mean, be in the now."

She turned toward him and let her head fall back in cheerless laughter. "You can say that now that you're high out of your gourd, you who wakes up several times a week shouting and in a cold sweat."

"Not going to do this!" He jumped up from the swing and ran toward the beach. He threw off his shirt, and then stopping at the water's edge, pulled down his jeans. He dove in the water in his underwear.

Byron and Georgette's drama was minor compared to the constant crises of their friends. There was the night they had to take Karina to emergency with a heroin overdose. A couple of months later Frankie swallowed a vial of pills because Lluc had broken up with him. Javi got caught with chunk of hash in his pocket coming back from Morocco, and Pili's boyfriend fled back to Germany when she told him she was pregnant.

Despite Byron's nightmares and Georgette's occasional bouts of worrying about their hedonistic lifestyle—easier to focus on than what really bothered her—they often managed to settle into what they would later describe as a time of innocence and reasonable happiness. But in the mid to late eighties, friends began to die, some from overdoses, but the majority from AIDS. Each time a friend passed, Byron swore off the saunas. By that time, their sex life had waned though not faded away. Byron still had a need for comfort sex, and Georgette needed a way to hold on. One day, in the mid-eighties, Byron came home with a box of condoms. "Just, you know, to make sure we don't end up with any little Byrons and Georgettes. We still agree on that, right?"

Georgette nodded and smiled wanly. She didn't mention that she had had tubal ligation soon after her rape. Both of them knew the condoms were really to avoid being the next statistic in the plague that hung over the decade.

At the beginning of the nineties, Byron and Georgette began to talk of going home. It was understood they meant New Orleans. Mississippi was out of the question. They briefly talked of New York, wondering if their fast-paced Barcelona life was an addiction they would need to feed. The conclusion was that winters were too cold.

Both of them would be giving up decent work, though Byron was getting fewer jobs in the fickle world of modeling. Georgette, on the other hand, had a high-profile client list that was growing. She had become known in Spain as the expert on interviews: what to say and how to say it in English, how to hedge for time, and even how to fake it if the question wasn't quite understood. Through their friend Jesus, who worked as a hairstylist on Almodóvar's films, Georgette had gotten to meet the master himself, not to mention Carmen Maura, Antonio Banderas, Victoria April, and Bibi Andersen. Sometimes Almodóvar's production company would fly her to Madrid when one of the stars had an interview with the English press. Often she would take Byron along, and at the parties they were invited to—*la movida* was in full swing—he would play the demure Southerner, politely deflecting all the attention lavished upon him for his looks.

Georgette also still had her tennis player clients, the Sánchez Vicario brothers and their sister Arantxa as well as Sergio Casal. And lined up behind these stars were a host of juniors ready to expand Spain's reputation as a tennis powerhouse, which meant more interviews in English. But Georgette didn't mind giving it all up. With both of them in their thirties—Georgette five years older than Byron—they felt old. The incessant partying had taken its toll. Georgette was obsessed with the crow's feet around her eyes, and Byron was twenty pounds overweight. They joked of getting a place on Decatur Street and sitting on the balcony under a hazy moon, drinking mint juleps and watching the Mississippi on its serpentine journey to the sea.

In the midst of Barcelona Olympic hysteria, Byron and Georgette packed up ten years of memories and headed to New Orleans. They stayed with Lidia, but spent most of their time in the Quarter, and they both knew that was where they wanted to live. One evening while dining at their favorite Cajun restaurant, the Bon Ton Café, Georgette wiped her mouth with a stiff napkin, imprinting it with a lovely red smear, and announced. "I'm going to take Daddy's apartment, you know, to give us some space." A year before she had gone home for her father's funeral. When the will was read, the family found out that he had secretly maintained a flat in the French Quarter.

Byron tried not to look stunned. "If that's what you want."

"Don't give me that puppy-dog look. We both know it's time. However," she said with a smile, "I'm not done with you yet, and I want you to look for a place close by."

"I will," he said half-heartedly. The thought of really being on his own terrified him. He loved his independence when he wanted it, but with a sympathetic someone to go home to.

"It'll be fine. You'll see." She actually seemed bubbly

with her decision and Byron didn't like it.

The next question was how they would fill their time. Georgette had finished her B.A. at Loyola before going to Barcelona. Now she wanted to go for a Master's, so she could keep teaching English. She encouraged Byron to take some classes. He only had a semester's worth of credits and the thought of getting a degree seemed daunting, not to mention the task of choosing what to study.

"You've got to do something besides deposit the checks you get from Manny," Georgette said.

"I've got an idea, something we talked about once. Spanish ceramics! I want to import them, and if I bought a building, I could open a shop downstairs and live above. Very European! And I could go on regular buying trips to Spain, go to all those places where we bought pottery together, like Talavera de la Reina, Sorbas, and Cordoba."

"And don't forget that lovely green stuff from Teruel. I'm jealous. It sounds a lot more exciting than teaching English."

"Somebody's got to mind the store when I'm away. You could be part of it."

"Oh, thanks a lot. How about you mind the store and I go on the buying trips? I'm a much better bargainer than you."

"This is true. But you sure dumped your teaching career mighty fast, sister."

"Baby, we're just dreaming."

"I'm not dreaming. I'm serious."

16 Building the Ark

In the dull, diffused afternoon light coming in from the courtyard, Byron stood hunched over a wooden crate with a crowbar in his hand. He shuddered at the thought of how much damage the piece of curved dark steel could do in the wrong hands, or in the hands of someone in the wrong state of mind. From where he stood, all the way to the front of the store, was a sea of glazed color, a delicate, vulnerable array of ceramic pieces he had accumulated over the last fifteen years: plates, bowls, pitchers, and assorted objects from Spain, Portugal, and North Africa.

He never tired of letting his eyes dance over each piece, remembering the trip he had purchased it, the artisans' workshops with their spinning wheels, muddy hands shaping cones and cylinders, lips and handles, the damp loamy smell of the clay, and the acrid kiln smoke curling up to the sky. These ceramic factory visits were both bitter and sweet, at times reminding him of a day when he and Thomas were teenagers, hitchhiking back from fishing.

Byron's car had broken down. A slender man in an old truck picked them up. He had long curly hair tied back, a bushy mustache, and rheumy eyes. They had put their fishing gear in the back and jumped in. There was a Willie Nelson song playing on the radio. Byron noticed that the man's overalls, which he wore without a shirt, were splattered with what looked like paint.

"I'm a potter," said the man. But because of his loose manner of speaking, Byron thought the man said "pothead" and glanced at Thomas to see if he heard the same thing. They had once talked of trying marijuana, but were both afraid of what might happen in Mississippi if they got caught. When the boys didn't respond, the man said. "I throw pots."

There was a dead silence in the car. "Damn!" he said. "What's got into you guys? I make pottery, you know, from clay, on a wheel."

"Oh," said Byron, though he still wasn't sure exactly what the man was talking about.

Then the man made a sudden U-turn and stepped on the gas.

"What are you doing?" Byron said in a panic.

"I'm gonna show you."

"But..."

"It's all right," said Thomas. "Sounds interesting." Byron had always marveled at Thomas' trusting nature and wondered if it would get him into trouble some day.

The man pulled onto a dirt road and, after about a mile, into a driveway by a small house that was little more than a cabin. "I kind of dropped out," the man offered. "Used to live in New Orleans, but got tired of all the shit, the noise, you know, stuff you got to put up with."

Around back was his open-air studio. He took Byron and Thomas through the whole process of making pots. Thomas was particularly fascinated and asked a lot of questions. The potter talked nonstop, lecturing about the importance of pottery throughout the ages, how you were taking something from the earth and turning it into something lasting, producing messages for the future. "For thousands of years, pottery has been indispensable to societies. Used it for everything, from transporting water to cooking and eating. People have used pots to keep the remains of loved ones. Pottery can be functional *and* a work of art. It says a lot about the culture that produces it."

"What do you mean by that?" asked Thomas.

"Archeologists study the pottery of a culture and find a wealth of information from it. The various glazes—that's what you call the outer covering that gives pottery smoothness and shine—can reveal things about a society." He raised his eyebrows to enhance the mystery.

"You mean you get information about a society just by looking at the outside of their pots? Like what?" asked Thomas.

"It can, for example, reveal information about trading partners. Shapes of vessels and decoration show the importance of art and style among different peoples. And sometimes they even paint their stories right on the pots."

"I never thought about that," said Byron. He marveled at becoming aware of something he had seen on a daily basis: the decorative pieces in his mother's house. Now he had an idea of how they were made and he was curious where they came from.

What they learned from the potter that day stuck with him; now, it was forever entwined with the memory of Thomas nodding his head at every word the man said. The store that Byron had opened was, in a sense, a memorial to Thomas, and the pottery that was formed from the earth and decorated with flora and fauna was a testament to the natural world that Thomas loved so much, his domain, the place where he found solace.

Byron wedged the neck of the crowbar under the edge of the crate and listened for the screech of nail against wood, a sound that always filled him with excitement, the thrill of opening a treasure chest. On his last trip to Spain, he had ventured to the dusty little town of Jun in Granada province and met Miguel Ruiz Jimenez, a master potter, architect, and historian who had revived a technique and style of ceramics developed in the Islamic world hundreds of years before. Byron had fallen in love with Ruiz Jimenez's replicas of *loza dorada nazari*, golden pottery with a transparent, metallic overglaze.

From the packing material he extracted a plate that came alive in the light from the ceiling spot, brilliant blues and golds depicting a stylized nature motif of leaves and an exterior border of interlaced Moorish arches. It was even more beautiful than he remembered. Next Byron brought into the light a jar with handles, its neck adorned with a band of triangles, and the body with symmetrical floral patterns. There was a lip of glistening gold where the lid met the jar.

After he had mined the crate of all its treasures, he arranged the fourteen pieces—bowls, plates, jars, and an octagonal oil lamp—in a cabinet with glass doors and LED lighting. He stood back in awe as if admiring Ali Baba's riches. He had paid much too much for them and knew they probably wouldn't sell. But the store had never been about making money. He was realizing a dream he had when he returned from Barcelona. The name of the shop was Tierra. Georgette had come up with it.

The thrill of opening the crate left him with the need for a cigarette, like after a gourmet dinner or great sex. He had cut down on smoking significantly by refusing to buy cigarettes, forcing him to bum one if he was desperate. He could go next door and see if Stella would indulge him one more time, but decided against it. Instead he looked in his wallet to see if he had enough for a pack.

It was a Friday afternoon and only a couple of customers had come in since he opened at 11:00. He put the "Back in 5 Minutes" sign on the door and went down to the corner store. The owner was preoccupied and couldn't take his eyes off the little portable TV behind the counter, which was tuned to the news. He barely looked at Byron as he grabbed the pack, took Byron's money, and gave change. The news was about a hurricane. Scenes of wind-whipped palm trees, downed traffic lights, and storm surges flooding streets.

"Where's that?" said Byron. He generally avoided watching the news as much as possible and had missed the story.

"Florida. Headed our way."

At the same moment, the whirligig on the screen indicated the path of the hurricane from south Florida, up the coast, then making a line for the Gulf Coast and possibly New Orleans. It was a slow mover, they said, winds around ninety miles an hour, still a Category 2, but could be upgraded at any minute.

"Yeah, well, it's the season," said Byron. He'd been through this many times. People always predicted disaster, even Armageddon, but at the last minute the storm would change course and New Orleans would be saved. Or, a hurricane would cause the usual wind damage, some flooding maybe. But the city knew how to recover. Storms like this had ripped through New Orleans since the early days of the city when it was made the capital of French Louisiana. In 1722 a hurricane leveled the town only to have it quickly rebuilt.

Out on the street, Ruthie was standing on the corner. She wore a yellowed and tattered wedding veil, but had eschewed the accompanying white satin gown that she frequently wore. In the old days she would get around the Quarter on roller skates, her wedding dress billowing out. But the old days were gone and people said they didn't expect Ruthie to be around much longer. Rumor had it she was already in a home, but there she was, Friday afternoon and wearing a mid-length, rose-colored cocktail dress. Her tiny frame was loaded down with baubles, costume jewelry that looked much weightier than it was. At her feet was a duck patiently waiting for Ruthie to decide which way she was going. She looked up at the sky. "This is it," she said. "It's coming."

"What's coming, Ruthie?" asked Byron.

"Well, you're a daft son of a bitch, aren't you?" When she was hustling drinks or cigs, she could be a charming Southern belle, but when she was perturbed her foul mouth ran.

She eyed the pack in his hand, and her transformation took place in a split second. "Might a gentleman offer a lady a cigarette?" she said in a sanguine drawl accompanied by batting eyelashes. They had run into each other on the streets of the French Quarter hundreds of times over the years, spoken many times. But she gave no indication that he was anything but a total stranger.

He opened the pack and took a step toward her. The duck quacked and moved in front of Ruthie to defend her. Its white feathers were tinged with yellow, showing its age.

"Shush," she said, and the duck quieted.

Byron put a couple of American Spirit blues in her tiny, weathered hand. She looked at the pack and then the sticks in her palm. She shook her head, but quickly made them disappear into a lace-trimmed pocket.

"This is it," she repeated.

"You talking about the hurricane?"

She gave him a look of a schoolmarm to a tardy student. "You're a swift one." She pointed to a gray churning sky. "Don't you feel it?"

"It's just a hurricane. We've survived before. We'll survive again."

"This one's different. Best you leave. I see a city under water."

"Are you leaving?"

She cackled and then launched into a coughing fit. "Never," she said between coughs. "I float. This one, too."

She looked down at the duck.

Her hand dived into her pocket and came up with one of the cigarettes. She put it to her painted lips—evening primrose to match her dress—and waited for him to light it. Then she took a deep drag, blew it out, and seemed to lose her train of thought. In a moment she had turned and was headed up Dumaine with the duck waddling behind.

Back at the store, he called Georgette.

"Have you been watching the news?" asked Byron.

"Who hasn't?"

"Me, until I saw something on the TV down at the store. But it was Ruthie who put it in context."

"Now she's always a reliable source of information."

"She says it's the big one. She envisions a city under water."

"It does seem to be serious. Category 3 now."

"You know, out of the mouths of babes and lunatics…"

"What are you thinking?" said Georgette.

"We should be okay here. The original settlers were crazy, but they weren't stupid. They knew where the high land was. But I'm worried about the Ninth Ward."

"The family." She knew exactly where his mind was, usually did. In a normal world, they would be happily married into old age. They were so in tune. But neither of them wanted a normal world. They had tried. Still, twenty-plus years after they first met, she was still the first person Byron would call in a time of crisis or to ask a silly question.

"I have to do something," said Byron. "If we get a direct hit, the Lower Ninth is going to flood. They live in one of the worst parts, near the canal."

After Byron had reconnected with his mother and Sofia, Sofia kept him abreast of the whereabouts of Thomas' family. She had given him their address, and he had driven by a couple of times, but couldn't bring himself to stop. What would he say? Sofia had told him the story of how the family got to New Orleans. Thomas' mother, Hattie, hadn't been well since her son's death, so Thomas' father, Joe, called his brother in New Orleans who owned a duplex. The brother managed to kick out the tenants who hadn't paid rent in four months, and Hattie, Joe, and Abigail moved in. Abigail, Thomas' sister, was twelve at the time, seven years younger than her brother.

"Go get them," said Georgette. "Bring them here. Commission the Grey Goose for the rescue." Byron had bought a 1965 Econoline van in perfect condition for a brief foray into the antique business before the pottery store got off the ground. The van had funny headlights, which Georgette said made it look like a goose. Byron kept the van in good repair, though rarely took it out of the garage.

"Oh, sure," Byron replied. "A stranger shows up at their door and pretends to be the great white savior. Would you just pack and hop on board if you were them?"

"I could go with you, maybe make it less threatening. We could say we're from some church group."

Byron laughed. "And what church would that be? The Church of the Poison Mind?"

"Any chance they'd recognize you?"

"Thomas' father worked for my daddy. I guess we spoke a few times over the years, but that was a long time ago. I'm sure they heard through Sofia that I disappeared, and if they thought about me at all since then, they probably figured I was swallowed up by the great beyond."

"Is the Goose gassed up?"

"I highly doubt it. I'm going to do that right now. In the meantime, start filling up anything that'll hold water. How are you set for food?"

"I've got the usual canned crap. Bunch a frozen stuff, but that'll only be good so long as the power stays on. I'll go down to Dino's and see if there's anything left on the shelves."

Byron got the Grey Goose started. She had about a quarter of a tank of gas. He went over to the Fuel Mart on

Rampart, but there was a line a block long. He tried the station on Esplanade near I-10. It was worse. Byron went back to Rampart and got in line. He inched forward. Even with all the windows open, the van radiated like an oven. Sweat rolled down his unshaven face.

It was after dark when Byron and Georgette pulled up in front of a double shotgun house on Jourdan Road facing the Industrial Canal. The house was painted a soothing celestial blue, but it couldn't erase the fact that the house was poorly constructed. It sat only four steps above the ground that was several feet below sea level in one of the most vulnerable parts of the city. If the levees broke or were topped by the storm surge, the place was doomed.

All the streets in the area were flat grey ribbons that stretched out from one body of water to another. Water was everywhere—Lake Pontchartrain, the Industrial Canal, the Mississippi Outlet Canal, the Main Outfall Canal, Fisherman's Bayou, and the river itself. You could see the sky in every direction, filled with blackening clouds tinged with pink. Byron took a last drag on his cigarette and threw it out the window.

"You're smoking a lot," said Georgette.

"What the hell do you expect?"

Georgette put her index finger to her cheek, tilted her head toward him, and gave Byron that twisted-mouth look he knew so well.

"Sorry," he said. "This isn't easy and I have no idea how to approach them."

"Let me handle it." She reached over and put her hand on his arm. "I'll think of something." Georgette pulled a clipboard out of her bag and a couple lanyards she had from a teaching conference. On her computer she had made fake IDs and slipped them into the plastic covers.

They stepped out of the van into air that was stifling and smelled of dampness, as if any minute the ground could open up and suck everything under, leaving behind nothing but a swamp. Byron and Georgette stood at the foot of the steps and felt the vulnerability of the soil under their feet. It was mosquito hour and Georgette juggled the clipboard so she could swat her bare legs. They climbed the cement steps and the porch wood gave, feeling slightly bouncy under their feet. Through the screen they saw lights and heard a TV. With the typical New Orleans architecture, there was a shotgun view all the way to the back door. When Georgette rang the bell, an overweight teenage girl got up from the sofa and peered out through the screen.

"Can I help you?" she said.

"We're looking for Mr. and Mrs. Davis," said Georgette, leafing through the papers on her board.

"You selling something? If you is, we ain't interested."

"No. No. We're volunteers from the Hurricane Preparedness Agency."

She turned and shouted toward the back of the house. "Momma, there some kinda agency people at the door."

Hattie came from the kitchen in back and passed through several rooms before getting to the door. She was a small slender woman in her sixties, though one might have guessed older. The pouches under her eyes looked like teabags and the skin sagged under her chin. Her thin arms stuck out of a sleeveless blouse and she wore baggy jeans cinched with a white plastic belt. There was a gentleness in her eyes that reminded Byron of Thomas.

"Agency, you say?" Her voice was calm, but suspicious. "Letisha, turn down that TV."

"Yes," said Georgette. She held up her ID. "I'm Georgette and this is my husband, Byron. We're from the HPA, the Hurricane Preparedness Agency. We just wanted to make sure you are informed about your options." It always came as a surprise to Byron when Georgette identified them as husband and wife. They had never gotten a divorce. The identification pleased him. He shuddered to think that one day Georgette might ask for a divorce to marry someone else.

Joe had come up behind Hattie, wearing a stretched-out, white tank top and khakis. He was considerably taller than Byron remembered and had gained weight.

Georgette swatted her legs again and continued. "If you are agreeable, we have a safe place on higher ground where you could wait out the hurricane." In the background, the TV program was interrupted by an update on Katrina.

Joe reached around his wife and unlocked the screen. He pushed the door open, not to invite them in it seemed, but to get a better look. The screen wasn't on a spring, so it arced all the way to the wall. "We been through this before. That one George back in '98—and what was that one last year, Hattie?"

"Ivan."

"Yeah, Ivan. One million people trying to get outta New Orleans all at the same time. World's biggest traffic jam. Don't know about you, but I'd rather be sitting at home than in some suffocating car."

"He gets claustrophobic," Hattie added.

"We're not talking about evacuation right now. They haven't called for that," said Byron. Joe looked at him hard for the first time in the conversation. He squinted. Byron wore a baseball cap and had a goatee. The man couldn't possibly recognize him from when he was a gangly teenager. "Just higher ground." Byron hesitated and seemed to lose his train of thought.

Georgette took over. "Some people are saying this one's different. If it follows the trajectory they're talking about, and it keeps picking up power like they say, it could challenge the levees, which everybody knows are weak. You live in one of the most at-risk areas."

Joe was still staring at Byron. "What higher ground you mean, for example?"

"Mr. Davis," said Georgette, trying to draw his attention from Byron, "volunteers who live in elevated areas near the river, places that traditionally don't flood, have opened their homes. We have a place for you and your family."

Through the open door, Byron saw three shadows watching the television: Letisha, who had answered the door; a woman who had to be Abigail; and a young man who sat in an armchair with his back to them.

"You can think about it tonight, and we can come back for you in the morning."

Joe turned to his wife. "You and the kids can go. No way I'm leaving this house what with looters and such."

Hattie laughed. "Now what we got that looters gonna want? A TV that's on the blink half the time? Or Letisha's banged-up computer that was a donation from down at the center?"

Letisha and Abigail, seated on the couch, occasionally glanced over, as if half- following the conversation at the door. The back of the boy's head did not move a fraction of an inch. "I ain't goin' without Lester," Abigail said.

Hattie rolled her eyes. "You even know where he is?"

"'Course I do."

Georgette took a pen from her bag. "Well, just in case some of you decide to go, might I get the names of the residents of the house?"

Hattie used her fingers to make the list: herself, Hattie Davis; her husband, Joe Davis; their daughter, Abigail; and her two children Letisha and Lamar.

"And Lester?" asked Georgette.

"He don't live here. He the father of Letisha and Lamar," said Hattie.

"So their last names are…?"

"Shaw," Abigail said loudly from the sofa. "And he mighty prouda his kids."

Lamar's head turned ever so slightly toward his mother and then quickly back to the TV. He stood up.

"Where you goin'?" said his mom.

"Glass a water." He turned toward the door and Byron felt a pinch in his gut that shot up to his heart. His legs became rubbery. He was back in the woods and he heard the blast of a rifle. Lamar gave them a blasé nod, and then sauntered down the hall to the kitchen.

Georgette sensed that Byron was on one of his "journeys," as she called them. Since he had come back from his trip to the States back in 1982, things would occasionally trigger his fog and his eyes would show a great pain. "Unless y'all have any questions," said Georgette, "we won't bother you any further. Think about what we said. We'll come by at nine in the morning to pick up anybody who wants to go."

"You can take my name off your list right now," said Joe. "But I appreciate your concern." He stuck out his hand and Georgette took it. She released it, and Joe put his hand out to Byron. Byron continued to stare down the hall toward the light at the back of the house.

"Byron," said Georgette.

"Oh, yeah. Sorry. Pleasure to meet you." He pumped Joe's hand.

"Goodnight," said Georgette. She steered Byron across the porch to the front steps.

They sat in the truck and saw Joe pull the screen door shut and lock it.

"What happened back there? You left," said Georgette.

"Did you see him?"

"The boy? He was cute, but—"

"God, Georgette, I'm not quite so shallow as to resort to my lowest desires at a time like this. It was Thomas!"

"I might beg to differ with you in your choice of the word 'lowest' but that's an argument for another time. You mean he looks something like Thomas?"

"Not something like. He is. The look, the voice, the way he swaggered down the hall. I first met Thomas when he was about the age of Lamar." He leaned his head against the steering wheel and groaned.

Joe had returned and opened the screen. He now stood looking out at them.

"Byron, we'd better go. Are you okay to drive?"

"It's him!" screamed Byron.

Joe came out on the porch.

"It's not him. It's his nephew. Get a hold of yourself," she said between her teeth. "Now let's go."

Byron took his head off the wheel and looked over at Joe, standing under a yellow porch light with bugs darting in and out of its beam. Byron started the van and eased back onto the ribbon of cement. Georgette waved at Joe.

"They can stay at my place and I'll stay with you. I don't think I can be around them."

"They might decide not to leave. The father was pretty committed to staying."

"They can't. They'll die," Byron said emphatically. "I don't claim to be clairvoyant, but sometimes I feel things strongly. The future. I mean."

17 And the Floodgates of the Heavens Opened

Byron and Georgette pulled up in front of the Davis house a little past nine in the morning; it was already in the mid-nineties. Lamar sat on the front stoop. As soon as he saw them, Lamar flip-flopped over to the car in plaid shorts, a blue tank top, and a pork pie hat. He put his hands on the roof of the car and chuckled harshly through the open window. Georgette leaned away from him. "What game you playing?" he said. "Hurricane Preparedness Agency? Yeah, right. Last night, went to my friend's house that got the Internet. Looked it up. Ain't no such thing."

"At least you're paying attention, Lamar. That's good," said Byron. He was calm now, able to hide the feeling that he was in a time warp with the past coming back to haunt him. "No, we're not from any agency. But the fact remains; we have to convince your family to leave. This thing is even more dire than we thought last night. The National Hurricane Center is urging people to leave and the airport's closed. Have you said anything to them?"

"Nah, Ma wanna go. She say maybe it time to leave this neighborhood for good, that maybe the Lord see fit to encourage people to move on. Granny near slap her."

Byron got out of the car. "Come on. Let's take a little walk."

Lamar looked suspicious. "Like where?"

"Just a little down the street. Want to talk to you."

Georgette got out, too, and said she'd go in to check on the family.

Up and down the street, people were packing up their cars. A neighbor hurried to a battered Nissan pickup, carrying an ice chest. He tripped over a pink tricycle in the front yard and frozen food spilled out onto the grass. He let out a string of obscenities and a little girl nearby started crying. The air was full of dripping heat and panic.

"I'm going to entrust you with some information that you have to keep to yourself. Can you do that?" asked Byron.

"Depends."

"No depends. You have to promise."

"Yeah, whatever."

"I'm from the same town as your grandparents. Your grandfather was a gardener for my parents. I knew your uncle."

"You knew Uncle Thomas?" said Lamar, showing excitement for the first time.

Byron took a deep breath. "Yes. We went to high school together."

"What's up with that anyway? Everbody get weird when his name come up. Ma, she get high sometimes, and start talking about her big brother like he some kinda saint. Granny get all quiet and sadlike. Grandpa go to the fridge and get a beer while Letisha go back to reading the Bible. It's like a house of lunatics. Maybe Ma is right. If Katrina coming to cause destruction, could be a good time to get out of this soup bowl."

"That's why we've got to get everyone to leave the neighborhood, at least for now. Tomorrow we might try leaving the city. But none of your family can know who I am or where I came from. I disappeared from Columbia and only a very few people in the world know that I'm still alive."

"How you know where we at?"

"Sofia. I guess she would be your second cousin. She worked for my family. Well, still does, but now it's just her and my mother. She keeps me informed."

"I don't get it. You trying to be some kinda guardian angel. Letisha all up in that guardian angel shit. Why you care?"

Byron breathed heavily. He would have loved to unburden himself from the load of history, tell Lamar about his uncle, but it wasn't the time or place. "I can't tell you any more now. We've got to get back."

"Damn, some mysterious shit goin' on."

"Lamar. I need you to help me. Is your grandfather still set on staying?"

"Yeah. Granny say she oughta stay, too."

"She can't. You've got to help me convince her."

Back at the house the front porch was loaded with bags of food and trash bags full of clothes. They only owned one suitcase and an old trunk, both of which they decided were too bulky, and would be left behind. Joe stood on the porch with his arms crossed, overseeing the exodus. Georgette urged them to take any important papers and bring containers for water, leaving some for Mr. Davis.

Byron and Lamar started up the steps. "He's still not going?" Byron said to Georgette.

"No, I ain't," said Joe. "My brother and me is staying." He pointed toward the other half of the double shotgun. "His family done left early this morning for Baton Rouge."

"Do you have access to the attic and an axe in case you need to break through to the roof?"

"All taken care of."

"And Mrs. Davis?" said Byron.

Hattie exited the screen door with a shoebox in her hands. She wore a lilac pantsuit and uncomfortable-looking black pumps, as if she were going to Sunday service. "My husband being stubborn like always. Say he won't go."

"Mrs. Davis, are you going to be comfortable in that?"

"Well, Georgette told me we goin' to the French Quarter. I don't want to make a bad impression."

"Don't worry about that. People should just bring comfortable clothes."

"I guess you people do have your HPA recommendations," Lamar said in his attempt at a white New Orleans accent.

"Yes," said Byron, giving Lamar a sharp look. "Water and food for a few days, important documents, and comfortable clothes. Oh, and do you have any candles?"

Abigail stepped to the edge of the porch and said to no one in particular, "Lester's goin' to the Superdome, but he glad his family gonna be in a safe place. He got a cell phone, so we can keep in touch."

"Looking out for number one as always," said Hattie.

"Hattie," Joe said in a warning tone.

Joe helped them pack up the van, said his goodbyes, and then went back up on the porch. Byron started to get in the driver's seat, but changed his mind and returned to the steps where Joe was standing. "I'll take care of them. Don't worry."

Joe nodded. Then he focused his eyes in on Byron. "You ain't from around here, is you?"

Byron hesitated. "No, sir, I'm not."

"Didn't think so." He continued to stare at Byron; a tiny smile worked its way to his mouth and then disappeared in a second. Byron stuck out his sweaty hand and they shook.

Under a bruised and swollen sky, the French Quarter seemed quieter than usual. Windows were taped or boarded up, and "Closed" signs hung on many of the establishments.

Lamar stuck his head out the window, gazing at groups of tourists who refused to give up the party spirit while his mother dangled her ruby press-on nails out the window on the other side.

"They sure don't act like they's scared," said Lamar.

Georgette chuckled and turned around to Lamar. "'Crazy flies toward peril like a moth to a flame,' my grandma always used to say."

"Lord, have mercy," said Hattie.

They pulled up in front of Byron's place and Georgette jumped out to unlock the gate.

Byron eased the van into the narrow driveway of his 19th-century red brick building with dark green shutters on Chartres Street. Cathedral bells down the street pealed with the insistence of an alarm, but they were just marking the noon hour. To the left of the driveway, a Magnolia tree grew out of the sidewalk so close to the front balcony that you could sip a Pimm's Cup and pick a blossom right from your chair. The tree was a constant reminder of the Magnolia under which Thomas lost his life, and Byron considered having it removed. In the end, he decided against it.

"Stop torturing yourself," Georgette had said. "Cut the damn thing down."

"I need to remember," Byron had countered. "Not just Thomas, but what I'm capable of, the bad things I've done."

Georgette had shaken her head and sighed. "Oh, Byron."

Through the alley Byron pulled into the back where the azalea bushes and calla lilies would soon share the patio with the unloaded trash bags and boxes holding what the family thought they ought to save if the worst happened.

"I'll put the van in the garage," said Byron, giving Georgette the keys. "Take the family on up."

"Don't look now, but Mrs. Kravitz is on the balcony," she said. It was the nickname they had given Carter, the nosy neighbor next door.

After garaging the car, Byron reappeared in the courtyard—Georgette had already led the family up the back stairs. He glanced at Carter, who looked down at him pucker-faced. Carter lifted a drink as if it were the torch of the Statue of Liberty and just as permanently attached.

"What the hell?" Carter said.

"Just helping out."

"That the family of one of your *friends*?" he scrunched up his nose.

"Just shut up. Doesn't concern you. You staying?"

"Hell yes. Johnny White's staying open and we're having a hurricane party." He let out the laugh of a wicked witch.

Byron shook his head. He was still unsure whether to leave or not. It was beginning to seem that only the crazies were staying. There was time to get out, though they were looking at hours on the road just to get to the edge of town. The state-devised contraflow, with all lanes designated for exiting the city, was supposed to start at four that afternoon.

Inside the apartment, the family stood gathering dust in the middle of the living room. Only Lamar sat on the brocade sofa with his legs stretched open. He listened to his iPod and bobbed his head. Abigail broke ranks and made a move toward the balcony to call Lester. She reported a few minutes later that he was in a line about a block long to get into the Superdome. People were fainting from the heat.

"Make yourself at home," said Byron. "Where's Georgette?"

Letisha pointed with her Bible toward the bathroom.

Hattie eased herself down onto the edge of a stiff-backed chair and rested the shoebox on her lap. The family formed a tableau of modern America: a grandmother lost in memories, a daughter steeped in misplaced devotion, a granddaughter opiated by religion, and a grandson trying to drown out the world with music. What Byron had taken on fell heavy on his shoulders.

Georgette came out of the bathroom. "Byron, why don't you tell everybody where they're going to sleep?"

Byron snapped to attention. "Good idea. I was thinking Abigail and Letisha could share the big bed in my room. Hattie can be in the guest room and Lamar on the sofa."

Lamar pulled one of the earbuds out and said, "This your place, huh? Where you gonna sleep?"

"I'll stay with Georgette."

"She your girlfriend or something?"

"Lamar, be polite and sit up straight," said Hattie.

"Actually we're married, but we live separately. Anything else you want to know?"

"That's cool." He tapped his foot to the music still coming through his left earbud while looking around the room. "What's with all this old sh…stuff?" He looked over at Hattie. She was watching him.

"God, Lamar!" said Abigail.

"Don't say 'God,' Mom," said Letisha.

Abigail moved her head from side to side and took a deep breath, punctuating the trials she had to put up with. "This old stuff is antiques and if you'd get your nose out of that Hip Hop music for two seconds, you might learn a little culture."

Lamar stood up with a purpose and put the right earbud back in.

"Where you goin'?" asked Abigail.

"Out," he said over the loud music in his head.

"There a hurricane coming and you goin' out wandering the streets. You got no more sense than your daddy."

"Maybe I'll go over there to the Dome and pay him a visit. Maybe he got that twenty-five dollars he owe me."

"Don't get smart with me."

Georgette approached Lamar. "I'll go with you if you want. The storm's not supposed to be here for at least twenty-four hours. Should be okay. Is that all right,

Abigail?"

"Don't stay out too long. I'm goin' call your Daddy in a couple hours. He'll probably want to talk to you. When the storm come, who knows what kind a service we goin' have." Abigail stood up. "In the meantime, I need to lay down on the bed if that's okay. I feel exhausted and this thing ain't even started."

"Go ahead," said Byron.

Letisha now sat at the dining table with her Bible spread open in front of her. Byron fell into the seat Lamar had just left. He grabbed the remote and turned on the TV. Georgette gave him a quizzical look, and he waved for her to go with Lamar. "We'll catch up on the latest," said Byron.

The news hadn't changed much. Governor Blanco and Mayor Nagin both made statements, encouraging people to leave, though falling short of a call for mandatory evacuation. Aerial shots of I-10 looked like an enormous parking lot, and long lines snaked into the Superdome. Then they cut to the National Hurricane Center. The whirligig image spun across a map of the Gulf and was now headed straight for New Orleans. Byron kept looking over at the box on Hattie's lap. "Mrs. Davis, don't you want to set that box down?"

"Please call me Hattie. It ain't heavy. Pichers mostly."

Byron felt a tingling going up and down his arms and legs. He couldn't stop himself. "Family photos, I suppose."

She stared past the TV, out the window at some faraway place. "I had another child," she said, distant, her voice barely a whisper. Letisha turned her head toward them, and there was something akin to fear in her eyes. Hattie's hands started opening the box as if they had a mind of their own. Her eyes still focused on the beyond.

Byron felt he had to stop her, was frantic to stop her, but he had no more ability to act than the Oriental rug on the floor. His blood raced, and then stopped and froze before going forward again, like a river gone haywire. He saw the Pearl River, and that summer he and Thomas had gone swimming. Thomas was grabbing him in a sudden hug as they lost their footing, falling to the ground.

Hattie looked down at her hands and a painful smile crossed her lips. "It's just some old pichers. Don't want to take up your time."

He could have easily gotten up and begged off with a task he had to complete, gone into his little alcove office off the living room, or onto the balcony for a smoke. But his legs wouldn't move. Perhaps more than most, Byron secretly loved the turbulent waters of emotion, loved diving into them, and then regretting it later.

"Time we got," he said. "Come on over here to the sofa, Hattie. I'd like to see them."

"Grandma, are you sure—?"

"Hush, chile."

She sat down next to Byron and pulled out the first photo, a picture of her wedding day. "Don't Joe look like a fish outta water in that suit," she said of her husband. Joe was tall and handsome. Hattie looked so proud, standing next to him. Hope reigned on her pretty face. The bouquet she held close to her bosom was about as wide as she was.

Hattie handed the photo to Byron and he studied it before setting it on the coffee table. Next was a photo of the wedding party, and he recognized Sofia as Hattie named the different relatives. Sofia wore the enigmatic smile that he knew so well, and he felt a warm and unsettling nostalgia. He knew he was just in the foothills of the mountain of painful memories he was about to climb. On the television, reporters were talking about the storm surge possibly topping the levees. The storm in the box of photos was already too big for any barriers to stop. Byron felt the foundations begin to erode when Hattie pulled out the first photo of a little boy standing in the yard, making a ridiculous face. "That's him," she said, as if speaking of a saint. "My boy, Thomas. The Lord took him from me."

Letisha squirmed in her chair causing the wood to creak. "Mr. Boudreaux, my grandmother has a heart condition. I really don't think this is a good idea."

Hattie acted like she didn't hear. "Look at this one. His tenth birthday party." Thomas' eyes popped as he blew out the candles.

With trembling hands, Byron held the first picture, lost in the boy that would become the cocksure adolescent mowing his lawn, and later, the playful young man that would wrestle him to the ground with a mix of urgency and tenderness. He discovered in the trepidation of that moment the strength to get through this session of aching reminiscence. It was a mission of gathering pieces to the puzzle, the mystery that was Thomas, still a part of his inner being, and yet someone he never really knew.

Byron was shaken from his reverie by the birthday photo passing into his hand. He looked at Hattie who was studying him. Byron smiled. "Nice-looking boy."

"And sweet, too. They started calling him Sweetness 2 after that Payton boy who they called Sweetness. Everybody thinking Thomas would be right in his footsteps." She shook her head and sighed. If Hattie only knew it was Byron that started using Sweetness 2 in his articles about Thomas in the school paper. It had raised some eyebrows, but stuck.

"Right. The football player," said Byron, referring to Payton. Though it seemed to make Hattie sad to talk about Thomas, it appeared to relax her at the same time. Byron, too, began to feel as if they had snuck into another world where empathy was a salve powerful enough to calm their aching hearts.

But even in this other world of detachment, the shock of the next photo could not be avoided. It was more faded than the others because it wasn't in a frame. Hattie brushed her hand across it to remove dust or lint or the memory itself. She gasped but didn't break down. "This is him, musta been a year or so before..." Her voice trailed off.

The photo took Byron back to the summer after graduation, the best summer of his life, when he and Thomas frequently went on fishing trips. The childhood memories of trips with his father were filled with heat, bugs, boredom, his father drinking beer and telling the same old stories he had heard a thousand times. And then when they caught one, he had to watch the thing flop around and look him in the eye. The hook poking through the fish's mouth sent a shiver up his spine.

All the bad memories disappeared in a flash when Thomas—smile overflowing with possibility—had suggested Byron give fishing another shot. With Thomas, Byron came to know fishing as an altogether different experience. Thomas respected nature, and the fish as part of it. Even taking the hook out of the fish's mouth was a gentle act, Thomas cradling the fish in his hands like a baby. He'd whisper to the thing as if he were apologizing. And sometimes, if he thought the fish was too young, he'd throw it back in, saying, "He got more growing to do," and then laugh the laugh he only let out in nature. He was closer to Earth, attached to it, whereas Byron always felt that he and his father had been invaders, using nature as a playground, never really bonding with it.

One day that summer Byron and Thomas had caught four good-sized catfish and decided to drop off two of them for Sofia to fry up for dinner. The other two would go to Thomas' mom. By the back door at his house, with Sofia admiring the fish, Byron said, "Wait a minute." He ran to get his camera and had Sofia snap a picture of them holding the catch. He had double copies made and gave one to Thomas. As far as he knew, that was the only existing photograph of them together. Where was Byron's copy? It had to be somewhere in his mother's house, if she hadn't thrown everything out.

"That was the best catfish I ever ate," said Hattie. Her eyes were full of tears, but she managed to keep them from flowing. She also seemed to make no association between the boy in the picture and Byron though, as every second ticked by, the possibility increased.

Byron felt his cell phone vibrate in his pocket; he was never so grateful for a phone call. It could have been the Devil himself calling. He jumped up and put the picture on the table. "Excuse me, Hattie. I have to take this call." It was Georgette. He went out on the balcony to talk.

"Is everything all right?" she said. "You sound a little shaky."

"I'm afraid we opened Pandora's box."

"Uh-oh. Is the secret out?"

"Not exactly, but close to it. Hattie has a photo of us."

"You and Thomas? No way! You never told me about a picture."

"I had forgotten… or blocked it out. I don't know. Just a moment ago, Hattie and I were sitting on the sofa, a few inches apart, looking at a photo of me and her son, talking about eating catfish. Is there nothing that can't happen in this world?"

"Like you're always saying, He's just up there in heaven, moving us around like pawns for his own personal amusement."

"Ain't it the truth!"

"Did she say anything about the white boy in the picture?"

"Didn't get a chance to go there. Saved by your call. The photo was faded and cracked. She must have looked at it a thousand times and wondered who that boy was and what he was doing with her son. But her eyes only seemed to focus on Thomas, his big beautiful smile in the proud moment of holding those fish."

"I've got to see the picture. I could get her to talk about it if you want. See what she knows."

"When I'm not around, okay?" He sighed. "So what are y'all doing? Is Lamar behaving himself?"

"There are people freaking partying all over the Quarter. It's like two parallel universes—the places that are closed and boarded up, owners gone, and the others paying no mind whatsoever to what's coming. People are walking the streets drinking Hurricanes. Unbelievable!"

"*Laissez les bons temps rouler.*"

"Yeah. Let the good times roll. Should we pick up some po-boys? I imagine everybody's hungry. We could go by Johnny's and see if they're sticking."

"Good idea."

Back in the living room, Hattie had packed up her photos. The box was resting on the coffee table. Abigail was up and sat stiffly on the sofa with her mom, watching the news with glazed eyes.

"I just want to say," Byron announced—and both their startled heads angled in his direction—"that as long as you're all here, I want you to feel at home. Feel free to eat or drink anything from the kitchen. If you want to use the computer, let me know. Don't know how much longer we'll have an Internet connection."

Byron looked up at the ceiling fan and thought of Katrina spinning its way toward them. Outdoors the wind was picking up; a shutter was banging against the wall. Sleeping in the same bed was something Byron and Georgette both felt comfortable with, though they didn't do it often. Sex hadn't been part of their relationship for a long time, but occasionally—usually in the cooler months after cocktails, dinner, and a bottle of wine—Byron would sleep over in Georgette's huge bed, a giant cloud allowing each of them to carve out with their arms and legs ample space.

"I've got to get that thing fixed," she said as a gust of wind buffeted the shutter.

"We better do something before tomorrow night or it's going to end up in Texas."

"Maybe we'll all end up in Texas."

"God, I hope not—for several reasons."

She sat up and put an extra pillow behind her. "I got Hattie to show me the photos." After their po-boys, Byron had excused himself and gone over to Georgette's place a couple blocks away. Georgette had stayed to help clean up. Hattie washed the dishes and Georgette dried.

"You did?" said Byron.

"Yeah, and lived to tell about it. Letisha had a silent fit. Guess it's not a sin in her Bible to kill people with looks. She's one of those quiet aggressive types that always give me the willies. Hattie was okay, didn't get too upset, though who could blame a woman expressing that saddest of all feelings, a mother grieving for her son. Of the two of us, I was the more agitated. Seeing the person I'd heard about all these years, together with you in a photo."

"You make it sound like I've talked about him incessantly since we met."

"Most of the time it's quiet—"

"But not aggressive, right?" He chuckled.

"Not aggressive. No, sir. But I did hear it every time I saw you look at a black man on the street."

"How do women like you stand to be with men like me? I mean, you must hate me sometimes."

"An old fag hag like me?"

"Oh, stop! I hate that term. You are the farthest thing from a hag, and I loathe referring to myself as a fag, even if I am one. It's a disgusting phrase that only stuck because it rhymes."

"Well, I guess a homosexual aficionado—does that work?—like me just can't help it any more than you can help, you know, drooling over some scrumptious guy on the street."

"See, you do hate me."

"Don't you want to know what Hattie said?"

He rose up on his elbow and cupped his hand under his chin. "Do I?"

"We got to that photo. Man, I've got to say, that picture should be in a museum. In black and white it would be a bomb. The energy in that image was electric with your smiles about a mile wide. Oh my goodness, it gave me goose bumps just looking at how happy you were. I asked Hattie if she knew who the other boy in the picture was. She said she never met him but her cousin, Sofia, worked for his family, and Joe was their gardener. She seemed to remember he died of a drug overdose while still in college. So sad, both cut down in the prime of life."

"A drug overdose? She must be confusing me with Bobby Ray."

"Crazy, huh? It's been a long time. People like to create their own versions of things, what they're comfortable with. When I pressed her on whether you two were good friends, she just talked about Thomas being a good boy, but that he kind of stuck to himself. She guessed you knew each other from high school, but couldn't imagine how it came about that you went fishing together. She wouldn't say any more though. Said she was suddenly very tired. Poor woman, and now all this! And by the way, why did you tell Lamar about knowing his family back in Mississippi?"

"What was I supposed to do? He was about to blow our cover, and then none of them would have trusted us."

"He asked me if you were gay."

"What?" Byron screamed and sat upright.

"Young people these days aren't afraid to ask those questions. He didn't say it with any malice."

"So what did you say?"

"I said he should ask you. Then he said, 'I guess that's a yes.' I think he's curious. Maybe he's got more of his uncle in him than even you thought."

Byron, Georgette, and Lamar sat on the sofa watching the frightening predictions coming from the National Hurricane Center and a report from an Air Force Hurricane

Hunter aircraft. Early in the morning, Katrina had reached near Cat 5 proportions, and though it would lose some steam when it hit land, it was still going to wallop New Orleans and the Gulf Coast. A meteorologist came on and talked about storm surges. The news showed an animated graphic of how a hurricane passed over open water, and how it reached down and sucked up the water that it would later dump on land. The graphic made the hurricane look like a vengeful animal.

Hattie had made eggs and grits for breakfast, and she and Letisha were cleaning the kitchen. Abigail was again on the phone with Lester, getting a report of the latest abominations happening in the Superdome.

"What should we do?" Byron said to Georgette.

"Yeah, boss," Lamar said to Byron, "why don't you just check your HPA protocol?"

Byron crossed his arms in front of his chest. "I'm pretty sure it says that anyone who's a smart aleck gets left behind."

"Ooh," Lamar said as if impressed. He tilted his head and looked sideways at Byron. "You dissing me?"

"No, I believe you're the one dissing me. What's with you? We're trying to save your ass." Georgette gave Byron a look that he was going too far.

"I'm just trying to figure out what's goin' on." He raised his hands and rattled them in the air. "All the mystery."

Georgette sighed. "Lamar, we've got a complicated situation that needs attention. All those questions can wait. Would you be kind enough to round up your family and get them in here so we can talk?"

18 Arise and Flee

A loaded-down Grey Goose turned from Rampart Street onto St. Bernard and came to an abrupt halt. They were still blocks from the I-10 ramp and cars were lined up like hot dogs on a grill, waves of heat rising off their shiny surfaces. It took another half hour before they eased into the bumper-to-bumper traffic of the elevated freeway.

None of them had been anxious to leave after watching the massive traffic jams on TV, and dread hung around them like a dampened cloth. Despite the high-force winds headed their way, there was not a hint of a breeze coming in the van windows.

Most of the evacuees seemed to be going west on I-10 toward Baton Rouge, and people reported eight to ten hour trips for a drive that should be two. Byron suggested they go east on I-10, then north on I-59 into Mississippi. Georgette and Byron had already spent a considerable amount of time convincing the family they needed to leave, all the while hiding their own doubts. When Byron had proposed driving north into Mississippi, Hattie's face fell and her hands twisted in her lap, but she remained quiet. It took them nearly two more hours to secure the apartments, covering up windows and locking all doors. Abigail insisted she talk to Lester one more time before they left, and Hattie called Joe to see if she could convince him to get out of town. He and his brother reiterated they were staying. Georgette overheard Hattie tell Joe they'd probably be back on Monday afternoon after the storm passed, and she raised her eyebrows at Byron. With a simple look they decided it was best to allow her to be optimistic.

In the long wait to get on the interstate, Byron entertained himself by studying the family in the rearview mirror. Lamar and his grandmother sat on the middle seat with Letisha and Abigail in the back. Abigail was tall and slender, a beauty who knew how to make the most of her attractiveness. She had told Georgette that even though she was just a checker at Winn-Dixie, she would get up two hours before her shift every day to do her hair and makeup. That morning, while Hattie and Letisha made breakfast, Abigail was in the bathroom preparing herself for the world, and that was before she even knew they were going out in public. Her corkscrew curls were both wild and perfectly arranged. Mauve eyeshadow accented her black eyes and a lavender stretch T-shirt emphasized her breasts, while gold hoop earrings gave her a kind of casual elegance. Lamar took after his mother, tall and thin, though his skin was darker. Letisha, on the other hand, didn't resemble her mother or brother, and her dowdy clothes put the final touches on the contrast. She had a flat nose and eyes that never seemed to open all the way, as if she were constantly praying.

They inched through East New Orleans, and in another hour the traffic started to pick up just as they came onto the Twin Span Bridge over the eastern end of Lake Pontchartrain. A sense of relief spread through the car, but before they could properly exhale, a hundred yards onto the span, everything came to a standstill again. There was a great expanse of water on either side of them dotted with small white caps, low angry clouds overhead, and a massive hurricane just a few hours away. Nobody said anything, but they were all thinking, "What if Katrina arrives earlier than expected? What if the traffic just doesn't move?"

The radio was tuned to WWL and the latest projection was that Katrina would hit somewhere between the I-10 span and the Gulf Coast. Hattie groaned. Raindrops started to fall.

"We've got time," Byron said. "I think I see Slidell."

"Guess you got x-ray vision 'cause I don't see nothing but grey," Lamar said. The clouds were heavy and low.

"Is Slidell in Mississippi?" said Abigail.

"No, but not much beyond that we'll be in Mississippi," Byron answered. He tried to hold back any trepidation of his own about returning to his home state.

"That's where you were born, right, Mom?" said Lamar.

"Uh-huh, though I don't remember much. Haven't been back since we left twenty-five years ago."

In the rearview mirror Byron glanced at Hattie's face, a roadmap of discomfort. "Anyway we're not going where you're from, Abigail," Byron said, hoping to lessen Hattie's pain.

Lamar leaned forward. "Oh, yeah? How you know where my mom was born?" He leaned back with a grin, and Byron gave him the evil eye through the mirror.

"Hattie told me yesterday when she was showing me the pictures."

"I did?" said Hattie.

"I don't like Mississippi," Abigail announced. "Not that crazy about New Orleans neither. Lester and me's talking about California. Maybe San Francisco."

"Yeah!" said Lamar, reaching back and giving his mom a high five.

Letisha got a prune face and shook her head, as if she were having visions of Sodom and Gomorrah. "California?" she whined.

"Lester win the lottery or somethin'?" said Hattie.

"Oh, Momma. We can dream, can't we?"

"That Lester's got him a motto: 'If wishes were horses, beggars might ride,' " said Hattie.

"No comment," said Abigail.

After a while the cars started moving, but so did the rain, pelting the windshield with fat drops. They got to Slidell, but on the north side of town, the I-10 and I-59 exchange was the biggest bottleneck yet. They sat in the devil's rain for another hour while hordes of evacuees from the Gulf Coast poured onto I-59, frantic to beat the storm.

Around Picayune, Mississippi, the traffic began to change from inching along to a steady crawl. On either side of the highway, a wall of deep-green trees, pines mostly, stood watch, a phalanx of tall, straight-backed soldiers, platoons of them that filled the low, wet land as far as you could see.

Lamar stared out the window with a forlorn look on his face. "I never knew so many trees existed in the whole world."

"Guess I shoulda taken you kids out more," said Abigail. "Practically your whole lives spent in the Lower Ninth. I did occasionally, in the summer, take you on the Elysian Fields bus out to the small beach on the Lakefront. I wouldn't get in the water, but I'd give an older kid a dollar to teach y'all to swim. Momma, we coulda brought them up here to show them where they come from."

"I guess I should thank you for not doing that," said Lamar. "There ain't nothing here but trees. Boring, boring, boring."

"You like to breathe?" said Byron.

"No," said Lamar like it was the stupidest thing he had ever heard. "I live on good vibes."

"All those boring trees produce oxygen. No oxygen, no life."

"Thank you, Professor."

Abigail reached over and gave him a little slap on the back of the head.

Every motel along I-59 had a "No Vacancy" sign. It was nearly 9:00 p.m. by the time they got to Hattiesburg and still they found no vacancies.

"Good Lord. Hattiesburg," said Hattie.

"Named after you, huh, Grandma?" said Lamar.

"I ain't that old," said Hattie weakly.

Georgette turned around and looked at Lamar. "Guess what county we're in?"

"I dunno. The county of no return?"

Georgette's face lit up. "We're in Lamar County!"

"For real?"

"For real."

"Guess we practically own this Godforsaken state," said Lamar.

"We've got roots here. That's for sure," said Abigail.

They got off the freeway on 198 and saw a sign pointing the opposite direction to Columbia.

"Good Lord," said Hattie again, shaking her head.

Highway 198 was a swath of suburban blight, cheap motels and fast food restaurants. They felt about as far away from the French Quarter as they could get, and despite the nearly eight-hour drive, they were a scant seventy-five miles away. Here, too, the red neon of "No Vacancy" colored their faces, but Byron decided to pull into Western Motel in hopes they might have something.

"Well, we got one room," said the desk clerk, "but I didn't want to rent it. Got some water damage in the bathroom."

"We're desperate," said Byron, but as soon as it was out of his mouth, he realized it was the wrong thing to say. The lobby was shabby with worn brown carpet, and it smelled heavily of Pine Sol, which always made Byron want to vomit. He imagined the hellish conditions of a room that, even in this motel, wasn't in rentable condition. But his body ached and he couldn't drive another mile. He looked out the windows—crisscrossed with masking tape—at the rain pouring down.

"I could give it to you for eighty."

"Eighty!" Georgette said. "Should be no more than thirty in a place like this."

"You know what rooms are going for in the area. I don't even wanna tell ya."

Byron threw up his hands. "We'll take it."

The man looked past them toward the van outside. "How many more people you got out there?"

"Don't you worry about it. You'll get your eighty bucks."

"Up front."

"Yeah, fine." He took out his wallet and paid.

"I was only asking 'cause there's only two beds. All the cots have been claimed."

"We'll manage."

They splashed through ankle-deep puddles and got all their things to the room.

"Holy shit, what's that smell?" said Lamar. It was obvious the room had been closed for a while, and the mildew was strong enough to taste. Georgette went to check out the water damage in the bathroom. She turned on the light and several giant roaches scurried for a crevice. The linoleum was buckled and the tub stained.

"My God," said Georgette, coming out of the bathroom. Letisha gave her a disapproving look. "It's pretty bad. Only two ratty towels. Plenty of roaches though."

"We got any food left?" asked Lamar. "I'm starving."

"We done ate most of it in the car," said Hattie.

"I'll go see if anything's open and ask for more towels

on the way back," said Byron.

Georgette put her arm around him. "I hate for you to go out there again after all that driving you did."

"I saw a chicken place down the road. It won't take long. Maybe somebody can get some sodas from the machines."

Byron pulled into a KFC, but just before he got to the door, a young kid locked it and turned the sign around. Byron pounded on the glass as the teenager walked away, shouting that they were closed. Byron motioned the teenager to the door and put his mouth to the crack of the double doors.

"Come on. We just drove eight hours from New Orleans and we're hungry."

"Sorry, mister. We're closed." He was a sharp-nosed blond kid with pimply skin—a poor ambassador for a diet of greasy chicken.

Byron saw a tray of dried-out legs and thighs under the red heat lamp. "What are you going to do with that?"

"Dump it." He started to walk back toward the counter.

"Hey, wait. Instead of dumping it, sell it to me."

"Register's closed. Can't take your money," the boy shouted.

"You're kidding, right? You can dump it, but you can't sell it."

The boy looked out toward the parking lot as though somebody might be watching, and then walked close to the door. "Meet me in the back by the dumpster," he said in a low voice with appropriate gestures, as the rain made it hard to hear.

Byron stood by the back door for five minutes getting soaked, but the kid did show up with two buckets of chicken.

"You're a lifesaver."

"Don't tell nobody, all right?" And then, as an afterthought he said with a smile, "Y'all come back now."

Back at the room there was a noticeable improvement of air quality with the air conditioner running full blast. The latest news was that the trajectory of Katrina seemed headed directly for Hattiesburg after it slammed into the Gulf Coast.

"Looks like we done jumped from the frying pan into the fire," said Abigail.

"I think," Letisha began meekly, "if we all pray, we'll be spared."

"Well, one prayer has been answered," said Hattie. "We have food."

They sat around the small table near the window while the rain beat against it. Lamar already had a piece of chicken in his hands when Letisha insisted they give thanks. Lamar put down the thigh and wiped his hands on his jeans. They held hands and bowed heads while she said a lengthy prayer. For everyone but Lamar the cold, greasy chicken took away their appetites after the first piece. They dropped the bones in a pile on a sheet of newspaper and cleaned their hands with toilet paper. Lamar wolfed down five pieces, took a few gulps of Coke, and let out a raucous belch.

"We'll just ignore that," said Abigail.

"Hey, it's a compliment to the Colonel," said Lamar. "Though I do prefer Popeye's."

"Nothing is quite right for you, is it, Lamar?" Byron said angrily. "You might appreciate that you had something to eat at all." He stood up as if to stomp off, but there was nowhere to go. The wind was so strong outside that it rustled the heavy curtains even though the windows were closed.

"Somebody got they panties in a twist," Lamar mumbled. Georgette turned toward Lamar as if she had been slapped. Everyone looked at Lamar with mouths agape.

"Enough, Lamar," said Abigail.

Hattie came out of her stupor. "What is the world's got into you, chile? Apologize to Mr. Byron."

"What? I can't make a joke? Everybody's so damned serious."

"You're right, Lamar," said Byron. "Let's lighten up, make a game of it. We're going to go around the circle, and each person is going to tell exactly what's going on in his or her head, and particularly why they find it necessary to be an asshole when the situation doesn't call for it." Byron stood over Lamar and they stared hard at each other.

Georgette reached up and took Byron's hand. "Teenagers! I'm convinced they don't even know where half the stuff they say comes from."

"That ain't no excuse. Your grandma's right. Apologize," said Abigail, but her voice lacked the conviction of authority, as if it didn't have the weight of experience behind it.

Lamar jumped up and pushed past Byron. He threw the door open and a gust of wind roared in, tossing up one of the greasy wads of toilet paper and blowing it across the room. Lamar ran out in the rain.

"Baby, come back here!" shouted Abigail.

"I'll go get him," said Georgette.

"Let him go," said Byron.

Georgette grabbed an umbrella sitting by the door, but as soon as she got outside the wind flipped it up in a saucer shape and rendered it useless. She threw it back in the room and visored her eyes with a hand, looking around the parking lot. Byron closed the door against the slanted rain darkening the carpet by the door.

"I'm so sorry," said Abigail. "She gonna be all right?"

"She's tough," said Byron. "Tougher than him or me."

Lamar sat hunched down in the passenger seat of the Grey Goose, which they had neglected to lock. Georgette opened the side door. "Can I join you?" She didn't wait for an answer, but climbed in the back, shook the rain out of her curls, and sat down, looking at the back of Lamar's head. "So what's going on?" she said.

"Just can't stand being cooped up with all those people. Granny only there half the time. Letisha zonked out on her Bible high. And my mom don't care about nobody 'cept her Lester."

"But Lester's your father, right?"

"If 'father' mean having his name on my birth certificate."

"All right, but right now your problem seems to be with Byron."

"Why he wanna do all this? I don't get it." A gust of wind buffeted the van and a harder rain pounded on the roof. "Now we in some fleabag motel far from home and we left Grandpa alone to fend for hisself."

"What your grandfather's doing is brave, but a little foolish. God help him if the levees don't hold. But I still wonder, what is your problem with Byron?"

"He act like the great savior. We didn't ask for no help."

"He's got his reasons. You're too young to understand."

"I am so sick of that! Everybody telling me, 'Lamar, you too young to understand.' Shit!"

"Lamar, you wanna come back here? I don't like talking to the back of your head."

"Damn!" said Lamar, falling onto the third seat, stretching out his legs in front of him. Georgette twisted around with her elbow on the back of the middle seat. She smiled at him.

"And you, why you trying to be nice to me?" said Lamar. "I ain't nobody to you, and I don't want to be no charity case."

"Is there anybody you trust? I mean, do you have one person in your life that you can talk to?"

He curled his lips into one big question mark. Then he hooked his thumb under his chin and pressed his fist against his mouth, part thoughtful and part suspicious of her question. "Hell, I don't know. My homies maybe. You make it sound like I got some shit I should be talking out. You like Byron, always looking at me like he know me. He don't know me and you don't either. Don't know nothing about me."

"You're right. We're from different worlds, but maybe not so different as you might think. Byron wants to help your family. He has his reasons. I can't really explain it to you right now. He's been through a lot."

"He told me something. There's some deal about my uncle, right?"

"Yes," Georgette said, her intonation cascading as if she had been the one who lived that terrible time.

"What? Like they had something going? No way my uncle was a faggot. He played football. I seen pictures in the old yearbooks."

She gave him a hard cold stare. "Lamar, I'm going to ask you a favor, just one. We're going to be spending time together. Who knows how long? Don't ever use that word in my presence again. And I would recommend you erase it from your vocabulary."

"Geez, everybody's so damn sensitive."

"No, it's not about being sensitive. It's about respecting people. You kids are always saying you want respect. You've got to give it to get it. So I ask you to respect my wishes on this one. I'm not trying to change your thinking. Just don't use that word around me. Got it?"

"Okay. Okay. I got it."

Another gust of wind hit the van and they looked out the rain-streaked windows. A traffic light bounced on a wire over the empty street. Debris from a tipped-over dumpster littered the parking lot. "We'd better go back inside. It's getting scary out here," said Georgette.

"From the looks of the motel, not sure it's any safer in there."

The TV was the principal light in the room. Byron was

stretched out on one of the beds, Abigail and her mother on the other. Letisha sat in one of the cushioned chairs, her Bible closed and resting in her lap. At first no one acknowledged Georgette and Lamar coming in the door.

They stood, dripping on the carpet and Georgette shivered. "It's nasty out there," she said.

"Not surprised," Abigail said. "Look at that." She pointed at the screen where they watched for the hundredth time the whirligig of Katrina moving toward the Gulf Coast and then northward. "Look like she don't want New Orleans. She coming straight for us."

"Byron, did you remember those extra towels?"

A grimace of failure overtook his face. "Sorry, George. With everything going on I forgot."

Letisha stood up, walked to the bathroom, and came back with the two thin musty towels. Georgette and Lamar gingerly wiped their heads and arms. "You guys okay?" said Letisha.

"Aside from being drowned rats, we are," said Georgette.

Byron got up and pulled the flowery polyester spread off the bed and dragged it over to Georgette. "You look chilled. We've got the air up pretty high. Wrap this around you."

"What about me?" said Lamar. "Don't I get wrapped up, too?"

Byron's jaw clenched and he pursed his lips, letting his brain search for the right response. There were times he wanted to discipline Lamar, paddle him or turn him over his knee, but in his head it immediately morphed in a pseudo-erotic fantasy. A tingling rose up Byron's spine, like hearing fingernails on a blackboard.

"Chill, man. I'm kidding." He smiled at Byron for the first time since they met.

"This thing's gigantic," said Georgette. "I could share."

"I'm good," said Lamar. He turned his attention to

Abigail with a tinge of mischief in his eye. "Hey, Ma, you talk to Lester?"

"Couldn't get through, thanks for asking. But would it kill you to call him Dad? You know he loves you."

"Don't go there, Ma."

"I'm just saying."

Around strangers, Abigail made attempts to reel in Lamar, but Byron imagined it was too much bother in the family circle. Hattie, too, occasionally commented on Lamar's behavior, though most of the time she looked at him as if he were from another dimension. Her gaze would sadden and Byron wondered if she was thinking of her lost son. The pall of Thomas' death hung over the family the way senseless and violent tragedies do, turning the survivors into ghosts who are drawn to joining him. This seemed particularly true of Hattie, and Byron wished he had known her when Thomas was still alive. In the many times Byron dropped Thomas off at his house, Thomas never invited him in, but he remembered a conversation with Thomas one lazy summer day on the banks of the Pearl River. Thomas had described a birthday party Hattie had organized for Abigail the previous weekend, saying that his mom loved parties and could even be encouraged to get up and dance though her church lady friends didn't approve. The description was a far cry from the woman now in front of him.

"Who wants to play cards?" asked Georgette. "Gin Rummy? A penny a point?"

Lamar rolled his eyes.

"Oh my," said Hattie. "I haven't played cards in years.

19 Temple of the Lord

The rain pelted the Grey Goose from all angles, even spraying the bottom with a furious grating sound while gusts rocked the metal hulk as if it were a toy. Byron was on Highway 98, alone, a scant thirty miles from home, a place he hadn't been in twenty-five years. Inside the van the air was stuffy and he struggled for the next breath; his hands gripped the wheel to stop them from shaking. His mind was on the box of photos on the top shelf of the closet in his old room, though he kept trying to drag it back to the more pressing issue of finding a place to move the family.

The hotel room was cramped and nerves were raw, creating a cauldron of emotions that the family only half understood. The connection to their common history still hadn't been made, but it couldn't be far down the road. If the air wasn't thick enough with pain and destruction, they were in Mississippi, a state none of them had fond feelings about. All that fear and loathing, combined with the heat, and concerns about food and water, made Byron feel like his head was going to explode. But he had no choice other than to keep going with the rope of responsibility he had taken in hand.

His childhood home was large; his mother and Sofia only occupied a small part of it. Why should they all be stuck in a decrepit motel room when his mother had room to spare? If his unannounced return home didn't give Camille a heart attack, his proposal surely would. She had never gotten over the terror of those days when her boy had been driven from town, or his disappearance where she had feared the worst. And then there were the mysterious deaths of the very same boys that had been, according to Byron, responsible for the death of Sofia's cousin. She told Byron that they had received anonymous threats, as if they were somehow involved in the men's deaths. Other callers claimed that if Byron returned, they would catch him and string up his "faggot ass." The sheriff had even paid them a visit, asking if they had heard from Byron. She had been mortified. After the death of Byron's father, Camille had settled into a quiet existence in the big house with Sofia, giving up most of her social obligations.

Byron's plan was to convince his mother that, with everybody preoccupied by the storm, nobody would notice—though even he had a hard time believing it. A white man driving an old van full of black people to stay in one of the oldest and most respectable homes in the town. They could, of course, arrive at night and park the van in the garage. It would only be a few days until they could go back to New Orleans.

He pulled off the road and started up the long driveway. The yard was scattered with branches and leaves. One of the old oaks had toppled over. Halfway up the drive he had to stop, get out, and drag a large branch off the gravel path. He stood in the rain gazing distantly on the lawn that Thomas used to mow, thinking of the day he refused to stop the mower, the day that changed his life.

Byron sat in the van at the back door, lost in another memory of Thomas: that first day in the garage, the awkward conversation, the racing feeling constricting his chest. He looked up and saw Sofia arrive at the kitchen window over the sink. She looked out, stretched her neck forward, and squinted. Their eyes met through the rain, and in a second she stepped out the back door.

"Goodness gracious alive! Get in here out of the rain. Does your mother know? She gonna have a fit. Hurry now." She closed the door behind him and ran to get a towel.

"Where is she?"

"She in her room. I think she still in bed. Ya know her room in the downstairs parlor. Long time now we don't use upstairs."

"Y'all weather the storm okay?"

"The ole house was a shakin' and leakin' here and there, but we okay. 'Lectricity went out for a few hours, but I was ready with the candles. I stocked up on food, too. Junior came over to check on us early this morning."

"There's a special place for you in heaven, Sofia." Byron hugged her loosely, knowing it made her uncomfortable. When he was growing up, she was always affectionate with him, sitting him on her lap to tie his shoe, or embracing him when he had some trauma that led to tears. But when he got to a certain age, she didn't think it was proper, "all this hugging people like to do nowadays."

Byron knocked lightly on the parlor door and then slid it open. The TV with the latest Katrina news cast a blue light on the room.

"Momma, you awake?"

"Good lord, Byron!" Her eyes and mouth took on the look of the girl in Edvard Munch's "The Scream of Nature" paintings. Her bed had been pushed up against a floor-to-ceiling multicolored tapestry, and she looked small and vulnerable, propped up against a pile of pillows. The light from the bedside lamp shone on the frayed edges of her nightgown. She dropped the book she was reading and tugged on the bedcovers. "Oh, sweetheart, you shouldn't be here," she said, recovering. "And look at me. I'm a mess. Haven't had a chance to do my hair yet."

"You mean I shouldn't be here to see you looking your natural self?" He went over to the bed and kissed her cheek.

"What if someone saw you?"

"Nobody's looking for me anymore. I've got the van. People'll think I'm a repairman or something."

"Well, you look the part." He wore a baseball cap and casual clothes. He hadn't shaved in a couple of days. "Go on now and talk to Sofia. Let me try to make myself decent. Tell her to put on some coffee."

A half hour later Camille appeared in the kitchen doorway in a fuchsia silk robe. She had teased her reddish hair into a globe and put on lipstick. Her face was pale and creased, her hands dotted with age spots. In recent years, he had only seen his mother in New Orleans. She always had her hair done the day before and wore a chic if old-fashioned ensemble, often with hat and gloves. Her aging process had been much less noticeable. Byron cringed to see her looking so old.

Camille sat down, and Sofia poured her some coffee. "I'm certainly glad you got out of New Orleans. The news is dreadful. Now they're talking about levees breached. Parts of the city under water."

Byron sat up straight and leaned forward. "What parts?"

"The lakefront, the Lower Ninth and such. I guess it's the canal levees that didn't hold."

Byron stood up. "I've got to see what going on."

"Where you going? We've got a little TV in here. Sofia?" Sofia turned on the Coby and the ten-inch screen sucked Byron's attention. "Anyway, I think the Quarter is fine. They said damage wasn't bad and no flooding."

Byron walked over closer to the screen. Helicopter footage showed tiny figures wading through waist-deep water, then switched to scenes where only the rooftops were above the water. It was the Lower Ninth Ward, near the Davis home. He wondered about Joe.

"What is it, son? You look worried."

He pointed at the screen. "Momma, I rescued a family from there, some of Sofia's relatives, and I've got them in a motel room over in Hattiesburg." He turned toward Sofia, who stared at him in shock. "Yes, Hattie, Abigail, Lamar and Letisha. They're fine, but Joe wouldn't leave."

"Lordy, that man always was stubborn," said Sofia.

"What in the world are you two talking about?"

Byron sighed deeply. "It's Thomas' family. I had a premonition something like this might happen."

Sofia jumped in. "Do you have any way to get in touch with Joe?"

Camille's forehead became a complicated series of worry canals. "Sofia, let me talk," she said. "I need to find out what's going on. You mean Thomas, the boy…" Her lips were still moving, but she didn't finish the sentence.

"Yes, Momma, that Thomas. I've got his family in a horrible motel over in Hattiesburg. The electricity is off—at least it was this morning—and we don't have any food or water."

"So that's why you're here. Not to see me, not to see if I survived the storm of the century."

"Please! You're the one that insisted I stay away all these years. It just seems silly for all of them to be suffering and you've got so much space here. Sofia says you don't even use the upstairs."

Camille looked as if she had been slapped in the face. "You want to move a colored family into my upstairs?"

"Oh Momma, have a little Christian kindness." He looked at Sofia with sad eyes as if to say he was sorry.

"I was just asking." Camille had a gurgle in her throat and tears in her eyes.

"I could call my sister," said Sofia. "She might have room."

"Georgette is with us, too. That's a lot of people, and I go where they go. I took on this responsibility, and I'm sticking to it."

Camille had her head in her hands. "Oh, Byron. It seems that your whole life you've been hell-bent on making things a trial for me. I've tried, Lord knows I've tried, to understand your...your...differences. When you would come home as a little boy and say the others were bullying you, I tried to find interests more suited for your specialness. I got you into piano lessons, and then tennis, thinking it was a sport more appropriate for you. None of it took. I got your Daddy to take you fishing, and he even attempted to get you into little league, but you refused to go. And there was the incident that nearly destroyed us all, the colored boy—"

"Thomas," Byron sang out.

"Yes, well, what were you thinking? We live in Mississippi, not some place where anything goes like...like California. If they had told me there was some shenanigans going on with one of the boys at the military school, I would have been shocked, but I guess not surprised. But when you called all emotional, wanting your Daddy to do something about the killing of that boy...Thomas, and telling us that you were there, it was devastating. I could put two and two together, but of course your father couldn't, even though it was staring him right in the face. And there are the other things that I don't even want to think about: your disappearance, your not speaking to your father up to his dying day, not to mention the things that made it impossible for you to step foot in this town, things I don't want to know and will never ask you. But if I could just understand why? Why that boy?"

"Let me ask you something, Momma. Why are you living out your golden years with a black woman? When Dad died, why didn't you go live with your own sister? I know she wanted you to. But no, you decided to stay here with Sofia, even begged her to stay when she thought it was time to move on." Sofia was sitting in the corner peeling apples for a pie. The scraping stopped and she looked up.

"That's entirely different!"

"What's different? You take care of each other, and besides the fact that you snip at each other like a cantankerous old couple, I think you are genuinely fond of each other."

"I have never for the likes of me understood what goes on in your head, son of mine. Are you saying that if that hadn't happened to Thomas, you would be growing old together? You are a dreamer."

"That's exactly the kind of attitude that killed him! Love is love, Momma."

They heard an "Ouch!" from the corner.

"Sofia, what did you do?" said Camille.

"Just a little nick."

"Come over here. Let me take a look at it," said Camille.

"It's nothing. I'll go get me a Band-Aid."

Byron and Camille stared at each other as if they had both made their point. Camille sighed heavily. "I'll have Sofia start getting the upstairs rooms ready."

"You'll do nothing of the kind. We're all completely capable of fending for ourselves."

"I'll be happy to see Georgette. I had so hoped…"

"Yes, Momma. We all did."

Camille's pride and joy in the house was the stairway that led to the second floor. It was wide and solid, carpeted in red, symbolic of the grand family name that she had married into, but in recent years had lost its shine. When she married, Camille had left her comfortable life in New Orleans and moved to her husband's town where she knew no one. The house and its magnificent stairway were a kind of compensation. She had once confessed to Byron that when she first saw it she imagined a daughter descending it in a wedding dress, a daughter who would give her grandchildren. What she got was a single son who would bear her none.

Byron stared up at the faded and dusty portraits of stiff ancestors in their finery, lining the wall at the top where the stairs divided into two wings. As a boy, the stairway had seemed huge and magical, but as a teenager it was merely tedious and somewhat embarrassing when friends came over and asked where Scarlet O'Hara was.

His room was in the back corner and pretty much as he had left it twenty-five years before. Gone were the posters of his teenage years, though you could still see the faded outlines on the wallpaper. One had been of a young Grace Slick giving the finger, and the other of the movie *Midnight Express*, which more or less summed up his thoughts about the world at that time.

On his dresser were several framed photos: Byron as young teenager, receiving an award for a short story he wrote in a citywide contest; a family Christmas portrait, possibly the only one they had sat for; and Byron as a young boy with his father, holding up the fish they caught. His mother had added that one after he left. There was one more of Byron in a tux with Julie, his date for the senior prom. But the picture he sought, the picture that now seemed the most important, had never been displayed. He went to his closet and found the shoebox (would he some day be like Hattie with her box, showing photos to strangers?) on the top shelf. Buried near the bottom of the box was the copy of the picture he had just seen a couple days before. It was strange that the composition of the photo of him and his father from their fishing trip was almost identical to the one with Thomas, though with Thomas he had a much happier expression on his face. His mother's words rang in his head: "Are you saying that if that hadn't happened to Thomas, you would be growing old together? You are a dreamer." Knowing what he now knew about relationships, he had to admit that the likelihood that they would have found happiness together was slim. But they never even had a chance; all the possible roads they could have taken had been struck down by a bullet. And at that desperately lonely teenage point in his life, even another month, week, day with Thomas would have been heaven. Instead he had been left with anger and hatred, and a torturous need for revenge.

He sat down in his desk chair and ran his fingers over the photo of Thomas, touching the lips that smiled often, but said little, the lips that kissed with an abandon, seemingly in conflict with the rest of his character. Byron remembered the day he had collected the quotes each senior had chosen to go under his or her picture in the yearbook. He came across Thomas': "A ship in a harbor is safe, but that's not what ships are built for." At the time, he knew little of the confusing passion that lay deep within Thomas, a mystery that would drive Byron crazy. And yet Thomas had seemed completely unaware of the obsession he had created in Byron.

Byron heard a noise outside, someone starting up a leaf blower, jolting him out of his memory. He still held the fishing photo in his hand. Byron took the picture with his father out of the frame and replaced it with the one of Thomas. Pleased with himself, he set it on the dresser and walked out of the room.

20 Before Thee in Truth

When Byron returned to the motel room, the electricity was back on. They had all seen the news about the levees. Abigail was nearly hysterical and Letisha and Georgette were trying to calm her down. Hattie sat quietly in a chair, staring off into a solitary future, and Lamar was wired into his ear buds, bobbing his head.

"That bitch Katrina," said Abigail through her tears, "done robbed us of our father and Lester in one fell swoop! It's the damn end of the world."

"We don't know that, Abby," said Georgette. "For heaven's sake, let's not jump to conclusions."

Abigail had tried numerous times to contact her Uncle Burt's cell phone, but only got a message that it was turned off or out of range. She had had no more success with Lester. The news out of the Superdome—shortages, armed gangs, rapes—plus the dire situation throughout New Orleans, were more than enough to provoke dread.

"Come on, everybody. Pack up. We're going to see Sofia. We can stay in my mother's house for a few days until we can go back in the city to look for Joe and Lester."

Georgette stared at him in shock. "Your mother agreed to that?"

"What choice did she have? We are people in need, Sofia's people. And where I go, they go."

"This is going to be interesting," said Georgette.

Abigail turned to Byron and looked him up and down. "Wait one minute! Our Sofia? What the…?" She lowered her voice. "You the Purvis boy. Ain't you dead? What's with the Boudreaux name?"

"Damn, a breakthrough in this mystery shit," said Lamar.

"Sofia?" said Hattie. The name brought her out of her stupor, but going back home presented a bit more of a quandary. "Columbia?" She shook her head and gummed her lips.

"Well, I think it's pretty obvious I'm not dead. An explanation is coming, but can we wait until we're packed and out of here? It's almost checkout time. I'll tell you in the car."

"Yes, Hattie," said Georgette. "We're going to see Sofia." Georgette turned to Byron. "I imagine Camille will be wanting us to keep a low profile."

"She's excited about seeing you."

"Even though I failed her?"

"No, I failed her. But you're right. This is going to be interesting! I just hope it's not a disaster."

Georgette drove while Byron leaned over the seat and told the family how he had known Thomas. He left it that they were friends at high school and had gone fishing a few times. Abigail was sullen; she had the look of someone who had been tricked. "So you been keeping tabs on us?"

"Sofia kept me informed. I'm sorry. The HPA was an invention. Lamar caught me out right away."

"Uh-huh," said Lamar.

"But I convinced him not to say anything. I had to get you out of New Orleans, and now you see why."

"Land of mercy!" said Hattie. "The fishing photo. You the one. Why you didn't say something?"

"Hattie, I'm sorry. I didn't want to stir up the past. Thomas was...I..I..." His voice began to quake.

Georgette jumped in, saving him from saying something he might regret later. "You see, Hattie, Byron quite admired Thomas and was upset by his death, as I'm sure many people were. He used to write articles about Thomas' football playing for the school newspaper. Right, Byron? I can't tell you how sorry I am too, though I never knew him."

"Hmm," said Abigail, twisting her lips. "There more to this story, and we goin' find out. But I think Momma had enough for now." She put her arm around Hattie, who seemed ready to collapse. "We need to concentrate on Daddy and Lester."

The garage door had been left open and they pulled directly inside per his mother's instructions. Byron got out and hurried to close the garage door.

"Relax, man," said Lamar. "This ain't the underground railroad."

"Kinda feels like it," said Georgette with a giggle.

Sofia greeted them at the kitchen door with the smell of cooking beans behind her. Abigail, Lamar, and Letisha knew Sofia thanks to the trips she and Camille used to make into New Orleans. While Byron, Lidia, and Camille went out to lunch, Sofia would head to the Lower Ninth and visit the Davis family, filling them in on the latest gossip from Columbia. True to her word, Sofia had never mentioned Byron, saying only that she accompanied Mrs. Purvis into town for shopping.

"Where's Momma?" Byron asked.

"Oh, she got her one them headaches," said Sofia. "Went to lay down. She gonna try and get up for dinner. We having a real New Orleans treat—beans and rice." She laughed, but only Georgette joined in.

"Just let us know what help you need," said Hattie. The idea of being useful in the kitchen seemed to animate her.

"You go on up and get settled. Byron'll show you the way. Byron, honey, Hattie and the girls can take the back bedroom with the queen and daybed. Your momma says Georgette should be in her old room. Lamar gonna be in the sewing room."

"The sewing room? What?" said Lamar.

"Hush or you be out in the garage." Sofia was never one to put up with Lamar's nonsense.

The group hesitated a moment at the bottom of the grand staircase, feeling the eyes of the portraits on them. Byron always hated the way the eyes followed you whichever way you went. Now he was more than happy to have them witness what they could never imagine in their lifetime—a family of black folks taking over the upstairs bedrooms while lady of the house slept on the ground floor. "Feast your eyes on this, Daddy, and weep." Byron directed his comment toward the latest family portrait of his father.

Georgette tilted her head and gave him an admonishing look. "Respect the dead, sweetie."

"See, that's why you get the master bedroom. Let's go, people," Byron said to the others, and they started up the stairs.

Byron stayed focused on his father's waxy face. The painter had tried to keep the same wooden style as the older portraits, which Byron thought looked absurd for this day and age. His father sat in a Louis XV knock-off chair with a wall of books behind him. The painting had been done about five years before he died of lung cancer. Needless to say, Byron had missed the funeral back in 1990. Even without the risk of returning to Columbia, he's not sure he would have made it. They hadn't spoken since Byron's frantic call from his Tulane dorm room three days after Thomas' death.

Byron walked into the dining room to see Sofia putting out the everyday flatware and dishes on the Chippendale table with its awkward-looking ball and claw legs. The heavy Italian damask drapes were drawn and lighting was low. "What's this? A clandestine dinner?"

"Your momma don't wanna draw no attention. You know people around here."

"I don't know which is more worrisome to her: someone spotting me or a black family taking over the Purvis Manor," said Byron. "Heck, she could just say I'm some distant relative. Nobody's going to recognize me after twenty-five years, at least not from afar. And as for the family, she can say they're your kinfolk fleeing New Orleans, which is the truth. What's the big deal?"

Sofia tilted her head and chuckled. "Are you really asking that?"

"Is she coming to dinner?"

"She say she plumb tuckered out. Gonna stay in her room."

"Can't say I'm surprised. Seriously Sofia, how is her health?"

"She complaining 'bout this and that from dawn to dusk, but she probably gonna be singing at all our funerals."

They sat at the table hunched over half-eaten plates of red beans and rice with andouille sausage. Since they'd seen the news about the levees, no one except Lamar had much of an appetite. Sofia brought out a bread pudding and a pot of heavy cream they were supposed to spill over it. Abigail's phone sang out and made them start like a firecracker had gone off under the table. She looked at the caller ID and shrugged. "Guess I better get this," she said.

Everybody zeroed in on her face and listened to her uh-huhs. Then she stood, turned her back, and walked toward the kitchen with the phone stuck to her ear.

"Where you going?" said Hattie.

Abigail kept walking and didn't answer. Sofia got up and followed her.

"Probably Lester," said Lamar.

Hattie shook her head. "If it is, there's trouble."

Lamar grabbed the dish of bread pudding. "Are we just gonna let this sit here?"

"Go ahead, Lamar," Georgette said.

Lamar had the spoon halfway into the pudding when they all heard a wail from the kitchen.

"It's comin' up a bad cloud," Hattie said softly. "Poor Lester, I suppose I was too hard on him."

Sofia came to the doorway. "It ain't Lester, Hattie. That was Uncle Burt. I took over the call when Abigail couldn't talk no more. I'm sorry, honey. Joe, well, he's gone missing. Burt gone over to a friend's live in Bywater the other side a Clairborne Bridge so as to call his family up in Baton Rouge and tell them he's okay. His cell was dead and no 'lectricity. When he leaving the friend's house they hears an explosion. He run back toward the bridge and by the time he get there, a big crowd was staring over to the other side. They all pointing at a hole in the cement wall, water gushing into the Ninth like the Red Sea on them Egyptians. Some of them saying the explosion was deliberate, that they flooding the Ninth to save the rest of the city. Burt's house is a direct line in front of the breach. Halfway cross the bridge he see his house knocked right off its foundation. He ran like crazy and get like two blocks from his house, but the water rising fast, up to his waist. If he keep goin' he gonna drown. He went back but couldn't get nobody to help. It already been two days. Said he didn't wanna call till he had some definite news."

Abigail was back in the room. "Daddy can't swim," she moaned.

Lamar's first spoonful of pudding was suspended in the air, cream dripping on the table.

Hattie stared at Lamar's spoon like she'd been knocked

silly. Letisha jumped up and went over to her side, put her hand on her grandmother's shoulder. "Grandpa's probably sitting up there on the roof like we seen people on TV," she said with little conviction.

"Yeah, he said he had an axe," said Byron.

"He didn't have no axe," said Hattie. "Just said that so we'd stop pestering him 'bout leaving. I guess the Lord's not done punishing me yet."

"Don't say that," said Letisha. "He has his ways."

"Isn't there someone we can call to find out what's going on?" said Georgette.

"Sometimes they give numbers on the TV," said Byron.

They all ran in the living room and turned on the old Motorola. Helicopter images showed people sitting on their rooftops, waving white rags on sticks at the sky like they were surrendering. The broadcast cut to Governor Blanco announcing she had requested federal aid—as much as they could send—rescue helicopters, and troops. In the meantime, they needed boats. She called on people with private boats not damaged in the storm to help out.

Byron sat chewing his lower lip. His father's old fishing boat sat on a trailer in the garage.

Camille came out into the living room. "What's all the commotion?"

"Look," said Byron, pointing to aerial photos of the flooded Lower Ninth. "We just heard that Joe's house got a direct hit and he's probably still in it."

"Who?" said Camille.

"Joe. Our old gardener. Hattie's husband."

"Oh. Dear me."

"Is that boat out in the garage in working condition?" Byron asked his mother.

"I don't know." She dug her fingernails into her mat of reddish hair and fluffed it up, trying to give it some shape. "Oh, no, no way. You're not thinking of going anywhere near that mess. Byron?"

It had hit Byron like a stroke of lightning. Maybe there was some kind of redemption in it, saving lives for those he had taken. Georgette stared at him, knowing full well what was going on behind his eyes. "You've already done a lot, Byron," she said. "The stories coming out of there are just too darn scary."

Byron stood up. "I've got to do something. Sofia, could you call Junior and get him to come over to look at that motor?"

"Byron, please no," Camille moaned.

"I wanna go, too," said Hattie softly. "I wanna see him, live or dead."

"No, Momma, it's too dangerous," said Abigail.

"I'm a nervous wreck, sitting here waiting for news. I can't take it no more. You can't talk me out of it. If that boat'll go, I'm in it."

"Y'all can't go alone," said Georgette. "If he's still in there, you'll need help getting him out. I'd go, but I don't think I'd be of much use."

Everyone turned to look at Lamar. "Uh-uh," he said. "What? Me?"

"No, baby. We don't expect you to go," said Abigail in the tenderest voice any of them had heard her use with her son.

"Why not?" said Hattie. "He all growed up."

"Well, guess it beats being all cooped up here," said Lamar. "I don't know though. Me and Byron in a boat?" He turned to Byron. "You wouldn't throw me over, would ya?"

"Can't you swim?" said Byron.

"'Course I can, but I'm not partial to swimming around in water with dead…uh, dogs floating around in it."

"Lamar, you better behave and do exactly what Mr. Byron say or I'll throw you over myself," said Hattie. She had come alive and seemed stronger and more focused than they'd seen her in days.

21 Lamentations

Junior came over and they got the motor running. "That Mariner's sixty horse power. It'll go pretty good," he said. "Might get twenty mile an hour."

They filled two cans with gas and hitched up the trailer to the back of his father's Oldsmobile, which his mother still used on the rare occasion she went out. Camille called Byron into her room. She opened the drawer of her nightstand and took out a pistol. "Your father gave me this for when I was home alone. I want you to take it."

Byron cringed and shook his head. He had sworn he'd never touch another weapon. "I can't."

"God forbid you should have to use it, but I'll rest better if you have it. Please!"

Byron opened his bag and let her drop it in.

"If anyone tries to mess with you, shoot the sons of bitches."

Byron looked like he had been goosed. "Momma!"

"Don't look so shocked. I never told you about the time someone broke in the house, the only time I ever used that gun. I missed him, of course, but he sure skedaddled." She let out a little laugh and covered her mouth. "Sofia found an old shotgun of your daddy's and now sleeps with it by her bed."

All along I-59 they saw the destruction left in Katrina's path. It was almost as if the storm had taken the interstate as its superhighway to the North. There were pools of water everywhere, power lines drooping, and telephone poles tipping. They could hear power saws cutting through downed trees and crows cawing from the ones still standing. They got on I-10 and headed into Slidell where they got an idea of what New Orleans might look like. Slidell had taken a beating. Some homes were reduced to matchsticks and others rearranged, an addition on the side of the house twisted around to the back. They saw boats teetering on piles of rubble and cars sticking out of collapsed garages. There were homes demolished and others nearby relatively untouched. "Passed over like the Israelites who marked their doors," said Hattie. But even the passed-over houses had busted windows and patches of bare roof where the shingles had taken flight. As they got near the lake, water was deep on either side of the highway. At a certain point they could go no further; I-10 was underwater. Byron pulled the car over and they got out. They stood in awe, surveying the surrounding lowlands. They saw a shirtless man carrying a large Doberman in his arms, wading through waist-deep water. He looked relieved to have found his dog, but the animal was shivering, a look of shock in its eyes and its ribcage showing, as if it hadn't eaten in days.

They launched the Starcraft sixteen footer. It would probably hold five, maybe six people. They motored slowly down toward the marina, watching for sunken cars, often detectable by their antennas sticking up. Byron had Lamar hold a paddle down in the water to see how deep it was. The Slidell marina looked like an angry child had picked up all his toy boats and thrown them down in a big pile. Even large cruisers were bunched up and atop one another as if caught in a stampede to escape the rage of the storm.

Once they were in the open, relatively calm water of Lake Pontchartrain, they picked up speed. In a little more than an hour, they angled around the Lakefront Airport and into the Inner Harbor Navigation Canal. On either side the water was deep with only the roofs of houses showing above the water line. Hattie's face grew dark under the fisherman's hat Sofia had given her, and she let out a groan, as if any hope it wouldn't be so bad had been drowned. On the surface of the greenish-brown water was floating debris: wood planks, shingles, clothes, garbage in plastic bags. A dead rat bobbed in the wake of their boat.

"Look, there's a baby," said Lamar.

"Good Lord!" said Hattie.

Byron turned the boat to get a closer look. It was a life-sized doll, its pale skin radiant against the brackish water marbled with the metallic blues and greens of oil and gasoline. The doll's blue eyes gazed up at the gray skies.

They passed under the Florida Street Bridge and came upon the first of the two levee breaches they had seen on TV. Byron turned the boat through the hole and they were in the Ninth ward. They headed south toward Clairborne, following the line of Jourdan Avenue underwater below them. Some of the homes had been pushed back halfway to Deslonde, the next street over, ripped from their foundations and crashed into other structures. Other homes had collapsed completely, taken down by the hurricane itself, and then given the coup de grace by the flood.

Lamar stuck his paddle down in the water as far as he could reach and didn't touch anything solid. "Must be like ten feet deep."

The pearl sky pressed its dampness upon them, narrowing their passage as if they were navigating an underground cave, and yet the sun was there, constant behind a layer of cloud. It was a silver disc you could barely see, but the heat from it bore down nonetheless. Byron wiped his neck with a handkerchief and it felt raw. He already had a sunburn.

They saw a few boats in the distance, but nobody on roofs. And then, on the port side, a boat similar to theirs headed straight toward them. There were three men in it.

"Lamar, put that tarp over the gas cans," said Byron. "And hand me my backpack." He reached in with one hand and made sure the gun was on top, but just touching the cool metal sent a chill up his spine. "And keep your comments to yourself."

"Jeesh," said Lamar. "I ain't stupid."

"I know you're not." The cords in his neck began to tense.

The boat came closer, and Byron slowed down. The other boat pulled alongside them, their bows facing in opposite directions. Byron tried to poker face the men, but he was distracted by the two long objects wrapped in heavy black plastic and tied with ropes in the belly of their boat. Hattie stared hard at the bundles.

"Y'all awright?" said the one at the wheel, speaking with a thick New Orleans accent. He was bald on top and had a fringe of stringy hair that hung down over his ears like a veil. His face was covered with patches of mangy dog beard. He had bloodshot eyes and wore a tank top the color of yellowed teeth.

The other white man greeted them, too. "Where y'at?" He was in his forties, had black curly hair and close-set eyes. His chin rolled down in waves to his neck. He was shirtless and his hairy man-breasts rested on a Buddha belly.

The third man nodded. He was older with café au lait skin, tight white curls on his head, and round, wire-rimmed glasses over his post-traumatic eyes. He was thin, and his threadbare T-shirt read "Don't Rain On My Parade" under an image of a fleur-de-lys jazz funeral umbrella.

"We're fine," said Byron. "Headed down yonder

looking for this lady's husband. He stayed behind when the rest of them left. He's gone missing."

"Howdy do?" said Hattie. "This here's my grandson."

"Where ya stay, ma'am?"

"Right here on Jourdan, down by that orange monstrosity." They had noticed a huge, rust-colored object floating peacefully in the old neighborhood. "What is that?" asked Hattie.

The man showed a smile with missing teeth. "Some say as dat barge, size a city block, busted dat second hole in the levee. Others round here say come through afta. Just sittin' dere empty. Sure hope ya can find ya husband. Dese here's ma marrain and parrain who raised me up afta ma folks passed on." He pointed at the bodies wrapped in thick plastic, his godparents. "Dey were up in a home ova in St Bernard. Dey's real sick and couldn't get out. At least the professor here got up ta da second floor."

"I tried to help," said the older man. "Nothin' I could do."

Hattie's face sank. "My profoundest sympathies" she said.

"Thank ya, dawlin'," said the man. "Got ta take dem to da collection site and da professor ta where dey's pickin' up people."

"Y'all need any water or anything?" said Byron.

"Professor say dey run outta everything ova dere. He up fer two days with almost nothin'."

Hattie opened the Styrofoam cooler Sofia had packed for them and pulled out a couple sandwiches and bottles of water. Lamar passed them over to the men.

"Much obliged. God bless!" said the professor.

"After I take care of ma people, we might head back dis way. We'll look for ya and see if we can help."

Byron bowed his head and spoke softly, feeling the eyes of Hattie upon him. "By the way, where exactly is it you're taking them?"

"Heard dey set somethin' up ova ta I-10 and 610, but people say FEMA's like a den of disturbed snakes dat don't know dey tail end from da head. But gotta go somewheres." He started the motor and it broke the relative silence with an angry roar. "Y'all have a blessed day. Maybe catcha later."

"Take care now," said Byron.

With everything under water, it took a couple of passes around the neighborhood before they found the house, off its foundation and leaning precariously to one side. Water was just a half-foot below the porch roof and one of the pillars leaned outward, no longer supporting the left corner. Byron pulled the boat close where they would have access to the attic window. Hattie was surprisingly calm, resigned.

Lamar jumped from the boat onto the roof. The window was broken, so he kicked in what was left of the frame, making a gap big enough to crawl through.

"Good Lord, be careful," said Hattie.

Lamar slid into the attic and was immediately punched with an odor that was far sight worse than the dead rat stuck in the wall the year before. He backed out and took a breath of air, not that the air outside was much better. The whole neighborhood was a bouquet of putrefaction packed in by the low clouds and the complete absence of a breeze.

"What is it?" said Byron.

"Nothing."

"You see somethin'?" asked Hattie.

"Not yet. Byron, throw me that flashlight."

Lamar edged back through the hole, holding his breath. As he crawled, he swore the house was rocking like boat. He got above the hallway where there was a trap door. He opened it and shined the flashlight. There, in the middle of the hall, was his grandfather, floating face down, in clothes that couldn't contain the body twice its normal size. "Grandpa," he said, though he knew it was useless. He felt dizzy and scrambled back out the window. He sat on the roof with his head in his hands. There was no need for words. Hattie stood up in the boat.

"Where are you going? You don't have to…" said Byron.

But she was determined. Byron tied a rope to one of the good pillars and held her arm as she stepped onto the roof. She sat down beside Lamar.

"I'm sorry, Grannie," he said.

They sat for a long time, heads down, arms gripping knees, side by side in their matching baggy shorts and tennis shoes. After a time, Hattie rose to her feet and steadied herself, holding onto Lamar's shoulder.

"Don't go in there, Grannie."

"I have to." She folded her frail body through the window. Byron and Lamar watched her tennis shoes disappear into the darkness.

She stayed inside so long that Byron told Lamar he'd better go after her.

They came back out and the three of them sat on the roof, staring at the immense orange barge in front of them. "What are we gonna do?" said Lamar. To get Joe, someone would have to jump down into the foul water, drag the body to the front door, and get him outside. Then they would have to figure out how to get him into the boat. Joe was a big man and now bloated into an even larger one. They each imagined how it would be done, ruminating the possibilities silently, and then shaking their heads.

"I don't see how," said Byron. "We need help."

Just then they heard a roar like a lawnmower magnified ten times, and a moment later, an airboat glided around the barge into view. There were several armed, uniformed men in it.

"The cavalry!" said Lamar.

Byron stood up and waved his hands. They didn't look his way and sped by. A second boat buzzed into view and came even closer to the house. Both Byron and Lamar jumped up and down and waved. One of the soldiers glanced at them a second, but the others stared straight ahead, though it was obvious the soldiers had seen them. The airboats powered out of sight.

"What the fuck?" said Lamar. "Sorry, Grannie."

"Maybe they'll come back. Or send somebody," said Byron.

Lamar raised his eyebrows. "Well, there one white person here. That's hopeful."

They nibbled on sandwiches and drank water while they waited, though the stench in the air squeezed their appetites. They wrapped up the leftovers and put them back in the cooler. Anxious to do something, they got back in the boat and motored around the neighborhood, but stayed close by in case somebody came back. Lamar and Hattie commented on the neighbors' houses. She saw her breadbox floating down the street. With that Hattie burst, finally, into the tears she had been holding for so long. Byron gave her his handkerchief, and she recovered quickly.

"Where're them soldiers?" she gurgled. "Surely, they'll come back."

"You expect something from the government? What they ever do for us?" said Lamar.

They knew they had to get out of the city by dark. Everybody back home had made them promise. They would have to leave Joe behind. Then they heard an outboard motor. The boat they had encountered before appeared, minus the man's godparents and the professor.

"Hey dere, podnas, ma'am," said the driver they came to know as Antoine. The heavyset man was Papite. "Glad we found ya. Dey's a pack a idiots ova dere. Hated to leave ma people. Y'all have any luck?"

"Wouldn't call it luck, but we found him," said Byron. "He passed. Just floating there in the house. We don't know how to get him out."

"So sorry fa your loss, dear lady. Dey just ain't words," said Antoine. "Let's go have a look."

Antoine came up with a plan. He tied a rope around his waist and had the three men lower him into the house. He lassoed Joe with another rope, tied the end to a paddle, and floated the paddle toward the open front door. Papite jumped into the water from the roof, swam through the door, found the paddle, and dragged Joe out of the house. From the water, the four men were able to get him onto the roof.

Papite pulled a body bag out of their boat. "Dem *couillons* refused to give us one, so we snitched it when nobody lookin'," said Papite with a toothy grin, his shorts still sending a cascade of green water down his legs. "Got a nice blue one. Hope he like blue."

They had rolled Joe over on his back and Hattie couldn't stop staring at his puffy, purple lips. "He love blue," she said in a deep foghorn voice that took them by surprise. "Blue his favorite color."

Joe lay nestled in the pouch, but they hadn't zipped it up yet. They sat in a circle around him, dripping and sweating. It was quiet. All the birds had gone. It felt like they were in a ship at sea, drifting toward shore, but still a long way to go. The stench seemed not so biting now and the milky sky had lifted some, the tiniest breeze tickled their arms. Hattie began to sing. "Swing low, sweet chariot, coming for to carry me home..." The men joined in. Byron looked over at Lamar and saw tears in his eyes, and in his sadness felt something sweet, something overwhelming, something simple. He knew what he'd be doing the next few days, weeks: rescuing, helping, and God willing, letting go of the pain and guilt he'd been carrying for so long.

II. The Book of Lamar

1 The Promised Land

The Apache helicopter angled down toward a cluster of low dusty buildings the same buff color as the desert that held them. From between two squat warehouses a truck emerged with several men in the bed. One shouldered an RPG and aimed it at the chopper. With the truck in his crosshairs, Lamar let loose a hellfire missile. There was no sound to the explosion, but he felt it like the rush of an orgasm, an all-consuming satisfaction. The truck became lost in a cloud of smoke, and out of the smoke dove several men, as if acrobats doing a routine. But after hitting the sand, their bodies remained still, crumpled.

Lamar lifted up toward the sky and caught sight of another helicopter, not friendly, rising from behind a giant dune. It was painted like a dragon, and the gun attached to its belly spit little balls of fire that quickly gathered speed and streaked by him without making contact.

Lamar shouted into his mouthpiece. "Cap, this is Nomad 5. Enemy bird approaching. I repeat enemy bird at eleven o'clock coming at me fast. Can you take 'em out?"

There was no answer.

"Cap, under heavy fire. Do you read me?"

The enemy helicopter sprayed at him again, but still didn't hit.

No answer from his captain. Lamar had a sweaty grip on the cyclic pitch control, but when he tried to move out of the incoming fire, nothing happened. Then he heard a triple thump of bullets hit the machine. The chopper shuddered and refused to respond when he frantically thrust the controls in one direction and then another. He started spinning, spiraling downward. Everything slowed to a standstill. He was weightless and unafraid. The sky and desert floated around him in an extremely slow rotation, a merry-go-round winding down. There was a sharp smell of burning flesh in the air.

The dragon chopper hovered next to him. In the cockpit he saw his grandfather and his uncle. His grandfather's face was bloated and his lips were purple. His uncle's lips were so red it looked like he wore lipstick. They were talking to him, beckoning him, telling him not to fear.

"I'm too young to die," he mumbled.

"Lamar, wake up," said Abigail. He opened his eyes and saw his mother at the window with a thumb and forefinger separating the blinds. "You thrashing around like you having a conniption fit."

Lamar rolled over on the sofa and pulled the blanket over his head. He had been up late at a neighbor's, playing Apache Air Assault. It was Saturday and all he wanted was to sleep in. Then it struck him that the flutter of the helicopters was real. There were sirens, too.

"What's that?" he mumbled in a froggy voice.

"Something goin' on in the park." She twisted her head, looking up at the sky through the blinds.

Lamar immediately thought of Lester who, since they had moved to Oakland, spent most of his time in the park. A few days before, Lamar had seen him with his new buddies sitting on a bench, drinking tall boys wrapped in paper sacks. A part of him hoped Lester was in trouble. They could be rid of him. He lifted his head and faced his mom. "Where's Lester?" he asked.

"Why, he out looking for a job."

"Uh-huh," said Lamar with a snort.

"Don't you uh-huh me. You sixteen now. Instead a being up in other people's business, you could get an after-school job, you know, contribute."

"I got basketball practice."

"Well, the money Byron give us ain't goin' last forever."

"Especially when it keep disappearing from Grannie's cookie jar."

Abigail turned away from the window. Her many bracelets tinkled as she moved her arm. Her earrings swayed and her perfectly coiffed hair had a coppery glow. Her long nails gleamed red. She looked like she was ready for a night on the town. But that was pretty much how she looked all the time. "You know, I don't like your attitude, like you insinuating something."

Hattie had come to Lamar a couple days before, asking him if he had used some of the money from the jar for food or something. She told him it was the second time in a month someone had cleaned her out. After they got settled in West Oakland, Byron had sent Hattie a check for two thousand dollars, which she deposited in a bank and took out little by little. Abigail, feeling that she was the only one competent enough to run the household, had been incensed that Byron hadn't sent the money to her. It had been Georgette who convinced Byron to make the check out to Hattie rather than Abigail. After they buried Joe back in Mississippi, Hattie had said it was time to move on. She didn't want to overstay their welcome at Byron's house. And Abigail was obsessed with getting to the Astrodome where Lester had been transferred. He said was like the Hilton compared to the Superdome and they should all come and join him. So they packed up the Gray Goose again, and Byron and Georgette drove them to Houston. Five minutes after meeting Lester, Georgette could see that Abigail was attracted to trouble like a June bug to a porch light. "Byron, honey," Georgette had said. "Best you make the check out to Hattie."

Lamar jumped up, pulled on some jeans, and went toward the front door.

"Don't go out there," said Abigail.

"I'm just goin' look."

He stepped out onto the porch of their lower unit in a four-unit building and looked up at the sky. He stumbled down the steps and traversed the walkway that led to a gate in the cyclone fence. On either side were small patches of sandy dirt full of holes from the neighbor's dogs. He went out the gate and looked toward the park less than half a block away. Three helicopters hovered overhead and he could see at least five police cars parked at various angles along the street next to the park.

Hattie heard the racket, too, and came out the front door behind him. "Stay close by, baby," his grandmother said to him.

"Wouldn't be surprised if Lester caught up in that," he said.

"So this the paradise they's hoping for? I'm 'bout ready to hightail it back to Mississippi, and I never thought I'd say that," said Hattie.

"If Lester involved over there, maybe the cookie jar won't get raided no more."

Hattie shook her head. "We don't know it was him."

"What? You think it was Letisha so as she could make a donation over at the church?" said Lamar.

With a tight smile across her face, Hattie nodded. She took Lamar's arm. "Please stay close, baby."

Thanks to the Guiding Light Baptist Church, they had

a one-bedroom apartment in West Oakland near Lowell Park. If there was one thing Lester was good at, it was talking a good talk. Once the family arrived in Houston, he went to the relocation office set up by the Red Cross and chatted up one of the volunteers, charming her with his slick manners and suggestive comments. He got her to write letters saying what a fine, church-going family they were. The Guiding Light responded that they could accommodate one more family, but all they had available was a minimally furnished one-bedroom. Abigail and Lester got the bedroom, and Hattie set up a cot in the utility room behind the kitchen. Lamar got the sofa in the living room, which was separated by sliding wooden doors from the dining room, where Letisha had a blow-up mattress on the floor.

Lamar and Hattie went back in the house, and Hattie started straightening up his sofa bed, folding the covers and picking up his dirty clothes.

In the kitchen Lamar ran into Lester coming in the back door. Lamar figured he must have climbed over the wood fence around the backyard.

"Hey," said Lester.

"What's up?" said Lamar. Lamar went to the sink and got a glass of water. The loud drone of the helicopters was still in the air. He opened the blinds over the sink and looked up at the sky. The room was flooded with light.

Lester shaded his eyes. "Shit! Cut the light." He was wound up like an alarm clock and his pupils were black moons.

Lamar turned to face his father. "What's going on out there?"

"Some idiot shot a cop." He smacked his dry lips and wiped his forehead with a handkerchief. "Guess some nosey-ass neighbors called the cops on some brothers in the park. Got nasty. The dude pulls a gun and they blast him. But not before he get off a shot. Damn, nothing get the boys in blue riled up like 'officer down' coming over the radio." He spoke in short hurried phrases with gasps of air in between. Lester's crack habit was nothing new. It had started back in New Orleans. Every Friday, soon after Abigail got her paycheck from Winn-Dixie, the money would be gone.

"They friends of yours?" said Lamar with a smirk.

"Lamar, be cool. I don't need your shit right now."

A toilet flushed and Abigail came out of the bathroom into the kitchen. "Lester, baby, I thought I heard your voice." She was purring like a kitten. "You want something to eat?"

"No, shug. I got to sleep." He was shielding his eyes from the light.

"You okay?" She went over to the window, reached around Lamar, and closed the blinds, giving him a cautionary look.

"Just tired," said Lester. He stared at a shiny metal garlic press lying on the counter. He picked it up and started nervously flipping the handle back and forth. "What the hell kinda contraption is that?"

"It come in a box of kitchen stuff they sent over from the church," said Abigail. "Momma say it for squeezing garlic."

Lester dropped it with a clang as if it suddenly burned his hand. It made Abigail jump. "Hope she ain't planning on filling up our food with garlic. You know I can't take that."

"She know that, baby." Abigail picked up the press and held it in front of Lester's dilated pupils. "Look, it never been used. I was goin' throw it out, but Momma say you can't just throw away donations like that."

Lester took a step back, and then looked suspiciously at a pot of beans simmering on the stove. "That smell funky. You sure she didn't put no garlic in it?"

"I'm sure." Abigail sighed. Even she, normally so

attentive to Lester, seemed to be bored with the garlic conversation.

Lamar finished his water and put the glass in the sink. "Ma, you seen my iPod?" He looked at Lester, but Lester was back to staring fixedly at the garlic press Abigail had laid back on the counter.

"Why no, baby. You need to clean up that mess around the sofa. I bet it's there."

"No, I looked."

Lamar went from leaning against the counter to standing up to his full height. He was already taller than his father. "You seen it?" he asked Lester.

"No, and I don't see why you can't keep track of your own shit."

Lamar took a step toward the center of the room. "It's pretty hard when so many things go missing around here."

Abigail narrowed her eyes. "Lamar, you better—"

"It's all right, Abby." Lester raised his eyes and smiled. "Son, I'm goin' buy you the latest iPod with everything on it. I got me a line on a job. Pay's good. And Abby, I got my eyes on a car the neighbors got for sale. Things are looking up. Just give me a little slack. Now if you don't mind, I'm goin' get some rest." He turned around and headed for the back bedroom.

Abigail stared at Lamar and shook her head. She raised her finger and wagged it at him.

Lamar walked out of the room.

Hattie's soft black duffle on wheels sat by the front door, holding all that she had in the world, including what she had accumulated in the few months she had lived in Oakland. She sat between Lamar and Letisha on the sofa. Letisha had a balled-up tissue in her hand and kept wiping her nose. Abigail was back in her bedroom; they were unsure if she would make an appearance to say goodbye.

Abigail and her mother had fought bitterly in the kitchen a few days before. When Hattie brought up leaving, she said that Lester was in part to blame. Abigail flew into a rage. She claimed that the reason Lester stayed away from the house so much was because Hattie made life uncomfortable for him, had never liked him, and was always trying to sabotage their relationship.

"You and Lester don't need no sabotaging," Hattie had said. "You two been a sinking ship for a long time with no help from nobody." Abigail was unpacking groceries, and she hurtled a box of frozen peas across the room, just missing Hattie's head by a few inches. Lamar had rushed into the kitchen. "What the hell you doing, Ma? Jesus!" Abigail had broken into tears, and fled to her room, slamming the door.

Now his grandmother, the only person in the family he could half-relate to, was going back to Mississippi. Hattie put her hand on Lamar's knee and squeezed it. A siren screamed over on Adeline. Lamar hated to see his grandmother tense up every time she heard one. And then another went by. He wanted to reach over and cover her ears. "You see?" said Hattie. "I don't even feel comfortable going to the corner store. I sure am goin' miss you kids, though. I hope to God you can talk some sense into your mother. You shouldn't have to bear that cross, but I been no good at it at all. There no reason you shouldn't be just fine what with the church still paying the rent and utilities, Abby's unemployment coming through, and the food stamps. Of course the money Mr. Byron give us is long gone, but still."

A silence fell on the room as it often did when the three of them were together. Letisha sniffled and Lamar tapped his foot. It was a Saturday morning, and with the sirens fading into the distance, all they could hear outside was the faint rush of traffic on I-880. Into the relative silence came the honking of a flock of geese flying over.

The Canadian geese had nearly taken over Lake Merritt and the parks in the surrounding area. They waddled around in the shade in Lowell Park, and left the grass full of goose droppings. Between the droppings and the suspicious element—including Lester—who congregated around the picnic tables in the afternoon and evening, most of the neighborhood families had ceased using it as a picnic spot.

"Momma's goin' take that cleaning job," said Letisha. A woman from the church had been cleaning for a lady in Piedmont, but she had to give it up for health reasons. Letisha told Abigail about it, and Abigail had gone to interview the week before. They were all surprised when she decided to take it. She had moaned and groaned about it being such a downward career move from her checker job at Winn-Dixie. But it was something she could do under the table while still getting her unemployment checks.

"That good news," said Hattie.

"Byron meeting you at the New Orleans airport, huh?" said Lamar.

"Yeah, he driving me up to Columbia, God love him. He already done so much, I hated to ask him."

"You didn't," said Lamar. "I did."

"Tell him 'God Bless' from me," said Letisha.

"Bet he glad he don't have to put up with me no more," Lamar said with a chuckle.

"Oh, y'all got off to a bad start, but every time I talk to him, he ask about you. He real fond of you," said Hattie.

Lamar laughed again. "Not too fond, I hope."

"All God's children deserve respect," said Hattie.

"Oh, Grannie, I was just kidding. He done real good by us."

Hattie sighed. "I'ma looking forward to being close to Joe. That's been hard, him so far away. Can't put no flowers on his grave."

Letisha's sniffling turned into full-blown tears.

A taxi pulled up in front of the house and honked.

"That the taxi or them geese?" joked Hattie.

"Guess that's you, Grannie," gurgled Letisha. They all stood up.

A door opened in the back of the apartment, and Abigail's red Chinese slippers slapped across the wood floors at a hurried pace. "Momma? That your cab?"

"'Fraid so."

"Glad I woke up in time to say goodbye." They all knew she hadn't been sleeping. As usual, she was made up and her hair looked perfect. She moved toward Hattie and embraced her tentatively. "Take care of yourself, Momma. And call as soon as you get there."

"Hope things work out with your new job." She seemed to have more to say, but stopped short.

"You take care, too," said Abigail.

Lamar was angry with his mother and blamed her for driving Grannie away. He stared at the way she was dressed and thought she looked like a whore. Once, when he had complained to cousin Sofia about his mother, she had explained a little about the family history.

"It a shame," Sofia had said, "how your ma and Hattie never been close. Hattie always been strict with her, taking charge of her punishments and not sparing the rod. It was to her father she always ran for comfort. Things didn't get no easier when Thomas' death struck the family. Abigail was about eleven when Thomas died. She knew her momma favored Thomas. Hattie couldn't help reminding Abby in small ways that she was somehow lesser. Still, Abby adored her older brother and felt his loss so deep. During that time your ma alternated from being barely a spec on her mother's radar to suddenly, without warning, being the target of her wrath.

"The decision to move the family to New Orleans again threw their lives into upheaval," Sofia continued.

"Abigail was desperate to be accepted at her new high school. Oh, did she love her some attention she got from boys. Her parents still in too much of a fog from Thomas' death and leaving behind the place where they had lived their whole lives, hardly noticed her becoming a woman. She took to slapping on lots of makeup and trying out different hairstyles. And some of those outfits she put together…I tell ya. Occasionally Hattie tell her she look like a common streetwalker, but didn't seem to have the energy or the desire to steer her on the right path.

"She about sixteen when she got pregnant with Letisha. She dropped out of school and moved in with Lester. He was older. It caused Hattie to snap out of her stupor, mostly because of how much Abigail's actions were hurting Joe. She began her campaign against Lester, but all it seemed to do was push Abby further into Lester's arms. But when Lester lost his job at the filling station and Abigail became pregnant with Lamar, she had no choice but to move home again. She kept saying it was just temporarily until Lester get back on his feet. Well, you kinda know the rest."

They walked Hattie out to the cab and said their goodbyes. Instead of going back in the house, Lamar headed down the street. He wasn't anxious to go back into a house that would seem empty without his grandmother. A walk might clear his head.

"Where you goin'?" said Abigail. "Don't go near that park."

"I won't."

2 Lips of the Adulterous Woman Drip Honey

A cool breeze came in the window and sent a chill through Lamar, still in his basketball shorts, still sweaty from his game in the park. Summer had arrived according to the school calendar, though its warmth was trapped in the June fog that rolled in every afternoon. They had been in Oakland almost a year and adjusting to the new climate hadn't been easy. At times he longed to feel the heat of New Orleans on his skin. But the memories of the day they retrieved his grandfather's body hung raw and heavy in his mind, making him glad they had left the city for a place where it was easier to breath.

He got up to close the window and looked outside. The tranquility of the house was about to come to an end. Coming in the front door from work, his mother adjusted the secondhand shopping bag—filled with cast-off articles given to her by the women she worked for—to her other arm so she could fish the keys from her purse.

"Hey, Ma," said Lamar.

Abigail sashayed into the room with a purpose. "Lamar, honey, you just the person I want to see."

Her puffed-out lips and the way her heels pounded the wood floors made him fall back on the couch with a silly laugh. "What is it now?"

She put her hand on her hip. "Are you high?"

"I was playing b-ball."

"Uh-huh. You plan on spending the whole summer playing pick-up ball and smoking weed behind the school? Oh yeah. I know all about that."

Lamar threw up his hands and looked toward the ceiling, praying for deliverance from whatever his mother was about to propose. She had that look in her eye.

"Don't you think it's time you start saving for college?" She spoke with the determination of someone who had broached the subject a hundred times and been ignored.

Lamar, however, couldn't remember her ever uttering the word "college," at least not in reference to him. "College? Really?"

"Some of the ladies I work for have yards that need work." She had a growing client list and had taken to cleaning houses more than anyone would have expected. "Why Miz Thompson's backyard look like a jungle, and I know just the person who can take care of it. I already told her I come from a family of landscapers, and that the day my daddy died he was doing yard work in Lakeview, one of the finest neighborhoods of New Orleans. He wasn't one to let a little thing like a hurricane called Katrina stop him. When the levees broke and Lakeview flooded, he was swept away."

"But that's a lie, Ma." After moving to New Orleans, Joe had given up yard work and instead worked with his brother in a small repair shop across the bridge in Bywater.

"I tell you, Miz Thompson put her French nails to her lips and shook her head all sympathetic like, close to tears."

"Why you got to lie about Grandpa?"

"I'm *trying* to get you work," she groaned. "I told her you used to help your granddaddy and know quite a bit about plants and such. And that you's a good worker." She lowered her voice and batted her eyelashes. "I also let it be known how big and strong you are, how you remind people of Taye Diggs."

"Say what?"

"She don't know who that is, so I tell her Denzel then. You ever bit as handsome as Denzel Washington. And she says to me with a laugh, 'Abby, you got a point about the yard. My husband travels all over the country for work, but he doesn't seem to be able to find his way to the backyard.' That one's in the bag. We got our first client."

"We?"

"Don't you want to get paid? Start that college fund?"

Abigail smiled as if thrilled with the brilliance of her new idea, but for Lamar, the idea of college was nothing new. He was in favor of anything that would get him away from Abigail, Letisha, and Lester.

The next Saturday, Lamar and his mother were on the AC Transit C bus lurching toward the tree-lined avenues of Piedmont. They were on the third leg of the journey to Mrs. Thompson's house.

"You got to go all this way every day, like two transfers and everything?" said Lamar.

"Uh-huh," said Abigail. "Now don't forget. You gotta be nice to Miz Thompson, seeing as how she such a lovely woman and all. She give me all kinds of stuff like jewelry and clothes she don't wear no more, though it look like new to me. The other day she give me a Kay Unger suit, I'll have you know!"

"Now where you gonna wear a Kate Ugger suit? Whatever that is."

"It's Kay Unger. And you never know."

"Why you gushing over this white woman? I thought

we left being servants to white people back in the South."

"Well, listen to you. Maybe when you go out and get a job, start pulling your own weight, you'll have a leg to stand on."

Lamar snorted. "You mean like Lester."

"Your Daddy's been sober a month and he been pounding the pavement. But I think there some kinda backlash against us Katrina people, like we been given too much already."

Lamar slapped his forehead. "Oh, that's why he don't got a job!" Lester had, for the most part, moved out of the apartment, though he made periodic visits, usually when he needed something. The last time he had stopped by, not two weeks before, he was as cranked up as ever.

"He your own flesh and blood and you can't even cut him a little slack. Shame on you." They rode the rest of the way in silence.

The house on La Salle Avenue was another ten-minute walk from the bus stop. The neighborhood made Lamar think it was just a matter of time before someone stopped them and said they shouldn't be there. They got to the house, and as much as Lamar didn't want to be impressed by white opulence, he couldn't help himself. The two-story Mediterranean mansion had a manicured lawn, trimmed hedges, and large trees. Why did they need Lamar?

The person who answered the door also took Lamar by surprise. At first glance, he figured she must be the daughter of the lady of such a fine house. She wore tight denim shorts and a flimsy yellow knit blouse that buttoned up the front. It was cut in a half-moon shape above the navel to expose her flat tummy, like he had seen girls at his high school wear. But his mother addressed her as Mrs. Thompson, and on closer examination, the crow's feet around her eyes betrayed her as a woman in her forties. Despite the affluence surrounding her, the turquoise rings on her tan fingers, the carefully applied makeup, Mrs. Thompson reminded Lamar of a girl at school they called TTB, short for Trailer Trash Barbie. It didn't matter how much makeup TTB wore or what she did with her hair, she couldn't hide the ordinary, almost sickly look of her face and her outdated sense of style. The teal blue eyeshadow was a dead giveaway. According to his mother, Mrs. Thompson came from an old money family and traced her line back to the Mayflower, but Lamar still saw something common in her, a simplicity that allowed her to go from point A to point B as long as there were no dips or curves. It didn't help that she was a bit hatchet-faced, with pallid skin that quickly flushed when she stuck out her hand upon meeting Lamar. On the upside, she had a shapely body and knew how to dress to accentuate it, even if the style was inappropriate for her age.

They walked down the hall past rooms that looked like something out of a magazine. The island in the middle of the kitchen was bigger than their whole kitchen at home.

"I better get working on the dishes," said Abigail. "Don't want to waste no more of your time."

Mrs. Thompson opened the French doors to the backyard. "Oh, Abby, relax. You work too hard."

"Well, you're not paying me to sit around and gab."

Lamar glanced over his shoulder and gave his mother a narrow look. He saw the same subservient side of her he had witnessed when she was around Lester, and he didn't like it. And yet, as she began to hum a Toni Braxton song and sway at the sink, he wondered if, behind those clumpy eyelashes and the waterproof eyeliner, she wasn't planning something.

The backyard was the polar opposite of the trimmed and manicured front. Mrs. Thompson explained that her husband wouldn't let the gardener touch it because he had a project in mind that he wanted to do himself. "He's so stubborn. I'm afraid hell will freeze over before he gets to it. I don't even like to go out here what with all the bugs and God knows what else running around. There could be a family of Mexicans camping out back here and I wouldn't even know it." The deep back area pushed up against a wooded hillside, and the fence at the end of it was barely visible. It was full of weeds and invasive plants: Japanese honeysuckle, Bishop's weed, and English ivy.

"I think you could start with the weeds, and then maybe trim back the honeysuckle. I'll show you where the tools are."

Lamar worked to the tunes of Lil' Wayne on the new, probably stolen iPod Lester had given him to replace the one that had gone missing. It was a hot day and Lamar quickly worked up a sweat. A little after noon, Mrs. Thompson came out with a sandwich and lemonade. She sat with him while he ate and stared at the triangle of sweat on his T-shirt. Lamar nervously took a sip of lemonade, but the jostle of ice cubes made half the sip spill out of his mouth and onto the crotch of his faux army fatigues. He looked down at the widening damp spot and she did, too.

"I forgot to bring you a napkin," she said, her cheeks coloring. "Anyway, I think you've done enough for today."

Lamar looked at the pile of weeds he had created and shrugged. He wiped his mouth with the back of his hand.

Mrs. Thompson stood up and touched a bead of sweat at her temple. "Man, it's hot. I bet you'd like a shower about now."

Lamar screwed up his face and said, "But I…"

She had already turned and headed for the house.

He put down his glass and looked toward the kitchen. Earlier, he had seen his mother and Mrs. Thompson talking and laughing on either side of the kitchen island.

Now Abigail was nowhere in sight. A big fat fly landed on the edge of his glass and he watched it rub its front legs together in anticipation. He mimicked the gesture by rubbing his hands together. A pigeon cooed from the eaves of the house.

Just inside the kitchen, Mrs. Thompson stood by the back stairs and stared at him through the glass. "I'll be damned," he said.

He stood up and went inside. She was halfway up the stairs, but he hesitated at the bottom.

"The shower's up here," she said over her shoulder. When still he hesitated, she sighed and turned around, looking down at him with tilted head as if he were a lost puppy. "What is it? Your mom? Don't worry. I sent her to the store. She won't be back for at least an hour."

She beckoned him up the stairway with a sureness passed down from her people and honed over the centuries. "Cat got your tongue?"

"No, ma'am."

"Ma'am? Lordy, boy," she said in a Georgia accent not that different from his people back in Mississippi. "Sorry, didn't mean to say "boy." But you are kind of a boy, aren't you? A fully developed boy, I imagine."

"Yes, ma'am." His development was growing by the second. The unexpected thrill of what looked like an end to the sexual drought that began when he moved to Oakland made him tingle all over. Back in New Orleans, he'd had flings with girls in hidden places that were either still under water or washed away by the flood. Lamar had seen photos of a nearly leveled Ninth Ward, and he lamented the fact that if he ever went back to New Orleans, he wouldn't be able to point out the exact places where he had had his first sweet tastes of sex. But those were girls. Now he anticipated being with a woman, even if she was a bit homely. He had no problem that she was more than double his age—in fact, he found the prospect of an older woman exciting, not to mentioned what she represented. She was the flipside of his life: a confident, privileged, rich woman who had superseded her physical shortcomings and knew what she wanted. He was drawn to her power. Though already 6'2" and a forward on the varsity basketball team—"solid as a live oak," Hattie liked to say—his strength didn't yet have substance. Off the court, he often felt like the ninety-pound weakling black boy that used to get picked on in grade school.

Mrs. Thompson giggled, raking her yellow hair out of her face with long jeweled fingers, and continued up the stairs.

When he exited the marble and glass shower stall, she stood in the doorway, holding the largest and fluffiest towel he had ever seen.

"My, my, my," she said. "Couldn't be better if I'd ordered you right out of a catalog."

In the shower he had managed to tamper down his excitement by thinking about basketball practice, but under her appreciative gaze, he began to rise again. He instinctively moved his hands to cover his crotch.

She laughed and tossed him the towel. Then she turned on her heels and walked across the hall to the guest bedroom.

"I'm sorry," he mumbled. He had exploded about ten seconds after entering her.

"Don't worry about it." She got up, grabbed the condom with a tissue, and walked across to the bathroom. He heard the toilet flush, followed by the water of the shower. He sat up on the side of the bed, a grin on his face and the unexpected thrill working its way up and down his body. In the next moment, a sobering vision of Byron popped into his head. Byron stood in front of him, arms akimbo and shaking his head as if to say, "Lamar, what are you doing?"

"Damn, go away," Lamar said out loud. "You got no business here."

After a few more pleasurable, and lengthier, times with Loretta Thompson, she turned to him one day with a twinkle in her eye and said, "My friend, Sybil, needs some work in her garden."

The summer progressed with Lamar honing his personal skills and building up his confidence in the Oakland hills while doing just enough yard work to make things look legitimate. The thrill of constant sex blinded him to what role his mother might be playing in his new life of pleasure. He was seeing the insides of fancy houses, being served lemonade, iced tea, and all he wanted to eat by rich ladies. It felt like a sweetest payback for the troubles he had been through since Katrina.

One day, on a break from his yard work at the Thompson's, he headed inside to go to the bathroom. He saw his mother and Loretta in the kitchen and snuck around the corner just out of sight.

"Here's for this week of cleaning and yard work," said Loretta. She gave Abigail a check. Then she pulled a few bills out of her wallet. Lamar peeked around the corner to see her fold them, take Abigail's hand, and put them into her palm. "And this is for Lamar's college fund," she giggled.

Abigail held the crumpled bills to her chest and bowed her head. "Oh, Miz Thompson, you been so good to us." She acted as if she might start to weep.

"Please, Abby. I told you to call me Loretta."

On the bus home, Lamar cleared his throat. "So, Ma, I was wondering how that college fund's going?"

Abigail had been looking out the window and made a sudden twist of her head toward Lamar. "She tell you something?"

"I kinda figured it out."

"Well, you said you'd be wanting to go to college. Now how we goin' do that? The yard work don't cut it."

"You shoulda told me."

"Lamar, baby, we been through some hard times. Coming out here was a good thing. I want you kids to have advantages I never had, and the only way to do that is with a little extra help."

"How much extra help she give you?"

"Not that much. More like you'll be going to junior college."

"How much, Ma?"

Abigail turned to look out the window again.

"Don't you worry about it. It going in a special account."

"And the other ladies, too?"

"Uh-huh."

"Damn. I'm a gigolo." He said it with a mix of surprise and pride.

"Shush. Don't say that."

Lamar laughed. He thought it was funny. His mom a pimp. He guessed that was what a black boy in Oakland— a Katrina refugee—had to do to go to college. "Damn," he thought. "I'm getting paid to have fun."

3 Betray Me to Mine Enemies

A couple years after Lamar's first venture into the pleasure market, he entered the kitchen and found his mother standing over the stove mixing up some Hamburger Helper, the Cheeseburger Macaroni variety. He asked her if there was enough in his college account to buy a used car to go back and forth to City College in San Francisco, the school where he had registered for the fall term. The city was a dream to him and he fantasized what it would be like to eventually move there. The day his mother first mentioned that she and Lester were thinking of San Francisco was so clear in his mind. They had been in Byron's van, escaping Katrina, and he turned around and high-fived her. It seemed like ancient history, but yes, they had made it—well, almost. West Oakland was an improvement over where he grew up, but there was still a long bridge between him and his goal.

Abigail turned down the fire and stirred the mess, which gave off a muddled smell of fatty hamburger and plastic cheese.

"Ma?" Lamar said, trying to look her in the eye.

"Yes, baby, well, not quite that much."

"How much?" He had a sinking feeling. He thought of all the times Lester had stopped by, slinking past Lamar without even looking at him, buzzed halfway to the sky. He would stay a couple of hours and then sneak out.

"Not sure exactly."

"Ma, look at me. After all those ladies? There's got to be money in there."

She turned around, still holding the wooden spoon in her hand as if to defend herself. "Life's so expensive here. I had no idea."

"What you saying?"

"I just had to borrow a little from time to time to make ends meet. I'll pay it back."

He grabbed the spoon hand and held it tight. "Goddamn it! How much is fucking left?" he screamed.

"Settle down, baby. I'm gonna ask for a raise from my ladies and start paying it back."

"It's that son of a bitch Lester, isn't it?"

With her free hand she slapped him across the face. "Don't ever talk about your father that way. He trying so hard."

He grabbed the hand that had just slapped him and pushed her back against the stove. "Bullshit. When you goin' to get into your head that man's toxic? All he do is take from us."

Letisha stood in the kitchen door. "Leave her alone," she said to Lamar.

There was a crusty burning smell in the air. Lamar dropped his mother's arms and turned toward his sister. "Oh, you're going to defend her now? Your mother, the pimp. Your mother giving my money to Lester so he can go out and buy drugs. What's the Bible say about that, Letisha?"

"Sarah," Letisha said calmly, as if she hadn't heard

Lamar's tirade.

"What?"

"My name is Sarah now. I changed it. There no Letisha in the Bible." Lamar stared at her in disbelief. "Anyway," she continued, "that's ill-begotten money. Dirty. Better you be rid of it."

"You're both crazy. Better I be rid of y'all." He turned back to his mother. "Tomorrow we're going to the bank and you're giving me every last penny that's left in the account."

Abigail turned off the stove and waved at the smoke coming off the burning meat. She flipped on the exhaust fan and it struggled, starting with loud grating noise, and then built up into something like a car without a muffler. "There is no account," she said softly.

Lamar turned off the fan. "What did you say?"

"There's no damn account!" she yelled.

Lamar balled his fists. Rage spread through him, a brushfire consuming his oxygen.

"Don't, Lamar," said Letisha.

Lamar turned and ran out of the room. He threw a couple things in a backpack and went out the door, slamming it behind him. He beat up the sidewalks with his sneakers, kicking cans out into the street. There was a garbage bin on the corner, and he knocked it over, spilling its contents onto the sidewalk: urine-soaked Pampers, beer bottles, soup cans, and the remnants of Chinese food spilling out of a Styrofoam container.

By the time he reached the BART station, he had calmed somewhat, but he was still ready to clobber the first person that looked at him funny. He got on a train to San Francisco.

In the city he transferred to a Haight Street bus and got off at Baker. Across from the stop was Buena Vista Park, a swath of dark green, tall trees and vegetation, primeval and foreboding in the late afternoon light. This was the place he had heard about.

He started up the wide stone steps, a sort of rustic outdoor version of the staircase in Byron's house in Columbia, reaching a landing and then splitting in two directions to the top. He pictured Byron standing at the foot of the stairs of the house in Columbia, posture slightly recoiled as he stared up at the portraits at the top. Damn! It had happened again, Byron coming into his brain for no reason. It had been over two years since they left New Orleans, and yet images of those ten days starting when Byron and Georgette picked his family up in the Ninth Ward and ending when they dropped them off in Houston were as real to Lamar as the last two years. Byron had even appeared in his dreams, a ghostly figure in the corner watching him have sex.

A Brown Creeper sang out from a Coast Live Oak at the top of the stairs, a sweet high squeak that could be a warning. He took the paved path to the right and continued up the hill, but quickly came to an intersection of three paths where he had to make another decision. He took the one that sloped up to the left. There was the occasional tweeting of birds and the rustle of leaves as squirrels scampered over them, but for the most part it was quiet. Then, in the distance, he heard an incongruous sound, which he soon realized was the thomp of tennis balls as he came upon an opening in the trees and looked down on two tennis courts, both occupied. He wondered how the players could see the ball in the failing light, and how they stood the cold wind coming off the ocean bringing with it the fog. He had left the house in such a rush that he forgot a jacket. Between the chilly breeze and his nervousness, Lamar shivered and bent his head down, picking up his pace as he climbed the path away from the courts.

As he got halfway up the hill he began to see people coming down the walkway: a pair of joggers, a woman walking six dogs of various sizes on an assortment of leashes, a man hand-in-hand with two small children. A woman with a golden Labrador walked briskly, and then when she saw him, slowed, giving him a wide berth as he went by. Others glanced at him, hands tightening on leashes, ears pricking up.

A gust of wind punctuated the tense air with the sound of Eucalyptus leaves rattling from a double-trunked old tree, shedding its bark and exposing a smooth, lighter underside. It didn't seem to be a park where many black people walked, or any people of color for that matter, and he felt conspicuous not running or walking a dog, or playing a sport. He wondered if he had been misinformed by what he had read on the Internet. All he saw were a bunch of white people in a park doing normal, white people park things.

Farther up the hill a man sat on a log under a Monterey Cypress while his terrier explored the area on a long leash. He was middle-aged and stocky with brown curly hair. Lamar got the first inkling that things weren't all lily-white when he felt the man's eyes follow him as he progressed up the hill. He glanced back and the man didn't break his stare, provoking a gut reaction of anger in Lamar. Why didn't the man mind his own business?

As he got near the top of the hill, Lamar saw more men by themselves, some with dogs and some not. They walked without purpose, like zombies, their heads down until someone passed and they furtively snuck a look. More stone steps took him up to the crown of the park where, on a small, round grassy meadow, a young couple was doing yoga. Lamar stopped a moment to capture the view of the white rolling fog blanketing the city as the downtown lights came to life. At one point he could see an expanse of skyline in one direction and, in the other, the steeples of a church with the towers of the Golden Gate Bridge in the background peeking above the fog. It hit him how far he had come—from New Orleans to a city of hills, a city on the rise, a cool city smothered in fog. He found a bench nearby that looked out over the city and sat with the idea that something was going to happen in this magical place. A grey squirrel hopped up on the end of the bench and stared at him as if it, too, wondered what a tall, muscular black teenager was doing in its park.

A short time later the man with the terrier walked in his direction. The squirrel jumped off the bench, and the terrier tugged at the end of its leash to chase it. The man stopped at the bench.

"Mind if I sit down?"

Lamar found himself without the ability to speak and merely nodded. With the squirrel now out of sight, the dog sniffed at Lamar's feet. He reached down and scratched its head.

"That's SuzyQ," said the man.

Lamar nodded again. He tried to act nonchalant, but his legs vibrated, poised to jump up and run.

"Nice view, huh?"

"Hmm," Lamar mumbled. It became clear that he couldn't go through with this. His whole body felt like the jittery images of characters in his video games after they were shot and just before they faded away. But his cheek still stung where his mother had slapped him, reminding him that he couldn't go home, at least not right away. He didn't even have enough money to take BART back across the bay.

"Aren't you cold?" said the man as he burrowed down into his jean jacket worn over a green hoodie. SuzyQ had curled up at his owner's feet.

"Nah. I'm cool."

The man laughed. "Was that supposed to be ironic?"

Lamar shrugged. A gust of wind swept through him and he tried his best not to react. "All right. Yeah, it's a little chilly."

"I think we're making progress. I'm Matt by the way."

"What you mean progress?"

"Just, you know, a normal conversation."

"Conversation? That why you're here?"

"Why are you here? I assume you didn't come here by chance on a chilly evening with no jacket just to take in the view."

"You mean people like me aren't supposed to be here?"

"It's a park. It's open to everybody."

"Yeah. Sure." Lamar turned his head to look at Matt for the first time. "You're not scared of me?"

"Is that what you're into? Making people scared?"

"No. I just needed to get away so I could think."

"Where do you live?"

"Oakland."

Matt laughed. "Come on. You came all the way over here from Oakland so you could think?"

"What do you want me to say?"

"Look. You can sit here and freeze your ass off if you think that will help. I'm going someplace warm. I'll buy you a cup of coffee if you want."

Over coffee at a place called Coffee to the People on Haight Street, Matt seemed relieved to find out that Lamar was eighteen. Lamar admitted that he was kind of running away from home.

"I don't think you call it that when you're eighteen," said Matt.

"Whatever."

"Do you want to talk about it?"

"Not really."

"What do you want to do?"

"Don't know."

"Is this where I'm supposed to invite you to my place?"

"If you're cool with that."

"You tell me. Should I be cool with that?"

"Depends."

"On what?"

"If you see something you like," said Lamar. In the warmth of the café and in the exchange of conversation, Lamar began to feel his mojo, the confidence he had gained with the ladies in Oakland. He wasn't sure how it would work with Matt, but he could tell from the expression on Matt's face that he was taken aback and pleased at the same time—the formula for excitement that had always worked before.

"I wasn't expecting that," said Matt.

"I know. You were just looking for a little conversation over an organic, fair trade, bullshit latte."

They stared at each other for a moment. Lamar could see Matt's mind working, calculating the risks while his loins were heating up. He found it exciting to put someone in that position, knowing someone wanted him. That's what always got him hot with the Housewives of Oakland as he called them, that exact moment when their eyes took a turn and desire pushed them over the edge.

"I don't pay," said Matt.

"Who said anything about money?" He had to play his cards right. Truth was, he was broke. If he was really going to leave home, he needed an income. But Matt was an experiment. Could he even do it with a man? He had to find that out first.

Outside the café, SuzyQ jumped up and yipped twice as Matt untied the leash. They walked to his place, a top-floor corner apartment of an art deco building on Buena Vista East. The views of Downtown and the East Bay were stunning even through the fog. Lamar stood at the window and fantasized living in such a place where all the people in his life who had put him down would have to look up to him, where he could silence the voice of his mother who said he would never amount to anything because he couldn't even support his own family.

"Do you want a beer?" said Matt. "Oh, wait. You're not old enough."

"Shut uuuup. You gonna tell me you didn't drink beer at eighteen? Or is that too far back to remember?"

"All right, you got me. Now we're even."

Matt went to the kitchen and came back with a beer in each hand, one dark and one light. He held them out for Lamar to choose.

"You're kidding me, right?" He took the light one.

"Perfect. I like dark."

Lamar rolled his eyes. "I just love a comedian," he said. He was working hard at playing casual, and in fact had lost much of his previous anxiety, feeling more in tune than he would have imagined.

They sat on the couch, drank beers, and watched *South Park* on TV. They smoked a joint and Lamar settled into a zone where he lost track of why he was there. They hadn't even touched. His eyes got heavy and he dozed off.

"Guess you better spend the night," said Matt.

Lamar sat up and rubbed his eyes. "Like I got somewhere to go."

Matt went in the other room and came back with sheets, a pillow, and a blanket.

"What's that?" said Lamar.

"I'm making up a bed for you here on the couch." Matt stood in front of Lamar with the pile of bedding in his arms, waiting for him to get up off the couch.

Lamar frowned. He was reminded of when Byron came to save his family, making him feel like he was just a young, lost kid that needed being taken care of. "I didn't come here to be your charity case."

"And I'm not here to be your experiment."

"What's that supposed to mean?"

"Have you ever been with a man before?"

"Sure. Lots of 'em."

"Come on. I know a greenhorn when I see one. I just want you to be sure."

Lamar jumped up and grabbed the bedding out of Matt's hands and threw it on the couch. Then he stood for a moment, rocking on his heels, unsure of his next move. The ladies liked it when he took charge and he had a feeling a man wanted the same thing. He had an intuitive understanding that older white people who were with a young buck like him were looking to fulfill a need deeper than sex, a stripping away of conventions, a journey down forbidden paths.

He put his arms around Matt and pulled him forcefully close. He closed his eyes and pressed his lips to Matt's. The stubble sent a momentary shiver through him, but the lips were soft, natural, not glossed over with fake color and that waxy taste like the women he had been with. It was a short kiss, and he moved his mouth to Matt's ear. "Where's the bedroom?"

Matt hesitated. His body was tense. "Are you sure?"

"Shit! If you won't tell me, I'll just have to find it." He lifted Matt off the ground and acted as if he were going to carry him like a sack of potatoes.

Matt giggled. "All right. All right. Put me down." He took Lamar's hand and led him down the hall.

Showered and dressed for work, Matt stood over the bed with a steaming cup of black coffee in his hand.

"Sorry to wake you, buddy." It seemed that he had forgotten the boy's name. "But I've got to get going."

Lamar bolted upright as if from the dead. "What?" He looked around, squinted at Matt, and then fell back on the pillows.

"Do you drink coffee?"

"Yeah, sure."

"I've got to go to work. What are your plans for the day?"

"Thought I'd rob a bank, go buy some crack, hang out at the park."

"Then for sure I'd better get you some coffee. You'll need the energy for such a big day."

While Matt got the coffee, he forced himself to get up and put on his boxers. He was tired, grumpy—he hated being woken up—unsure, and fearful about the future. But there was one thing that was missing from his state of being: guilt. He should have been feeling nasty, anxious to cleanse his mind of the images of what they had done, or in complete denial that anything had happened. Instead, he smiled. He thought of Matt's eyes going wide, the agony and ecstasy stretching his face like a comic book character in distress, the moans, the slide from rough passion onto a sleepy cloud. As much as he didn't want to admit it, he felt a tight knot in his chest coming undone, a loose, reckless awe. Before he could stop it, he was hard again.

Matt came into the room with his coffee. Lamar pointed with his eyes down toward his crotch. "No way, buddy," said Matt.

"Lamar."

"Right. Lamar. I've got to go to work. What are you doing tonight?"

Lamar nodded his head, an affirmation of the ease of conquest. "You tell me."

"Are you going to go home or what?"

"Not ready for that. Guess I better get a job."

Matt took out his wallet and gave Lamar a Costco business card. It said Matt Linsky, General Manager. "Come by this afternoon. If you're willing to work hard and start at the bottom, I might be able to set you up with something."

Lamar sipped his coffee and slowly finished dressing.

"Come on," said Matt. "I'm already late."

"All right, boss," Lamar said with a snigger.

Matt and Lamar stepped out into the cool, damp morning and Lamar paused a moment, staring at the fog raking through the treetops in the park.

"Don't even think about it," Matt said with a laugh. "There's hardly anybody there in the daytime."

"Get your mind outta the gutter, man. Just looking at nature."

Lamar shoved his hands in his pockets as they walked down to the bus stop. His fingers touched the forty dollars Matt had given him—too little to be considered a payment for sex, though a little more than he needed for the stated purpose of a day's transportation and food. But economics is economics. It couldn't have come at a better time since he was down to two dollars and thirty-nine cents. A few bills in his pocket and a possible job; he could live with that. He could more than live with that. He took off in a jog to the bus stop, and then turned and waited for Matt.

They got on a 71 Haight bus and rode quietly until Matt's stop at 11th Street. "So I'll see you later?" Matt said with questioning eyes.

"Definitely."

"Around three would be good. Show them the card at the door."

"Gotcha."

Lamar sat on the ground in Lowell Park with his head up against a tree. It was still early and he was waiting for his mother to leave the house. Letisha was probably at church already. He didn't want to run into anybody when he went in the house to change clothes and get a jacket.

He dozed off until a shadow over him caused his eyes to pop open and his head to jerk forward. Lester was hovering above him with crazy eyes, a look on his face like he wanted to do Lamar harm.

"You scared the shit out of me," said Lamar. "What you doing?"

Lester's face splintered into raw laughter. "You ain't got nothing to fear from me. You're my boy."

Lamar wasn't sure about the "nothing to fear" part. The glint he usually saw in Lester's eyes looked more like a disguised hate than love. In his senior English class at McClymonds, the teacher had tried to get them interested in Greek mythology. Good luck with that in West Oakland, Lamar had thought. But he did remember the story of Oedipus killing his father after his father had tried to get rid of him because of some prophecy.

Lamar could tell that Lester was still on the upside of his high, but he often pondered what would happen if he caught him on the downside on the wrong day at the wrong time. Lamar was taller than his father, but he didn't have the bulk (even though Lester's mass had long ago started its journey to flab). But in sheer craziness he had Lamar beat by a mile. Unpredictability was the thing his basketball coach always talked about. And the most dangerous

Lamar stood up. "What you doing up so early?"

"Got some meetings today."

"Meetings?"

Lamar knew that Lester didn't like being questioned. His father narrowed his eyes and spoke in an irritated voice. "You should be glad I brought you out here to California, land of opportunity. Saved your ass, yes I did. Got us outta that cesspool. We could be underwater. Underwater! I made this happen. Me. I don't know what you want from me. Look where you is. Goddamned Oakland instead of that shithole Ninth Ward of fucking New Orleans. Look around you, boy. Opportunity. The Big Easy, my ass. If you don't drown in the floods, you drown in your own sweat. Something big coming for us here. I goin' fix it so your momma don't have to work no more. Get us a nice big house. I got meetings. Possibilities. Every day I'm out there." He paced around Lamar and pointed his finger at him. Every couple of minutes he shook out his shoulders.

A flock of geese flew overhead and Lester looked up at the sky. His feet stopped. The life drained out of his face just as sure as the honking of the geese faded into silence. Lamar had the feeling that Lester was shifting into the downward spiral, and he was anxious to get away. The day would come that he would stand up to his father, tell him how he was full of shit, maybe even flatten him if it came to that, but he wasn't there yet. And not now, when Lester was so volatile.

Seeing Lester so jumpy made him wonder that he had never laid a hand on his mother, at least that he knew of. Possibly Lester's only attribute was knowing when he was too crazy to be around her and removing himself from the scene. With Lamar it was different. He had been saved from Lester's fists only by the fact that they were hardly alone together. One day when Lamar was twelve, Lester came to the house when everyone else was out. He wanted Lamar to tell him where Hattie kept the house money. Lamar gave him a smart answer and Lester went off on him, had him up against the wall with his hand at Lamar's throat. Joe walked in, grabbed Lester from behind, and threw him out the door. "I see you lay hands on that boy again, there'll be hell to pay. And if you ever touch Abby, I'll kill ya."

Lester's head had rolled around on his shoulders. He rubbed the back of his neck. "Wouldn't never hurt her," Lester had said, sounding like he meant it.

But now, alone in the park, there was no one to come to the rescue. Lester seemed to get more agitated by the minute. "You feel me? You hear what I'm saying?" Lester continued in his rant. "What you doing to make things better? Just givin' your ma a hard time, stressing her out. She done everything for you. Workin' her fingers to the bone for you kids." He now seemed unable to get his breath. He coughed. "You got a cigarette?"

"You know I don't smoke. Look, I gotta go."

Lester grabbed his arm in firm grip. "Wait. Don't you mind the shit I's saying. Just…just cut me a little slack. I need a couple bucks for the bus. Got that meeting." In the blink of an eye he had gone from tirading monster to pathetic supplicant. He looked like he might burst into tears. Lamar didn't know what would be worse—his father breaking down or popping him one. He reached in his pocket and took out a twenty.

"Here. Take it. Do what you have to do."

Lester took the bill and kissed it. His lower lip hung down in abject appreciation. Lamar was afraid Lester might pull him into an awkward fatherly embrace, and he moved quickly to be out of range.

Lamar took a few steps toward the house and then felt his sneaker come down on something soft and mushy.

"Tell your momma I'm goin' drop by the weekend."

"Yeah. Whatever." The sharp smell of dog shit rose up from his shoe.

"Fuck!" Lamar said out loud. He had given away half his money to the asshole who had smoked and snorted up his whole college fund. He was no better than his mother, falling prey to Lester's needs. "That's it. I'm out of here." He vowed to never give Lester another penny. Running into him was a sure sign that it was time to go.

He opened the door to the apartment with a feeling that he no longer lived there. Letisha surprised him by calling out from the kitchen.

"That you, Lamar?"

"What you doing here? No work?"

"I called in sick." Letisha had started out volunteering at the church, but after a year they had given her a job in the office filing, answering phones, organizing.

She came into the living room and saw Lamar gathering the rest of his things: clothes, shoes, a basketball, a few workout magazines. "You all right?" she asked.

"Yeah. It's just time for me to go."

"Momma say she real sorry. She know she done wrong."

"What? About the ladies or giving my money to Lester?"

"Everything, I guess."

"I just ran into Lester in the park."

"How is he?"

"He in a bad way. Don't leave any money laying around the house." Lamar looked thoughtful. "He ever hurt you?"

"Nah, well, there was that one time. I walked in on him rifling through the drawers in the church office. I knowed he was looking for the petty cash. I told him he stooping pretty low to be stealing from the Lord's work. When he kept at it, I threatened to call someone. He pushed me into a chair and told me to shut up. I tried to get up and he pushed me so hard the chair tipped over and I bumped my head, but I never told nobody."

"He get anything?"

"There was a noise out in the hall, the pastor coming, so he run off."

"You think he'd ever hurt Ma?"

"Not as long as she give him money. When you were…you know…with the ladies, and the church was still paying the rent, I guess she always had money to give him. Now most all we make go to paying the bills. What she goin' do when she ain't got nothing to cough up?"

"If anything happen, call me. No, call 911 first, then me. Don't hesitate. Run over to the neighbors if you have to. Benny next door would help."

"Where are you going?"

"Don't know yet. Got a chance at a job this afternoon. In San Francisco."

She screwed up her face. "Over there?"

"I'm putting a bridge between me and this life. But call me if you need anything."

"Momma's not gonna like it, not knowing where you at."

"She shoulda thought of that before."

Lamar looked down at his duffle bag; it wasn't even full. "Ain't that pitiful? All I got in the world."

"Blessed are you who are poor, for yours is the kingdom of God."

"You don't really believe that."

"It is easier for a camel to go through the eye of a needle, than for a rich man to enter the kingdom of God." She gave a rare smile, always happiest when she was quoting Scripture.

"You're too much. Say one thing though—you're consistent."

4 Lest the Land Fall to Whoredom

With fingers pressed to his temples in an attempt to alleviate a day-long headache, Lamar stared at an apartment-share listing on the Costco lunchroom bulletin board. Six hundred and fifty dollars for a room? You could rent a whole house for that back in New Orleans! No way he could afford it, but Matt said he could only stay until the end of the week. At Matt's, through mutual agreement, he was now sleeping in the living room. Matt was not looking for a relationship, and Lamar was still learning to navigate the murky waters of sex with men. Though he claimed he was perfectly cool with it, certain things sent a queasy vibration through Lamar: the whiskers on a man's face, hairy buttocks, the smell of another man's spunk in the room.

Despite the new and sometimes-awkward sensations, he had surprised himself that arousal was so easy—the same rush of blood, the same accelerated heartbeat he had experienced with women. But there was the additional forbidden thrill that enhanced his pleasure. A long time before meeting Matt, he had decided that he had no intention of living a life others considered normal.

"Bisexual" was the word that came to mind when Matt asked him if he still planned on having girlfriends. "Why should I limit myself?" he had said.

As the circular motion of his fingers brought a slight relief to the pain in his head, he continued reading the ad. Near Buena Vista Park—sounded good. Views—double good. Furnished room—necessary since he had shit to his name. He figured it wouldn't hurt to look. The guy's name was Jeff, and he worked in Produce. He called and arranged to visit the next day.

Lamar had no trouble finding the place on Roosevelt Way, just the other side of the hill from Matt's place. Jeff answered the door in flip-flops, baggy shorts, and a tank top. He was in his thirties, a sandy-haired man-boy with a little paunch. He was mild-mannered and prone to slip into an awkward laugh when he didn't know what to say. But the eyes! Two little swimming pools you could dive into. They made Lamar think about one of his Oakland ladies, a quirky woman with so much money she didn't know what to do with it. In her round yard she had two side-by-side Jacuzzis put in with a curved pool next to them. She said she did it because, when an airplane flew over, people would see a happy-face.

The room for rent was small and a little dark, since it looked out on the heavy vegetation of the hill in back. But the view from the front deck was similar to the one at Matt's, and he got that same tingling sensation he'd experienced waking up in the middle of the night and looking out at the city lights from his place on the couch. Lamar imagined enjoying the view from Jeff's deck, with a midnight snack or a drink, staring at the twinkling lights and marveling in the sudden turn his life had taken.

"Want a beer?" asked Jeff. And then he titled his head and asked, "How old are you anyway?"

"Twenty-two." It was the age on his fake ID and so far no one had challenged him. Lamar was tall and filling out well from his workouts. He had the tough face of his father, which he tried to accentuate by looking serious and squinting his eyes.

"Great. So you just started working at Costco?"

"Yeah, and I haven't got my first paycheck yet. How much would you want to move in?"

Jeff's face took a little dive. "Man, I would need at least the first month's rent."

"Oh, no problem. Just don't think I could do the deposit right now. In a couple weeks, though, when I get my check."

Jeff raised his forehead in a show of hope. He seemed to like Lamar and was willing to give him a chance. "You got any references?"

"Yeah, no problem." He was bullshitting his way through the interview. Hattie had always told him to look people in the eye when he talked to them. He had learned to do that and more, developing a soft, disarming stare that drew people in. The metamorphosis from a lackadaisical teenager to a man with an effectual presence had begun with the Oakland ladies and been furthered along staying with Matt. Matt never confronted him directly about his ghetto speech, but would drop little hints like, "I don't think it's such a good idea to use 'ain't' in a job interview." Lamar started paying attention to how he spoke. He had been working on his slouch, too. Across the table from Jeff, he felt his butt creeping to the edge of the chair and quickly sat up straight. He put his hands on the table, stretched out his long fingers with their broad, shiny nails. People noticed his hands. One of his favorite Oakland ladies, Lisa, always commented on how beautiful his hands were. She dabbled in palm reading and said that the shape of his fingernails showed he had the ability to remain calm even in the most trying of situations. She had trusted him the moment she saw his hands.

Jeff took a sip of his beer, looked down at Lamar's

hands, and laughed. "Well, hey, you seem like a good guy. Can you get the money to me by this weekend? I'll hold the room for you."

Lamar took a sip and licked his lips. He broke into a rare, but controlled smile. He angled his head the tiniest amount and raised his eyebrows a fraction. "Don't worry. I'll come by with the money on Saturday. How's that?'

Jeff chuckled and his baby blues got brighter. "I think this is going to work out."

Lamar left Jeff's place high on his little conquest, but the wind whipping the fog over the hill slapped him in the face. How was he going to get six hundred and fifty dollars? He thought of Loretta and Sybil, and the other ladies his mom worked for. There was no way he could go to them without his mother finding out. It was possible she had already sullied his reputation by creating a bogus story, letting it slip that he had to go to the clinic because of a man problem just so they wouldn't see him. Her little revenge for his leaving home. But he had learned a few things, and like his mother, knew how to deal with people, how to get what he wanted.

When he and Matt first met, Matt told him that he didn't pay for sex. Later in bed one night, he admitted that he had once, and when Lamar pushed him Matt had said, "Well, a couple of times." Lamar fished for information, trying not to be too obvious. There were websites where you could find escorts, according to Matt—several of them. Lamar couldn't believe it. A few months back he could hardly imagine gay sex. Now he found out you could shop online for it like you were ordering a pair of sneakers from Zappo.

The next day, Lamar went to the library where they had free computer access, and set up a profile, glancing over his shoulder constantly to see if anybody was looking. That night he got his first call. The next day, two. By Thursday he had over eight hundred dollars in his pocket. It had been relatively easy. Not always pleasant, but easy. The outward aggression/inward detachment he had learned from taking care of his Oakland ladies transferred to his encounters with men. But there was a whole new universe of negotiations and predicaments, personalities and schedules. With the Oakland ladies he just had to show up, maybe do a little gardening to make it look legit. His mother made the arrangements, and what they wanted, for the most part, was straightforward. His foray into sex with men had more…quirks.

On Friday, he decided to take one more request before turning over the rent to Jeff on Saturday. He arrived at a place in the Mission district and rang the bell. The buzzer persisted long after he had pushed the door open, making it seem like the unknown hand at the top of the stairs was stuck to the button. The vibrating sound coursed through his head, adding one more rumple in a day that refused to smooth out. Tiredness had followed him around like a lost dog since that morning when his cell phone had cut into his dream, a perfectly good dream steeped in erotic potential. And there was the inexplicable mid-afternoon traffic that had made him late, the chilly wind off the ocean that crept up his back, the ache in his left leg from a basketball game. He was on the verge of shouting and pounding on the wall to let the person know that he was inside and could he please, please cut the buzzer. But even with his limited experience, he knew that propriety must reign. Be polite. Be cool.

The droning stopped, but with the door still open, the sound was immediately replaced by the slap and rumble of skateboards tearing up the sidewalk in front of the building. He could also hear a drunk in front of the bar on the corner bellowing in foul language his take on nothing in particular. On top of all that, the notion that something was not quite right rubbed his raw nerves. He usually liked to hear the voice before meeting a person. He felt he could tell a lot from the voice. But the man, who said his name was Jerry, insisted on setting everything up by texting.

Lamar squinted, trying to bring into focus the figure at the top of a narrow dark stairway, a faceless shadow framed in an aura of candlelight. The shape of the man—he seemed to be clothed in sweats—indicated someone not grossly overweight or comprised of any obvious deformity. He was relieved that he was not meeting a monster.

The draft from the street flickered the candlelight and played with his mind. He had his hand on the open door. It would be easy to back out, always his first impulse each time he stood with the door still open, even when there were no doubts. He eased the multi-paned glass door into its jamb. The flames stopped dancing and settled into an upright, steady burn. And then, a memory came to life so vividly that his legs froze and were rendered useless, as if the muscle tissue had forgotten how to work in its normal alternating pattern of contracting and relaxing that would get him up the stairs. He tried to fight through the daze, but his feet wouldn't move, neither forward nor back. He lost sight of where he was and exactly what he was doing there. Out of the foggy past, he heard Mrs. Thompson's giggly voice: "Come on, Lamar." He marveled at how much his life had changed since that day he stood at the bottom of a different stairway, looking toward uncertainty.

With the door now closed, a moment of quiet overtook him, until he heard, just faintly, Middle Eastern chillout music coming from somewhere in the belly of the apartment. At the top of the stairs the music was louder, and he could distinguish the sounds: the painful lament of a flute, the tinny sound of a chalice drum, and the melodic chords of an oud. Lamar didn't know about much in life, but he knew music. He spent hours every day downloading and listening to songs, focusing on dance music because his goal was to be a DJ, but listening to everything, knowing that almost any kind of music could be mixed into a dance number.

He followed a trail of votive candles that led down the hall to a bedroom. The man had gone to a lot of trouble to achieve a sense of mystery—the music, the candles, the insistence on texting—but Lamar was suspicious of too much in the way of frills. He had already learned that he didn't have to be soft with men, exchanging pleasantries, talking about his damn goals, what he wanted out of life. Sure, he had dreams, but he didn't want to talk about them. No talking. Just let the chests collide. He felt a surge in his body when he could provoke, within seconds, a rise out of his partner with just a touch or a hug. It was like a drug. Men. He knew where he stood with them. But in some ways, they weren't so different from the Oakland ladies. He knew to touch every part of their sometimes weathered and disproportionate bodies, never allowing the idea that some misshapen emotion brought about in a flash of passion could bud into something more. He knew how to stay in the moment—engaged, but emotionally detached.

The man sat on the edge of the bed, his head down and his hands between his knees, like a boy in a doctor's office sitting on an examining table, trying not to crinkle the stiff white paper under him. The man raised his nervous eyes and gasped quietly, as if he hadn't expected Lamar to be as good as his pictures, a surprise mixed with a dash of suspicion, as if a man who looked that good couldn't actually be that good. Lamar knew the look, and it made him smile with the power of being desired.

"How ya doing?" said Lamar.

The man picked up a note from the bedside table and handed it to Lamar. It was a neatly typed paragraph saying that he was a non-hearing, non-speaking person, but could read lips fairly well. He hoped that Lamar didn't have a problem with that. The note was signed, "Jerry."

Lamar shrugged and produced a tight little smile. "We aren't here to have a conversation," he said, not knowing if Jerry could discern what he was saying.

Jerry nodded, and Lamar felt assured that he had been understood. But at the same time a pang shot through him, the pang that shook him when he saw someone with a disability, or an amputee, or a person with a badly disfigured face. Of course, he didn't suffer that sympathetic twinge when he encountered a person who was grossly overweight, or wrinkled with age, or short with stubby legs, or awkwardly tall. He wasn't sure how he would handle it if he encountered a person so physically reprehensible that he had to turn around and walk out. When one of his Wednesday clients had suggested that he must be able to go beyond physical beauty and see the true beauty of the person inside, he had shaken his head and said, "Well, that has a nice ring to it, but isn't exactly how I'd put it. True, I met some pretty unattractive people that were real sweet inside, but you can't really go there."

"Do you do women as well?" the client had asked.

"Uh, yeah."

"I can't imagine having sex with someone you're not attracted to."

"It's like jogging on a path that might be new, but you been jogging so long your feet know the trail without looking down. Your feet just sense where they must go."

Despite the awkwardness with Jerry's disability, he wasn't bad to look at. In fact he could be considered handsome, with a head of wavy brown hair, soft eyes winged with long lashes. He was average height, wiry and in good shape for someone in his forties. It seemed so wrong that he should be stuck with an impairment of abilities that everyone takes for granted.

"What would you like to do?" Lamar mumbled, staring at a candle that popped and crackled across the room.

Jerry pointed to his lips.

Lamar let his shoulders fall in a sad, sorry, slightly frustrated expression.

Jerry shook his head violently and made a tiny guttural sound. He grabbed a pad of paper and scribbled, "Not here to feel sorry for me."

Lamar felt Jerry's burning stare. "I know. I know." He reached down and took the man's hands. He lifted him up into a tight embrace and began to gently knead Jerry's bony shoulders and upper back. "Take off your clothes and lie down. I'll massage you."

Jerry tilted his head back and looked up at Lamar. Again he pointed to his eyes, and then at Lamar's lips.

"Oh, right." Lamar nodded toward the bed. "Massage."

Jerry smiled and gave the thumbs up sign. He took Lamar's hands and prompted him to undress him. Lamar began to lift Jerry's T-shirt, and Jerry pushed him back hard, shaking his head, and making a strange guttural sound.

Lamar looked stricken. "What? What did I do?"

Jerry's dark eyes were on fire. And then his body started to shake. A wheezing noise escaped from deep inside. Lamar took another step back in horror. Jerry broke his stare and reached out for Lamar's hands. The shaking stopped and a smile overtook Jerry's face as he pulled Lamar toward him. And then it hit Lamar that Jerry was laughing, playing with him. It had never occurred to him that a person who couldn't speak also couldn't laugh in the same way other people did.

"Oh. I get it," said Lamar. He more forcefully grabbed Jerry's shirt. Jerry wiggled and fought, but he was no match for Lamar, who pushed him face down on the bed and pinned him. He got the shirt over his head and threw it behind him. Now Jerry was nodding emphatically, making a faint pleasurable groan. Lamar took the waistband of his sweatpants and underwear at the same time and yanked them down, revealing a hairy, nicely formed butt. Jerry reached around and tried to pull his pants back up, kicking his legs at the same time. But Lamar took Jerry's arm in a tight grip, and then threw it aside. He slid the pants down over Jerry's white delicate feet. Lamar stood up and quickly tore off his own clothes. Jerry wriggled and scooted as if trying to get away, but Lamar pounced, straddling him. He laid his hands on Jerry's back, and with a rocking downward pressure, produced cracks all along his spine.

Lamar worked on Jerry's back and dug deep into his muscles. He positioned himself lower on Jerry's body and gave his ass a couple of quick slaps before working his fingers deep into the glutes. Jerry had stopped struggling and his eyes were closed. The harder Lamar massaged the more relaxed his face became. Lamar could be sweet or belligerent or a combination of both. It didn't matter to him as long as he felt the vibe of happiness rising off the person's skin.

5 Wise in His Own Eyes

Lamar sat on the edge of his bed, transferring information into his new iPhone. Jeff came to the door with a beer in hand. It was his day off and the beer probably wasn't his first. Scattered on top of Lamar's rumpled sheets were shiny blue running shorts, a pair of Nikes, a pair of Lucky You jeans, and a couple of Nautica polo shirts, all displaying the tags.

"Hey, Lamar."

"What's doing, Jeff?" Lamar's head did not lift up from the screen.

"I was thinking of ordering out Chinese. You want to join me? My treat."

"Uh, sure."

Lamar finished a sequence and looked up. He noticed that Jeff's eyes were flitting from one article on his bed to another like a dragonfly over a pond. "Payday, huh?" said Jeff.

"Oh, shit. The deposit. I think I went overboard." He dropped the phone in his lap and picked up one of the polo shirts. "Maybe I should take some of this back."

"No big deal."

Lamar didn't like the way Jeff so easily let him off the hook. There was a blue jay squawking from a branch just outside his window. The neighbor's tabby was on the prowl. "No, man. My bad. You'll have your money. Give me a couple of days."

Jeff took a swig of beer. His eyes were bloodshot and he seemed a little unstable on his feet. "Really, don't worry about it."

The jay squawked again. Lamar wanted the cat to pounce if only to shut the bird up. It was the one thing he didn't like about his new room, the damn bird screeching outside the window all the time, the eternal dance of the cat creeping and bird protesting. They both seemed to like the teasing.

"Hey, you don't have to treat me like a runaway. I know my obligations and I'll comply." Lamar surprised himself. He not only sounded honorable, but intelligent.

"Sorry. Didn't mean to suggest that you wouldn't, or couldn't. I know you're just starting out and things can be tough." He glanced down at the pile of new clothes again, and then quickly toward the squawking outside the window.

"You don't need to apologize," said Lamar. He picked up his phone and went back to the screen, but it had gone black. In his reflection he saw a little smirk. Damn, how easily they fell.

Jeff lingered in the doorway, rubbing the whiskers of his chin.

Lamar looked up and raised his brows. "The Chinese?"

"Right. I'll get on it. What do you like?"

"Oh, I'm eclectic." He liked trying out new words he had heard while hanging around with Matt.

Jeff stopped stroking his chin. "Okay, then. I'll just order my usual and hope you like it."

Lamar downloaded the app of the website where he

had his profile. He made it active again. "Gotta do what ya gotta do," he said out loud.

On a cool, foggy Sunday morning Lamar woke up, and through crusty eyes peered at the person sleeping next to him who looked both familiar and foreign at the same time. Lamar pretended for a moment that he didn't know how he got there. But of course he knew. The inevitability of it had been buzzing around the apartment for the past week like a fat fly that refused to leave out the balcony door they had left open. Jeff lay in a dead man pose, his hands folded over his chest, honking like an Oakland goose.

Outside the glass doors of Jeff's bedroom, Lamar had a view of the East Bay, a distant land shrouded in mist. It reminded him of the hidden valley he had just dreamed about, a place he could see from a cliff, but not get to. Every trail he chose led nowhere. Several times he felt the gravel of a downward path slip under his feet, followed by the sensation of falling. His mother and sister were in the valley looking up at him, and he worried that the pebbles and dust kicked up by his near-fall would rain down on them and get in their eyes, blinding them.

It had been only three weeks since he made his escape from Oakland, and yet Abigail and Letisha had already faded from his conscious into the world of dreams. He was still too angry with his mother to suffer anything akin to missing her, and with Letisha he had never been close. He only felt a vague absence, like a habit he had finally been able to rid himself of; he was happy to be free, though it would take some getting used to.

Letisha had called once. He answered for fear that something bad had happened. No, their mother was okay. No Lester sightings.

"But that Shawna is driving me nuts," said Letisha. Shawna was a girl down the street who had her eye on

Lamar. "She even been coming to church, probably just to track me down so she can ask about you. I don't know what to tell her."

"I know. She's left me a bunch of messages. Just tell her that I went back to Mississippi to visit Grannie."

Visiting Grannie was something he fully intended to do. She was the one person he really missed. But the thought of traveling over deserts and mountains and rivers all the way back to Mississippi was daunting. How would he do it? By car? By train? Could he afford to fly? It saddened him that she was so far away, but he was glad she wasn't around to witness Abigail's questionable survival tactics, Lester's further degeneration, and his own behavior. On one level, he was horrified that she might find out what he had been doing since she left. The few times they spoke on the phone, he quickly ran out of safe topics: the weather, his work, her life in Columbia. Juxtaposed to the real conversations were the ones he had in his head, where he told her the true facts of his life, and she understood and comforted him. He imagined sitting in the kitchen of her simple house in the Owens Street neighborhood where she had lived before they moved to New Orleans. He would talk freely, tell her everything. She would smile wanly and change the subject as she often did when things came up that she didn't understand. She would fall into her favorite topic of conversation: the days of Katrina, reminiscing how wonderful Byron had been, saving their lives, giving them shelter, putting himself in harm's way to help find Joe. Lamar would nod in agreement. Then he imagined what Byron's face would look like if he saw him waking up in the bed of a man.

Jeff made a loud guttural snort, and then rolled over on his side.

Byron seemed to have taken up residence—albeit as a rather quiet, brooding occupier—in the corner of Lamar's conscience, popping up at inopportune moments to shake his head in disapproval. The youth in Lamar still wanted to shock Byron, say things and do things that would rile him. But Lamar had matured since those days they spent together during Katrina. Since that day on the roof with the floodwaters all around them, and Joe's body floating in the house below, he could no longer dismiss Byron as simply a sanctimonious, white do-gooder helping poor black folks. He and Grannie and Byron, an unlikely trio brought together by disaster, had formed a bond that changed Lamar's impressions of Byron forever

At Joe's funeral, Georgette had sat on one side of Bryon, holding his hand in an anxious grip, while Lamar sat on the other. Lamar sensed that Byron's desolate and bloodshot eyes were not for Joe's passing, but for the person in the grave next to Joe, his Uncle Thomas. Though Lamar couldn't do it, he felt a strong urge to throw his arm around Byron's shoulder to comfort him. Back then the notion that his uncle and Byron had a relationship was still disturbing; the mental image of his football star uncle and Byron having sex set off uncontrollable spasms in his gut. Now, after his own experiences with Matt and Jeff, and others, he had, if not a real understanding, at least an awareness of how it could have happened.

Last night he and Jeff had sat in the neighbor's hot tub, drinking beers under a starry sky. They smoked a joint that kept going out with their damp fingers. Soon after, they were rolling around on Jeff's bed, the smell of chlorine and beer-breath and pot in the air.

All this talk of "coming out of the closet" or "being born with the gay gene" was fine for people who found some comfort in it. But sometimes it was just a matter of being in a situation and acting on it. Did Lamar feel like he had been born gay? No. Did he enjoy sex with women? Yes. Did he feel like he had been in the closet? No. Did he like sex with men? Yes. Maybe it had been the same for his uncle. Maybe Thomas and Byron had gone fishing one day, and then swimming. Maybe they really liked each other and were curious. And Byron, being a sensitive type, took it to heart, probably fell in love, and years later still could not control his emotions. It was impressive, but it was the emotional part that Lamar couldn't get his head around. He loved sex. How could it be bad as long as you weren't forcing yourself on or hurting anyone? Grannie, who had taught him so much about life, sat him down one day and laid it out in no uncertain terms.

She had gazed at his strong body as if it had developed overnight. "Never ever let me hear that you used your strength to force yourself on a girl," she began, with the intensity of a revved-up preacher at church. "It is not who we are. Your grandpa would never do that, nor your uncle, God rest his soul. Even Lester, for all his shortcomings, ain't that kind of person, though high on drugs who knows what he might do. I beg you, Lamar, never ever put yourself in that situation."

Lamar shook himself out of the past and came back to the bedroom on Roosevelt Way. He kicked off the covers and sat up on the side of the bed. He heard the rustle of sheets and then, "Hi, sweetie."

Lamar looked over his shoulder with a twisted smile. "Sweetie?"

Jeff feigned embarrassment and gave a tiny shrug, but he was so content that Lamar could have slapped him across the face and it wouldn't have knocked the sparkle from his eyes.

"Now don't go getting any ideas," said Lamar.

"Oh, come on. Let me be happy for a little while at least. That was about the best night of my life."

"Jesus!" Lamar stood up, grabbed his clothes from the floor, and held them in front of his crotch as he lumbered out of the room. But deep down Jeff's words had touched him. He had given someone the best night of his life.

Jeff was so sincere, so innocent. He didn't seem to

have a mean bone in his body. And Lamar was getting accustomed to Jeff's nervous chuckle, the swimming pool eyes that followed him around the apartment. He had awakened in the middle of the night caressing Jeff's furry little belly, though had quickly dropped his hand and rolled over to face the other way.

After his shower, Lamar followed the scent of coffee into the kitchen. Jeff sat at the counter hunched over his laptop, but his head shot up as soon as Lamar came in the room.

"I was thinking we could go have brunch and then hit Dolores Park," said Jeff, his voice like the maple syrup sinking into a stack of pancakes pictured on the box sitting next to the stove.

"Uh, I'm going to shoot some hoops, maybe a pick-up game."

Lamar had been to the Panhandle courts a couple of times during the week, where the cat-piss odor of eucalyptus and the cacophony of constant traffic on either side were annoying, but the crowd was mixed and the level of trash talk was tolerable. They had told him there were some pretty good five-on-five games on the weekend.

Jeff refused to be let down. "Okay. How about dinner?"

"Dinner. Yeah, well, that's a distinct possibility." Again Lamar was unsure where this was going, but a friend was something he needed. He had drifted from the few attachments he had made during his two-plus years in Oakland. His basketball buddies in the East Bay, Tommy and Jaden, had both texted him, asking where he was. He hadn't answered. They would want to know what he was doing. What could he say to them?

Two months later Lamar still hadn't given Jeff the deposit, and Jeff hadn't bothered him about it, probably because they were sleeping together several nights a week and the sex was good.

Lamar always managed to come up with rent, but every time he had a little extra cash, he would find himself walking down the street with bags of new stuff. Sometimes he would wait until he knew Jeff wasn't home to bring in his bags from Macy's or Nordstrom's or the Nike store. Half the things he bought would sit under his bed unworn with the tags still on. Nothing Lamar did or wore went unobserved by Jeff. It was as if he couldn't control policing Lamar with his eyes. Lamar recognized the same puppy-love face, the droopy and unrelenting smile that he had witnessed in Shawna, his ersatz Oakland girlfriend.

It was particularly obvious that love stares but does not see when Lamar gave Jeff an expensive watch for his birthday. Jeff was so excited Lamar swore he saw Jeff's heart thumping under his T-shirt.

The next evening Lamar received a text from one of his b-ball buddies inviting him to have a beer.

"I thought we were going to have dinner," said Jeff.

"Sorry. Gotta go."

Lamar came home late and was pouring a glass of juice when Jeff came into the kitchen.

"Uh, hi. You know I love my watch," said Jeff, cradling it in his hand, expanding and contracting the wristband. "It was sweet of you, but I think you should take it back."

Lamar slowly recapped the juice, opened the fridge, and placed the bottle on the top shelf. Hesitating a moment, he then moved it to the door before letting the door close a little harder than he should have. The sound of tinkling bottles echoed through the room. Still with his back to Jeff, he picked up the glass, took a sip, and turned around.

"Why's that?" said Lamar.

"It's way too expensive. You can't afford it. I don't know how you do it on your salary."

Lamar's eyes rose to the ceiling as if searching for something. "Those damn credit cards are dangerous. I know I shouldn't be using them so much, but I wanted you to have a nice birthday."

"Credit cards?"

"Yeah. Why?"

"I've never seen you use a credit card."

Lamar watched Jeff's eyes darting this way and that. Why was he pursuing a conversation that could only go badly? "That doesn't mean I don't have one."

"I looked in your wallet."

"You what? You went into my shit? Fuck! You can't do that! That's it. I'm goin' git me my own place." His anger made him slip into ghetto.

"Wait. I'm sorry. That was wrong. But I was worried about you. Please tell me you're not dealing drugs."

"Shit! You think every bitch-ass nigger that's what we do, all we can do. Well, fuck you!"

Jeff's face turned even whiter than his normal pale self, his eyes like azure marbles about to shoot out of his head. "I'm sorry," he whispered.

"Fuck your sorry," said Lamar. He snorted and took a breath. The truth was that Jeff looked so comical in his devastation that Lamar had a hard time keeping a straight face. "You should see yourself. You look like Large Marge in Pee Wee's Big Adventure, you know, when her eyes pop out."

"Please don't move out," Jeff whined. "I mean, it's such a drag going through the hassle of finding another roommate."

"So that's what I am to you. A roommate?"

"No."

"Then?" Lamar put his glass in the sink and hopped up on the counter.

Jeff's voice squeaked like opening a rusty metal door. "When we're together, I feel so close to you. There's got to be something there. But it's like you have this whole other life. You never invite me to go out with your friends."

"Whoa, baby! We just met and you want to get married? I'm too young," he laughed. "I'm not even sure I'm…you know…"

"So you're seeing girls?"

"Not recently."

Jeff slumped to the floor and covered his face with his hands. "See what you do to me? I've become a nagging bitch."

Lamar shook his head. "It ain't me doing it."

Jeff forced himself off the floor. He slapped his own face a couple times. "You're right. What you do is none of my business. I promise I won't bug you, and we can just do our own things. And if our desires coincide from time to time, fine."

"Coinciding desires? That sounds so much better than fucking."

"Don't make fun of me. I'm trying to figure this out, too."

Lamar drummed his fingers on the counter between his legs. "Okay, here's the scoop. Yes, I have extra income. Nothing like drugs. I didn't tell you because I didn't think you could handle it." He paused and cleared his throat. "I provide services to lonely people."

Jeff's head snapped back and he crossed his arms in front of him as a shield against Lamar's gut-punching words. Lamar stared at him without flinching and Jeff's eyes fell to the floor. "Now who's mincing words?" Jeff said softly. "You fuck people for money."

"You make it sound like you'd prefer I was selling drugs. Look, I play safe, so you don't have to worry about that."

"How considerate! God, do you at least take a shower

before jumping into bed with me?"

"See, I knew you couldn't handle it. You think it's easy coming from where I come from?"

"You've got a job, a place to live. You don't need all that shit you buy."

The day he realized that his mother was getting cash for his pleasuring the Oakland ladies, he understood something about the world. Everybody loved sex and those who claimed not to were just afraid. What he provided was no different than any service people paid for. "I'm not ashamed of what I do. You're right, though. I don't need all that stuff. I'll give you that. But would you have let me move in here if I hadn't come up with the rent? I had to do something or I woulda been sleeping on the street. And besides, there are things I want to do and my goal in life is *not* to work at Costco. No offense."

"Jesus! What *do* you want? How many guys your age have what you have? I saw your real age, by the way, on your driver's license."

"This is me!" shouted Lamar. "This is who I am! You can't handle it. It's best I look for another place to live."

"Oh, so that's what you do? Run away?" Jeff sniffed. His swimming pools were about to spill over.

"Jeff, don't do that, please."

"I know you think I'm sappy, but these last two months have been the best of my life. I've never really connected with anybody before."

"Man, this has gotten way too heavy, too fast." Though his words put on the brakes, a part of him wanted to tell Jeff how important it had been to find a friend, how lost he had been when he moved in. He enjoyed the sleepovers in Jeff's room. Jeff had taught him how to be intimate with another person after sex, the part that had always felt so awkward. The first time Jeff tried to cuddle with him, Lamar pushed him away. Jeff tried the encroaching method: inch forward, rest, legs touch, stop, rest, an arm lightly on back, wait, then arm full around, chest pressed to back. In the morning Lamar would wake up, surprised to find the roles reversed with his chest pressed to Jeff's back. With time he became increasingly comfortable with knowing that someone wanted him for more than just sex. At the same time, he knew he couldn't tell Jeff any of that, couldn't open the door any more than he already had. Jeff was one of the emotional types like he imagined Byron to be, someone who latched on like a bulldog. Lamar knew he would never be like that. All the love he was ever going to feel would be in the moment, like waking up and rubbing Jeff's tummy or taking in the expression on his face when he was about to explode. Within a few minutes that warm feeling inside him dissipated like the fog on a summer afternoon. Others could take that moment and stretch it out over days or months or years, make it grow, fertilize it. The next thing you knew, it was an invasive vine that strangled you. But that didn't mean he didn't feel something as he looked at Jeff's teary eyes across the kitchen.

Lamar opened his arms. "Come here."

Jeff pushed off the counter, crossed the room, and wedged himself between Lamar's knees.

"Don't be sad. I do like you," said Lamar.

"That's a start."

Lamar didn't want to tell him that it would never be more than a start.

6 Lead Us Not Into Temptation

The kid—whose name turned out to actually be Kid—stood in the parking lot of a truck stop outside of Barstow, looking like an extra in a film set in the sixties. He had shoulder-length curly reddish hair, tattered jeans, and a corduroy jacket with elbow patches over a tie-dyed T-shirt. His John Lennon glasses glinted in the harsh desert sun, and he was pale, with a few golden hairs sprouting from his chin and cheeks. Lamar wondered how he managed to support the large backpack on his thin frame.

"You looking for a ride?" Lamar asked. He made a low burp and tasted the greasy hamburger he had just eaten.

"Yeah, well, I guess. I mean…"

"Where you going?"

"Phoenix."

"Me, too."

"Oh." Kid looked at him in wonder, half sizing him up and half on the verge of turning around and running for his life.

"Well, my car's over there if you decide what you

want to do in the next two minutes." Lamar took out his keys and remotely unlocked his Dodge Magnum. A weekend in Los Angeles with a Hollywood executive had earned him enough to buy the used 2004 RT.

Kid followed him. "It's just that…"

Lamar whirled around and the boy jumped back a step. "What? You afraid of me or something?"

"No," he said emphatically. "I'm just surprised a guy like you—"

"You mean a black guy?" Lamar laughed. "Of course, if you prefer one of those potbellied redneck truck drivers that'll insist you talk their ear off to stay awake, and later want to jump your bones…"

Kid put his hand to his forehead to shade his eyes from the sun. "How did you know?"

"What?"

"That's exactly what happened. I started off in Eugene, Oregon—that's where I'm from—and got a ride from a truck driver who seemed pretty cool, but we didn't have a whole lot to talk about. When I told him I was studying psychology in college, he started going on about his roommate who had threatened to commit suicide several times. I told him I was just in my second year and wasn't qualified to give advice. But he kept going on about this roommate and how he was jealous when he went out on dates with girls. I got a little uncomfortable because I didn't know why he was telling me all this personal stuff. And then he asked me to describe in detail every girl I ever had sex with."

"Uh-huh," laughed Lamar. "What was that, like two?"

"More than that," Kid said with a smile. "But I did have to invent some to keep the stories going. And then, when he decided to pull over and sleep, he wanted me to climb in back with him. No way. He actually started touching my leg and shit. I'm not into that. I mean, nothing wrong with it, I guess. It's just not for me. After that I decided I should be a little pickier about who I ride with. Don't want to get in that situation again."

"You worried I might be one of *them*?"

"No way. I mean, look at you."

They threw Kid's backpack in the backseat and got in. Lamar adjusted the bulge in his basketball shorts and Kid pretended he didn't notice. The conversation had gotten Lamar hard. "Fuck," Lamar said to himself. "I've got to wait until Phoenix unless..." He had never been with a redhead before.

His stop in Phoenix for the weekend was partly business, as he would need gas money to make it all the way to Mississippi. He had set up his profile to show that he would be in town. He had already gotten a couple of calls and put in his ear buds in case he got more, though he would have to keep his conversations cryptic with Kid in the car. He was looking forward to having company on the drive and didn't want to scare him away.

Kid fell asleep within a half hour of getting on I-40, but before he drifted off he kept commenting on how cool the music was. Lamar was playing one of his upbeat playlists that included the Cold War Kids, Haim, and The Mowgli's—bands Kid had never heard of.

Soon after they got into Arizona, Lamar noticed a cop car following him. A minute later, Lamar saw the dreaded lights in his rearview mirror.

"Shit!" said Lamar. Kid woke up, looked around, and wiped the drool from his chin.

"What is it?"

"Cop."

"Were you speeding?"

"No, Mom, I was not. Funny thing is, I've been speeding most of the way, but in the last few miles I've been going the limit."

Lamar turned the music off and rolled down the window.

The state trooper, short and a little overweight, looked inside the car. "Did I do something wrong?" asked Lamar.

He ignored the question. "License and registration," he barked.

Lamar fished them out of the glove compartment, brushing Kid's leg, which he quickly moved out of the way.

The officer looked at his license. "Mr. Lamar Shaw from Oakland, Cali-for-nye-ay," he said with a nasty let's-have-some-fun tone.

"Yes," said Lamar.

The cop bent down, though he didn't have to bend down far, and looked at Kid. "Who are you?"

Lamar began, "I'm just giving him—"

"Did I ask you? I'm talking to Red there."

Kid's voice was troubled. "I'm Kid Rogers from Eugene, Oregon."

The cop shook his head. "Are you bullshitting me? Sounds like a dumb-ass rock star name."

"That's what my parents named me. I can show you my ID."

The cop ignored him and turned back to Lamar. "You know you can't be driving and listening to that jungle bunny music on your earphones."

Lamar gripped the lower part of the steering wheel and heard Grannie's voice saying, *Be calm, Lamar. Don't mouth off.*

"I wasn't listening to music. I was expecting a phone call. Hands free. Isn't that what we're supposed to do?"

"And who you expecting a call from? Your dealer?"

Grannie whispered, *Cool down, sweetie.*

"My grandma." Though it was possibly the truth, the way he said it had a sarcastic edge. A couple days before he had awakened from a terrible dream. Grannie was on a raft made of old tires in the middle of a large body of water. The sky was angry and threatening. Lamar stood on the shore watching her drift farther and farther away. His feet were buried in mud up to his ankles and he couldn't move. He tried to call out to her, but his voice stuck in his throat. It had been years since he had seen his grandmother, and things weren't going well with Jeff. It seemed the perfect time to pay her a visit.

The trooper's face distorted and he growled, "Don't get smart with me, boy. Get out of the car."

"I'm serious. I'm on my way to visit my grandma in Mississippi."

"I said get out of the car!"

The indignation he suffered in the next half hour made his fists flex involuntarily and his toes burn. If it weren't for Grannie's voice in his head telling him to be calm, he would have ended up in jail or dead. He wanted nothing more than to punch the officer in the face. The man pushed him up against the car and searched him, going up and down his legs, patting his arms, chest, and back.

Staring at Lamar's balled up fists, the trooper said, "You're looking a little tense there, buddy. Gonna have to put these on you while I search the car." He slapped handcuffs on Lamar and told him to sit by the side of the road.

Kid got out of the car. "What are you doing? He didn't do anything."

"Just shut up and join your friend over there. If I don't find nothing, you'll be free to go."

Lamar could feel the Arizona dust caking in his nostrils and the sound of traffic whooshing by while he and Kid sat by the side of the road, looking out at the pine-covered Hualapai Mountains and occasionally exchanging disgusted glances. The trooper rifled the glove compartment and let things spill out onto the floor. He went through their bags, taking his time and leaving their clothes strewn over the back of the car.

With a huffy lament that he had found nothing, the cop slammed the car door. "Guess you can be on your way to grandma's house," he said with a chuckle. "Just watch out for the big bad wolf. And…show some respect the next time you get pulled over." He spoke as if it were a foregone conclusion.

Lamar and Kid sat in the car, watching the police car get back on the road and accelerate rapidly to join the traffic.

Lamar rubbed his wrists. "Bastard!"

"Man, I'm sorry," said Kid. "That's harassment pure and simple. I admire you for keeping your cool."

"It's called self-preservation. I'm too young to die."

"He wouldn't really shoot you," said Kid, and as an afterthought, "Would he?"

"Black guys get blown away all the time for less."

"I mean, I hear about this stuff, but you can't believe it until you see it." Kid shuddered as if he just realized how close he had been to a disaster. "Damn, I need to get high." He reached inside his jeans and down into his underwear.

"Now don't be telling me you got drugs on you. Shit!"

He pulled out a plastic bag and extracted a joint. "Just a little pot. They're never going to look in your underwear unless it's a border or something."

Lamar shook his head, turned the key, and made the car roar. "Well, you gonna fire that thing up or just sit there contemplating it?"

The high was stronger than Lamar had expected, and he began to imagine cop cars under every overpass. He had always lived in cities, so the classic American road trip was both exciting and terrifying—the open spaces, seeing mostly white people and a few Latinos on the roads, the dry scorched earth. He realized the pot was making the experience lean toward the terrifying. "You're not going to fall asleep on me again, are you?" Lamar's voice came out surprisingly shaky.

"Don't worry. I'm here with you." Kid bounced his leg to the music and seemed devoid of any of the paranoia Lamar felt. He examined the map sitting on his lap. "We should take 93 South."

"What? Where's that? You sure?"

"Are you okay?"

"Yeah, sure." He saw a car ahead on the side of the road and slowed down. "I'm pulling into the next rest stop. I've got to pee."

"Me, too. Maybe you should get a coke or a snack. You seem a little wigged out."

Lamar didn't respond. He pulled into a space in the parking lot, got out, and stomped toward the men's room.

Kid came up beside him at the urinal. They both stared at the tiled wall as if it held a message. There was a crack in one tile that looked to Lamar like a snake. He heard the sound of Kid peeing next to him and tried not to think about sex, but the more he tried not to think about it, the more his member started to enlarge. And then, from one of the stalls came a fart that rumbled and echoed off the walls. Lamar imagined a noxious gas filling the room, sending them to their knees. Kid immediately made a choking sound, trying to hold back his laughter. Lamar turned his head toward Kid and snorted at the sight of Kid's reddening face.

"Oh my God. Let's get out of here," said Lamar.

They exited the men's room laughing so hard they could barely stand upright. They stumbled over to a picnic table and fell onto the bench. "God, did you hear that?" said Lamar.

"Hear it? I swear I could feel it. It was like an earthquake." They burst into a fit of laughter that wouldn't stop. Kid started coughing and it sounded like he was choking. Lamar clapped him on the back, and when the coughing subsided, he left his arm on Kid's shoulder. Kid leaned his head toward Lamar and they ended up in a half embrace, their bodies still shaking with laughter.

"Stop!" said Kid.

Lamar dropped his arm and pulled away.

"I meant stop laughing. I can't stop until you stop."

"Oh," said Lamar. But the moment had passed. Inside him the desire still raged, but the pot made him uncertain. Was this kid into it? He thought about suggesting they crawl in back of the car and try to sleep.

"Guess we'd better get back on the road. I told my mom I'd try to be there by dinner time."

"Your mom? I thought you lived in Oregon."

"I was living with my dad in Oregon. My mom lives in Phoenix."

The sun was low in the sky and passed through two pine trees, making Kid's hair into a golden halo. He turned his green eyes toward the car. Lamar took in his angular profile and the long white neck he wanted to sink his teeth into. Lamar shook his head from side to side as if trying to get a crick out of his neck. He stood up quickly. Kid turned his head back and looked up at Lamar. Their eyes met for second and a kind of understanding passed from one to the other that, for Lamar, felt like a mild electric shock. Kid's face turned soft and tender. It was the kind of connection that turns some people's minds toward sex. For Kid, though, it seemed enough that they were physically close, laughing, sharing the absurdities of life.

The intensity in Lamar's eyes made Kid look away, and he heard a sound in the direction of the restrooms. "Oh shit! Here he comes."

A large man with a look of relief on his face emerged from the men's room and appeared to be headed in their direction. Kid stood up, and they hurried toward the car.

They went south through high desert surrounded by pine-blanketed mountains toward Wikieup, a name they found impossible to say without chuckling. U.S. 93 was a rollercoaster of hills and valleys, skirting cliffs and dry riverbeds that cut through where the Sonoran and Mojave deserts overlapped. Hardy creosote bushes carpeted the desert floor, and standing among them were Saguaro cactuses flexing their prickly muscled arms in the hot dry afternoon. Lamar created in his head a video game called "Cactus Invaders" where cactus people from another planet arrived to take over Earth. It was up to him to stop them, and he began blasting them with a flamethrower that turned them to charred statues. The ocotillos then attacked with spindly barbed arms, rippling like the tentacles of sea anemones. Their fluidity allowed them to dodge his fire shots that turned the sky red with his constant fire.

"What are you thinking about?" said Kid. "You look so intense."

"Oh, nothing."

"Yeah, out here is a whole lot of nothing."

Two minutes later they saw a sign for a town called Nothing, Arizona. They looked at each other in wide-eyed amazement, thinking that their high still played tricks with their minds.

"Did you just see what I saw?" said Kid.

Lamar pulled off the road, toward a boarded-up gas station and store. The old sign said, "Population 4," but it appeared that the last four had left. Another sign read, "Thru-the-years-these dedicated people had faith in Nothing, hoped for Nothing, worked at Nothing, for Nothing."

"That is so Kafkaesque!" said Kid.

"Say what?" Lamar asked.

"You know, kind of *Twilight Zone* bizarre, but with a sense of humor."

"Whatever," said Lamar. "Damn, I wanted a Coke." He put his face close to the boarded window and tried to look through the crack. "There's a machine in there."

Kid twisted his head and squinted at Lamar. "We have entered an alternative universe and all you can say is that you want a Coke?"

Lamar shrugged. "I bet you didn't even see the Cactus Invaders back there, trying to take over Earth. I torched a bunch of them."

"You're crazy," said Kid. He grabbed Lamar and hugged him. "You're crazy, but I like you." And just as quickly he dropped his arms and started back to the car.

Spread out in front of them, Phoenix was a twinkling carpet of lights that seemed to go on forever. Kid told Lamar he could drop him off in Surprise.

"You're kidding me, right?"

"That's where my mom lives, Surprise, Arizona." He laughed.

"This state is crazy. Are you sure you don't want to go to Mississippi with me?" Though he said it in jest, he harbored a sinking feeling that tweaked his insides, a strange sense of impending loss.

"I would except that my mom is getting married. I have to be there. It's been a hell of a trip, though."

They found the Shell station where Kid's mom had agreed to pick him up. They shook hands. Kid got out and gave Lamar a little wave.

Lamar stood at the window in his room at the Clarendon Hotel in midtown Phoenix. He felt as if he were on a spaceship above a distant planet, drifting in a slow orbit, his head light and airy. Everything and everyone he knew were hundreds of miles away. Except Kid. He allowed himself about two minutes to feel sad, a sense of loneliness. Images of the day went through his mind: the chance meeting, the incident with the state trooper, getting high, the town of Nothing, laughing hysterically, the brief hug. It seemed a whole relationship had passed in a few hours, and then disappeared into the desert night without them even exchanging phone numbers.

Lamar's phone pinged with a message. He turned away from the window and back to his reality, his momentary nostalgia quickly forgotten. Someone was coming for a massage in less than an hour. He pulled his shirt over his head, threw it on the upholstered chair, and headed for the shower.

Lamar and Hattie sat on two rusty folding chairs they brought with them so they could sit a spell by the graves. In front of them were the side-by-side simple tombstones of Joe and Thomas. Lamar looked up toward the treetops where a sinuous drone like a synthesizer line in the back of a new age video danced on the air.

"What is that sound?" Lamar asked.

Hattie turned to him with a slight chuckle. "Oh, that's right. You a city boy. Them's cicadas."

"Like bugs or something?"

"Uh-huh."

"Don't they take a rest?"

"It just go on and on til they decide to crawl back underground for another fifteen years or whatever. This their time to shine." Her face dropped and she began to chew the soft flesh on the inside of her lips. "They was here to see off Thomas, when we put him in the ground. We was sitting right here and them things buzzing to beat the band. Wouldn't give us no peace…as if there coulda been any."

With his hands clasped in front of him, Lamar nodded at Thomas' grave. "Why didn't y'all talk about him?"

"It was just so darn hard," said Hattie. "To lose a child ain't something you can imagine. And in that way!" She moved her head from side to side in slow, graceful arcs. "So senseless. It's enough of a cross we got to bear being black in this country. But you add the violence people suffer for being…being different on top of that…my Lord!"

"What did Byron tell you?"

"Pretty much everything. I drug it out of him."

"He shouldn'ta been telling you that stuff," Lamar said with an angry bite in his voice.

She gave him a quizzical look. "You think I can't take it, like I ain't seen just about everything in my life. Who people want to love is their business. It's not something I really understand, but of course I never had no education."

"Don't have nothing to do with education."

"I guess." She bent down and rearranged the flowers for the third time. "So you got a girl out there in California?"

"Nope."

The stem of one of the roses they had bought at the Piggly Wiggly had broken in the car. She plucked the bud and threw it aside. "But you're doing okay?"

"Yeah, 'cept me and Mom aren't getting along too well."

"Getting along? She say you don't even speak."

"We have our differences."

"Your momma made a bad choice a long time ago and can't seem to get out of it."

"Don't I know it."

"I hope you ain't gonna let her failings discourage you from having a family."

"Funny you'd say that after all you've suffered with your kids."

"But if I hadn't had Abby, I wouldn't be sitting next to my beautiful grandson right now. There's a silver lining to every cloud."

"Don't feel much like a silver lining."

"You're doing just fine. Any grandmother would be proud to have the likes of you for a grandson. And you ain't bad-looking either," she said with a smile. "Might get me some beautiful great-grandkids yet."

"I'm kinda leaning toward a dog right now."

"Well, there's time."

7 The Wicked Shall Not Be Unpunished

"He don't know who he's messing with," shouted Lamar over the radio blaring Depeche Mode's "Enjoy the Silence." *All I ever wanted, all I ever needed, is here in my arms.* Just a couple weeks before, he and Jeff had lain in bed listening to a playlist Lamar had made, and the Depeche Mode song had come on.

Jeff gave Lamar a little squeeze and said, "That says it all."

"Oh really?" Lamar stopped stroking the head of thick, blond hair that lay on his chest. He moved his fingers close to his nose and sniffed. He loved the oily smell, the musky essence that was the olfactory equivalent of tweaking his nipples. He felt like having sex, but all Jeff seemed to want to do of late was engage in long embraces and extended sighs. Why did he have to turn everything into something emotional? They were not a couple, as he had let Jeff know multiple times. Still, he hadn't exactly curtailed his visits to Jeff's bedroom.

The weekend after Jeff's here-in-my-arms declaration, Lamar had been invited on an all-inclusive trip to Palm

Springs with an investment banker. He didn't tell Jeff where he was going or when he would be back. Lamar returned on Sunday afternoon and went straight to his evening shift at work. It was late when he got to the apartment and Jeff's door was untypically closed. Because of their conflicting schedules, it was a couple days before they saw each other. Jeff was cold and only said something about the bathroom needing cleaning. The next week they barely spoke.

"Damn him," said Lamar as he accelerated, weaving his Magnum through Bay Bridge traffic.

The irony was that he had planned to talk to Jeff when he got home after working a day shift. Maybe apologize. For what, he wasn't quite sure. He would explain again that they weren't boyfriends, but they could still have fun together. Instead he found a note that made him explode. Jeff proclaimed, in his childlike scrawl, that he had packed up Lamar's things and was going to drop them off at his mother's house. Lamar had no idea how Jeff had gotten the address—more snooping most likely—but the tactic was obviously chosen to inflict maximum damage.

Lamar had to get to his mother's house before Jeff did. He gunned the engine, passed a couple cars, and then cut in front of them to exit I-80 onto West Grand Avenue. He turned right on Mandela Parkway and two blocks later came upon Jeff's SUV parked on the side of the road. Jeff was inside, consulting the GPS of his phone. Lamar pulled over in front of him and jumped out. Jeff dropped his phone and locked the doors.

"Get out of the car!"

Jeff refused to look at him. He stared straight ahead and held the wheel in a death grip.

Lamar pounded on the window with his fist. "This is crazy. Get out."

Jeff sat in a trance.

Lamar went to his trunk and took out a tire iron. He

went to Jeff's back window, smashed it, and then reached around to unlock the door. Jeff still sat in a catatonic state.

"What the fuck do you think you're doing?" screamed Lamar. He grabbed Jeff by his jean jacket, pulled him out of the car, dragged him over to the curb, and pushed him down. He proceeded to transfer his belongings from the SUV to his Magnum. Jeff sat on the curb with his head down, his body shaking.

Lamar tried not to look at him. He hated making people cry, but he hated being disrespected even more, which set off a chain of reactions inside him that had a life of their own. After putting the last box in his car, he took the house keys out of his pocket and threw them over next to Jeff. "Sorry about the window," he said.

Lamar got in the driver's seat and started the car. It sounded like a jet getting ready to take off. In the same instant, two police cars arrived, one pulling in front of him and the other at his side, forcing him to stop. A young Latina cop jumped out of one car and a large football-worthy black man got out of the other.

What the police saw was the obvious: a black man had shattered the window of a white man's car and removed the contents to put in his own. Needless to say, it did not look good. They had him out of the car in a flash, his face smashed to the ground. The black cop got on top of him and put on the cuffs.

"Don't hurt him!" shouted Jeff.

"You know this guy?" said the Latina.

"Yeah."

She rolled her eyes.

"It's my stuff," grunted Lamar.

"Shut up," said the black cop. And then he turned to Jeff. "That true?"

"Yeah."

"What the hell's going on here?" said the cop. He told the Latina to put Lamar in the back of the squad car while he went over to question Jeff.

"Did he assault you?"

"Not really. Just pushed me a little."

"That's assault. And he broke the window. Did he threaten you with the tire iron?"

"No."

"Are you sure?"

Jeff nodded. The anger and desperation on his face had now turned to fear. "I don't want to press charges," he said.

"That's up to you. But we've got witnesses that say he smashed your window and dragged you out of the car. He's going to jail."

Jeff's eyes now showed panic. "No, really. It's his stuff."

"That doesn't excuse criminal behavior. We'll be in touch."

As the black cop got in the car, he said to his partner, "Looks like we got a fag domestic."

Sitting in the back of a police car was Lamar's worst nightmare. He had tried so hard to avoid the cliché: young black man with an arrest on his record before he even turned twenty-one. Why had he let Jeff get to him? He could have pleaded through the window, turned on the charm, worked it. Why didn't he? His pride? His bad temper? His feelings of betrayal? He had known for a while that Jeff's emotions were out of control, and he let the relationship continue, not wanting to give up regular sex with someone who actually cared. But this was a lesson: Don't get involved. Or better said, don't let someone get involved with you.

On the ride to the station, the black cop told fag jokes and his partner sniggered. Lamar tried to block them out while he thought of who he would call. He hadn't talked to his mother in months. Lester? That was a joke. The idea of calling Byron entered his head. But he wouldn't be able to stand the disappointment in Byron's voice, let alone the told-you-so attitude. Anyway, what could he do from New Orleans? That left Matt. Lamar occasionally ran into him at work, and they had gone out for drinks once, though sex was no longer part of their relationship. Matt also knew Jeff from work, so Lamar had thought their talks might give him some perspective.

"Are you gay now?" Matt had said one evening while they sat at the bar at Moby Dick's.

Lamar stared at the large fish tank above the shelves of bottles. There was a phallic-shaped rock inside it. "Jeez, why you asking that?"

"Well?"

Lamar shrugged. "Just keeping my options. If I say I'm gay, that sounds so…I don't know…weird."

"Sitting on the fence isn't easy," said Matt. "I wish you luck."

Matt answered the phone in his usual cheery manner, but must have detected something right away. "What's wrong? Where are you?"

"Okay. Don't freak out. I'm at the Oakland police station."

"Lamar, what did you do?" Matt said, his intonation now scraping the ground.

"Hear me out before you judge. You know how I told you Jeff was kind of obsessed?"

"Uh-huh."

"Well, he did something stupid. And I did something stupid. So here I am."

"That's it? That's your story."

"Please, Matt. I have no one. Don't make me beg."

"Is Jeff okay?"

"He's fine, I mean physically. Just kind of emotionally screwed up."

"I knew that was headed for disaster, but what could I do?"

"Save the commentary. Just get me out of here."

"I'll be there as soon as I can."

"Please say something," said Lamar, rolling down the window. The air in the car was infused with the odor of dirty socks from Matt's gym bag on the backseat.

"I talked to Jeff. He's not going to press charges, but he wants you to pay for the window."

"Of course. Is he really pissed?"

"More like hurt."

"I told him from the beginning…"

"I know. He knows. He actually got a friend of his to take BART over and drive his car back while he drove yours. Your other key was on the ring with the house keys. It's parked in front of his house."

"Is that where we're going?"

"Yeah."

"I can't go back there."

"You don't want your car?"

"I mean to live."

"That's between you and him. But you need to get your keys and it might be a good chance to talk. You don't want him to change his mind about pressing charges."

"Right. I have a hearing anyway thanks to the black cop who was such an asshole. You know a lawyer?"

The street was quiet. Fog had blanketed the hill. He stared at his car and the apartment where he had lived with Jeff on the other side of the street. The lights were still on. He walked across and rang the bell.

Jeff only opened the door halfway. He cleared his throat and said, "Hey."

"Thanks for taking care of my car," said Lamar.

"I'll go get the keys."

"Can I come in?"

"Don't think that's a good idea." It was obvious that

he was working to keep his voice low and steady.

"Just wanted to say I'm sorry."

Jeff was close to melting into a puddle on the floor. "Don't," he said. "I can't talk to you now. Wait here." He got the keys and returned. "You got someplace to go?"

"Sure. Thanks." A car alarm went off down the street and they both turned to look. "Not mine," Lamar said with a little laugh. "Guess I should go."

Jeff nodded and closed the door.

Lamar got in his car and called Letisha. "How's everything?" he said.

"The same," she said in a scratchy voice like she had just woken up.

"And Mom?"

"She know I talk to you sometime and she bugging me for info. I tell her you don't tell me nothing which is pretty much true."

"Look, Letisha—"

"Please call me Sarah."

"Oh, right. I keep forgetting. Well, I need a place to stay for a while. Think Mom would be okay with that?"

"After she give you a piece of her mind she probably come around. You know how she is."

In the background Lamar heard Abigail's voice. "Who you talking to?"

"Just a wrong number, Ma. Go back to bed."

"I'm getting off the phone," said Lamar quickly. "I'll be over tomorrow."

Abigail grabbed the phone. "Lamar, baby, is that you?"

He hung up.

"Why you sleeping in the car with your home right in front of your nose?" said Abigail.

Lamar sat up quickly and rolled down the window. "Didn't want to wake you." He got out of the car and walked around to the other side. "Plus, I didn't want to leave all this stuff in the car."

"Well, ain't you sitting pretty? You left here with nothing and now you got a fancy car filled up with all kinds of stuff." She cupped his cheek with her hand.

"I've been working."

"I see."

"Got a job at Costco."

"Ain't that something."

"I was renting a room in the city, but the guy came back from Europe. This is just temporary." He dragged a box off the backseat and set it on the sidewalk. Letisha came out of the house and started to help. She looked like she had gained a few pounds. The three of them carried Lamar's belongings into the living room.

"You could stay," said Abigail flatly.

"Driving back and forth to work across the bridge could get old really fast."

"Lotta people do it," said Abigail. "But I suppose you got bigger fish to fry. We just been struggling along here."

Lamar took a bundle of cash out of his pocket. "I've been meaning to give this to you. Just been so busy."

Abigail took the money in her palm and held it up to her cheek with her elbow resting on the arm across her chest. "What? They make you president of the company already?"

Lamar avoided her eyes. "Been working a lot of overtime. All I do is work."

She continued staring at him. Letisha stood off to one side, her eyes also fixed on Lamar. "You look different," said Letisha.

"Work changes you, I guess." He dug into one of his bags, searching for a change of clothes.

"Uh-huh," said Abigail. "But I see something more than that. You got some lovin' in your life?"

"Nah, Ma. What are you talking about?"

"Look at that, Sarah. He embarrassed. Something going on." She laughed, but stopped quickly and looked at the clock. "Damn. I got to go to work. I'm at Miz Thompson's today. You remember her, don't you?"

Lamar found the red T-shirt he was looking for and held it like a matador's cape in front of him, shaking it out. He raised his head and narrowed his eyes as a sort of warning. "I'm working the afternoon shift. I get home late."

"Well, don't that beat all. We all got different schedules. Sarah got her some banker's hours. And you president of Costco. Must be nice. I'm still scrubbing pots and cleaning toilets."

"I'm just a stock clerk, Ma. You should take some classes over at the community college. That's what I'm doing over at City College in the fall."

At his hearing on the following Monday, Lamar said he had a job, was back living with his mother and sister, and was registered for classes at City College in the fall. The lawyer, a friend of Matt's who agreed to take his case pro bono, also managed to insert that Lamar's family had struggled after Katrina made them homeless. Lamar was required to pay for the broken window and was put on probation for six months.

His probation officer looked like a hairy Justin Timberlake in nerd glasses, but Lamar thought his Jew-fro was definitely not flattering. His name was Benjamin Moss. He greeted Lamar with a slightly asthmatic voice and a loose handshake that had the quality of shyness rather than weakness. He asked Lamar a series of questions and keyed in the answers, barely looking up from his computer. He only showed interest when Lamar revealed he was going to take classes at City College.

"That's where I got my Associate Degree." He pointed to a framed certificate on the wall.

"And the others?" Lamar asked, looking at the wall.

"One's my B.A. from SF State and the other is a Master's from Long Beach."

"Guess you must be an expert on bad boys like me," Lamar said with chuckle.

Ben looked directly at Lamar for the first time. "Truth is, I don't do a lot of hands-on…"

Lamar's eyebrows shot up and he cracked a smile.

Ben flushed. "I mean…I'm mostly a supervisor, but we're short on staff…summer vacations…"

"I see."

"And I'd hardly put you in the bad boy category. Sounds like you've been through some hard times what with Katrina and all."

"Have you thought about cutting your hair short?"

"What?" Ben said, like he had been knocked off his chair. "Where did that come from?" He picked up a pen off his desk and started twirling it through his fingers.

"Sorry. Just thinking out loud."

"That's rarely a good idea."

"Or I could grow mine and we could have a fro-off, since we're going to be seeing each other regular."

"First, you don't seem to be taking this seriously. Probation is serious. And second, you will most likely be assigned to another officer. Like I told you, I'm just filling in."

"I believe your words were you 'don't do a lot of hands on.'"

Ben squirmed in his chair and it squeaked. "All right, Lamar," he said in a defeated voice. "We're done for today. We'll see you next time…or someone will…probably not me."

Lamar stood up and leaned over the desk. He was having fun and was sorry it was ending. "That's a shame. Hope I don't have to go through all these questions again."

"No. No. It's all in the computer."

"Sorry if I made you uncomfortable."

"What? Me?" he scoffed. "I've talked to all kinds."

"None like me." Lamar laughed and started toward the door. "See ya."

Lamar sauntered down the hall, thinking about the reckless abandon he felt around older white men. Words just tumbled out of his mouth, but were moderated by the casual push and pull of his eyes and the half-smiles that never bloomed. Around black men, like the cop who had arrested him, he froze up, anger always sitting on the horizon like a blood-red sun inching up. It was probably another one of Grannie's little talks that had saved him the day he got arrested.

Grannie, in her wisdom, had sat Lamar down one afternoon after they had lived in Oakland a couple months. She had already scoped out the territory, the volatility of their neighborhood. "Whites are uncomfortable with the black man being free. They can be pretty nasty. But black men in authority think they got something to prove and in the wink of an eye can turn dangerous. If any officer, particularly a black one, stops you, remember your "yes sirs" even if it kills you to say it. It might kill you if you don't."

8 Come Near That I May Feel Thee

Around the corner from Ben's office, Lamar sat in a scooped-out orange plastic seat under institutional lighting and leaned his head back against the sickly green wall. It was his second appointment with his probation officer, and though Ben said it was unlikely they would see each other again, Lamar could hear his nasally voice in conversation with one of his co-workers.

"You taking off, Carlos?" Ben said.

"Yeah, man. You should be heading out, too. Looks like everybody else is gone. Long weekend, you know."

"Still got one more client this afternoon."

Lamar's ears perked up and he gave a little snort-laugh, though not loud enough to hear.

"You work too hard."

Ben chuckled.

"I mean, living alone, I guess you must really have a lot of time on your hands."

There was a long pause. Lamar could hear Ben's chair squeak as he leaned back. "Oh!" said Ben, as though he were barking. "Since I don't have three screaming kids running around the house, or a wife that's constantly on my case to fix something, or relatives coming by all the time to borrow stuff, my life must be empty?"

Now there was silence on Carlos' part. Lamar had the urge to laugh out loud at Ben's outburst, but he didn't want to give away his position.

"Where did all that come from?" said Carlos in a voice as raggedy and limp as an old dishcloth.

"Well, you complain about it day in and day out."

"Excuse me for living!" Carlos huffed. He came around the corner, a squat man, working his jaw. Lamar stared at him as he quickly walked past. The man's puffy eyes looked as if they might tear up.

"Carlos, I'm sorry," Ben said. The chair squeaked again as he got up. "That was uncalled for. Have a nice weekend."

"Whatever," Carlos said over his shoulder.

Ben came into the waiting room and stopped short when he saw Lamar with a big smile on his face. "What are you doing?" Ben said accusingly.

"I have an appointment."

"I mean, I didn't hear you come in."

Ben hurried through the interview.

"I thought I was going to be assigned to someone else," said Lamar when it seemed Ben was finished with him.

"Still short on staff. Most people left early because of the weekend."

"You mean it's just us?" Lamar said with a smirk.

Ben took his eyes away from the computer and glanced at Lamar for the first time. "We're done, Lamar. You can go." He spoke sternly, though the authority in his voice was forced.

Lamar leaned forward in an attempt to get Ben to look him in the eye. "Are you okay, Mr. Moss?"

Ben stood up abruptly. "Look, I would like to get out

of here before too late. Do you mind?" He pointed to the door.

Lamar stood up and adjusted his crotch, pulling at the underwear under the thin polyester of his warm-up pants. "Yeah, sure. Have a nice weekend, Mr. Moss." He had a way of drawing out the "Mr." as if it were a provocation rather than a sign of respect.

"Goodbye, Lamar."

Lamar was halfway out the door when he turned around. "Enjoy your peace and quiet."

After getting on BART at the West Oakland station, Lamar hurried to send Matt a text before the train went into the tube under the bay. He was going to be in the city and wondered if Matt wanted to have a drink. They hadn't seen each other since Matt picked him up at the police station.

Lamar was on his way to San Francisco—he continued to live at his mother's house during his probation—in response to a text from a guy named Steve who lived in the Mission and wanted a massage. He hated driving across the bridge at rush hour, but the tunnel under the bay also had drawbacks. He couldn't stop thinking about the millions of gallons of water around him; it made his palms sweat and his heart rate increase. He closed his eyes and saw his grandfather floating in ten feet of water.

When the roar of speed diminished and the train slid into Embarcadero station, he took a breath and looked at the commuters lined up along the platform. He noticed how few black people there were. The doors opened and the workers rushed onto the car, avoiding the seat next to Lamar until it was the last one left.

At Mission and Twenty-Fourth Street, Lamar got off and weaved through the crowd that inhabited the plaza like a pestilence—homeless drunks sprawled out on the pavement, sidewalk preachers shouting through bullhorns in Spanish, a street musician singing "If I Had a Hammer," and young men whispering mota to potential customers. He didn't feel the least bit guilty about charging an extra fifty bucks for an outcall.

It was a short walk to the address on Shotwell Street, an Edwardian with a fading paint job—sickly lilac with purple trim. He rang the doorbell, and it was immediately followed by buzzer to let him in. He stood at the bottom of a long stairway and almost laughed. Why didn't anyone live on the ground floor?

A voice said to come on up. At the top of the stairs was a dimly lit living room where a tall man stood looking out a window. He turned toward Lamar and the two men stared at each other in shock. Ben's bony shoulders rose to his ears. "What the...?"

"Fuck, I guess I'm busted," said Lamar. "What kind of game are you playing here, uh, Steve?"

"You had no face pic in your profile," Ben mumbled. "How was I...and you didn't exactly include this as an income source."

"We all want to be anonymous, right?" Lamar chuckled. "So this is how you spend your long weekends. Maybe it's you that's busted."

"This is the first time."

"Uh-huh. Heard that one before. You don't have to feel embarrassed about it. We all got needs."

"I swear. I've looked a lot. But I could never...anyway, why am I explaining myself to you? This is a violation of your probation."

"Really, Ben...can I call you Ben...or Steve? This is what you're gonna fall back on? Our roles in society?"

Ben stepped back and sat on the edge of the sofa as if his legs wouldn't carry him anymore. "Just go, Lamar. We'll forget this ever happened. You'll be assigned to another probation officer."

Lamar took out his phone, found Ben's number, and

deleted it. He showed the screen to Ben. "See? I've erased texts. No record. But I suppose it doesn't erase any needs you might've been having." Lamar sat down in a chair opposite him, leaned forward and rested his elbows on his knees. It was almost as if he could see Ben's dick twitch in his pants. And Ben's shoulders had already dropped a fraction as if resistance were futile.

Ben shook his head. "For you to even be here is so breaking every rule in the book. I need you to stand up and walk out that door right now."

"Is that what you really want?" Lamar got up and took a step closer to Ben. His crotch was at eye level. He enjoyed seeing the internal gymnastics Ben was going through reflected in his face, the slight moisture in his eyes, a tiny tremor in his jaw. But he also really wanted to hold Ben in his arms and make him feel better about himself. He took another step forward. "I'm here now. I won't hurt you. I can be very discreet."

"It all makes sense now."

"What?"

"Reading your file something was strange. Your fight with that guy. The broken window. The emotional escalation."

Lamar put his hand on Ben's shoulder. "You're not at work. This is not an interview. You need some attention."

Ben shrugged off the hand. "Please."

"Please what? Go or stay?"

Ben closed his eyes. Lamar gently turned him around and started massaging his shoulders.

As soon as he closed the door of his newly acquired studio apartment in the Lower Haight, the bare, off-white walls began to close in on him. He felt utterly alone as he stared at the five unpacked boxes distributed at odd angles on the battered and paint-splattered wood floor. Matt had helped him carry in his new futon sofa bed, leaving him a box of dishes and odds and ends that he no longer used, before rushing off to a meeting.

Lamar's six-month probation period had just ended and he decided it was time to separate himself from Oakland. With Lester in jail for possession, the last couple months were relatively calm at his mother's house, and even though she bemoaned Lester being locked up, she was noticeably more relaxed. She got up early and went to clean houses as she always did, but now the money she made went to clothes and shoes and improving the apartment.

Lamar couldn't bear tackling the boxes, so he pulled out his MacBook Pro and sat on the futon. He opened his Virtual DJ program and loaded one of the songs from a playlist. He almost pined for those days in Oakland, the time between when his mother and Letisha left for work and before he had to go to his job at two, when he had the apartment to himself. He spent hours searching for music, making playlists, and learning Virtual DJ. He had already DJed a couple of birthday parties for a hundred bucks (he had to start somewhere) and Shawna had arranged for him to do a friend's wedding. In return he had taken her out a couple of times, but would decline her offers for sex at the end of the night, saying he was dating someone in San Francisco. He neglected to mention that it was his parole officer (his ex-parole officer) and it wasn't exactly dating. He would stop by Ben's after work and occasionally spend the night. There was not, and never had been, an exchange of dollars with him. He did it because he liked seeing Ben emerge from his shell—the stunned and wonderful look on his face when he realized his body deserved pleasure. It was like teaching someone to swim, and then watching them splash out on their own. It had been a while since he had been with a girl, but he still told himself he liked girls, just not ones that wanted to tie him down.

He loaded another song onto the second virtual

turntable and tried mixing them, but he couldn't get the beats right. His phone lit up with a text message. Someone wanted a massage as soon as he could get there. Perfect, he thought. The room felt cold and the light was fading. He had no lamps. From one of the boxes he pulled some clothes and went to take a shower.

The older Asian man in an apartment near Alamo Square was nice enough—shy, not demanding—but Lamar was distracted by thoughts of Ben. As each new image of Ben entered his head, it felt full of splinters, his thoughts catching on them, thoughts that were too troublesome to put into words. Better to let them die, and continue to smile, play the only part that seemed to make sense.

He also realized that part of his discomfort was due to the music. "You can cut the swag music," said Lamar. "I'm not on the down low." He fumbled for his iPhone and put it on the base as if he were in his own home. His music was softer.

"Much better," the man said.

With the softer music Lamar could hear the sounds he really craved: the breath irregular, fabric pulling away from skin, the hollow rush of a hand rubbing and fingering the tiny springs on his wooly head. This one couldn't get enough of rubbing Lamar's head. Said he used to sit behind the only black kid in his school and fantasize about touching his hair.

The man asked a couple of questions, but Lamar's short answers made it clear he didn't want to talk, didn't want to talk about how his day was or where he was from. The room fell quiet except for the sounds of Nina Simone singing "Feelin' Good." Peace. Lamar cradled the man's butt cheeks and lifted him, backed him up to the bed, and let him fall. He pulled the man's arms out like wings and put his knee between his legs. He started kneading his hairless chest.

Lamar paused and looked out the window.

"You tired?" the man asked.

He was tired, and yet his hands began to move again with ease, gliding over curves of flesh and bone, skin smooth as silk. And then, their limbs were entangled; his earlier feelings of being lonely now rode clouds of nothingness, going nowhere. Peace. He thought of how many came to him, solicited him, begged for him—or at least, the anatomy of him, the potion he offered against the solitary life.

Their breathing settled and the room cooled. Lamar pulled the covers up over them. "Mind if I spend the night?" he asked.

"I have no money for that."

"Freebie," Lamar mumbled, and fell asleep.

9 Smite This People with Blindness

Lamar felt the power of a god as he looked down from his box high above the circular dance floor, a crater bathed in red light, a bubbling, undulating sea of molten lava. They were in the drop of "What Can We Do," the second-to-last song. The beat was pounding and he cranked up the bass another notch. On the video screens were black-and-white cityscapes, urban hipsters dancing free, skateboarders in stark alleys. The screen visuals were a sharp contrast to what was going to happen next. The lights on the crowd eased into purple and the sky exploded into a meteor show of spinning balls and lasers raining down on the writhing bodies. The volcano was about to blow. Lamar slipped the Beats off his ears and let them rest on his shoulders so he could listen to and feel the thumping heart of the room while the three comp whiskey sodas he had downed kept him mellowed and in the moment. His hands danced over the levers and buttons, pushing the music to the max. And then it was breakdown time. He brought in the loop of Anastacia belting out "Pride, a deeper love" over and over, pushing up the vocals. The lyrics made him tingle, reminding him of the love he wanted so badly to feel for himself. He saw below him hundreds of lips mouthing the words and his arms shot out to embrace the energy.

On the last "love" he held it and hit the reverb. With his Beats back on, he got ready for the mix-in. But first he cut everything. The screens went black and the music and light show stopped. The crowd, now bathed in blue, stared up at him. The universe stopped for eight beats and the faces of the people fell as if something had gone wrong, their highs suddenly canceled. And then he started the world again with a repetitive a 126 beats-per-minute synth pattern of deep chords in G. People came out of their shock and began to move again. He let it loop about thirty seconds, a good beat match for the finale. The screens came alive with brown tinted footage of abandoned buildings, and he slid the crossfade bar to Deck B. An ethereal synth melody floated in the air, and immediately the arms of the dancers shot up, knowing what was coming. A chorus of voices began softly, "There's a place in the distance / a place that I've been dreaming of." He repeated the chorus several times pumping up the volume each time. The drop hit with a heavy drumbeat and the lighting guy brought in color with a slowly rotating Iosphere ball and a moonflower LED splash effect. In the video, urban warriors prepared for battle, running through empty streets. But their weapons were pods of colored powder. They pelted each other with pastels, changing the drab clothes and surrounding landscape into pallets of color. It was a war where no one was hurt and the city was transformed.

Lamar left the song on its own and took a sip of whiskey. He swished it around in his mouth and smiled. This was it, better than sex or drugs. Better than anything. And yet, at the edge of his happiness was the knowledge that the night was coming to an end and soon he would be out in the cool Oakland night alone. Bar-backs worked frantically to gather up glasses. He saw them coming for his and he took one last sip. The song let everyone down with a chorus of violins and faded out. A few people looked up toward him and clapped. He waved and bowed his thanks.

He packed up his MacBook Pro and headed down the stairs. The bouncer, Seymour, was coming in the back door.

"Anybody out there?" Lamar asked.

"Yep, they're there."

"Shit!"

The last few weeks a pair of cougars had been hanging around the back entrance when he left. He hadn't figured out a polite way to discourage them. Maybe he didn't want to completely discourage them. Maybe he liked the attention. Maybe he liked the idea that hot older women thought they had a chance with him. And in a sense they did. He could get it up with women. No problem there. But it was the five minutes after sex that he had a problem with. They wanted his phone number. They wanted to see him again, be his girlfriend, get married and have kids before it was too late, move to the suburbs. God, no. That's not what cougars were supposed to do, but it's what they did with him. He had friends who were good at the bang 'em and leave 'em thing. Why didn't it work for him? He had convinced himself that he went with guys because they were less complicated. They wanted what he wanted, and they could leave it at the door.

"Hi, Lamar," said Lina. She was a dark Puerto Rican with a sexy accent and a voluptuous body on the edge of tumbling into overweight. Her sidekick, Brenda, was a dyed blond, tall and slender, on the shy side until she had had a few drinks.

"Hello, ladies. What's cooking?"

"That would be you, handsome," said Brenda. She teetered on her heels and put one hand on his shoulder to steady herself.

"It's chilly out here," said Lina. "Let's go someplace and get warm, kick back, have a drink. How 'bout it, Lamar?"

"Man, I'm beat," said Lamar.

"Oh, baby. We'll take good care of you. Come on." Brenda tilted her head and gave him a kitten look. She was high.

"Lina, I think you need to get Brenda home. Chill, you know. Maybe another night."

"That's what you always say."

"What the fuck?" chimed in Brenda. "I'm okay. Maybe we're just not good enough for you."

"Or the right sex," said Lina.

He was stunned, but quickly recovered and put his arm around Brenda's waist. "You guys are babes. Don't get me wrong. But I got somebody waiting."

"Male or female?"

He dropped his arm and moved away. "Goodnight, ladies. Be safe and get out of this alley."

"Just tell us," Lina shouted after him.

He got out to the main street where a few people lingered on the downtown sidewalks, smoking and talking in drunk-loud voices. A patrol car flashed its lights down the block. He started walking the opposite direction toward his car that was parked a little farther than he would have liked. He had the laptop case slung over his shoulder. Still with a brisk high he moved at a good pace past dark alleys and sidewalks with fewer and fewer people. His car was a half a block away; he pulled out his keys, pushed the button to unlock it. A few steps from the car, two men came out from behind a van and cut him off before he could reach the door. One of them pulled out a gun and pointed to the bag. There was nobody else on the street, a universe that included only Lamar and his attackers.

"No way," said Lamar.

"Give us the bag, nigger," said the one with the gun. The other one grabbed the strap.

"Who you calling "nigger"? Shit, stealing from you own kind." Lamar held on tight. His Virtual DJ program and all the music he had worked on for months was on the laptop, most of it not backed up.

The gunman gave up a snarly laugh. "Own kind? You blind, nigger? We ain't no faggots. Nothing worse than a nigger fag." He put the gun to Lamar's head. "The bag now!"

The other one was still tugging at the strap and Lamar kicked him in the balls as hard as he could. There was a flash, a loud crack and then blackness. But before the blackness there was his life, all twenty-three years of it in a quadruple fast video. The impact knocked him back up against a slender tree, and then he slid to the ground. The bony tree felt uncomfortable against his back. Liquid ran down his face and dripped on his shirt. His ears still rang from the explosion. And then, slowly, he heard things, the city's night music of distant sirens, traffic, and the bass of a passing car's stereo system. Lina's voice sounded both distant and a whisper in his ear. "Oh my God, that was Lamar's bag!"

"What are you talking about?" said Brenda.

"That sound we heard wasn't a car backfiring. Shit. Call 911."

Lamar wasn't sure who they were talking about. A shot? He felt around him for his bag. Dirt. A sticky wrapper. A few sprigs of grass. He was sitting on a patch of dirt. "Why can't I see?" he thought. The dripping continued off his chin. The clomping of heels came toward him, and then stopped. Brenda screamed.

"Shut up," said Lina.

"Oh my God. Is he dead?" asked Brenda in a softer but shaky voice.

"No," said Lamar. "Unless you're angels."

They hurried over and knelt beside him. "Oh, Lamar," said Lina.

"What's happened?" said Lamar.

"We called 911. They should be here any minute."

Lamar reached and touched the side of his head. It was warm and wet, a wound. "I've been shot."

"Don't touch it," said Lina. She took his hand.

Brenda walked a few paces away and vomited. She began to cry. "I'm so sorry. Please forgive me."

"For what?"

"For what I said before."

"Brenda, just...just be quiet, okay?" said Lina. "Stay with me, Lamar. Don't talk. Don't...I don't know...don't waste your energy."

"I can't see," he whispered, "but it doesn't hurt. It's weird."

"You're in shock, but you're going to be all right." Lina was a nurse, though she only worked in a retirement home and never saw gunshot wounds.

"Can't we do something?" wailed Brenda.

"Please, Brenda." Lina went from a kneeling position to sitting beside Lamar. She very gently put her arms around him and moved his head to lie on her breasts. They heard a siren. "Brenda, get up and flag them down."

Lamar moaned. "Stay with me, baby." she said. "Everything's gonna be fine."

"Fine? My eyes are gone. They're gone, damnit." He began to whimper. "Am I dying? Christ! This sucks."

"*Tranquilo, niño.*"

"What?"

"It's what I always say to my little boy when he's in pain."

The siren had changed to a whop, whop, whop. "They're here. See the lights?"

"No..." he whined like a little boy.

"Oh, God. I mean, sorry. They're here."

The paramedics took over and a police car pulled up a minute later. While the paramedics braced his head and put him on a stretcher, he heard the officers questioning Brenda and Lina. They said they had seen two men running away with Lamar's bag. Lamar's memory was fuzzy, but bits of the story came to him: the muggers, their twisted faces, the explosion in his head. And the laptop. Gone.

Lamar didn't believe in Letisha's Bible nonsense, but as he lay in the hospital bed his mind sank into a dark place where he considered the possibility that he was being punished for something. He felt guilty for not treating his family better. Since that chunk of cash he gave his mother and sister a couple of years back, he hadn't exactly been forthcoming with more help. The few months he lived with them after his arrest had ended with another fight with his mother. Lamar found out that Abigail had used most of the money he gave her on Lester's defense after he was arrested for possession. Lamar's probation was coming to an end, and he had packed his car and left, staying in a motel on Lombard Street while he looked for a place in the city.

He had spoken to Letisha a couple of times in the past year, but not his mother. In one of their conversations, she dropped in a couple of quotes from the Bible about homosexuality, ostensibly in reference to Byron and his lifestyle, but perhaps they were really intended for him. Was it possible that he was being punished for all the sex he had had with men? All his life he had heard it was sinful, and yet it didn't feel wrong. It was curious that he had never heard his grandmother, the person who had taught him so much about life, speak badly about homosexuals. Her main message was not to hurt people, especially those who couldn't defend themselves. Was he hurting people by accepting money for giving them what they wanted?

Maybe he should have stuck with the Costco job and not gotten into DJing. Starting off as a DJ he had to take gigs in places that he didn't necessarily like, leaving the discos after most people had gone home in sketchy neighborhoods late at night. But with Costco…what? Move up the ladder? Maybe save up enough to buy a house in the East Bay because San Francisco was too expensive, be stuck in a mortgage with two weeks of vacay a year. He wasn't cut out for a nine-to-five. Now everything he loved was taken away: DJing, basketball, regular sex. Who would want to have sex with a blind person?

Lamar felt someone in the room. Ben had a habit of coming up behind him in the living room when he was watching TV or the bedroom while he was sleeping. He would stand and stare at him. It always gave Lamar an eerie feeling when he would open his eyes or look over his shoulder, and find Ben there like a peeping Tom, trying to peer into his head. Now, when he felt stared at, he didn't have the luxury of opening his eyes or looking over his shoulder, and it drove him crazy.

"That you, Ben?"

"No."

"Who are you?"

"How are you doing, Lamar?"

"Are you shitting me? Byron?"

"Wasn't sure you'd want to see me, but I came as soon as I heard."

"I *can't* see you."

"Oh, right."

"And I'll never be able to. Lucky for me, huh?"

"I thought there was a chance for your left eye."

"Who've you been talking to? Who called you anyway?" His words were drug-slurred.

"Your mom." The truth was that Hattie had called him, though she wasn't supposed to know. Lamar was adamant with his mom that Grannie not be told. She was recovering from a bout of pneumonia and needed to rest, not feel bad that she couldn't come to his bedside. But more than that, he was embarrassed. Everything that she had warned him against had happened to him in the last couple years: an arrest, police harassment, street violence.

"I just hope no one tells Grannie."

"Hey, if there's any chance you could get vision back in one eye, that's something."

"Five percent. Is that something?" The bullet had entered his right temple and exited the left. His right eye was shattered and had to be surgically removed. It could be replaced with a prosthetic eye, the doctor explained. The left had suffered severe trauma to the tissue and nerves. When the swelling went down they would have a better idea of his prognosis, but the doctor admitted it didn't look good.

"But you're alive! I could just as easily be coming to your funeral. It was that close. I'm really happy that's not the case."

"You can be happy all you want. I want to kill those motherfuckers."

Byron remembered feeling exactly the same when he was about Lamar's age. A lecture started forming in his brain about the emptiness of revenge, but he decided it wasn't the time. It was probably good that Lamar was angry. Better than being depressed. "Go ahead and shout at the world. I don't blame you."

"I want to do more than shout."

"Of course you do. But you've got to heal first."

"Come over here," said Lamar. "I hate it when people just stand in the middle of the room like I'm a leper or something." He motioned to the side of the bed. "Sit. There's a chair there, isn't there?"

"Yes."

The rough edges of Lamar's anger began to soften and he curiously felt an urge to cry. Must have been the drugs. "I can't believe you're here. I was such a jerk back then."

"That was a long time ago."

"Not that long. Hearing your voice brings it all back. How's Georgette?"

"She'll be here tomorrow. She couldn't get away yesterday, so I came on ahead."

"Coincidence you planned a trip here now."

"Don't be an idiot. We're here for you."

Lamar started to say something nasty about still being a charity case, but he heard Grannie's voice telling him to shut up. It was more knee-jerk reaction than his true feeling. He couldn't help being skeptical why people like Byron and Georgette would be interested in him.

"She's a fine woman," said Lamar instead.

"Yes, she is."

"Guess my mom and Letisha will be over later. I hadn't seen them in months, but when I came out of surgery, there they were."

They fell silent. The long pause flitted around the room like a butterfly, and then landed on his bandaged head. He swore he could feel it.

Lamar reached out his hand. "You still there?"

Byron took Lamar's hand in an arm-wrestle handshake, and despite the initial awkwardness, held on to it. Lamar also made no attempt to extricate his moist and calloused hand. It eased into something surprisingly normal. Something about the hospital bedside allowed it, along with the painkillers that took Lamar's nervous energy down a notch.

Byron felt there had been an overall change in Lamar that he couldn't quite put a finger on. And then it came to him. He spoke differently, having dropped a lot of the ghetto talk and teenage attitude in his voice. He must have been hanging around with a different crowd.

Lamar heard someone come into the room and dropped Byron's hand.

"Hello," said Ben.

"Oh, Ben. This is Byron."

"I know." There was tension in Ben's voice.

"You two met?"

"No. It's just that you've talked about him so much."

"Me?" said Byron in genuine shock.

"And some of it was even good," said Lamar. The anxious air in the room swallowed his joke.

In an instant, from the look on Ben's face and the edge in his voice, Byron knew that Ben was in love with Lamar, that they had had sex, that they might even be boyfriends. The first thing Ben had seen upon entering the room was Byron and Lamar holding hands. Terror had flashed across his brow. Byron also sensed that, although Lamar was fond of Ben, he didn't feel the same way.

Ben dropped a bag on the bedside table. "I brought you some stuff." He stood on the opposite side of the bed from Byron, his gaze focused on the bandages around Lamar's head.

"Thanks," said Lamar. "Did you bring my iPod?"

Ben fished it out of the bag and put it in Lamar's hands.

"The doctor says you can go home tomorrow."

"But…"

"I mean my place. You'll need help."

Lamar's jaw dropped and trembled. "Yeah, I guess," he said in a shaky voice. He saw the future laid out in front of him like a great desert with no hope. And the thought of being dependent on someone sent fearful vibrations through his body. "Maybe I should stay here for a while."

Ben looked at Byron for a little support. "Well, you know how hospitals are these days. Get them in and out. Right, Byron?"

"Nothing fun about a hospital," said Byron. He jumped up. "I'm going to get some coffee. Anybody want anything?"

"You don't have to go," said Ben.

Byron communicated with his eyes that Ben and Lamar needed some time to talk. "No, really. I'm feeling a little jet-lagged. I'll be back." He patted Lamar's arm on the way out.

Lamar had been pleasantly surprised by Byron's visit; it had temporarily lifted his mood. Now he felt himself plunging into an abyss. When Ben mentioned going to his apartment, it brought up a million questions, questions that he would have to deal with for the rest of his life.

"I know," said Ben. "It's a lot to think about."

Byron's stomach had been in a state of revolution since he arrived in San Francisco, and the hospital cafeteria coffee set off a new round of agitation. It gurgled and surged like a chemistry experiment, making him spend a lot more time in the men's room than he would have liked. When things calmed somewhat, he felt it was safe to return to Lamar's room. He came around the corner and saw two women emerge from the room. For a moment he had the bizarre notion that Lamar had hired a couple of prostitutes. But the absurd image of the bandaged Lamar cavorting on the narrow hospital bed with the women while Ben looked on quickly passed when he noticed the serious expressions on their faces. The woman who looked Latina touched her blond friend's arm and whispered something.

When Byron entered the room, Lamar was on his cell phone. Ben was gone. One of the women must have dialed the number for him. He spoke in a low angry voice, but as soon as he realized Byron's presence, he ended the conversation.

"Where's Ben?" asked Byron.

"He had to go. Actually, he offered to pick up Abigail and Letisha who, by the way, now wants to be called Sarah. You know, like in the Bible. They've never met, so it should be interesting."

The sun came out from behind a cloud and burst through the window, bathing Lamar's head in an unsettling golden light, a light that intensified the already yellowish tinge to his skin. He had a habit of touching his bandages, attempting to adjust them every few minutes as if it itched underneath. And then his hands would settle on his stomach, fingers crossed. It was a pattern Byron had witnessed a number of times since he had been there.

"Are we going to talk about it or just let it sit in the corner?" said Byron.

"It being…?"

"Change. What's been going on in your life since I last saw you. Ben."

"He's a friend."

"I see. He nearly freaked when he walked in and saw you holding my hand."

Lamar shrugged.

"Does anybody in your family know what's going on?"

"Going on? Nothing's going on. Look, I don't stick my nose in anybody's business and they better not do it in mine."

"How did you guys meet?"

"What did I just say?"

"Okay. Forget it."

Lamar touched his bandages again, and Byron got up to close the blinds. The room immediately seemed cooler. The TV from the other side of the curtain was blaring a talk show in Spanish.

"Were those women visiting you…" Byron lowered his voice and said, "…or the person over there?

"God, Byron, you're back in my life for an hour and

you're already heavy with the questions."

"And why would that be?"

"'Cause you're a nosey son-of-a-bitch?"

"Wouldn't have anything to do with the fact that I care about you. I feel bad that I wasn't better about keeping in touch."

"I didn't need nobody keeping tabs on me. I was doing just fine. I got a job. I was taking a few classes. I started DJing and living on my own. Meeting some interesting people. My life was just getting cool. And now everything's fucked up." He took a long shaky breath.

"I'm truly sorry. I am."

"Those ladies found me when I was shot. They were at the club. Regulars. They used to stand by the back door where I come out."

"A little cougar action, huh?"

"I never did nothing...anything with them. If I had gone with them that night, I would still have my eyes." He paused and took another deep breath. "They just told me something."

What had been so important a moment ago—finding out about the two women—now seemed unimportant as his mind drifted. With half of Lamar's face buried under the bandages, Byron struggled not to see Thomas, fantasize that he hadn't died of his wounds, that he was right there and that Byron would take care of him. He stared at the strong arms and long-fingered brown hands against the whiteness of the sheets, his unshaven chin, the slightly purple lips. As long as no one else was around, he could stare all he wanted and no one would know.

"Byron?" said Lamar.

"I'm here. What did they tell you?"

"They saw the guys running away. Lina knows one of them." His right fist was clenched and he ground it into the palm of his other hand. "He lives down the street from her."

"Is she going to the police?"

"She has a son. She's afraid the bastards would get off and then come after her."

"But she wasn't afraid to tell you."

Lamar shrugged. "She likes me."

Byron's stomach turned upside down and he thought he might have to run to the bathroom. "You're not thinking of doing anything?"

"Right. Look at me."

"Or have someone else do something?"

"Why would you say that?" asked Lamar.

Byron looked at Lamar's phone on the bedside table and had to fight the urge to pick it up and look at his recent calls.

10 Fearfulness Hath Surprised the Hypocrites

Lamar probed the food with a fork. He was learning to recognize the items Ben had put on his plate by texture: mashed potatoes, chicken breasts cut into pieces, salad that liked to fall off his fork. Little of the food was going into his mouth. For the first time in his life, he was without an appetite. Ben kept telling him he was losing weight and needed to eat.

"Maybe you should just put a bib on me and feed me baby food," Lamar said with disgust.

Ben kept eating, acting as if the comment didn't deserve a response.

"Where's my wine?" Lamar demanded.

"It's above your plate on the right."

Lamar touched the smooth thick-based, lowball glass. "So I'm not allowed a wineglass anymore?" The night before he had knocked over a stemmed glass, sending a swath of red across the table.

"Until you get used to..." Ben didn't know the right phrase. It was all new to him, too.

"Used to what? A life of one accident after another? Where I can't walk two feet for fear of bumping into something?" Though half his face was still covered in bandages, the lower part was as tight as a drum. His chest moved up and down, and then his arm swept across the table, sending plate, glass, and silverware to the floor. "I can't do this!"

"Yes, you can!" Ben shot back.

Lamar groaned. "This in not a fucking Obama campaign slogan. This is my life. I wish they had aimed a couple inches to the left."

Ben got up and started picking up the mess. "Don't say that."

"And how long before you get sick of taking care of me?"

"Things'll get better."

Lamar slipped off the chair to his knees. He stretched out his hand and came upon a piece of broken plate.

"Don't. I've got it," said Ben.

Lamar picked up another piece of the plate and clumsily put the pieces on the table.

"Lamar, stop. You'll hurt yourself." He grabbed Lamar under his arm and lifted him back into his chair. Lamar snatched his arm back and pushed him away. "I'm not an invalid."

Ben stood strong and firmly gripped Lamar's shoulder. "You're angry. Who wouldn't be? But the bullet didn't go an inch or two to the left for a reason."

"And what reason would that be?"

"We don't know that yet."

"It's not like I'm going to be the next Stevie Wonder or anything. For everything I like to do I need my eyes. Don't you get it?"

"Everything?"

"What?"

Normally Ben would have winked or raised his bushy eyebrows or smirked. The ways they could communicate now were limited to words and touch. "You don't need your eyes to have sex."

"Where's the fun in that?" Lamar loved having the lights on, the visual feast of bodies in motion in the mirror, his partner's orgasm, the contorted face, the eyes rolling back, the shooting semen landing on naked skin. Just thinking of the visuals normally got him hard. Since the attack he felt nothing down there.

The TV in the living room was on and an interview was in progress. Lamar tilted his head and listened. Ben started to say something and Lamar hushed him.

"What does he look like?"

"Who?"

"Can you see the TV? The guy who's talking."

"Balding. About forty-five. Thin face. Glasses."

"I knew it. Take me in there."

They sat on the sofa in front of the screen while the man droned on about the sanctity of marriage and the vile gay agenda. They were the same robotic catchphrases they had heard a thousand times. But they were coming out of the mouth of someone Lamar knew.

"We don't have to watch this crap," said Ben.

"Wait. I want to hear it."

Ben got up and started for the kitchen. "I'm going to clean up."

Lamar was taken back to a hotel suite at the Hilton. It was the third or fourth time they had met. The man from the TV had lain naked in the bed while Lamar put on his clothes. He was U.S. Congressman Reggie Port. Lamar had only learned who he was the week before their meeting when he saw him on TV for the first time. The man disgusted him and he had debated accepting another call, but his car payment was due.

That evening, Lamar sat in the canary-yellow armchair by the window looking out over the lights of the city. He bent over to tie his shoes.

"I saw you on TV," said Lamar.

"And?"

"How can you do that? Talk shit about gay people?"

"What do you care?" Port said, rubbing his crotch under the sheet as if he wanted more. "You're no homo."

"I am a homo. A homo sapien. People should be able to do what they want in their own damn bedroom."

"The problem is, they don't leave it in the bedroom. They take it out to the streets, parade it around, try to push it on other people. White conservative men like me speak out and we get bashed for it. That's not right."

"You know what I think? You're a hypocrite."

"I don't pay you to think."

"Fair enough. But you would have to pay me a hell of a lot more to stop me from thinking."

"You little shit. If you're considering blackmailing me, you'd better think twice."

"Who said anything about blackmail? You're paranoid."

Port took his cell phone from the bedside table and began thumbing through his messages. After a minute he looked up. "You still here? Your money's on the table by the door."

Lamar went out in the hall and counted it. "Cheapskate!" he mumbled as he went out the door. "He didn't even leave me a tip."

The next time Port called, Lamar didn't answer. He had to put up with a lot in his line of work, but hypocrisy was one thing he refused to abide. The congressman called a couple more times and then stopped. That same week he read online that a blogger had outed Port and claimed that a couple of male prostitutes were ready to talk.

"Damn! Damn!" Lamar shouted.

Ben ran out from the kitchen. "What is it?"

"Where's the remote? Turn that thing off. I've got to think."

"I thought you wanted to watch it."

"Turn it off!" Lamar screamed.

"All right. Calm down." Ben went back to the kitchen.

The night he was shot came back to him. He distinctly heard one of the attackers say, "You sure that's the motherfucker?"

In the flurry of the attack and the aftermath, he had completely forgotten the brief exchange. Maybe it wasn't a random mugging as everybody assumed. Maybe they were looking specifically for him. Lamar had been wracking his brain, wondering if it had been some punk who had it out for him. He had gotten into a scuffle a few days before when he accidentally elbowed a guy in a pick-up game. The others had quickly broken it up, tensions had dissipated, and they had shaken hands. He couldn't think of anybody else who might hold a grudge against him.

The conversation with the congressman presented another scenario. Could he have hired thugs to off him? "What the fuck? It couldn't be. No way!"

Ben came in drying his hands on a kitchen towel. "What are you yelling about now?"

Georgette sat on the sofa with Lamar helping him with the VoiceOver program on his new MacBook. He swore and banged the keyboard after he kept hitting the wrong keys. She wondered if he had taken his anti-anxiety medicine. The doorbell rang and she got up to let Byron in. They had agreed to spend time with Lamar in shifts while Ben went to work. She motioned for Byron to stay in the hall and she stepped out to talk to him.

"We've been working on the program on his new computer. He gets furious when he hits the wrong keys," said Georgette.

"I thought that was the point, that you used voice commands."

"But you still have to use some keys. If you don't

know the keyboard, it's frustrating. Be gentle with him."

Byron looked at her like she was being ridiculous. "Don't worry. I can pretty much say that we've buried the hatchet."

"I hate that expression. It always makes me think of Lizzie Borden."

"Oh, my dear sweet gentle soul with a morose imagination."

"Yeah, well, I'm counting on you to calm him down."

Georgette said her goodbyes and Byron went into the kitchen. "I brought you some of that Chinese food you like from the corner. Do you want to eat now?"

"Not really hungry. Later," said Lamar with a voice sunk in hopelessness.

Byron sat down on the sofa and stared at the open computer on the coffee table. "Did you have a nice time with Georgette?"

"I guess. What was she telling you at the door? That I was an asshole?"

"That most certainly is not what she said."

"I hope she'll come back."

"Of course she will."

Lamar crossed his hands in his lap and took a breath. "So you were with him that day, huh?"

Though it was a fly snatched out of the air, Byron knew exactly what he meant. A low-pitched buzz hung about every time they were in a room together. "Yes," said Byron softly.

"You ran away? Just left him there?"

"No. It wasn't like that."

"A good little faggot just ran away." Lamar's words had taken on the same aggressive attitude as when they first met except this time they were fitted with spurs to dig deep.

Byron stood up, determined not to be dragged in. It was Lamar's frustration, the drugs. He didn't mean it. "I'm going in the other room until you calm down."

"Run away. There you go."

"Shut up, Lamar. You don't know what you're talking about."

"Fuck that. I wanna know what happened. I wanna know why he died and you survived."

"You know why I survived, though I could easily have not. And yes, I did run, so that I could get help. I would have done anything to save Thomas. He was still alive, but they wouldn't let me go. I got to the point where I didn't care if they shot me, too. But I was no good to him dead. I eventually got away and called 911. They sent an ambulance, but by the time they got him to the hospital he was gone."

Lamar's jaw loosened. "Tell me about that day, everything."

Byron started like a car left out in a winter storm, at first failing to ignite, then chugging, his words slow and nearly dying until they began to flow—the afternoon of fishing, the sex under the trees, the hum of the cicadas, the shot ringing out, the blood, his pleading with Kelly and the boys to get help, how he eventually shook them. Since it was now obvious that Lamar had sex with men (he still insisted Ben was just a friend), Byron knew he wouldn't be shocked by the story.

Though Lamar was intrigued, noise outside the window kept swaying his attention. Occasionally, a city bus would grind to a halt outside the window and announce in a computer voice, "27 Bryant to Jackson and Van Ness," as if the people didn't know what bus they were getting on or where it was going. He had a hard time concentrating these days. Byron's voice shifted as he paced around the room, and Lamar could only imagine Byron's gestures stirring up the air. Finally, Byron slumped down on the sofa and sobbed into his hands. After all these years, the pain was still that of a wound being teased open.

Lamar's head was pounding, and his eye sockets burned and itched. "You loved him."

"More than you'll ever know," said Byron in a voice that sounded like he was drowning. "Why did you make me tell it? It kills me every time."

"I had to know. If I hadn't provoked you, you never would have told me."

"You shit," said Byron, but without malice.

"Yeah, I'm a blind shit-assed nigger with a humdinger of a future ahead of me. But at least I know what all the mystery was about." He stretched out his arm along the back of the sofa and searched until he found Byron's shoulders. He rested his arm on them and gave them a little squeeze. "Sorry."

"I should have told you sooner, but I didn't think you'd understand."

"I knew you didn't run away. And I know that you stepped up like a man."

"What do you mean?"

"Taking care of things."

Byron shrugged off Lamar's arm, sat up and looked at him. "Who have you been talking to?"

"Grannie."

"You called her?"

"I had to tell her what happened to me. Didn't want her to hear from somebody else. And I needed to know some things."

"Like what?"

"What happened to the murderers."

"What did she say?"

"She say three white boys got burnt up in a trailer. Columbia's a small town and people had their suspicions that it was those same three boys who killed Thomas. Grannie say an accident like that was divine retribution. But I say no way. That was my boy Byron."

"You said that to her?"

"Nah, just what I was thinking."

"Well, you're wrong."

"I don't think so. Something you said the other day about revenge not being all it's cracked up to be."

Byron sighed and leaned back against Lamar's arm. He had come clean about everything else. He might as well tell Lamar the truth in hopes that he could deter him from doing something stupid. "It's not. I regret my actions."

"You regret putting those motherfuckers who killed the person you loved out of their misery? What are you talking about? Revenge is sweet. It says so in the Bible."

"I'm sure you're thinking of the 'eye for an eye' quote. Turns out there are a hell of a lot more biblical passages *against* vengeance, like 'Do not repay evil for evil or reviling for reviling, but on the contrary, bless, for this you were called, that you may obtain a blessing.'"

"Sounds real nice, but that's bullshit, and you know it."

"Not at all. I was going through a really hard time in Barcelona. Georgette introduced me to a priest—one of the good ones who was part of the Liberation Theology movement. He had been in Central America where several of his fellow priests and nuns were murdered. He knew something about the gut reaction of wanting revenge and could quote about fifty passages that warned against it."

"But come on! What about justice?"

"We're not talking about Thomas anymore, are we? I don't know what you're thinking, but don't."

"I thought you'd be behind me on this."

"Let the police handle it."

"Yeah, like the police give a shit about one black man shooting another," said Lamar. He touched the dime-sized crusty scar on his right temple. Then he ran his fingers over the right eye patch that he had to wear until he got his prosthetic eye. He lowered his head and mumbled, "And it could be a lot more complicated than that."

"Meaning?"

"Something makes me think it wasn't a random act of violence. It wasn't the laptop they wanted. They were after me."

"Why? You piss somebody off?"

"I didn't mean to, but you know I speak my mind."

"I'll give you that. So what happened?"

"If I tell you, I have to reveal a whole lot of shit I didn't want you to know."

"You think you can shock me?"

"Yep. I think I can."

The irony of Lamar now being the one with secrets wasn't lost on Byron. Lamar proceeded to tell Byron everything, from the ladies of Oakland to Congressman Port, and everything in between. When he stopped talking, a middle-of-the-night silence fell on the room, though it was only late afternoon, with the sun sitting just above a bank of fog hovering over Twin Peaks.

"You still with me, Byron? I can't even hear you breathing."

"Wow. I'm so sorry."

"For what? That my mom pimped me out or stole my money? Or the arrest? Or the sleazy congressman? Or that I could still be in danger? Or for my whole fucking sad life?"

"Your life is not sad. You're alive and you have people who care about you. Ben is a good man. Georgette always loved you. God knows why," said Byron with a chuckle. "Hattie loves you with all her heart, and despite what she did, I know Abigail does too. I can imagine what pressure Lester put on her."

"People say I look a lot like my uncle." His voice had fallen to almost a whisper. He could feel the turn of Byron's head toward him, imagine the mouth drop open.

"And your point?" said Byron.

"Maybe people just like me because I remind them of

him. You for instance. You think I didn't see how you looked at me? I still feel it even though I can't see it now."

"Of course, at the beginning, it was about helping Thomas' family, something I had to do. And then I began to care about y'all as individual people. I have a great affection for your grandmother. And yes, you have an uncanny resemblance to Thomas. But you are your own person, and I want the best for you. I'll be the first to admit I have no idea what a young black man has to do to survive in this world. The deck is stacked against you. To be honest, I admire you. You got out of Oakland. You found people who could help you. You made your own money, though some people wouldn't approve."

"I had a real job at Costco, too," Lamar reminded him.

"And your DJing. I know that's a passion for you."

"Was."

"Blind people do all kinds of things. Why couldn't you continue as a DJ? You've got your ears. Don't you manipulate those levers and wheels on your machines a lot by feel anyway? And the computer technology? You'll have that down in no time."

"I don't know. It might all be a moot point if they come after me again."

"I've got an idea. Do you still have the name of the lawyer who helped you out before?"

"Should be in my phone."

"And you've got to tell Ben about the congressman, as difficult as it may be."

"He knows about my past, just not the specifics. The congressman thing was before we got together."

Byron contacted Lamar's lawyer and asked him to write a letter to Congressman Port stating something to the effect that Lamar had never spoken to the press, nor would he, concerning the controversy surrounding Port. If contacted by the press, Lamar would deny knowing the congressman. He had no interest whatsoever in the scandal or any possible benefits that he might reap from it. There should be no further contact between the two parties if in fact there had ever been any. It was a shame to let Port off the hook, but they had to think of Lamar's safety. The congressman's career was ruined anyway, and it seemed that others were willing to come forward and implicate him.

Ben and Byron also went behind Lamar's back and contacted the police. They had talked to Lina and gotten the name and address of Lamar's shooters, promising her that her name would not be mentioned. The police were skeptical when Ben and Byron refused to reveal the source, but they agreed to at least check into it. Not the most brilliant of criminals, the two wanna-be gangsters, Zeppo and his cousin BG, still had Lamar's computer, but no gun. Zeppo had aspirations of being a DJ and claimed he had bought the computer on the street from an addict for a hundred bucks. The police couldn't disprove that, and without an eyewitness and a weapon, it was hard to make a case. When Byron told Lamar the news, he said, "See I told you. They're walking free. The popo don't have time for black-on-black crime." Byron again went into his lecture about revenge to which Lamar answered, "Your damage wasn't a disability."

"Not one that you can see," said Byron.

11 It Shall Be Forgiven Him

A foggy breeze swept through the open door and over their table of cold *mezes* at a Turkish restaurant on Guerrero. Georgette slipped her arms into her beaded vintage cashmere sweater and shivered. "I had no idea San Francisco was so cold," she said.

The waiter, who had hardly taken his eyes off her since they came in, ran over and pulled the door closed. "Sorry, madam," he said in a hoarse, accented English.

She gave him a winning if dismissive smile.

"You've still got it, baby!" said Byron.

"Why thank you, Mr. Boudreaux. I might say the same about you. And here we are in the city of love, especially the manly kind."

"What are you suggesting?"

Georgette picked up a piece of warm bread and slathered it with *cevizli ezme*, a shiny red paste of walnuts, red pepper, and garlic. "Wasn't that guy you met in Cuba from San Francisco?"

After all these years, Byron was still flabbergasted at how Georgette could read his mind. He hadn't told her that he had rummaged through a drawer of old papers in his desk on the day he left. He had found the address and stuck it in his wallet. "Rafael," said Byron. "Yes, I believe you're right."

Georgette giggled. "You believe?"

"I mean, what are the chances he's still here? San Francisco people move a lot. It's a transient city, unlike New Orleans where they sink into the swamps. And, I hate to say it, there was the plague that wiped out a good part of a generation. Sometimes it's best not to dig into the past."

"Aren't you curious?"

"It was a long time ago. I didn't treat him very kindly."

"He knew you were going through a hard time. I'm certain he wouldn't hold a grudge for thirty years."

Byron moaned. "Is there anything I haven't told you over the years? Every last secret you've squeezed out of me and left me as dry as an old sponge."

"I bet you've even got an address for him."

The waiter stopped at their table, but before he could ask how everything was, Byron looked up into his glistening black eyes, realizing suddenly how handsome he was, and locked him into a flirtatious stare, encouraged by the bottle of wine they had almost finished. "Would you mind removing this woman from my presence?" Byron said, waving his hand toward Georgette.

The waiter's forehead shot up, lifting his bushy eyebrows, and a falling jaw stretched his scruffy face in the other direction. He gave Georgette a shy, pitying look. He took a step back and looked down.

Byron and Georgette burst into laughter.

"Don't listen to him," said Georgette. "He's just being silly."

"Oh, maybe good for me," said the waiter, joining in the joke with a chuckle. "I mean, she's a beautiful woman."

"And she's my wife. Aren't you, darling?" Byron only played the wife card when he could somehow use it to his advantage or make someone uncomfortable.

The man stopped laughing, but remained jovial. "You're a lucky man."

"Could I get some more water?" said Georgette. She wasn't pleased with Byron's behavior, wine or not.

"Water it is. Anything else?"

"No, dear. Everything is fantastic," said Georgette. When the waiter had gone, she narrowed her eyes at Byron. "You need to get laid."

"What a lovely idea! Maybe we could take Ali Baba home with us."

"Byron, you're being a jerk. Seriously. Do something. Call Rafael. You know you want to."

"Seriously? I have an address from thirty years ago. No phone number. Even if I thought it was a good idea, which I don't, it's a pretty impossible task."

"Look him up on Facebook."

"Oh, I had forgotten you succumbed to that abomination of social non-communication. Do we have lots and lots of imaginary friends that wish you the happiest of birthdays when they've never even met you, I mean, in *real life*?"

"Oh, shut up. I'll have you know that I reconnected with Frankie in Barcelona after all these years thanks to Facebook and we chat all the time. Don't be such a stick in the mud."

"What do you expect? I'm from Mississippi. The Stick in the Mud state."

Byron sat in an antique chair upholstered in teal silk, positioned by a window looking out over Guerrero Street and the lights of the city's downtown beyond. In his hand was a worn scrap of paper with a name and address on it. Georgette slept in the next room, the other half of their two-bedroom suite at a Victorian bed and breakfast decorated in a style of faded elegance that reminded them of New Orleans. He regretted his behavior at dinner, possibly prompted by a phone call Georgette had received on the way to the restaurant. At the end of the call, he heard her say "Me, too," undoubtedly a response to "I miss you" or even "I love you." A sharp pain passed through his chest, and he wondered if this was the angina his doctor had warned him about if he didn't start taking better care of himself.

In the recovery period after Katrina, Georgette had started seeing a jazz musician named Clive. Neither of them was looking to get married or even live together, but the relationship had continued, and despite Byron's initial expression of support, there was a deep, possessive center in his male brain that resented it. He knew it was absurd to have pangs of jealousy, especially when he had had his own series of trysts with younger men, some of whom actually stayed around for a week or so. But he had never gushed over the phone, saying that he missed them or loved them. The love he felt for Georgette was admittedly complicated, and like the moon, changing, waxing, waning, and even disappearing for short periods, but always there in some form or other. In his disproportioned annoyance, he was convinced that Georgette only encouraged him to seek out Rafael to assuage her own guilt for abandoning him.

In his rush to get back at Georgette, he had left some crucial information out of their dinner conversation. The previous afternoon he had paced back and forth in front of the address on the paper, a three-flat Edwardian on South Van Ness. A young man had come out of the low gate that sectioned off a tiny spot of yard in front of the building. "Excuse me. Do you know the people who live in the lower flat?" Byron had asked.

When the man seemed confused by his question, he

switched to Spanish.

The man stared at Byron suspiciously. "I think it's a Cuban lady," he answered in English, but with a Mexican accent. Byron glanced at the bay windows and thought he saw a shadow. He shivered.

"Does she live alone?"

"I dunno, man. Why you asking?"

Byron showed the Mexican the paper. "I have this address from many years ago. The person who gave it to me might be her relative." He remembered that Rafael had mentioned living with relatives when he first went to San Francisco.

"She's mostly alone, but has visitors sometimes. I think she has a son."

"A son?"

"He don't live here. Gotta go. I'm late for work."

"Thanks," said Byron. He stood in front of the building for several minutes, but couldn't make himself approach the door.

As the week progressed, Lamar gave small indications that he was glad to have Byron and Georgette around, rationing his appreciation like squares of chocolate, one at a time. He still had moments of being ornery and demanding, but who could blame him under the circumstances? Georgette, since she first met Lamar back in New Orleans, had been able to deal with his moods and teenage posturing. For Byron it was a learning process, and he still rankled at times when Lamar seemed ungrateful or challenged Byron, which he was prone to do several times a day. It was Georgette who made Byron recognize that under his gruff exterior was a sweet young man, maybe in some ways like his uncle. Aside from the physical similarities, Byron had rejected any comparison to Thomas.

But there were days when Lamar would say

something funny and they would laugh, or Byron would insist they go out for a walk and Lamar would hold on to him tight, seeming to relish the physical connection. He kept telling Byron that he could feel the tightness in his body and he needed to relax. These were the moments when Lamar seemed to channel Thomas, and Byron would swallow hard, feeling Lamar's strong arm in his as something almost painful.

When Georgette would come in for her afternoon shift, Byron would rush from the apartment, gasping for the cool San Francisco air and bathing in the freedom of the streets. He would also be left with a craving for an animalistic joining of bodies, where the smell of sweat and sex hung in the air so thick you could taste it. What further disturbed him was that the image entering his head from the distant past was not Thomas, but Rafael, a Rafael who was most likely far away, or dead and buried.

That evening Georgette came back to the guesthouse with a Cheshire Cat smile on her face. "I found something."

"What? A new friend on Facebook."

"Maybe. I found several Rafael Arteagas in the Bay Area. One is seven, one is sixty-five, two declined to give their ages, but from their pictures, I would guess they are in their thirties or forties, and one is fifty-two." She beamed like she had just discovered the cure for cancer.

"And?"

"Do you want to see his picture?"

"No."

"You're not curious?"

"It was so long ago."

The name on the mailbox was Arteaga, but the light-skinned woman with snowy hair who answered the door took Byron by surprise. She blinked her green eyes and said, "Can I help you, young man?"

He detected a Cuban accent though he still had difficulty believing it was Rafael's mother. As she had referred to him as a young man, he also questioned her eyesight. And then he remembered how familiar, even flirtatious, Cubans could be at any age, in any situation. He smiled without finding the words to begin. It had taken him two days after his conversation with Georgette to summon the courage to knock on her door. Curiosity got the better of him. He had to know if the man Georgette found on Facebook was in fact his Rafael, if life had treated him well, if he had found happiness, and if he held any bitterness about their past.

"Are you Mrs. Arteaga?"

She nodded.

"And you have a son Rafael?"

She stepped back and clutched the neck of her turtleneck sweater. "Has something happened?" Her eyes had the initial glint of shock.

"Oh, no. No. I met your son a long time ago. He gave me this address. I was living in Europe. Never got in touch. But I'm in San Francisco now, obviously." He knew he was rambling and the more she stared at him in awe, the more he rambled. "I mean, I'm just here on a visit. Well, actually a friend had an accident. I just thought I might look up Rafael, if he still lives in the city."

"*Dios mío*, you gave me a scare!"

"I'm so sorry."

"He's fine then?" she said.

"Uh, I haven't seen him since we met many years ago."

"Where did you meet?"

"In Cuba."

"Cuba?"

"I mean, when he was back there for the Venceremos Brigade."

"Oh my. That was a long time ago. I think he went

there several times. He didn't tell us until years later."

It was a warm day, but the house behind her looked dark and cool. She stared at him as if she wasn't quite seeing him clearly in the late afternoon light. Byron thought he heard someone in the interior of the house. He wanted to scream, "Can someone just tell me? Is he alive or dead?" But he calmed himself and forced a smile. "Is he…?"

"Rafael? He doesn't live here. I'm alone. His father passed a few years back."

"My condolences."

"I had finally convinced my husband to go back for a visit. But we never got a chance to take the trip."

"To Cuba?"

"*Mi hijo* offered to take me."

"Rafael?"

"Yes. There's just the one."

Hallelujah, Byron thought. They were making some progress. "So is he nearby?"

"Who are you again?"

"I'm terribly sorry. I didn't introduce myself. I'm Byron Boudreaux. I worked with your son for a few weeks. In Cuba. A long time ago."

"Oh, yes. You said that."

"Is there any way to get in touch with him?" Byron held his breath.

"He lives in…" She pointed down the street. "The hill there. What's it called?"

"I'm not familiar—"

"Bernal Heights!" she shouted as if answering a question on a game show.

"Would it be possible to get his address?"

"Give me a minute." She closed the door, and he heard her walk down the hall.

After a few minutes a young girl came to the door. "Can I help you?" She spoke with a strong accent. "*La señora* say there's a man at the door, but she no remember why."

Byron's heart was thumping as if he were about to have a heart attack. He took a deep breath and began his story again. Halfway through his story he switched to Spanish, a natural transition.

The girl went to get the address and Mrs. Arteaga returned to the door. "He'll be over on Sunday," she offered. "He always comes for dinner on Sunday."

"That's very nice. I'm so sorry to have troubled you."

"No trouble at all."

The girl came back with address. *"Es un amigo de Rafaelito,"* Mrs. Arteaga said to the girl.

"Aquí lo tiene," said the girl, handing him a scrap of paper. It was only an address. He was glad there was no phone number as a call would be awkward, but perhaps only slightly more so than just showing up at his door.

Byron sat in a rented car outside a small two-unit Victorian on Andover Street. The late-afternoon fog was quickly conquering the blue sky in its sweep to the east, and a chilly breeze came through the open window in irregular gusts. He sipped his coffee from a local café and watched the house.

He had no pictures of his time in Cuba and his memories had suffered the harassment of time. Would he even recognize a much-older Rafael? In his head he had preserved Rafael as an ideal mate who came along at the wrong time, and yet he was aware of his propensity for idealizing the past. What he remembered most clearly was that he was the first openly gay-and-proud man he had met. It had frightened and confused him at a time of upheaval in his life. He had lost Thomas, fled from his family and the world that he knew, and thrown himself into a world of conflicts and unimagined experiences. In those few short weeks, Rafael had taught him a lot, and in return Byron had abandoned him without a note and had never gotten in touch. Tangled thoughts snaked through his head as he studied every man who made his way down the street to see if he was the one he waited for—a fat Rafael, a longhaired Rafael, a hunchbacked Rafael, a disabled Rafael, a Rafael who wore his anger like a cloak. Each person who passed filled Byron with a new fear until the oncoming person passed by without stopping at the house. The only thing he could be certain of was that he was looking for a man in his fifties.

In Georgette's Facebook research, she found that Rafael worked for a progressive cell phone company. It sounded like a nine to five. It was nearly six when a bicycle raced down the street and with screeching brakes pulled into the driveway of the building. On a keypad the cyclist punched in a code and the garage opened. He pulled off his helmet and ran his hands through his longish, thick hair, now streaked with gray. Even after all these years, there was something about his movements that was unmistakably Rafael.

Byron pushed open his car door, but he had left the keys in the ignition and it began to beep. Rafael turned toward the street. Byron grabbed the keys and got out. Rafael got off his bike and leaned it against the side of the garage. He stood with his arms across his chest. Byron started across the street at a snail's pace. Rafael took off his wrap-around sunglasses.

"Hello, uh, Rafael?" Byron called out. "Not sure if you remember me…"

Rafael laughed. "Byron, you haven't changed a bit. Assume nothing. Take your sweet time."

"I'm sorry."

"And apologizing!"

They stood close enough now to see the lines in each other's faces, battle scars that at least Rafael seemed to wear proudly. He had a mustache and a close-cropped beard also flecked with gray. He was trim, his eyes content.

"Where does one start?" asked Byron.

"With a hug?"

In the strong embrace, Byron felt no reluctance from Rafael, no hint of bitterness from the past. His body gave off warmth and a slight pungent smell from his ride.

"You don't seem surprised," Byron said after they separated.

"*Mi mamá* told me a stranger with a Southern accent had come to the door, someone from long ago, but she couldn't remember your name."

"And you guessed it was me?"

"Was hoping."

"You haven't changed either, giving people the benefit of the doubt."

"Life is too short and too precious to hold a grudge. I forgave you a long time ago for taking off without a word." He stopped and narrowed his eyes. "But not answering my letter is another thing."

"Letter?"

Rafael held up his hand. "Come in and have some tea, and breathe, Byron." He put his hands on Byron's shoulders and pushed them down. "Relax."

Rafael dashed from window to window, opening them, allowing the odors of last night's dinner, that morning's coffee, and the mustiness of old furniture to escape. Byron took notice of the cozy Mission-style sofa and chairs embracing the fireplace and a variety of blooming orchids holding court in contrast to the simple lines of the Shaker table on which they sat.

Rafael told Byron to make himself comfortable in the living room, but Byron followed him into the kitchen. "But what letter?" he said anxiously.

"Don't worry about. It's history. No doubt you were going through some difficult times."

"I never got a letter! I can't guarantee I would have responded, but it would have meant something to me. I swear I didn't get it."

"You're serious. Okay." He filled the kettle and turned on the gas. "Maybe Malik gave me the wrong address. He never did seem to like us being together. Jealous no doubt." Rafael laughed.

"Oh, come on." Byron turned a little red.

"Look at you. You still get embarrassed. I love it."

"When did you write?"

"The next year I went back with the Brigade. I ran into Malik and he said you were in Barcelona, that you two had been writing."

Byron's eyes burned with the memory of why they had been corresponding. "So what did you say?"

"To Malik?"

"In the letter, you jerk."

"Oh, a bunch of crap about how you were the sexiest man I had ever met. And if I didn't see you again, I'd go mad." He bugged his eyes and rattled his head.

"Come on, really."

"I said I thought you should come to San Francisco. That it would be a great place to sort yourself out. Later I was glad you didn't come. Soon after that, the horror started. You might have ended up one of its victims."

"But you survived."

"Survived, but tainted. I've got the virus."

The news no longer had the punch it did years before, but it still made Byron shudder in sympathy. Despite his years of stumbling through the dark wasteland of anonymous sex, some miracle had allowed him not to fall. "You look fine. Healthy." Byron wanted to tell Rafael he was as handsome as ever, but checked himself.

"Thanks. I'll take that as a compliment. I've been lucky. No other way to put it."

They sat at the kitchen table, oak, heavy, square. "I've

been lucky, too. I mean, somehow I avoided it. I married a woman. In Barcelona."

"That's how you avoided it?"

"I didn't mean that, but maybe, I don't know."

Rafael shook his head. "Poor girl."

Byron felt a stab from the remark. "You know nothing about it."

"You're right, I shouldn't have said that."

"She knew what I was…am."

"Yes, they know, don't they? But they still go ahead."

"We never got divorced. She's here in San Francisco with me." Byron wanted Rafael to squirm a bit.

Rafael poured the scalding tea from high above the cups, creating the sound of an angry waterfall. "Well, if it works for you."

Byron put his hand on Rafael's knee. "We haven't lived together for the longest time, but we're still best friends. What do they say nowadays, BFF? Sounds corny, I know. The reason she's here in San Francisco right now is a long story I'll tell you later. In fact, she has been pushing me to look you up."

"You didn't want to."

"Afraid."

"Of what? That I would be angry at you…or that I wouldn't?"

"You never were one to beat around the bush," said Byron, grinning, in small increments relaxing.

"Like I said. Life is short. AIDS taught us that."

"Georgette—that's my wife—and I lost a number of friends in Barcelona. It was part of the reason we returned to the States. Been living in New Orleans since."

"Were you there during Katrina?"

"Oh, yeah. Well, just before the storm hit, I left the city and went to Mississippi." He was reluctant to mention taking Thomas' family out of the city, not knowing how much Rafael remembered of the story he had told him when they were in Cuba, a story that he wasn't ready to delve into.

"You're from Mississippi, right?"

"You remembered."

"I remember making some wisecrack about the South and you getting immediately defensive. You were so cute."

"I was such a mess back then."

"I thought about what you told me many times over the years and I wondered if I was sufficiently supportive, if I could have done more to help you, if I was too selfish about what I wanted. But especially if I was too hard on you in our last conversation."

"You were fine. You were great. I admired you so much for your openness, but it took a long time for me to incorporate any of it into my own life. I was screwed up for a long time."

The conversation was getting dangerously close to things he wasn't prepared to talk about. He remembered talking to Rafael about revenge and thought he must have wondered if Byron actually did anything about it. He wondered if Malik had told him anything. Of course Rafael had counseled against it, telling him how sick he was of the Miami Cubans and their revenge complex, how that had driven him away from his family. He had been adamant that his escape to San Francisco was not about being gay, but about finding a place where he could breathe air untainted by rage against Fidel Castro.

"I guess you reconciled with your parents because they ended up out here," said Byron.

"They eventually got tired of the constant whining about how much had been lost in the Revolution. But the last straw was when an uncle of mine criticized me, calling me not only a commie, but a *maricón*. My father defended me and broke off with his brother. They moved out here a couple years later into the house you saw on Van Ness."

"There is so much to tell you, but I'll save that for

another day."

Rafael nodded and sank back into the sofa. He put his bare feet up on the coffee table. "There'll be another day then?"

Byron stared at the tufts of black hair on Rafael's toes and the patch on top of his foot. "You have beautiful feet," he said. "I had forgotten that."

12 Bathe His Feet in the Blood of the Wicked

In Byron's room, Georgette dozed in the chair by the window, stretched out as if in a nineteenth-century painting, her eyes closed, a book resting on her belly. The baby-blue throw on her legs, the lavender of her silk blouse, and the teal of the chair bathed in the violet light of a midsummer sunset, formed a palette of low wavelength colors.

He closed the door and her eyes sprang open. "Oh, sorry. The chair in here is so much nicer than the one in my room." She rubbed her eyes, sat up, and stared at him. "Oh my God, you saw him!"

"What are you talking about?" He lifted the book from her stomach to look at the cover. *The Confederacy of Dunces.* "You reading that again? Missing New Orleans?"

"Honey, you think I don't know you like the back of my hand? You not only saw him, you had a good time. Did you have sex?"

"Georgette! Jesus!" Byron turned the book over and read the notes on the back cover. "'Leaving New Orleans also frightened me considerably. Outside of the city limits the heart of darkness, the true wasteland begins. John

Kennedy Toole.'"

"I do believe you're blushing, Mr. Boudreaux."

"We did not have sex."

"Does he have a partner?"

Byron put the book down. "No."

"What did you do?" Her voice jiggled like she was a teenager.

"Just talked. Drank tea."

"At his house?"

"Uh-huh. Was Lamar okay when you left him?"

She was fully awake now and leaned forward, her eyes burrowing into him. "I know you're dying to tell me. So just do it!"

He fell into the chair across from her. A grin bloomed on his face. "He has the most beautiful feet."

"Details, sweetheart."

"It's the strangest thing. When you're young, you assume that attraction is about sex. Actually, you don't assume anything, don't think about it, just do it. But I was so fucked up at the time I met Rafael. I didn't want to feel anything, at least not for someone else. It would have taken the edge off the anger, the hurt. I wanted to stew in it. So in my hurt, I hurt someone who cared for me. Thirty years later, whatever it was that brought us together was still there, and yet it was different, mellowed like..."

"A fine wine?" She rolled her eyes and giggled.

"I felt so happy—God, I can't believe I'm saying this— to be a mature man. All the bullshit of youth, the pressures coming at you from all sides, have faded away. By the end of our talk, we were holding hands. It was the most natural thing in the world." He sighed and leaned back in the chair. "But..."

"I knew there was a 'but' coming."

"There's a whole string of them. The downside of being a mature man."

"If you are at the 'but' stage, that means you've

already considered the possibilities."

"Not really. He has his life here and mine is there. My business. His job. I mean, yeah, there's something there, but we all know the hundreds of pitfalls between point A and point B even in the most convenient of situations. Oh, and he's HIV positive."

"Really, Byron. In this day and age, you're going to let that be an obstacle?"

"I'm here to support Lamar," he protested. "Not rekindle an old romance."

"So it was a romance, not just a fling."

"Stop pushing, George!"

"I just want you to be happy."

"I'm happy. I'm fine. I like my life." He got up and poured himself three fingers of vodka. "You want one?"

"If I hadn't lived with you for the last thirty years, I would accept that answer. You suffered a terrible loss under grotesque circumstances, but that was a long time ago. I was always afraid to say this, but my dear, you need to move on. Let someone into your life."

"I let you in." He handed her a drink.

"And I am truly grateful. We found each other when we both needed comfort, and we both knew it would never be more than friendship, friendship at its highest level, friendship so overwhelming that I thought I was in love with you, but friendship nonetheless."

"Are you in love with Clive?"

She took a sip, leaving a lipstick stain on the glass. "Yes, it has taken a while, but I think I am."

"That's great. I'm happy for you. I really am. An older woman and man getting together is fine. I mean, sexually imaginable. But two old men, diddling with each others willies, playing hide the sausage—it gives me the creeps."

"I can't believe you said that. That is so juvenile! Number one, you and Rafael are not old. And number two, you've got a youth addiction and it's not pretty. It will always disappoint and it will always leave you wanting more. I have watched you do it for too long and I don't see it bringing you the slightest bit of happiness."

Byron looked down into his empty glass, and then got up to fix another. He knew she was right. And he knew what he liked.

"Look at it this way," she said. "You've got a unique opportunity here. You were with Rafael when you both were young. Just close your eyes and remember how it was."

"It doesn't work like that."

Georgette let out an exasperated growl. "Don't be an idiot and let this pass you by. If you don't at least try, I'll…I'll…"

"What?"

"I'll be so upset with you."

His eyes opened to a darkness softened by the sweet warm scent of sandalwood. His position in time and space eluded him for a minute, and then he remembered standing at a sink, washing his hands with a buff-colored soap, a woody smell expanding to fill the room and even those nearby.

He lay on his side with a hairy arm thrown over him. He was fully clothed. The other's breathing was somewhere between a purr and a contented snore. The pieces of the puzzle to how he got there gradually fell into place and he smiled at his reluctance, the nervous chitter in his brain that he might be forced into something he wasn't prepared for.

Rafael had asked him to come over after work as they had plans to go out to dinner. Rafael was late, and Byron had sat waiting on the front steps. When Rafael had stored his bicycle, he trudged up the stairs. Byron noticed his weighty eyelids and his weary voice. "Are you okay?" he asked.

Rafael put his hand on Byron's shoulder and squeezed it. "I just need to lie down for a few minutes. I didn't sleep well last night."

"Oh," said Byron.

Inside the apartment Byron felt trapped. His mind stumbled through a variety of scenarios all of which made him uncomfortable. Rafael took his hand as if to lead him to the bedroom. "You want to join me?"

Byron retrieved his hand as gently as he could. "I can just wait out here." A few days before, he had been ready to pounce on the waiter, but now he felt like a sexless blob incapable of intimacy.

Rafael grabbed his hand anew and searched his eyes. "Byron, when I ask you to join me for a nap, I mean a nap. If it were something else, you would know it. I need to relax and it would be nice if you were there beside me. I've got a big bed."

Byron nodded. It was true that when they were in Cuba, Rafael never used tricks or subtleties; he was always very direct in what he wanted.

Rafael kicked off his shoes and flopped on the bed, patting the space beside him. "Don't be afraid, *mi amor*." He was reminded how casually Cubans used endearments. It always confused him. "My love" was a phrase Byron never used.

Byron took a step toward the door. "Maybe we could go out another night. I should go and let you get some sleep."

"Don't go. I'll be fine in a half hour. Take off your shoes. Lie down and shut up."

Byron did as he was told. Rafael fell asleep in a couple of minutes. Byron turned on his side and drifted off, too.

Trying not to wake Rafael, he slowly reached for his phone on the nightstand. The time glowed brilliant white on his screen, and at first he thought it had to be a mistake or his eyes were deceiving him. Two hours had passed since they lay down, and in that time he had received five messages. The first was from Georgette. She had spent the afternoon with Lamar. "Ben's not home yet. I have to leave. Guess L. will be OK. Where are you?"

The next was from Ben. "Going to be much later than I thought. Georgette had to leave. Could you possibly stop by and check on Lamar?"

And then Georgette almost an hour later. "L's not picking up. Maybe I should go back over there when I'm done here. Respond, please."

Ben shortly after Georgette's message. "Lamar's not answering."

Twenty minutes later from Georgette. "At Ben's. Lamar not here. Little worried."

Since Lamar had come home from the hospital, he had spent almost no time alone and had never left the apartment by himself. "Shit," said Byron.

"What?" said Rafael. He reached over and turned on the light. Byron was already dialing Georgette.

"Glad you called," said Georgette. "This is a little weird. Ben just got home."

"Still no sign of Lamar?"

"No. We thought maybe someone stopped by and took him out. We called Abigail, and then Matt. No one's heard from him. He's still not answering."

"He couldn't go out by himself," said Byron. "Somebody must have come by." Lamar had learned to get around the house and could probably find his way to the street door of the building. But out onto the street? So far he had rejected the idea of using a cane and had no practice with one anyway. "How was he today?"

"The last couple of days he was irritated," said Georgette. "But today he was okay. Distracted, but okay. It seems like he would have told me or Ben if he was going out...unless he didn't want us to know. Are you with Rafael?"

"Yeah. We fell asleep. No. Not what you're thinking." Rafael was sitting up now and smiling. "I'll come over."

"There's nothing you can do. We're going to keep calling people he might be with. I'll let you know if anything turns up."

"Sorry," said Byron when he got off the phone. "It must sound strange to you."

"Sounds like someone is lost," Rafael said.

Byron hadn't really explained why he was in San Francisco except in general terms, but he decided it was time to tell Rafael. He relayed what happened to Lamar, that he was part of the family he and Georgette had rescued during Katrina, and that they had spent a week with them in Mississippi, keeping in touch when they moved to Oakland. When the inevitable question arose as to why this particular family, Byron had to follow the story thread back to the event that caused him to end up in Cuba.

"So, that guy…what was his name?"

"Thomas."

"Thomas is still part of your life, in a manner of speaking."

"I never thought of it that way. I couldn't stand by and do nothing. They would have likely drowned. Thomas' father in fact did. I took Hattie and Lamar into the city during the worst of the aftermath to retrieve his body." He picked up his phone to check if there were any new messages. "You think I'm dwelling in the past, don't you?"

Rafael sat cross-legged on the bed and hugged a pillow to his chest. "I didn't mean it in any negative way. I think it's admirable what you did, especially going to retrieve Thomas' father."

Byron gave him an appreciative smile, but inside he felt guilty. He had left out the whole part of the story where he went back to Mississippi for revenge. He expected Rafael to bring it up any second, but he didn't. "Are you hungry?"

"A little. But I don't want to keep you if you feel you should go over there."

"They'll call me if there are any developments."

Lamar sat alone on Ben's couch, sinking into his self-pity, the silence and the eternal darkness he now lived in pressing down on him. All the freedom he had worked so hard to achieve—his apartment, his own money, doing the things he liked to do—had been taken away in a few seconds. And now being stuck in the apartment had gotten unbearable—doing nothing, being taken care of, reduced to the status of an invalid child. At the same time, he felt guilty for his internal railings. His endless frustration with being dependent on others made him less appreciative than he should have been that Byron and Georgette had stayed an extra ten days to help to take care of him.

A few days before, Georgette had rearranged the drawers Ben had cleared for him, rolling his pairs of socks into little bundles so he wouldn't mismatch them. And knowing how important looking good was for him, she had stacked his T-shirts according to the colors of the rainbow (she had been particularly proud of this innovation)—red ones on top, violet on the bottom. She slid a piece of paper between colors. The only problem was that he had to keep asking Siri what the order of the rainbow colors was. Georgette had similarly stacked his basketball shorts and sweats—still his preferred form of dress. God forbid that he should put on a red T-shirt with purple shorts.

All the kindness of Ben, Byron, Georgette, Matt and others did little to assuage his anger that those responsible for his misery were free while he was hardly more than a prisoner. A few minutes after Georgette left, he heard the Ben-specific tone of a text message. VoiceOver helped him find the Message app on his iPhone, and he double-tapped it. A nasally woman's voice read Ben's message in a robotic monotone. "I'm stuck at work. Will be late. Asking Byron if he can come by for a couple hours." Lamar found the reply and then voice buttons, dictating his response. "Not necessary. Jesus, I'm fine."

He immediately told Siri to call Jaden. This time she got it right, so he didn't have to scream at the program that she was a silly-assed bitch. Jaden and Tommy, his old basketball buddies from Oakland, had told him a hundred times they were there for him, that whatever he wanted to do they could handle. But he hadn't had a moment to himself since he got out of the hospital.

Jaden and Tommy were tough, streetwise, but managed to stay out of trouble unless someone was asking for it. They were also cool. They never asked him his business or why he had disappeared for a couple years or why he was now living with Ben. "Come and rescue me now!" he told Jaden.

An hour later they walked into the Blind Cat bar on 24th Street. It was the first bar they came to in the neighborhood and Tommy almost had a fit to keep from laughing.

"What the hell's going on?" asked Lamar.

"Brother, you ain't goin' believe it," said Jaden. "We in the Blind Cat."

"What?"

"That the name of the bar."

"Not funny. What you trying to do to me?" said Lamar, and then stopped. He sensed that the conversations among the few early evening patrons had stopped. Lamar, Jaden, and Tommy were three large black men from the hood. Lamar was wearing sunglasses. He didn't need to see to know that everyone was looking at them. "What kind of bar is this?" he said.

"This here's a hipster bar and everybody lookin' like

we just walked in with Uzis. Bartender's hands below the bar workin' overtime getting ready to dial 911. Shit."

Tommy walked up to the bar and with a smile said, "Three PBR's, please."

Lamar gave Tommy his wallet. "I'll pay for 'em." He turned to Jaden. "How am I supposed to know a one from a twenty? Shit."

"Huh," said Jaden. "Like payin' for pussy in a dark room and you don't even know what bills you givin' her."

Lamar laughed. "But you also don't have to worry if she pretty or not."

They took the beers to a table.

"We been doin' some investigatin'," said Tommy. "Those bitches that popped you, they's amateurs."

"Yeah, but they got a gun," said Lamar.

"They ain't the only ones," said Tommy.

"Shit. You got it on you?" said Lamar.

"No way," said Jaden. "Chill. It's in the car. The trunk."

"I ain't going to prison. It's bad enough being a blind nigger out here, but in there..."

"So what do you want to do?"

"This music sucks," said Tommy. They were playing Duran Duran's "Hungry Like a Wolf."

"What do you care, man?" said Jaden. "We ain't here to dance. Focus, nigger!"

Lamar rubbed the bridge of his nose under the glasses. "Just want to send them a message."

"I assume you mean non-verbal communication. Some bitches just don't get it 'less you pound it into 'em."

"Kind of what I was thinking," said Lamar.

Lamar, Jaden, and Tommy pulled in front of Zeppo and BG's rundown California bungalow on 75th Avenue in East Oakland. They were cousins and lived with Zeppo's mom, who had been out of town for months according to Lina. The front porch was littered with junk and the windows were covered with sheets. There were lights on in the living room.

"We goin' see if we can look in a window," said Tommy.

A few minutes later they came back and said they saw through a back window that Zeppo and BG were in the living room getting high. "The place reeks of weed," said Jaden. "Think we can get in the back. Piece a cake. You stay here. When things are ready, we coming to get you so you can throw in your own message."

"Yeah, whatever. Stay cool. Just the message, nothing more." Byron's constant warnings had made him rethink what his gut kept telling him: To put them out of their misery.

About five minutes later, Lamar heard yelling and then a double pop. "Oh, fuck," he said. Then things were relatively quiet. He could hear a TV in one of the neighboring houses. He had no way of knowing if Jaden and Tommy were ignoring his wishes or the other guys had been ready and shot his friends. Either way he felt like he was in danger. He knew Lina lived close by, but he didn't know which way. He opened the back door and got out on the street side, crawling along the ground toward the front of the car. Gravel stuck in his palms and his nostrils were assaulted by the smell of gasoline and oil. When he got to the bumper he reached out and touched another vehicle parked in front, a truck, and continued crawling along the side. He did that for several more car lengths without a clear plan. Maybe if he heard someone walking by he could ask if they knew Lina.

Then there was a car coming down the street. He turned his head in that direction and instead of darkness saw a reddish yellow glow. He wedged himself between two cars, shaking and screaming inside how much easier things would be if he had his eyes. He wanted to run so bad, but he shook with fear and cowered between two bumpers. The car stopped alongside him and a car door opened. This was it. Probably buddies of Zeppo and BG come to finish him off. How had things gone so wrong? But the voice he heard was Byron's. "Lamar, get in. Quick." He got out and grabbed Lamar's arm, dragged him to the car, and pushed him in the backseat. It all happened fast, and he felt so relieved that he didn't even think how they had found him.

Ben started yelling, "What the fuck are you doing?"

"Just drive, Ben," said Byron. "Get us out of here."

"I should dump your ass out in the street and let the cops get you."

"Ben," said Georgette from the front seat. "Relax. We can talk later, but we need to leave."

"Wait. Wait. Wait," said Lamar. "My friends are back there."

"Some friends! They let you get messed up in this," Byron said.

"I heard shots. They might be—"

Ben growled. "You're fucking kidding me. Shots?" He stepped on the gas and turned at the next corner. In the distance they heard a siren.

"Please," said Lamar. "I can't just leave them. They're my friends."

"Goddamn it, Lamar. I told you—" Byron began.

"No, they were just going to rough them up a bit." Lamar wrestled the phone from his pocket. He turned it on and shook it, trying to hurry the screen. "Can't we just go around the block?"

"The siren sounds pretty distant," Georgette offered. Ben looked at her like she had betrayed them all.

Lamar got the message app and dictated to Jaden, "Get out if you can. Police coming. My friends picked me up. Hurry." With trembling hands he pushed the send button.

Ben slowed the car and turned right again. "This is unbelievable. It's so wrong."

"Please, Ben," Lamar said.

Just then a text came through and the robotic woman's voice filled the car. "We're out. Fucked them up good. The shots were just warning. No worries. Why you call your friends?" In her voice the message sounded hilarious, but no one felt like laughing.

"I didn't," Lamar dictated. "They found me." Send.

"Yeah, what are you guys doing here?" said Lamar. "How did you find me?"

Nobody said anything, so Georgette jumped in. "Byron had a feeling. He got Lina's number from your iPad. She was at work, but gave him the address of these people."

"Damn, why won't you guys stay out of my business?" said Lamar.

Byron pounded the armrest. "Because what you're doing is so stupid. You could have gotten killed."

As Byron's anger rose, Ben seemed to have calmed down. They were far away enough from the scene now to take a breath. "Lamar, nobody's blaming you for having those feelings," said Ben. "None of us can imagine what it's like for a young active guy to lose his sight. It's terrible. But we all love you and couldn't stand anything worse happening to you."

Lamar nodded, touched and angry at the same time.

While Georgette made lunch, Lamar sat in the living room with his iPad on his lap supposedly practicing his VoiceOver program. But what he really wanted to do was smash his fist into the screen. His little venture with Jaden and Tommy had brought him no satisfaction—he hadn't even been able to participate in the beat-down—and in fact the whole incident left his nerves more exposed than before. Maybe those punks got a lesson not to mess with people, though he doubted it would have any lasting effect.

More than the frustration of his tepid revenge, he had been thrown into the terror of not being able to cope on his own—the first time no one was at his side since the accident. Stuck between cars in a neighborhood he didn't know, he could neither run nor hide, let alone help his friends who were risking their lives on his account and were possibly in trouble. He felt so utterly useless and afraid. And it wasn't lost on him that Byron had again saved his ass. The thought of being dependent on other people for the rest of his life sat like a ball of clay in his stomach.

He slapped the iPad case closed. Sure he could read his messages, make phone calls, and search for music on the Internet, but his physical energy, his youth, was like a tiger in a cage, pacing back and forth, disgusted, because it couldn't hunt the raw meat thrown in its direction.

Georgette came into the room and announced, "Lunch is ready."

Being aware of his foul mood, she had made Philly cheesesteak, combining frizzled beef, onions, and oozing yellow cheese on a soft roll. She found the assortment of ingredients disgusting, but it was his favorite and sandwiches were the easiest things for him to eat. Nobody needed to tell him which quadrant of the plate each food was in. Once Ben had served him peas and Lamar screamed at him, accusing Ben of torturing him and threatening to call the abuse line.

Lamar stuffed a big chunk of the sandwich in his mouth, and then heard Georgette crunch down on a piece of carrot. "What? You're not having one?"

With his words so tangled up in greasy meat and cheese and the bread sticking to the roof of his mouth, she could barely interpret what he was saying. "I'm having a salad. Want some?"

The last time he had tried a salad, more landed on his lap than in his mouth. "No, thanks," he managed, and then swallowed hard. "This is our last meal, huh?"

"For this trip," she said.

"That's good."

"You're sick of me?" she said with false tragedy in her voice.

"I mean you need to get back to your life. You got a man back there, don't you?"

"Yeah, but the main reason is that classes are starting. Got to work."

"So your man is not that important?"

She groaned. "Please call him Clive. 'Your man' sounds like a Country and Western song."

"All right. So you miss Clive?"

"Sure. He's a good person."

"But not that exciting."

"At my age good is good."

Lamar had finished half his sandwich and felt full. "And he's not Byron."

A raggedy puff of surprise and exasperation escaped her throat, sounding almost as if she were passing gas.

"You still in love with him?"

She picked up her fork and realized her appetite had left her. "Not sure I was ever in love with him. It just became a habit."

"What I saw was not a habit. Of course that was when I could see shit. But there's still something I hear in both your voices."

"See, you think you've lost everything, but you're very perceptive, even if you are wrong!"

He laughed and then caught himself, not wanting to sound like he was having too much fun.

"Wipe your face, honey. Napkin on your right." A string of cheese was stuck to his chin. He picked it off and dropped it in his mouth as if it were a worm.

"So is Byron going back, too?"

"Nope. He's staying."

"Oh, Superman thinks he's got more saving to do."

"It's not that. He met somebody."

"What? Our Byron?"

"I should say he re-met somebody, somebody from a long time ago. Somebody he met in Cuba."

"I thought something was going on. He's just been acting a little bit too chipper. Must be getting some. Everybody need that."

Georgette smiled. "Uh-huh. Who knows where it's going though? He is one to keep things bottled up inside."

"Keeps his secrets tight. Man of mystery and all that. The first time I met him I thought he needs a good…well, you know. But I feel something new. He's got to let go."

"There you go again, Mr. Perceptive. Next thing you'll be hanging out a shingle and charging therapist rates."

"Hmm." He wondered if she knew anything about the kind of therapy he had previously offered. Had Byron told her?

Just the other day they were watching TV and Byron had said to him, "You know, you could totally do that."

An ad had come on TV for Hawaiian Airlines, and it showed a couple getting massages on tables canopied in gauzy material with a white beach and blue sea as a backdrop.

"Do what?"

Byron had forgotten for a moment that Lamar couldn't see what they were watching and cringed. "Sorry. This hunky guy is giving massages on the beach in Hawaii."

"Bastard."

"Seriously. You could go to massage school, get certified. It's something you could totally do. I think it's hot, a blind masseur."

"Shit. The other day you were trying to convince me I

could still be a DJ."

"Well, you could. There's so much you can do."

"Easy for you to say."

13 Light Shines in the Darkness

The absence of a light source told him it was still night. He had them leave the shades open so that he could turn his head toward the window and know if it was day or night. Ben was not happy that he insisted on sleeping in the spare bedroom. "What if you wake up in the middle of the night and need to go to the bathroom?" Ben had reasoned. "I can take you." Lamar said that he was quite capable of feeling his way down the hall and he was fine as long as no one left anything like shoes or clothes on the floor for him to trip on. He also explained that he didn't want to wake Ben up with his bad dreams. He had them frequently and they weren't always about getting shot. Sometimes he was riding a bicycle down a steep hill and lost control, or a dance crowd turned ugly because they didn't like his music, or Lester snuck up behind him and stabbed him in the back. But no matter what kind of dream he had, in his dreams he could always, always see.

And each time he awoke, he became depressingly and immediately aware that the only thing he could detect of his surroundings was the light of day or the darkness of night. He would put the pillow over his head and long to escape into an even darker place than what his world had become. These were the times he really didn't want Ben around, asking him what was wrong, as if he didn't know, telling him things would get better, putting a hand on his back that felt like the hot sticky palm of the devil. These days he couldn't stand being touched.

Even though it wasn't morning yet, he was done sleeping. He lay on his back, opening and closing his left eyelid, begging God for a miracle that the next time he opened it there would be light and color and form. And then the words of the second-opinion doctor would come into his head. "I wish I could say there was a chance. It would have to be a miracle."

He let his hands slide down his body under the covers, thinking that release would let him go back to sleep, though he sometimes wondered what was worse, the harsh reality of being awake or the frightening, unpredictable nature of his dreams. He took his limp member in his hand and began to stroke. He had always been proud of his instant erections, and the ladies of Oakland and his massage clients were appreciative as well. Now he felt dead. Using his other hand to pinch his nipple, he tried to create a fantasy of a naked person—unsure if it was a man or a woman—face-down on the massage table with two beautiful soft white globes above two long legs. He stroked and pinched furiously, trying to push the buttons of his memories, but nothing worked.

With a moan of disgust, he drew his hand away from his cock as if he could no longer bear to touch it. Thinking back to what Byron had said a few days before, he wondered if people would be interested in a limp-dicked masseur. Even if he kept his clothes on, a client would inevitably brush his hand against his crotch or grab it outright, and then sigh with disappointment.

When he had started spending time with Ben and

getting more DJ work, he had stopped responding to requests, but he hadn't canceled his account on the male massage site. The phone he used exclusively for clients sat in a drawer at his apartment, undoubtedly without a charge, and he hadn't checked his inbox on the site for weeks. Now he desperately wanted to check his messages, dying to feel the excitement of people wanting him, no matter how crass and unimaginative their messages were, expressing little more than a simple animalistic urge to be with him.

He reached for his iPad and put on earphones so Ben wouldn't hear the VoiceOver. Siri helped him get to the site, and he softly dictated his password. The voice started reading. URL not found on this server. Seizedserver.com. He tried again and got the same message. Then he went back to Siri and asked for stories about Hotmanmassage.com. He found it. Homeland Security had raided the Los Angeles offices of Hotmanmassage, busting the CEO and five employees on the basis that they were promoting prostitution. Uniformed Homeland Security agents had confiscated boxes of files. With a certain sense of delight he imagined that all his messages would now provide saucy reading material for the agents in drab windowless rooms, sitting around metal tables loaded with coffee and junk food. He also had a moment of paranoia, but then he thought how there must be thousands of masseurs and many thousands more clients across the United States. It wouldn't be possible to go after all of them.

The timing, so soon after the scandal involving Congressman Reggie Port, struck Lamar as suspicious. "Siri, stories about Congressman Reggie Port," said Lamar. In a new article he found that the scandal had widened, with more escorts saying Port had been their client. Though the article didn't mention any other congressmen by name, a nuanced sentence implied that Port wasn't the only rabidly anti-gay politician who used masseur/escort services. The article also identified Port as a member of the House Committee on Homeland Security. "Well, ain't that too cute?" Lamar said aloud. Lamar knew it was unlikely that anybody would be able to trace his shooting back to Port. If Zeppo and BG had been part of deliberate attack, they most probably didn't know why or who was behind it. In the meantime, Lamar was still blind.

At Byron's insistence, Lamar was going to the gym for the first time since the attack. "You're getting flabby," Byron said. It was his afternoon to hang with Lamar.

"Fuck you," said Lamar with his mouth full. He sat on the sofa with a bowl of sugary cereal held close to his chin to catch any drips.

Byron chuckled. "Okay. Maybe flabby is a slight exaggeration, but you will be if you keep sitting around the house all day eating." When he first came home from the hospital, Lamar had no appetite, but lately all he did was eat. "Come on. I'll go with you and help you work out."

"And you know your way around a gym?"

Byron pulled in his stomach even though nobody could see it. "I'll have you know that when I was modeling in Barcelona, I used to go to the gym all the time. I did martial arts. Of course that all went to hell when I moved back to New Orleans. Nobody cared there. Probably the city with the lowest percentage of men with gym bodies in the country."

"Whatever." Lamar slurped the sweetened milk from the bowl like a cat.

Byron continued to badger him, saying how he could walk him around, set the weights, spot for him, and in the end Lamar relented. He felt the lack of exercise more than he let on.

A short time later Lamar stood at the front door, gym

bag on his shoulder, with the trepidation of a child waiting to be taken to his first day of school. He listened to Byron filling up water bottles in the kitchen. And then he heard someone coming up the front steps. It wasn't time for the mail carrier and he didn't recognize the hesitant climb as anyone he knew; he had become able to identify whoever arrived with an almost hundred percent accuracy. The doorbell rang. To Lamar, it sounded like a fire alarm.

"Who would that be?" said Byron, coming into the foyer.

He opened the door to a scruffy young man whose eyes were already searching the apartment behind him. "I'm looking for Lamar Shaw. Is he around?"

Lamar stood behind the door out of sight.

"And who are you?" asked Byron.

"I'm Rip Sorenson, a reporter for the Huffington Post."

Byron blocked the doorway with one hand on the door and the other on the threshold. "What's this about?"

"I'm doing a story on Congressman Reggie Port. Perhaps you've heard about the scandals. I'd like to ask Lamar a few questions."

Lamar moved deeper into the shadow behind the door.

"He doesn't know anything about the congressman," said Byron, narrowing his eyes on the reporter, "except what everybody's heard in the news. Plus, he's just been through a terrible ordeal—he's lost his sight."

"I'm aware of that. Really a shame. I'd still like to ask him a few questions if he's up to it of course."

Byron gripped the door strongly. "If you have a card or something, I could give him the message."

"Yeah, okay." The reporter took a card out of the pocket of his messenger bag. He held it out, but didn't put it in Byron's outstretched hand. "You know, I was just wondering if Lamar thought there might be any connection between his attack and the congressman's problems."

Byron grabbed the card and stared at it. "I wouldn't know. As I said, I'll give him the message."

"Like what?" Lamar said loudly, coming out of the shadows. He faced the light beyond the door, as if the stranger were offering the gift of illumination.

"Ah, Lamar," said Rip. "Could we talk a little bit?"

Byron turned to Lamar. "Not a good idea."

"He seems to know a lot already. Maybe he could tell me a few things."

"Look," Rip jumped in. "This will be off the record. A few questions. Later, if you feel you want your story out there, we can use an alias. Your name doesn't have to be in the article."

Lamar reached up and touched Byron's arm blocking the door. "Come in," Lamar said.

Byron stood firm. "I think we should talk to Ben about this."

"This is my house as long as I'm living here. Isn't that what everybody's always telling me? And it's my life. Let him in."

Rip started in the door, giving Byron a shrug as if to say Lamar had a good point. "Looks like you were on your way to the gym or something."

"It can wait," said Lamar.

Once settled in the living room Lamar asked, "So what've you got?"

Rip produced a wry smile. "A story breaks that an outspoken anti-gay congressman likes to take trips to San Francisco and use masseur services. A young man is brutally attacked in Oakland. The scandal breaks wide open when several escorts or masseurs identify the congressman as one of their clients. Homeland Security busts an escort/massage service that some believe the congressman used. Might be nothing there, but I'd like to find out. Oh, and I forgot. Two punks who the police had questioned as possible perpetrators of the attack were badly beaten up the other night in what looked a little like revenge."

"Interesting story," said Lamar.

"I don't think you have one," said Byron.

"How did you get to me?" said Lamar.

"Rumor has it that the congressman particularly likes young muscular black men. Before they took the site down, hotmanmassage.com, I found a profile that looked very much like you and then matched it with the photo in the paper about your attack. Now if I were the congressman and had that predilection, I don't think I would pass up a nice young man like yourself."

Though Lamar seemed to be enjoying the attention—he was more animated than he'd been in days—Byron didn't like where the conversation was going. He flashed Rip a dirty look. He was annoyed that Lamar was being talked about as if he were a cut of meat. When Lamar had first told him how Abigail had set him up with the Oakland ladies, using her own son so she could keep forwarding money to Lester, it sickened him. He now had a hard time looking Abigail in the eye, and felt the urge to lash out at her, tell her how disgusted Thomas would be with her. But when Lamar told him about his voluntary plunge into the world of male prostitution (for what else could you call it, even if Lamar like to use the term "man massage"?) he had tried to not act shocked, tried to be sympathetic to Lamar's circumstances. Deep down he felt disgusted, not with the world for putting Lamar in that position, but with himself for not continuing to support the family, and particularly Lamar. It's what Thomas would have wanted, isn't it? He could have sent more money. He could have shown more of an interest, taken more a fatherly role toward Lamar, guiding him to…to what? The path of righteousness? How sanctimonious he sounded! What was it that really bothered him so much about men paying Lamar to be with them? Jealousy that he wasn't one of them? It had been Rafael who made this last suggestion when Byron discussed the matter with him. The comment had made Byron so angry that he had gotten up to leave until Rafael apologized and admitted he didn't have the right to say that.

"What have you found out about the two punks?" said Lamar.

"I have not found the smoking gun, so to speak," said Rip. "The police dropped it, too. And if Port has a brain in his head—and there are many who have posed that question—there would be no money trail. So I'm left with you. Is there anything you remember about that night that would make you think it wasn't a random mugging?"

Byron cleared his throat. "Come on, man. It all happened so fast. He was shot in the head. What's he going to remember?"

"Lamar?" said Rip.

Lamar was impressed by the reporter, but he wasn't quite ready to give him another piece of the puzzle. He would love to see the bigot exposed, but if the story came out, alias or no, he could be in danger. "Hmm," he said. "Like Byron says, it's hard to remember anything except the explosion in my head."

"Now what about those two ladies that found you?"

"Did you talk to them?" asked Lamar.

"No, they refused. They're friends of yours, right?"

"Sort of." Lamar thought of Lina's little boy. Of course she didn't want anyone finding out she had identified Zeppo and BG. "They don't know anything. They just happened by. Good thing, too."

Byron stood up. "We have things we need to do."

"I appreciate your time, Lamar, I really hope we can talk more later. Call me anytime."

After Rip had left, Byron said, "I don't like this one

bit."

"But they're exposing that asshole. Isn't that a good thing?"

"He's just trying to get a scoop that will further his career. Do you think he really cares about you and what you've been through?"

"He's a reporter. It's not his job to care."

14 Wash and Make Yourselves Clean

The rose light from the bedside lamp gave Hattie's face a mauve tone. Her damp eyes looked as if they were struggling to hide a dull pain from her visitor. She unclenched the covers and reached out her thin arm to take Georgette's hand.

"I came as soon as I could get away," said Georgette. Sofia had called her and told her about Hattie's stroke.

"Oh, honey, you didn't have to drive all that way." Hattie's voice was as thin as a thread. "But I'm mighty glad you did." She struggled to sit up. Georgette helped her arrange the pillows and plucked a tuft of down from her hair, casting it aside.

"How are you, Hattie?"

She ignored the question and motioned for Georgette to lean closer. "I have just two wishes for my funeral."

"Funeral? Sofia told me—"

"Now just listen. I don't want people wearing black. It's depressing." She stopped to take a breath. "And my second wish is that everybody who shows up to the church be treated with respect."

"Why in the world would anybody disrespect your

friends and family?"

"When I come back here, I went back to the church that was such a big part of my life before...well, before we moved to New Orleans. Didn't take me more'n two minutes to see they was the same, but I'd changed."

"What do you mean, Hattie?" Georgette asked.

"Unlike them," she hooked her thumb toward the neighbor ladies in the other room. As soon as Georgette had arrived, Hattie had shooed the neighbors from her bedroom into the living room. "I seen a bit of the world now, a lot more of God's creation. Living in New Orleans and Oakland, spending time with my grandkids and you and Byron, opened up my eyes. All God's creatures deserve respect."

"Hattie, you shouldn't be worrying—"

"I know more than you maybe think I do." Her voice was stronger now. "I talked to Lamar the other day, told him not to come out here 'cause I'm just fine. Don't want to put him to no trouble what with all he been through. When I told him I wish I coulda been there to take care a him, he say he got Ben. There was something in the way he say it, like he want to tell me more but can't find the words. When he come out to see me last time, he say not to be expecting no great-grandkids, said he more likely to get a dog, the way he put it. I just want him happy, specially now with his blindness." She took a labored breath.

"Hattie, maybe you should relax. You don't have to talk."

She took Georgette's hand again. "I got things to say and now the time."

"The doctors say you're going to be fine. But you need to rest."

"Doctors!" she said with disgust. "What do they know?" She had slid down and Georgette helped her scoot up again into more of a sitting position. "I want to talk 'bout Byron, seeing as how I might not get the chance to tell him myself. He been so good to us. Another thing my church friends wouldn't understand is how I come to terms with him and Thomas. I was blind to that fishing picture all those years, but now it's so obvious." She let out something resembling a chuckle. "At Joe's funeral I saw the hurt in Byron's soul as he look on Thomas' grave. They was special to each other and it give me comfort to know in Thomas' short life he had the chance to have someone special. That a lot more important than what the Bible say."

"Hattie," said Georgette with tears in her eyes. "God love ya!"

Georgette told Hattie she needed to rest and said her goodbyes. She promised to come back the next day. She had arranged to spend the night with Byron's mother and Sofia, and called Byron as soon as she got to the house. She told him what Hattie had said and he became very quiet.

Finally he took a deep breath. "Why is she saying all this now? I thought the doctors said she was going to be fine."

"Her vitals are good. I just confirmed with Sofia again what the doctors said. But the way she was talking scared me."

"You think Lamar should come?"

"I hate to think something might happen and Lamar not have a chance to say goodbye."

The following day Sofia called Lamar.

"Sweetheart, your Grannie passed last night," said Sofia.

Lamar slumped to the floor, dropping his phone. Sofia's distant voice kept talking to him and he could easily have located the phone from the sound. But he didn't want to touch it.

"Lamar, honey. Are you there?"

If he didn't reach for the phone, didn't listen to her,

maybe it wouldn't be true.

Hearing the crash, Ben rushed into the room. "What happened? Are you okay? Your phone. Somebody's talking."

"Don't touch it. Go away."

The faraway mournful voice said, "Lamar? You still there? I'm so sorry."

Lamar lay curled in a fetal position on the floor with his hands over his ears, but he was still able to sense Ben leaning over to pick up the phone. "No. No. No."

"Hello, this is Ben. Lamar's friend. Has something happened?"

"Oh, hello, Ben. This'd be Sofia. Lamar's grandma passed last night. I feel terrible being the one to give the news. He okay?"

"Thank you so much for calling. I think he just needs a little time. My condolences to the family." With Lamar in pain on the floor, he was anxious to get off the phone. "I'll have Lamar call you. Goodbye." Ben sat down next to Lamar and put his hand on his arm.

"Don't," said Lamar.

"I'm so sorry. I know how much she meant to you."

"You have no idea. I should have been there. Why didn't someone tell me to go?" he screamed, too angry to cry.

"We understood she was going to be all right," said Ben softly.

"She was alone. She shouldn't have been alone."

"I know…we need to make travel arrangements."

"We? You don't have to go. I'll manage."

"I want to go. I want to pay my respects," said Ben.

In the waiting area of Louis Armstrong International Airport Georgette danced from foot to foot, imagining she could hear Satchmo's gravelly voice singing "What a Wonderful World." She hugged herself as if trying to hold all her emotions, the good and the bad, inside her. She had the most powerful urge to smoke a cigarette, though she hadn't had one in years.

Byron and Rafael emerged first and she lost control. Something shook inside her, a strange mixture of giddiness and tears, gasping and choking. Her feelings for Byron had always been complicated, but what she felt when she saw him at that moment was pure joy. He looked happy, smiling, his shoulders loose. It was of course too soon to think of Byron and Rafael as a couple, but every fiber in her body wished for his happiness. She was so pleased that Rafael had insisted on making the trip, even though Byron had objected, telling her over the phone in a vexed tone that Rafael was using the trip as a sneaky excuse to know where he came from, connect the dots, and meet his mother. "Well, if he really wants to know the whole sordid story, so be it," Byron had lamented.

And then she saw through the blur of her tears Lamar and Ben. She cried again for Hattie and for Lamar's blindness, though he seemed to be doing well with the cane. When Ben took his arm he shook it off, showing his independence and perhaps a lingering reluctance to be seen as part of a male couple. And then she laughed again as she saw Byron turn to admonish Lamar for not letting Ben help, and Lamar turn his head to Byron with a nasty comment, most likely telling him to mind his own business. She knew, as she always had, that the banter between Byron and Lamar did not come from genuine dislike, but rather fear that they might actually have to admit they were fond of each other.

She hurried toward them and fell into Byron's arms. "Well, sugar," he said, holding her tight. "Look at you. You're a mess."

"Y'all looked so beautiful walking out that door, I nearly peed my pants," she said in a gurgly voice. "Then I remembered we're supposed to be sad, and I am, of course. I'm devastated—but happy, too."

"Girl…"

She pulled herself out of Byron's hug and went to Lamar. "Sweetie," she said, reaching up to throw her arms around him. "I saw Hattie the day before she passed, and she was so calm, so clear in her thoughts. I think you know it, but she had a love so deep for you that she embraced everything you are. She wanted nothing more than to see you happy."

Lamar took a wobbly breath, but managed not to cry. "Georgette, the first moment I saw you I knew you were a good woman, and Grannie knew it, too."

She stepped back and looked behind them. "Are your momma and Sarah here already?" Georgette was the only one who always remembered to call her Sarah.

"They came in on an earlier flight out of Oakland. Cousin Ruth picked them up, drove them straight to Columbia."

"Ah, too bad you couldn't all come together." But in truth, she was happy. She wanted her men all to herself.

Georgette hugged Ben, and then Rafael. She whispered in Rafael's ear, "Now you tie a knot on him and don't let him go. That is, if you want to." They both laughed.

"Hey, no secrets," said Byron.

The New Deliverance Church looked more like someone's living room, a social gathering where women in their best hats and men in ill-fitting suits walked around and greeted friends while the choir sang "Take me To the King" softly in the background. Though a lot of the congregation had missed the word about no black, Hattie's family and friends arrived together dressed in shades of beige, following Abigail's lead. She looked stunning in the off-white Kay Unger suit that Mrs. Thompson had given her with a lavender silk blouse, and she held on tightly to Lamar's arm, allowing him to forgo his cane. Letisha and Sofia followed right behind. Except for Sofia, they weren't known in the church, so everyone turned to watch them slide into the family section. But necks were really craned when the family was followed by Byron and his mother, Georgette, Rafael, and Ben. Camille drew the most attention. There had been rumors she had paid for the casket, but everyone looked shocked that she had shown up at the funeral. Byron acknowledged the commotion with a little smile, and at the same moment, felt his mother tense up. There were whispers, especially among the older members of the congregation who remembered the demise of Thomas, Hattie and Joe's move to New Orleans, the disappearance of Byron Purvis, and the mysterious deaths of the three white boys who had found Thomas in the woods. It had become the material of legend and myth.

Now they had the players in the old drama right before their eyes, accompanied by three more people that nobody knew. The church was abuzz and the choir director prompted the singers to pick up the volume. The pastor, a short wiry man who nevertheless commanded a presence, walked to the podium, stood up straight, and sent a message with his eyes for them to calm down. With a simple motion of the director, the voices of the choir fell back into the melodious whispering of angels that had greeted the guests when they came in.

The pastor stretched out his hands, and the last of the stragglers and neck-craners took their seats and faced front. The only movement in the crowd was a woman in white pacing the aisles with a box of tissues in one hand and a plastic bag for discards in the other. When she saw someone in need, she would stop, pluck the little white cloud from the box, and with the tiniest snap of her wrist, flatten it out and let it float into the hand of the weeper.

He began to speak in a mighty baritone, "Brothers and

sisters, though we feel with all our hearts the loss of Sister Hattie Davis, we must rejoice in her coming home to the Lord. Her departure from us, sad as it be, she's moved on to greener pastures, into the arms of Jesus and the everlasting glory of our Lord. I welcome you one and all to this celebration of her life. To begin our program today, we will join together in the song, 'Goin' Up Yonder.' Its words ring so very true for our sister, 'I can take the pain, the heartaches they bring' and Lord knows she had her share of pain. But we are heartened by the words 'As God gives me grace, I'll run this race, until I see my Savior face to face.' Everybody raise your voices for Sister Hattie."

The choir led the congregation through a handclapping version of the song, followed by two readings from the Scriptures by one of the church elders: Corinthians 15 and then Psalm 23. By the end of the second reading, Georgette could feel Byron beginning to fidget, and when she looked over at Camille, she appeared to be in shock. The pastor's wife read a resolution from the church with a host of "be it resolveds," each new one causing Byron to sigh. A soloist from the choir then sang a moving rendition of "Swing Low, Sweet Chariot" and Byron relaxed a bit, bowing his head, remembering the day he, Lamar, and Hattie had found Joe's body.

Pastor Jenkins then asked, almost as an afterthought, if anyone from the family would like to speak. Abigail and Lamar stood up. She led him up to the lectern, said a few words of sorrow about her mother, and then introduced Lamar.

"As my mother said, I'm Lamar Shaw, and I'd like to say a few words representing the family. I can say that I'm mighty proud to be Hattie Davis' grandson. I've been mixed up about a lot of things in life, but there is one thing I know. My grandmother was a beautiful person. She was always there for me. She taught me so much about life."

"Amens" echoed about the church, some soft and low,

others loud and joyful.

"And even though she had many trials in life, she kept her head up. First she suffered the loss of her son, my uncle Thomas, through a violent act that had no reason to it. He was shot down and there were some people who were even so cruel as to say some sh…bad stuff, like he must've been where he shouldn't be or doing something he shouldn't. It made the pain of losing her first-born even worse, and made my grandfather feel compelled to move the family to New Orleans. Columbia went from being a place she called home to a place of bad memories."

The "amens" faded, replaced with the clearing of throats and whispers. Without a doubt, he had their attention.

"Her suffering continued when Katrina led to the death of my grandfather, one of the many souls—poor black folk mostly—who lost their lives due to an incompetent government. Any normal person, you know, she'd get bitter, but my Grannie continued to love, continued to guide my sister and me. I was so lucky that she accompanied us to Oakland, uprooted again, and at least for that transition period we had her close by. We certainly didn't blame her when she wanted to go back to Columbia, to be near her husband, who she joins today in everlasting peace. That's how she came back to y'all, and she told me she was comforted to return to the church she attended before."

A couple of people couldn't help blurting out an "amen" or two.

"I could stand here all day and talk about the good things she did, but if you knew her, you know what I'm talking about. I'm sure, however, that Grannie would be put out with me if I didn't mention a few people here today. When Katrina was at our doorstep, Byron and Georgette, sitting over there, offered us an escape from the danger, though my grandfather refused to go. They put us up in the French Quarter, but when things got dicey, they took us out of the city and we ended up here in Columbia. Byron's mother, Mrs. Purvis, took us in and my cousin, Sofia, who worked there, fed us. My family is forever grateful."

There was some creaking of wood as people turned to pick out the individuals Lamar had mentioned. Georgette had tears in her eyes, and her heart grew large seeing how Lamar had matured. She never would have imagined that the incorrigible youth she had met a few years back would be giving a composed speech in front of a room full of people.

"Yes, Grannie returned to her church. She loved her Scriptures and was known to quote them from time to time."

So many members of the choir said "amen" that it seemed they'd break into song.

Lamar interrupted the chorus, raising his voice. "But when there was a conflict between Scripture and the people she loved, the people won out every time. In my last conversation with her, she expressed her sorrow about not being with me after I, too, was a victim of violence, leaving me blind. I know it hurt her not to be there. But I told her not to worry, that people were taking good care of me. Byron and Georgette were good enough to come out to help. But I'd particularly like to thank a man sitting over there, Benjamin Moss, who took me in. Much of the time, in my recuperation, I was a pain to be around, but he stuck by me. I told Grannie all that, and at the end of the conversation she said, 'Love is love.' I'll leave it to you good people to figure out what she meant by that. Love is love. Amen."

Silence hung on the air heavy with floral scents, and even the paper fans had stopped midair. Georgette couldn't choke back the tears any longer and Byron struggled to hold back his. He took Georgette's hand and held it tight.

The pastor jumped up and made a motion to the choir. The director led them into "Soon and Very Soon." "Soon and very soon, we are going to see the king. Hallelujah. Hallelujah. We're going to see the king."

Lamar stood at the lectern, turning his head from side to side as if looking for someone to rescue him. His mother sat glued to her seat, head down. It was clear she didn't like the implications of his speech. Lamar had told Georgette during one of their afternoons in San Francisco that Abigail had no idea he had sex with men. (He still was reluctant to describe himself as gay.) He had tried to talk to her about it once, but she changed the subject.

Georgette reached over Rafael and squeezed Ben's leg, bringing him out of his stupor. Ben stood up and hesitated, looking as if he wasn't sure whether he was allowed into the sanctuary. The minister nodded to him, and he helped Lamar back to the pew. As soon as Lamar sat down, Georgette put her hand on his shoulder and whispered, "That was beautiful, baby."

The pallbearers, dressed in identical rust-colored suits, moved into position around the casket. With military precision, they lifted it to their shoulders and began a slow rhythmic procession down the aisle. The six men with football-player bodies walked with a lightness of step, swaying slightly, in time to the music, eyes forward and with faces of stone.

After the service, a frazzled-looking Camille insisted that Byron drive her home and he hadn't complained, as standing next to Thomas' grave wasn't something he was anxious to do. He did, however, return for the continuation of Hattie's "coming home" celebration held under the ghastly florescent lights of the church basement. The closed space smelled of fried chicken, deviled eggs, and Revlon Jontue. He spied Georgette, Ben, and Rafael huddled in a corner, their hands awkwardly supporting plates filled with chicken wings, potato salad, cornbread, and globs of assorted casseroles that the church ladies had made. On the other side of the room, Abigail, Letisha, and Lamar received condolences. Lamar stood at a slight distance from his mother and sister, his cane tucked nervously under his arm.

"We should go rescue him," said Georgette.

"Poor guy," said Byron. "Have you noticed the dagger looks coming from Abigail?"

"Oh, honey, you're being paranoid. She did just bury her mother," said Georgette.

"No. She hates me. Ever since she found out Thomas and I were friends, she's had a hard time being civil to me. And now that Lamar dropped his little bomb, his quasi coming-out speech, she probably thinks it's all my fault, that I corrupted her whole damn family. I never told you about the time she cornered me outside Lamar's hospital room. It was so dreadful I tried to block it out, pretend it never happened. She said that whatever fantasy I had about her brother was totally in my mind. He wasn't that way. And if I ever laid a finger on her son, she would hunt me down."

"And what? Sick Lester on you? Poor Abigail."

"Poor Abigail! What about me?"

"I feel sorry for her. I really do. With—"

Byron interrupted. "Did you see that? If looks could kill...she knows we're talking about her."

"With a mother like Hattie...I mean, she seems to have gotten none of her sweetness. I just don't know what happened."

"I think Hattie went away for a while, I mean mentally, after Thomas' death, just withdrew at a time Abigail really needed her. And then the Lester thing was a rebellion that turned into a nightmare."

"Anybody got a flask?" asked Ben, holding up his

glass of Hawaiian Punch.

"I wish," said Byron.

"At a Cuban funeral," said Rafael, "we would have less food and more rum. Drown your sorrows by getting stinking drunk. Here all you can do is clog your arteries."

Georgette chuckled and dropped her untouched plate on a table. "Where's the Kleenex lady? I'm perspiring like a mint julep."

"There she is again," said Byron. "Glancing at us like we're a bunch of fools. I'm giving it ten more minutes, and then we're taking Lamar out of here—before Abigail has a chance to be alone with him and read him the riot act."

"I'll tell you one thing," said Georgette. "He does not take shit from her." She noticed the untouched food on Ben's plate and his gaping eyes. "How are you holding up, Ben?"

"I was thinking how good it is that Lamar got out of the South," said Ben. "What if they had all stayed in Mississippi? What would he be like? Aren't you glad you left Mississippi, Byron?"

"Yes, but I didn't exactly have a choice." Rafael put his arm on Byron's shoulder. "What are you doing?" Byron said in a panic.

"Relax, *cariño*, I was just going to say that I'm going to wait outside. I need air."

"Sorry I snapped at you," said Byron. "This whole thing is making me jittery."

"When we get back to your place, I'll give you a massage. I promise."

"I would kill for a whiskey sour," said Georgette.

"Ten minutes," said Byron. "You'll have to be the one to fetch Lamar. Don't imagine she'd scratch your eyes out."

"Don't be mean. She's his momma."

"And wasn't she being a good momma when she set him up with those ladies in Oakland!"

"What?" cried Ben.

"Byron!" said Georgette. The three of them looked at each other like someone had just dropped a rose. Georgette started backing up. "I'm just going to mosey over toward Lamar. Talk amongst yourselves."

"Oh shit, Ben. I'm sorry. I thought you knew."

"Knew what?"

"Well, I mean, when they first came out here, they were suffering financially, especially with Lester siphoning off what little they had. Abigail used to offer some extra services to the lonely ladies she worked for via Lamar."

"Oh, God. Stop. Can I pretend I didn't hear that?" His dazed expression turned to one of disgust, and he took a handkerchief out of his pocket to wipe the sweat off his forehead. "If Lamar wants to tell me someday, then so be it. I mean, he did mention that he had some experience with older women, but..."

"Me and my big mouth. When I first heard about it, I was so pissed off with Abigail, but out of respect for Hattie, I held my tongue. Now that she's gone, I'm of a mind to..."

They watched Lamar unfold his cane and make his way over to them with Georgette at his side. Abigail said something to him, and he called back over his shoulder, "I'll call you, Ma."

Abigail puffed up like a cobra about to attack, but Sofia stepped in and steered her toward a group of church ladies in frilly hats. Byron caught Sofia's eye, and she waved them to go on.

Once outside they practically ran to the car, the sound of Lamar's cane scraping over the parking lot pavement alongside them. Ben stayed close by in case Lamar veered.

In the backseat, Lamar let his head fall back. "Thank you so much. They's about to drive me crazy."

The laughing in the car was cut short when Lamar's phone buzzed and Siri announced that Abigail was calling.

"Uh-uh. No way." He turned it off. Ben put his arm around him, and Lamar leaned in. Now that Grannie was gone, he felt more than ever that his family was here in the car and not back at the reception.

"Oh, Lord," said Byron. "We'll drive back to the city. We've got beer and stuff at my place. No disrespect, Hattie," he shouted out the window, "but we need to go home."

"I need to go home home," said Lamar. "Grannie's in the ground. There's nothing for me here."

"Don't be in such a hurry," said Georgette. "I kind of like having you around."

"I got to get ready for a gig coming up," said Lamar.

"What?" everybody said at once.

"Don't act so surprised. It's just a wedding, but it's something. A gay wedding at that!"

"Anybody I know?" asked Georgette. Byron gave her a threatening look.

"Nope. Friends of mine. They actually went to Iowa to get married what with California being so backward and all." He laughed. "They're having the celebration in San Francisco though."

"It's coming," said Rafael. "I predict next year."

"Just in time," said Georgette with a giggle. Byron shot her another look.

"What about Louisiana?" asked Ben.

"Ha! In the South we like to keep our traditions," said Byron.

Rafael sat up straight. "I cannot believe you are saying that!"

"He's being sarcastic," said Georgette. "Don't listen to a word he says. I showed him a YouTube video the other day of a man proposing to his boyfriend and he cried his eyes out."

"That is a boldface lie. It's your fantasy, not mine. Anyway, this is about Lamar DJing a wedding. That's great! But how are you going to do that, Lamar?"

"Now you're doubting? You were the one kept telling me I could do anything," said Lamar.

"I'm not doubting. Just curious."

"Tell him," said Ben. "It's amazing!"

"Now that I got my laptop back from the police, I hook it up to the controller, my Numark. Still got my old library of songs and some new bangers in crates, organized by types of music. Serato lists them according to beats per minute, and VoiceOver will tell the name of song, bpm's and stuff. Double tapping, I load the songs onto the Numark. I never thought about it, but I pretty much know the locations of the platters, crossfader, buttons, and knobs for mixing and effects, and anyway I was always doing it a lot by feel rather than looking at the board. It's just practice, you know, like typing without looking at the keyboard. The only thing I don't have is the visuals on the computer screen for cueing and beatmatching, but my ear is already trained for that. I can't be as spontaneous as I was before with loops and scratching and whatnot, but I'm practicing."

Georgette turned around to the backseat. "Now could you explain all that in English?"

"I'll show you sometime."

"Can we all go watch you at the wedding?" asked Byron. "We could be your crew."

"I already asked if Ben could come. So a couple more shouldn't be a big deal."

"You are coming back to San Francisco?" Rafael said to Byron.

"Thought I might. Get away from the heat."

"You want to come, too, Georgette?" asked Lamar.

She took a moment to answer. After a deep breath to stabilize her emotions, she smiled and said, "No, honey. Got things to do here."

They reached the part of I-59 where stands of pine

trees lined the flat road, and Byron thought about all the times those tall thin guards of the land had looked down on him—watched him as a boy escape to New Orleans when his mother took him away from the cicadas, shed needles like tears when he fled with his heart in shambles after Thomas' murder, turned their backs on him when he ran for his life after the revenge that in the end he hadn't even wanted. And then, when the escape was in reverse, as he led the family north away from Katrina, the trees had been a symbol of strength—roots gripping the earth, braced for the storm. He smiled, remembering how Lamar had been so young and naïve, how he had talked about the seemingly endless mass of trees surrounding them. Now he had matured into a young man of whom Byron was immensely proud.

The sky quickly turned gray and fat drops hit the roof, sending the car into silence. Within seconds they were driving through a downpour with the wipers working frantically, the wind blowing the rain in quivering sheets, tires spraying water like fins rising up on the sides of cars. He wasn't sure if he was escaping a storm or driving into one. He glanced at Georgette and she turned her head slowly, examining his face as though she knew what he was thinking. In that moment, he was overtaken by a great sadness. He would miss her terribly. For nearly thirty years, they had been at each other's side, for better or worse. He would offer her the store if she wanted to run it. She could use his apartment. They would talk every day. But things would never be the same. In the rearview mirror, he looked at Rafael who stared back at him. Rafael tilted his head slightly in question. Byron, with a half-smile on his lips, nodded. The wind and rain battered the car, but having Rafael there with him made him feel somehow safer, more relaxed.

He turned his attention to Lamar. With the storm buffeting the car, he now sat up straight, his head turned toward the window, panic marching across his face as if he imagined water flooding the car, plunged into a darkness none of them could comprehend, left without the simple gift of vision to help him escape. Ben squeezed him tighter, tried to settle him back.

"We're okay," said Rafael, patting Lamar's leg. "It's just a tropical storm. In California we forget what those are like, the beautiful cleansing they bring."

Lamar nodded. "Washing away our sins," he mumbled.

Byron jerked the steering wheel and pulled the car onto the shoulder. He threw the door open and went around the side of the car to the edge where the shoulder dropped off to a ditch. Muddy water had begun to flow. He looked out toward the trees and threw up his hands as the rain plastered his hair, ran down his face, and drenched his clothes. Rafael jumped out of the car to join him. Ben grabbed Lamar's hand and pulled him out of the car. The four of them stood in a row, baptized by the pounding rain, howling and dancing and shouting until they fell into hysterical laughter.

Georgette stayed in the car and shook her head. "Men!"

ACKNOWLEDGEMENTS

I would like to thank my editor, Stefany Anne Golberg, for her wisdom and direction as she patiently made her way through my long manuscript. A number of others have read part or all of the book and made invaluable suggestions: Richard May, Wayne Goodman, Donnelle McGee, Waqar Ahmed, Nathan Wisman, Erik Pihel, Rachel Callaghan, Timothy Kay, Bethany Edstrom, Jacob Schott. I would also like to thank Jamaal Bradshaw for his technical advice related to the work of a disc jockey.

In doing my research for the book, the people of Columbia, Mississippi were helpful and kind. I apologize if I have cast the town in a negative light. As a reminder, it is a work of fiction and none of the events I have described actually happened there.

I also must acknowledge my partner and my family for their continued support of my writing. My mother, Virginia Meis, has spent hours listening to me read out loud parts of the manuscript.

Vincent Meis is a teacher, editor, and writer, not to mention world traveler looking for the setting of his next story. He has published travel articles, short stories, and three previous novels. He lives with his partner in Oakland, California. More information at www.vincentmeis.com.

9 780999 767280